PRAISE FOR ERIN KINSLEY:

'Brilliant, utterly compelling, heart-wrenching writing'

'Full of twists and ... compelling rea...

'Took me on the kind of twisting journey that kept me
turning the pages until the early hours'
Chris Whitaker

'This may be the perfect staycation read'
The Times

'An unputdownable thriller . . . will stay with you
for a very long time'
Elly Griffiths

'Sensitive and moving . . . but with a core of pure tension'
Sunday Times

'A page turner that is equally remarkable for the beauty
and consideration given to the writing'
Jo Spain

'A tense and intriguing thriller you'll find difficult to put down'
Woman's Weekly

'This razor-sharp thriller keeps you guessing until the last page'
Woman's Own

Erin Kinsley is a full-time writer. She grew up in Yorkshire and currently lives in Greece.

Also by Erin Kinsley:

Found
Innocent
Missing
Someone You Know

someone

you

know

ERIN KINSLEY

HEADLINE

First published in Great Britain in 2023 by
HEADLINE PUBLISHING GROUP

This paperback edition published in 2024 by
HEADLINE PUBLISHING GROUP

2

Cataloguing in Publication Data is available from the British Library

ISBN 978 1 4722 9254 4

Typeset in Adobe Garamond by CC Book Production

Printed and bound in Great Britain by Clays Lrd, Elcograf S.p.A.

MIX
Paper | Supporting
responsible forestry
FSC
www.fsc.org
FSC® C104740

HEADLINE PUBLISHING GROUP
An Hachette UK Company
Carmelite House
50 Victoria Embankment
London EC4Y 0DZ

www.headline.co.uk
www.hachette.co.uk

For all my family, who mean the world to me

Be patient where you sit in the dark. Dawn is coming.

Rumi (1207–73)

PRELUDE

Here in the dark, the only thing you see is a sliver of light at the edge of the ill-fitting door.

But that slender, bright line is a message of hope, telling you morning is here again, offering the possibility – you might dare think it's a probability – that soon the door will open and let in the dazzling sunshine.

Because what you fear above all is the dark: more than the loathsome spiders, which might already have dropped on your hair and be crawling to tickle your face; more than the scuttlings behind the wall's damp plaster, which probably are mice, but what if they're rats?

Rats are a whole different story.

In this cavernous darkness, silence amplifies what scant sounds there are. Sometimes you're certain you can hear someone close by, before you realise the in-and-out flow of breathing is your own. At least, you pray it is. If there were someone in here with you, how could you tell? Might the first you know be a whisper in your ear, a hand clamped over your mouth, the terrifying gentleness of fingertips on the back of your hand?

Yes, that narrow, arrow-straight shaft of light is saving your sanity, dispelling the blindness of full night.

It's a glimmer in the dark.

All that's needed to rekindle hope that soon, someone will open that door, and you'll be free.

PART 1
Lost and Found

ONE

A day in early spring, towards the end of March.

Wilf has come to feed the swans, as he always does on Thursdays. He's a man of regularity and routine, and this weekly ritual is a habit formed early in his life.

The riverbank is muddy below the red-brick bridge, which village folk claim has spanned the river for a thousand years.

But Wickney folk don't know much.

Wilf treads very carefully as he makes his way to the water's edge, anxious not to slip or dirty the polished leather of his shoes. Only last week, the river was glazed with ice; now the celandines blooming by the war memorial offer a hint of warmer seasons. Wilf, though, still feels the cold. Under his overcoat, he wears a lambswool sweater over his shirt, and his old university scarf – the black, blue and white of Bristol's School of Arts – is draped over his shoulders in case of need.

Dipping his hand into a Tesco carrier bag, he scatters an arc of yellow corn kernels over the ground.

The five swans dabbling in the reeds on the river's far side are already on their way, barely rippling the sluggish water as they glide across. The single male swan reaches Wilf first, and as it waddles from the water, he feels a frisson of intimidation at the creature's size. If it chose, the swan could do him significant harm, but Wilf has learned a balance over the years between standing his ground and not appearing to be a threat, and so the birds have come to trust him, or at least tolerate him in return for food.

Like many fenland villages, Wickney straddles the river. The main road passing through runs along the eastern bank as far as the bridge, where it takes a right angle to cross over to the village's western half. Along that far stretch, a white van is approaching, braking to make the turn. Partially hidden by the bridge's parapets, it soon reappears and continues along the eastern carriageway, making its way past a row of shops – a pork butcher, the Spar, a pizza takeaway, an empty premises for sale, the Mystique hair salon and a hardware store – and disappears out of sight.

Greedy for the corn, the swans surround Wilf on the bank, close enough that he could touch them if he dared. Throwing them the final handful, he begins to break up the heel of a stale loaf.

As he tosses the birds the first pieces of crust, he realises he's being watched.

Only a few metres away stands a little girl, pretty as a picture in her utilitarian grey school dress, eyes wide with lively curiosity.

A little girl Wilf knows.

Her name is Ruby.

Ruby's mum, Natalie, is caught up in conversation with the school-gate mums she calls her friends: Hannah, Jess, Sarah,

April. Jess is going through a bad patch at home, and wants to know Natalie's opinion on whether she's better off staying with Paddy, or making the break and going it alone.

'Best thing I ever did, leaving Justin,' declares Natalie. 'What do men do for you? They just hold you down, stop you being yourself. Who wants a life like that? Life's for being free, being who you want to be. Their idea of what's good for you ends up being what's best for them, if you ask me.'

'But what about money?' Jess asks. 'Me and the kids couldn't live on my wage.'

'You're a good-looking woman,' says Natalie. 'You'll never have a problem finding work.'

A white van is coming along the lane, making its way through the tight spaces left by the parked school-run cars. As the van reaches Natalie and her friends, it slows to a crawl and the driver beeps his horn. The women turn round, and the man in the passenger seat – blond hair in a ponytail, stud earrings and a confident smile showing teeth in need of work – blows Natalie a kiss.

Natalie laughs and, blushing, turns her back.

'Who's that?' asks April, following the van with her eyes as it makes a turn for the main road.

'Eric,' says Natalie, apparently uninterested. 'I've been seeing him for a couple of weeks.'

'What, another one?' asks Hannah. 'I don't know where you get the energy.'

They talk for a few minutes more, giving the kids a chance to let off steam before they head for home. By the time Sarah notices Ruby isn't with the other children, Ruby might have been gone two minutes, maybe five. Worst-case scenario, ten.

'Nat,' asks Sarah, 'where's Ruby?'

Natalie looks round the playground, over towards the climbing frame, down the lane beyond the fence. Ruby's nowhere to be seen among the other children chatting and playing.

'That little madam,' says Natalie, seriously annoyed. 'Always wandering off.'

Walking away to find her daughter, she calls back over her shoulder, 'See you tomorrow, ladies.'

As if all time to come is hers.

'Hello, Ruby,' says Wilf.

Ruby's slight build is unusual for this area, where so many of the children, even the girls, are – in Wilf's view – overfed and bulked out like wrestlers. She reminds him an awful lot of Margot. On the piano at home there's a photograph of Margot at a similar age – four, he supposes, or five – in a similar uniform, and they have the same elfin daintiness about them, the same delightful air of fun and mischief.

And seemingly Ruby is intrigued by him.

Which is a novelty.

'You're our next-door neighbour,' she says. 'I've seen you from my bedroom window.'

Wilf smiles. 'I am.'

'My name's Ruby.'

'I know,' says Wilf. 'I've heard your mother . . .' about to say *shouting at you*, he corrects himself. '. . . Calling you for dinner. I'm very pleased to meet you, Ruby. My name is Wilf.'

Ruby lifts the skirt of her dress and bends her knees in a curtsey. A lump comes to Wilf's throat as he remembers

Margot doing the same, decades ago in an apple orchard with petals of white blossom on her head. Life's passage is hard and cruel, and Time will play the same dirty tricks on this child as it did on Margot, stealing away her innocence and loveliness, leaving her the sagging flesh and painful infirmities of old age in their place.

But Ruby has no inkling of that future yet.

'That's what princesses do when they meet people,' she says. 'Why are you feeding the swans? Can I help?'

Wilf is happy to hand her his last remaining piece of bread, and Ruby throws it at the feet of the nearest swan, who gobbles it and looks to her for more.

'That's it, I'm afraid,' says Wilf, folding the carrier bag for reuse.

'I like your tie,' says Ruby, gazing at his immaculately tied silk bow. 'Yellow's one of my favourites. My dad has a tie like that but he only wears it sometimes and his is black. Do you wear yours every day?'

'As a matter of fact, I do. I think a bow tie makes every day extra special. Ruby, where's your mother?'

'Talking.' Ruby manages to make talking sound tedious beyond bearing, and Wilf laughs. 'When she's talking, I'm not to interrupt. I expect she'll come looking for me in a minute, though. Your garden's much bigger than ours. Ours is tiny. If our garden was bigger, I'd have a duck pond like yours.'

'You're welcome to come and feed my ducks, if you'd like. They're always hungry. Maybe your mum would bring you.'

'I want a kitten but she won't let me. Mila Ferguson's cat's got kittens and Mila said I could have a ginger one but Mum said no.'

'I have a cat,' says Wilf. 'But he's much bigger than a kitten. He's an old man of twelve and very grumpy.'

'What's his name?'

'Mr Grimes.'

'Is he ginger?'

'He's a big ball of grey fluff.'

'Can I stroke him?'

Wilf looks doubtful. 'I'm afraid he does occasionally bite. Probably better not.'

Realising there's no more food, the swans have wandered back to the water.

'I remember,' says Wilf, pointing to the reeds where the birds are rummaging, 'when my sister and I were the same age as you, we used to come and pick the reeds here sometimes and make them into candles.'

Ruby's eyes widen. 'How do you do that?'

'I'll show you.' He bends and picks one of the slender stems. Digging his thumbnail into the epidermis, he runs it to the top of the stalk, splitting the outer green from base to tip before peeling it back to show the fragile creamy pith beneath. 'All you do is peel the skin right off, dip the pith in the leftover fat when you have pork chops or lamb for Sunday lunch, and when it dries it will burn for hours. Nature's candles. People in villages like Wickney used them as lights for centuries, in the days before we had electricity.'

'Ruby!' The voice is strident and Ruby winces. 'What the hell are you doing?'

Natalie is standing on the road above the riverbank.

Wilf turns round to face her, and smiles.

He knows her by sight; he's watched her many times from

his windows as she takes Ruby to school, carries in shopping, comes and goes in taxis at weekends. In her red coat and black patent boots, she's very striking, and plainly the origin of Ruby's dark eyes and hair. But in Wilf's eyes, like so many modern women she spoils herself with too much fakery: stuck-on lashes, sprayed-on tan, plastic nails. Take all that away, and she'd be beautiful. At least, she would if she didn't always look so irritable.

'Who the hell are you?' demands Natalie. 'Get away from my daughter. Ruby, get over here.'

Without looking back, Ruby walks slowly up the bank and goes to stand by her mother. Seen side by side, the likeness between them is remarkable.

Wilf moves to follow her, his hand extended. 'We haven't formally met. I'm your next-door neighbour, Wilfred Hickling. Please do call me Wilf.'

Natalie glares. 'So you're the peeper. Don't think I haven't seen you, hiding behind your curtains, getting an eyeful.'

Wilf feels a deep flush of indignation and embarrassment spread from his neck up into his face. 'My dear lady, I must object in the strongest terms . . .'

Natalie's expression is of surprised amusement.

'You what? Are you for real?' Pushing Ruby ahead of her, she begins to walk away, putting insufficient distance between them for Wilf not to hear when she mutters, 'Disgusting old perv.'

'I've told you not to go wandering off! Why can't you listen?'

Natalie has Ruby tightly by the wrist, pulling her fast along the road towards where the car is parked. Ruby's pink unicorn schoolbag bounces on her back as she trots to keep up.

'Mummy, you're hurting me. I was talking to Wilf. He was telling me about candles. He said I can go round and help him feed the ducks.'

Natalie keeps firm hold of Ruby's wrist. 'Well, you can't.'

'Why not? I bet Daddy would let me.'

'Not all men are nice, Ruby. Some men are bad people.'

'Wilf is nice.'

'You don't know that.'

'Daddy's nice too.'

Silence.

'And Grandpa. Do you think he's finished painting my bedroom?'

'I sincerely hope so, he's been at it long enough. Days and days he's been doing it, and that room's hardly as big as our fridge.'

'He told me he's taking his time so he can keep an eye on us.'

'Did he now? He and I might have to have a word about that. I don't think we need keeping an eye on, do you?'

'Don't you think it's kind of Grandpa to be looking after us? I like having him there. He makes me laugh. Wilf's cat is called Mr Grimes. I think it must be that fluffy one that watches for mice by the hole in the fence. I asked if I could stroke him but Wilf says I'd better not. Sometimes Mr Grimes bites. I don't think he'd bite me though.'

Natalie's hunting for the car keys in her handbag.

'Shall we invite Wilf for tea one day?' asks Ruby. 'I think he'd like to come. I think he might be lonely, all by himself in that big house. We could make fairy cakes with pink icing and those silver sprinkles Daddy put on my birthday cake.'

Natalie finds her keys. As she unlocks the car, her phone begins to ring. When she glances at the screen, the corners of her mouth lift in an almost-smile.

As she climbs into the car, Ruby listens to the one side of the conversation she can hear and frowns.

'Hello you . . . I'm good . . . Not tonight, babe . . . You know I would (giggles) . . . How can I get a babysitter at this short notice? Anyway, I have other commitments . . . Yeah, those kind of commitments . . . I know you don't . . . Because no, simple as. You'll just have to wait . . . Anyway, you can keep it nice and hot for me till then . . . Yeah, no worries . . . You be good too . . . Miss you too, babe. See you soon. Bye. Bye.'

Ruby is staring through the windscreen, watching a woman walking a small white dog.

As Natalie starts the car, Ruby says, 'Am I going to Daddy's tomorrow?'

'Yes.'

Ruby's voice is without its usual fizz. 'I knew I would be.'

Natalie pulls out of her parking space. The road's quiet, no other traffic. As they drive over the bridge, Ruby turns her head to see if Wilf is still watching the swans. And he's there, smart and dignified as an old soldier, though his head is bowed as if he's feeling sad.

'How did you know?' asks Natalie.

'Because you're seeing that man.'

'His name's Eric, Ruby. And he happens to be a very nice man.'

'Eric's a stupid name.' For a few moments Ruby's silent, until they turn away from the bridge and Wilf and the swans are out of sight. 'And if Eric's nice and Grandpa's nice and Daddy's nice, why should Wilf be the only one who's not nice? I don't think Eric's very nice. He smells like toilet cleaner.'

'He does not smell like toilet cleaner.'

'He does to me. Why don't you love Daddy?'

Natalie's going almost too fast to make the turn into Saddler's Drove.

'For God's sake,' she says, braking so hard Ruby's pitched forward in her seat. 'Not this again. Give it a rest for once, will you? All your questions are giving me a stinking headache.'

TWO

At the café in the town-centre marketplace, the service is surly but the coffee's fragrant and hot. In this part of the world, where the choice of venues is limited, you forgive plenty for drinkable coffee.

Natalie's mother, Dee, sits down opposite her oldest friend, Tina, and removes her dark glasses, so incongruous on this deteriorating March day.

Tina studies Dee's face, blinks her kohl-lined eyelids and says, 'I ordered you a latte. What happened to your face?'

Dee has tried the same useless trick that failed to fool her mother thirty years ago when she was trying to cover teenage love bites on her neck, and has dabbed a mixture of foundation and toothpaste on the bruising around her eye.

The waitress brings two coffees in tall glasses, not apologising for the milky spills in the saucers, nor offering to fetch a cloth to wipe up the crumbs left on the table by previous customers.

'Did you want anything to eat?' Tina asks Dee, but the waitress is already gone.

Dee brushes the crumbs on her side of the table on to the floor. 'It's not what you think.'

'I'm thinking Frank.'

'Only indirectly.'

'An indirect black eye. That's a new one.' Tina takes two packets of brown sugar from the bowl at the centre of the table, rips off their corners and pours both into her drink. As she stirs, Dee picks up her own long-handled spoon and stirs her coffee too, even though she's no reason to except to buy a few moments to muster her thoughts. Tina knows a thing or two about men who'll take a swing, but that's never been Frank.

Frank's bad behaviour lies in a different direction.

'I know you won't believe me, but it was just a stupid thing. I dropped my glasses and when I bent down to pick them up, I caught myself on the corner of the dining table. That's it.'

'A likely story.'

'Dull but true.'

'So where does Frank come in?'

Dee takes a sip of her coffee. 'I was putting on my glasses so I could read the messages on his phone. Serves me right for trying to spy on him.'

Tina looks at her in that way she has, weighing things up, choosing her words. People judge her by her appearance, thinking her long skirts and bangles and sandals mean she's nothing but a hippy stuck in the past, but Tina has an uncanny gift for untangling human relationships.

'You think he's having another affair,' she says, reaching across the table to touch her friend's hand. 'How do you know? Are you absolutely sure? Is there a chance you're being oversensitive, seeing things that aren't there? Not that I would blame you, with his past form.'

'It's the same old stuff,' says Dee. 'Phone calls he won't

answer while I'm around. Messages pinging at odd times, long silences, extra showers. And he keeps going AWOL, hours and hours he can't account for. I don't really think there's any doubt.'

Recounting the evidence rekindles the hurt. How could he take her for such a fool?

She tries to smile through the tears pricking her eyes.

'I'm such an idiot,' she says, though her voice comes out small. 'He promised me he wouldn't, and he swears blind he isn't. But how can I believe him when all the same signs are there?'

'Oh, Dee, I'm so sorry. What a bastard. You must want to kill him.'

'Not this time. I'm not angry at him so much as myself, for giving him another chance. And I told him last time if it happened again, I'd divorce him, but now it looks like the time has come, I feel afraid to be alone. And I don't want to upset Ruby.'

'What about Nat? What would she say? I expect she'd want you two to stay together.'

Dee shakes her head. 'Natalie wouldn't care. Hard as nails, that girl is, and if her father upped and left, it wouldn't surprise me to hear her tell him good riddance.'

'What will you do?' asks Tina. 'You can stay with me a while, if you need time to think. You know it's not luxurious, but there's always wine and chocolate.'

Dee gives her a grateful smile. 'Thank you. It helps to know there's somewhere I could go. But I suppose I'm going to wait and see what the next few days bring.' Her smile fades. 'I've left it too late, haven't I, to leave him?'

'Not if that's what you want.'

Dee's eyes become distant, looking back into the past. 'Why is it so hard to put your finger on where things go wrong? When we were first married, Frank and I were really good together, and Nat was such a bright and sunny child, always full of fun. I thought that was it, happy ever after. But then, I thought we were happy when Frank started playing his games, which goes to show what I know. Now I wonder why I put up with it, why I didn't throw him out, but I never quite dared. Sometimes I think if only I'd had the confidence, I could have had a different life, got a little flat for me and Nat, been independent. I always wanted to go travelling. All those places I wanted to see, Venice, Florida, even just Edinburgh Castle. But Frank wasn't keen and I'd no one else to go with.'

'You could still go. I'd go with you, if I could afford it.'

Dee nods an acknowledgement and goes on, wistfully. 'Shall I tell you something, something I've never told anyone? Once upon a time, years ago, I got caught in a downpour, and I did something I never do, I took shelter in a pub. Soon as I was through the door I wished I hadn't gone in. It was full of businessmen drinking their lunchtime pints, barely another woman in the place, and when I got to the bar, I felt really awkward. The barman hadn't noticed me and I was going to leave, but then a man standing next to me asked if he could buy me a drink. He was nice-looking, handsome even. Frank and I were going through one of our bad times, and I thought what the hell, and I said yes. I asked for a glass of wine and this guy made a big show of making the barman open a fresh bottle of something I'd never tried before. It was lovely wine, and he was a lovely man. He was actually interested in me, asked me questions about where I was from, what I did for a living. We chatted until our glasses were empty, and then he offered to buy me another. And I so wanted to say yes, to be irresponsible, forget about where I was supposed to be and what I had to do later and just give myself up to whatever it was that was happening, because that's what Frank would have done. Because I was already thinking I really, really liked this man, and he really liked me.

'His name was John. But when he offered me that second drink, I told him I couldn't stay, even though he did his best to persuade me.

'I walked out on him. And from that day to this, I've never forgotten him. A few times after that, I went in there, hoping I'd see him again, but I never did.'

Among the chatter from other tables, a melancholy silence hangs over them, until Tina says, 'That's such a sad little tale. A missed opportunity.'

'Story of my life,' says Dee.

Wilf feels the spattering of rain.

Hands deep in the pockets of his overcoat, he wanders up the riverbank, crossing the road to go into the Spar, hesitating when he reaches the shop door.

His encounter with Natalie has unsettled and embarrassed him. Did anyone witness how she spoke to him? Do other people view him the same way?

Inside, the shop is warm. Martine is behind the counter, chatting as she serves a young woman holding a boy about Ruby's age by the hand, scanning and bagging fish fingers and spaghetti hoops. There is, Wilf notices, a bit of a queue. If

19

he'd come earlier, he'd have avoided what passes in Wickney for a rush hour.

Somehow, though, he wants to be part of the crowd.

He picks up a wire basket and takes his time browsing, even though he already knows what's on the shelves. He takes a small Hovis loaf, a pint of semi-skimmed milk, a bag of frozen peas. By the cat food he dithers a while, undecided between pilchard, rabbit and turkey, in the end choosing none of them and plumping for beef. On his way to the till, he passes the bakery section again and decides he will after all have the packet of almond slices he resisted when he picked up the bread.

The queue has grown shorter. He stands at its end. No one speaks to him.

When his turn comes to be served, Martine smiles, as always. In the last three years she has buried her farmer husband and all but lost her teenage daughter to drugs, and behind the home-tinted hair and supermarket lipstick she has the air of a conscripted soldier, trying to make the best of whatever life pummels her with. But her cheeks retain the ruddiness of a life spent outdoors, and Wilf wonders how she gets through her shifts in this place, with the fluorescent lights and cramped aisles and lack of windows.

'Hello, Mr Hickling.' She scans the cat food, the peas, the almond slices. 'How are you keeping?'

'Oh, as well as can be expected,' says Wilf. 'It's still rather cold, though, isn't it? I suppose that's why I haven't seen you out our way recently. You'll be staying closer to home.'

Martine scans the bread and the milk. 'That bridle path can be so muddy this time of year. I'm afraid Rocky will slip and do himself a damage, and that's the last thing I need. But I expect he'd enjoy a change. Maybe we'll have a ride over sometime soon.'

'I've got some Polo mints for him in the cupboard.'

Martine manages another smile. 'He'll be your friend forever. Anything else?'

'No, thank you.'

As he picks up his shopping, Wilf wishes her good afternoon, but Martine's moved on to the next customer and doesn't reply.

He drives his Toyota over the bridge and then steadily along the rain-glossed lanes, taking the same route as Natalie out of the village. Daffodils blow along the roadside dyke, and he recalls – years ago – planting some of those bulbs, him and Margot and Ma and Pa clambering up and down the steep bank sides, Ma complaining all the while how her back was killing her. For all that hard work, she saw them bloom only once before she was gone.

Beyond the dyke, flat fen farmland stretches to a sky which some might call drab but where Wilf always sees shades of blue, even when they're bleached almost to grey. There was a time when spring saw these fields ablaze with tulips, a glorious spread of crimson and pink. For days, sometimes into weeks, they were a sight to behold.

Now it's just the monochrome green of leeks.

There are only two houses on Stickpike Lane. As he passes Turle's Cottage, he notices Natalie's little Peugeot is in the drive.

Turning through the gateway of Nine Brethren House, he

drives over the gravel to park in his usual spot, well out of sight of potential thieves.

Mr Grimes is yowling on the doorstep. Wilf's pleased by the welcome, and chatters away to him, asking the cat how his day has been as he fumbles for his keys.

He sets the kettle to boil and puts away his shopping.

Mr Grimes is rubbing round his legs. Wilf spoons cat food into a dish and places it on the cold kitchen floor.

Mention of Natalie has made Dee think she could call her, go over there, delay the inevitable return home. Natalie will have picked Ruby up from school, and time spent with her granddaughter is always cheering.

When Dee dials the number, Natalie answers on the second ring.

'Hi, Mum.' She doesn't sound pleased to hear from Dee; she seems distracted, like she's been interrupted.

'Hi,' says Dee, far more brightly than she's feeling. 'I'm just thinking about popping over, if you're home.'

'What for?'

The blunt question takes Dee aback. 'No special reason. Just to see you and Ruby. Cup of tea and a chinwag type of thing.'

In the background, Dee hears Ruby ask, 'Who is it?' and when Natalie tells her it's her grandmother, she calls out, 'Hi, Grandma!'

'Hi, sweetheart,' says Dee. 'How was school?'

'Ruby, go and get changed out of your uniform,' says Natalie. 'I'm sorry, Mum, this isn't a good time. I have work to do.'

Natalie's new work seems to take up a lot of her time.

'Why don't I come and get Ruby, then?' suggests Dee. 'I'll give her something to eat. She can come to us for a sleepover.' *And keep the peace between me and Frank.* 'Then she won't get on your nerves.'

Natalie hesitates, and Dee thinks she's going to say yes.

But instead she says, 'Another time, Mum, OK?'

'Won't she be in your way?' Dee persists. 'I'll be there in no time, get her out of your hair. Just put her some pyjamas and her uniform in a bag, and I'll whisk her away.'

'It won't work for me tonight. Sorry but I have to go.'

'Are you all right, Natalie?'

'Why shouldn't I be?'

'You just sound so stressed.'

'I'm not stressed, Mum, I'm busy.'

'And I was offering to help.'

'Well, thank you. I have to go.'

Dee takes a deep breath. 'Nat, your dad . . .' But now isn't the time.

'What?'

'Nothing.'

'C'mon, tell me. What?'

'It doesn't matter. Never mind. I'll talk to you tomorrow, maybe.'

'Bye,' says her daughter, and ends the call.

Leaving Dee to head back to the house she's no longer sure is home.

THREE

Over the weekend, intervals of sunshine fail to lift the outside temperature. Wilf decides to venture into the garden anyway, thinking he should refill the bird feeders and cut back the elder he's been meaning to prune for weeks.

He wears a fleece-lined gilet and hat against the cold breeze, and puts on a second pair of socks before pulling on his wellingtons. Mr Grimes sits on the conservatory windowsill staring out at the early blossom on the apricot tree, but although Wilf tries to tempt him, he shows no inclination to leave the house's warmth.

So Wilf goes outside alone.

The elder grows in the border adjoining the lane. Readying his cutters, he pats his pocket to make sure the Polo mints are there. It's not a bad day. Martine might possibly bring Rocky out this way.

Wondering if they could already be on their way – this is about their usual time, somewhere around mid-afternoon – he steps into the road, scanning the distance for a horse and its rider.

Someone is there, but it's not Martine and Rocky.

Still a fair distance off, a woman is walking slowly, pushing a buggy.

Wilf begins to cut at the tree, stepping back from time to time to check the shape he's creating, working carefully to keep it even.

After a while he hears the rumble of small wheels and peeps through the thinned branches to see who's there.

The woman with the buggy has stopped outside Turle's Cottage. The little girl in the buggy is fast asleep.

Wilf's seen the woman here before, though not often; he assumes she's a friend of Natalie's, though with her lank hair and shapeless clothes she seems a curious companion for his glamorous neighbour.

She's looking at the upstairs windows, biting her nails, hesitant.

Wilf steps out to show himself. 'Good afternoon. Lovely day.'

Startled, the woman turns to him with a hand on her plump chest. She gives a nervous laugh. 'I didn't see you there. You made me jump.'

'If you're looking for Natalie, I think you'll find she's not home.'

'Really? Her car's here.'

'That doesn't mean much. She often gets picked up at weekends, taxis or boyfriends, I assume. She seems to have a glittering social life.'

The woman's face takes on an expression Wilf can't quite name. Resentment? Disapproval? The hurt of being left out?

'I might just knock anyway,' she says.

'Up to you, of course,' says Wilf, and he goes back to his pruning.

FOUR

Monday, 2.38 a.m.

Dee can hear noises outside.

She wasn't fast asleep but drifting between uneasy dreams and short interludes of wakefulness – not quite insomnia but a close and equally unwelcome relation. She isn't a woman who sleeps well alone. Since Frank moved to the spare room, she misses the secure warmth of a companion.

During her sleepless episodes, she's had ample time to become familiar with the noises of the night: the clatter of rubbish tumbled by a rummaging fox; the banshee wails of warring cats; the faraway drone of an overflying plane, usually a sign that morning is near. Some of the noises she likes; rain pattering on the window makes her feel safe and protected, even though she's alone in this bed which was meant for two. And when the moon is full, she loves its otherworldly, metallic gleam behind the curtains.

But the glare through the curtains now is not moonlight. Something's triggered the security lights, and the sound which troubled her was the sliding open and the closing of the patio doors.

Could someone have broken in? Not likely. Frank's obsessive about locking those doors, about locking every door in the house and checking every window lock, and he won't sleep unless his nightly ritual's complete.

She listens. All seems quiet.

The security lights click off.

A moment later, they come back on.

She decides she'll go and wake Frank.

Climbing from the bed, she crosses to the window. Being sure to stay out of sight, she moves the edge of the curtain to peep out.

Frank's down there on the patio, hands in the pockets of his old dressing-gown, staring out into the darkness at the garden's end.

He doesn't look up.

Frank being awake in the small hours is not normal. Frank is a total stranger to insomnia, and sleeps like the dead. And (as always) unlike her, in times of stress he sleeps longer and more deeply, taking shelter in unconsciousness from the pressures of the world.

So it seems their row yesterday – they seem to be rowing almost daily – really got to him. They covered a lot of ground, in between the door-slamming and the yelling. His absences. Her coldness. What's going on with Natalie and what they should or shouldn't do about it. This time, when they finally both ran out of grievances and insults, she felt they'd crossed a line into territory where they had rarely ventured before. The things he said made ashes of what love she still had for him. They headed for separate rooms on the very cusp of calling it quits.

And at this point, she doesn't really care.

Maybe he doesn't either. Maybe he's down there thinking about leaving for good.

Because for certain there's something – someone – on his mind.

She watches him take out his phone and glance at the screen. Is he checking the time or looking for messages? He switches off the phone and returns it to his pocket.

Dee climbs back into the empty bed and tries to fix her mind on pleasant things – what book she'll read to Ruby tomorrow, whether she has the ingredients for them to make scones – and before long she begins to feel mercifully drowsy.

As she's drifting away, somewhere close by she hears a car start.

Or maybe that's in her dreams.

In the morning, she's up late and Frank's apparently already left for work. No note to say he's sorry, no text on her phone.

Screw him.

As she makes coffee, she turns on the kitchen TV, spends five minutes not engaging with *Good Morning Britain* and switches it off again.

Wherever her marriage is heading, whether she gives a damn or not, she feels agitated, unsettled.

She needs something to occupy her mind.

Maybe Natalie would come over.

After the brush-off she got on Thursday, Dee hasn't tried to get in touch, except for sending a couple of *How's things?* messages yesterday morning.

Picking up her phone, she sees Natalie hasn't replied.

The messages are unread. That's out of character.

She thinks about Ruby, wondering if Nat's got her to school on time.

Natalie's phone, when she dials it, goes straight to answerphone. Uneasiness begins to whisper, and she wonders if everything's OK.

Wouldn't any mother be concerned?

FIVE

The biggest compliment anyone's ever paid Dee was to tell her she looked like Sharon Osbourne, though of course it wasn't Frank who said it. Frank wouldn't know Sharon Osbourne from the Princess of Wales, and anyway the comparison was made some years ago, before Sharon had all that dubious work done and lost a load more weight. Dee's face has met no resistance to its fifty-something sags and bags, and for every kilo Sharon's lost, Dee feels she's gained two.

Even so, the guy holding the *Go* sign at the temporary road works gives her a grin as he waves her through. He's in his sixties and no catch, but Dee takes it as a win anyway, a little boost to brighten her day. Maybe there could be a life after Frank, after all.

Natalie's new place is a twenty-five-minute drive away, and why she (or anyone else) would want to live in such a backwater is unfathomable to Dee. She's always enjoyed the facilities and liveliness even a small town offers – even when the town is nothing special – and she thought Natalie felt the same way.

But Natalie's changed since her break-up with Justin. She's

become obsessed with privacy, with living her own life – except of course when she's wanting her dad to do some job around the house or needs a babysitter. And she's needing a babysitter far too often to be good for Ruby.

As Dee turns off the dual carriageway in the direction of Wickney, the rain becomes heavier. Dense, low clouds hang over the dismal fenlands, and even with the wipers going full speed, it's hard to see the road, especially since her old car's demister has failed as usual to clear the windscreen. She slows down, and rubs a hole in the fog on the glass just in time to see a muddied tractor emerging from a field gateway, blocking the carriageway as it makes the turn.

She slams on the brakes, coming to a sliding stop far too close to the huge wheels. Headphones on, high up in his cab, the tractor driver's oblivious, and rumbles away in the direction Dee's just come from.

She's badly shaken. If she weren't over halfway there, she'd go home and forget about Natalie. She'll get no thanks for her visit anyway. Nat will tell her she's old enough to look after herself, and she'll be perfectly right. Or possibly she won't even be home, and this trip will be a wild-goose chase.

Dee envies those women who are their daughters' best friends, sharing shopping trips and spa days and hot chocolate in snuggly pyjamas on cold winter nights. To some extent, she always felt at war with her own mother, right from the day the puberty hormones kicked in. Even then, a part of her sensed her mother's heartbreak at the loss of her innocent little girl, the child who'd get excited at the prospect of a picnic or a day at the seaside, who transformed overnight into a rude and hate-filled stranger. By the time Dee emerged from that phase almost a decade later, the relationship was already beyond repair, destined to remain until her mother's death never better than an uneasy truce, with too many emotional battle scars and too much hurt – on her mother's side, at least – for them to ever again enjoy any real connection.

So as Natalie approached that troublesome age – when the pouts and sulks were beginning, when the first slammed door and the inevitable *Leave me alone!* echoed through the house – Dee thought she was prepared. There'd be no war between her and Nat. Times had moved on; young people had a right to their freedoms, and there was no point in behaving like her own mother had done, issuing draconian curfews, grounding Dee when inevitably they were ignored.

Except that Dee quickly came to see her own mother's point of view. Lying awake in the dark as one hour after curfew became two – praying to hear a car pull up outside or for the phone to ring, anything to let her know her child wasn't dead in a ditch – her sympathy with her own mother grew. And when eventually Natalie did come home, it was a shock to realise how quickly fear and dread for her safety could morph into pissed-off rage, and how easy it was to say – in an echo of home, thirty years before – *Where the hell have you been till this time?*

History repeats itself.

And yet there were still days when she and Nat were close: shared interests, silly jokes, companionable times. Especially while she was with Justin. With him, Nat was calmer, sunnier, easier to get along with.

Justin was good for her.

But then she wanted to be free.

*   *   *

32

By the time Dee turns into Stickpike Lane, the rain's all but stopped. From a distance – you can always see for miles across these flatlands – she can see Natalie's car's parked in front of the cottage. So there's a chance at least she's home.

Even so, doubting her welcome, Dee seriously reconsiders turning round and going home herself. Visiting without calling ahead isn't cool these days. But if Natalie's near a window, she'll have recognised the car, and that will seem odd. Better to go on, and if she gets a frigid reception she'll risk being brutally honest and tell Natalie she was worried, that if she doesn't want unannounced visitors she should answer her phone, that she might at least put the kettle on and offer her mother a coffee.

Straight lines and rectangles make up the tapestry of the fens, designed by male minds for efficiency, and Nine Brethren House stands where Stickpike Lane bends in a right angle. The house is a gentleman's residence on three floors, red brick and gambrel-roofed in the Dutch style. Dee knows from her schooldays that the roof dates it to the eighteenth century, when engineers were hired from Holland to manage the drainage of the fens.

The house is striking, yet its latticed windows and high chimneys seem to leak despondency. Before Turle's Cottage was built, Nine Brethren was a solitary dwelling for two hundred years, isolated against the empty sky, too lonely even these days to anticipate many visitors. As Dee drives by, the gate across the driveway is closed.

A short distance along the lane, Dee pulls in behind Natalie's car on the gravelled frontage, and switches off the engine.

The cottage is little changed from when it was built in

the early 1900s: two bedrooms, a small kitchen and a living room, a downstairs bathroom in what must once have been the scullery, space for a washing machine in the inadequately converted coal cellar. At least there have been improvements to deal with damp and vermin.

But this was a house built for labourers, who made what living they could off the land and waterways. When Natalie moved in, a sepia photograph hung on the landing. Its subject was a man – a rough, stooping, ragged creature wearing waders up to his thighs, a long wicker basket and trident on the ground beside him. Even behind glass, you could almost smell the dirt and dankness on him, see the river mud ingrained in his palms and in the wrinkles around his disturbing, pale eyes. *Stephen Turle,* the picture was labelled: a renowned eel-catcher in his time, and first resident of this cottage.

Ruby hated that photograph, insisting Turle's eyes followed her up and down the stairs, fearing he would come at night to slip wriggling, slimy eels into her bed. Soon, she began to have nightmares, blamed by Natalie on the photograph, which she relegated to the back of a cupboard. But sometimes the nightmares still come. Dee doesn't blame the photograph; she blames the house. This godforsaken outpost is too far from any friends – and doting grandparents – for any sociable child.

The curtains at the front windows upstairs and down are open, and that's a good sign. If Nat were sleeping off a wild weekend, she'd be a monster to deal with.

Dee heads for the back door, expecting to see through the kitchen window Natalie putting the kettle on, even if reluctantly.

But she's not there.

Dee knocks at the door. Over the fence in next-door's garden, a flurry of goldfinches chatter in the branches of a pear tree. Still no sign of Natalie.

Maybe Nat and Ruby got picked up by a friend this morning, so the mums could go shopping after they dropped the kids off at school.

Maybe the car's broken down again, and Nat called a taxi.

Maybe Justin picked them up. Maybe there's a reconciliation on the cards. But wishing and hoping won't make that so.

Of course there's a chance she's not well, though with Natalie, that's usually self-inflicted. If she's hungover, Dee will struggle to keep her temper. What kind of an example does it set for Ruby, losing entire days like Natalie too often does to the after-effects of alcohol? Why does she do that? But Dee knows the answer to that question, having occasionally been there herself. Some people try to drown their sorrows. If only she could figure out what Natalie's sorrows are.

She'll have to let herself in or she'll have completely wasted her time, coming all this way and not finding out if Nat's OK.

Dee knows where the key safe is, but before she resorts to that, she tries the door.

And it opens.

Standing in the doorway, she calls out. 'Natalie? Nat, are you there?'

No answer.

Dee steps inside.

On the table, a glass vase holds the drying remains of a florist's bouquet, dead from lack of water.

Natalie never mentioned anyone had sent her flowers. That's unlike her; normally with such a gift, the first thing she'd do would be to ping Dee a photo and post on Instagram. Not this time, it seems, and Dee wonders about the sender.

Aside from the fading flowers, the kitchen is clean. The dishes have been washed and stacked in the draining rack rather than being piled dirty in the sink, and the worktops are clear and wiped. But that's unusual for a Monday morning, with the rush to get Ruby ready for school. Spills of Coco Pops, carbonised crusts of toast and abandoned coffee would be more normal. And the absence of Ruby's favourite unicorn mug and bowl suggest Ruby wasn't here for breakfast. If Natalie let Justin down again in their childcare arrangements, there's likely to be trouble.

Sometimes it's hard to believe Nat cares about anything but her own convenience.

The calendar hanging on the cellar door is scrawled on in Natalie's hand: birthdays and school events, a hairdresser's appointment and Ruby's end-of-term outing. Nothing for today.

In the lounge, she finds a similar story. By Natalie's standards, it's tidy.

The door to the cupboard under the stairs – a dark hole where Natalie keeps the vacuum cleaner and shoves anything she doesn't have a place for – is slightly ajar. When Dee goes to close it, she finds it blocked by the corner of Ruby's duvet.

Puzzled, she opens the door wide, finding a pillow to match the duvet spread over the terracotta-tiled floor. On the pillow lies Ruby's favourite Lottie doll, alongside a torch and the wrapper from a pack of strawberry Oreos. The cupboard smells unpleasantly musty. In an upper corner, cobwebs tremble as spiders scuttle away. The light she's let in reflects on glass:

the unsettling image of Stephen Turle is propped against the rear wall.

Why has Ruby been playing in this grim hole? Pulling out the doll, duvet and pillow, Dee carries them upstairs.

Frank's been decorating Ruby's bedroom and it stinks of paint. He's almost but not quite finished; just a couple of square metres of the original cream emulsion remain on one wall, so if he'd taken another fifteen minutes he'd have been done, and all his clutter – the stepladder, paint cans, a roller and tray now dried to uselessness – could have been removed.

Yet Frank's a man of careful habits, who cleans his tools and clears away.

From the way everything's been left, you might assume he left in a hurry.

To freshen the room, Dee goes to open the window, where the view is of next door's lovely garden – a summerhouse set on a lawn brightened with early aconites, and a pond with ducks settled on its banks.

Ruby often talks about those ducks, drawing endless pictures of them and telling Dee and Frank that one day she'll be going to feed them. And as Dee watches, a man in his sixties comes out of the house carrying a bowl, calling the ducks as he scatters handfuls of pellets on the ground. The ungainly birds hurry towards him, and when his bowl is empty, he stands for a while, watching them hunt for any feed they've missed before waddling back to the water.

Then he looks up at her.

What strikes her is that his eyes didn't pan across the house, didn't check the kitchen window or Natalie's bedroom. He looked straight up here, at Ruby's room. And he must sense someone is here because his hand lifts in the beginning of a wave, until he realises it isn't Ruby he can see. His hand drops and he turns away, walking briskly towards a barn-like building at the garden's far end before disappearing inside.

Almost as if he's run to hide.

At the time, she thinks nothing of it. About to spread Ruby's duvet on the bed, she notices a stain on the bottom sheet, a spill of milk or juice, and makes up her mind to put all the bedding through the washer and hang it out before she leaves. Then it will be clean for when Ruby comes home.

Whenever that is. The poor child doesn't know if she's coming or going.

With the bed stripped, she carries the laundry on to the landing. Natalie's bedroom door is closed. Dee knocks, then cautiously tries the door.

'Nat? Are you there, love?'

The bedroom's like the rest of the house: compared to Natalie's usual lax standards, it's tidy and in good order, all clothes and shoes put away. But Dee hates what Natalie's done to this room – the purple curtains at the windows, the red shades on the lamps and the black carpet she's had laid. Why must everything be so dark?

The bedding in here smells fabric-softener fresh. In Dee's view, that makes it unlikely Natalie slept in this house either last night.

So where is she?

At this window, she looks out again to see if the man next door has come out of hiding, but the garden is empty.

A scattering of crimson powder lies on the windowsill: pollen from the dead flowers in the kitchen.

The flowers, of course, are a clue. No doubt there's a man behind this mysterious absence. Probably Natalie's cleared off for a long weekend with some bloke. No wonder she didn't tell her and Frank. She knew she'd get a lecture on responsibilities.

Dee carries Ruby's bed linen downstairs, not caring that she'll get no thanks for interfering.

When she opens the cellar door, the unpleasantness of the underground space leaks out: mildew, and the sharpness of ammonia which she hopes isn't rats. And undeniably, unexpectedly, the sickening stink of piss and vomit.

Seems like Natalie's had visitors who've used her place like a Saturday-night back alley. No way she's tackling a mess like that. She'll forget the laundry, go home and get the news from Justin as to what's been going on.

But a noise comes from the cellar: the metallic ring of something hitting the washing machine casing.

Something's fallen.

Or someone's down there.

Dee's instinct is to slam the door shut and leave. Yet how can she leave her daughter's house to an intruder?

Dropping the sheets, she glances round the kitchen, searching for something to bar the cellar door if she doesn't like what's down there, and spots the wooden wedge Natalie uses to prop open the back door. That would work. Along with the frying pan as a potential weapon.

Standing over the cellar steps, she calls down. 'Who's there?'

In response, she's shocked to hear an outbreath, an expulsion of air from liquid-filled lungs, like the death-rattle of a lifetime smoker; undoubtedly a human noise, and yet nothing she's ever heard before.

She puts a foot on the topmost step, her hand uncertain over the light switch. Does she want to see who makes such a noise? Summoning courage, she flicks the switch.

Ten steps down, the utility room is lit up: the washer, the dryer, the detergent and softener on the shelf.

And on the vinyl-covered floor: Natalie, on her back and barely conscious, her right leg bent at a distressing angle, dark patches of piss on her jeans, vomit in her hair and round her head.

When her mother calls her name she doesn't respond.

Dee has to leave Natalie to get signal on her mobile. In the lounge, as she dials 999, her hands are shaking in a way she can't remember them ever doing before.

The dispatcher's calmness is exasperating. Why doesn't he understand the need for urgency?

'Is the patient conscious and breathing?'

Dee pictures Natalie's corpse-like face, the relief when she saw her eyelids flicker.

'Not conscious, no. Please, send them quickly. It's my daughter. I think she's had a fall.'

'First responders are on their way,' says the dispatcher, deadpan. 'Is your daughter breathing?'

'Barely. She's in a really bad way.' Dee wants to cry, but she needs to hold it together. Then words come out of her mouth she can't believe she'd ever say. 'I think she might be dying.'

'Are there any dogs in the house?'

'Dogs? What?' Dee shakes her head. 'No, no dogs.'

'Is there someone who can wait outside for the first responder?'

'I'm here alone. I want to stay with my daughter. How long will they be?'

'There's one in your area now. She's on her way.'

'How long?'

'She's on her way now.'

'Tell them there are two cars outside, one red, one blue. Tell them to come round the back. I need to call my husband. He doesn't know.'

'Please stay on the phone with me for the time being, Dee.'

Dee hears a vehicle outside, but there are no blue lights, no ambulance. Through the window, she sees a woman in high-vis climbing from a white Peugeot, dragging out a hefty kit-bag.

But she's alone.

'Someone's here,' Dee says to the dispatcher.

'Is it the first responder?'

Dee begins to be angry. 'We need an ambulance. Two big men to carry her upstairs. I told you, she's in a cellar. You've sent me a middle-aged woman.'

'The first responder will help your daughter until the ambulance crew get there.'

Dee can hear the signing-off in the dispatcher's voice.

'My daughter needs an ambulance, maybe the air ambulance,' she insists. 'We're miles from anywhere. When will they be here?'

'We're experiencing very high call volumes at the moment. Current estimate is about forty minutes.'

'She could be dying!' shouts Dee. 'Do you understand me?'

'They're on their way,' says the dispatcher, and Dee hears apology and frustration in his voice. 'They know you're a priority call. The first responder will make your daughter comfortable in the meantime.'

41

Frank. He'll know what to do.

Dee disconnects the call and dials Frank's number. The phone rings and rings before going to answerphone.

The first responder knocks at the door.

Dee's message to Frank is garbled, almost incomprehensible with panic. 'Frank, for Christ's sake, where are you? Just pick up, please. OK, ring me right now. Natalie's had an accident and it's serious. For God's sake, Frank, where on earth are you?'

SIX

Wilf has come in from feeding the ducks to eat a late breakfast: a free-range egg on wholewheat toast, a glass of grapefruit juice, a pot of Earl Grey tea.

Outside, Mr Grimes is stalking the nest of blackbirds in the walnut tree. Fearing the babies will be easy prey, Wilf raps on the window to make the cat move on.

Mr Grimes pretends not to hear.

Carrying his dishes from the dining room to the kitchen, Wilf decides to put on his outdoor shoes and fetch the cat inside where he can do no harm.

He's tying his laces when he hears sirens blaring on the A-road two miles away across the fields. The sound is too familiar. The road is the only major thoroughfare in this part of the county and is notorious for crawling tractors and agricultural vehicles. Sometimes drivers stuck in slow traffic get impatient, lose their tempers, take crazy risks. Sometimes it doesn't end well.

Usually the sirens wail a while and then fade into the distance. This time, though, they're growing closer.

Outside, Wilf claps his hands at Mr Grimes, who runs

scowling away under the hedge. Wilf walks to the front gate. The sirens have stopped, but he sees repeating flashes of acid yellow as a vehicle passes behind the trees on the top road, and a strobing blue. An ambulance is passing very close indeed. He keeps watching, expecting it to go out of sight, but it slows and makes the turn into Stickpike Lane.

They must be going next door.

Hurrying upstairs, he heads for the first-floor spare bed-room window, from where he'll have the best view.

Justin. Justin needs to know.

He picks up on the third ring, bright and cheerful as always, on the outside at least.

'Hello, Dee. Long time no speak. How's things?'

'Justin, it's Natalie. She's had an accident.'

A short silence. 'What kind of accident?'

Dee is so overwhelmed, she can only ramble. 'She was wearing those stupid shoes. Only she'd be daft enough to carry laundry in those damned high heels.'

Justin sounds flustered, concerned. 'But what happened? Is she OK?'

'She fell down the cellar steps.'

'Christ. Is she OK, though? Shall I come over?'

'We're waiting for an ambulance. They say it might be a while.' Dee feels tears running down her face, beyond her control. 'I think she might be dying.'

'Dying? No, come on, Dee, just from a fall? I'm sure it's not that bad.'

'I don't know how long she's been down there. When did you last speak to her?'

'Oh my gosh. I have to think. Thursday, was it? Maybe Friday? Listen, let me close up here and—'

Dee cuts him off. 'The ambulance is here. I have to go. Can you pick Ruby up from school and take care of her tonight?'

'Of course. Ring me and let me know how Nat's doing. As soon as you know anything. Do you want me to come to the hospital? I can take a couple of hours off, no bother.'

'If we need you, I'll let you know. Just please look after Ruby. I have to go now. Bye.'

'Natalie? Natalie, can you hear me?'

Down the cellar steps, Dee can see the paramedics are doing all they can to rouse her.

And then, in a wonderful moment, Nat murmurs a response. She's alive.

Dee makes a third call to Frank and leaves a second message.

A few minutes later, one of the green-uniformed paramedics comes up the cellar steps, excusing himself as he passes her.

'Is she going to be OK?' Dee asks.

The paramedic's smile is strained. 'We're doing all we can.'

'Can I go down to her?'

'Better not just at the moment.' He holds up his phone. 'I need to make a call. Where will I get signal?'

Dee gestures towards the lounge. 'Through there, if you stand by the window.'

He glances at her and something flashes across his face, something she can't read. 'I'll try outside.'

'Shall I make tea?' Dee asks, but he doesn't answer.

Dee knows they don't have time to drink tea, but how can she do nothing? She finds milk in the fridge, alongside Ruby's favourite cherry yogurts and Babybel cheeses, foil containers from some takeaway and two bottles of Chardonnay, one unopened, one two thirds empty. And several cans of Budweiser. Since when did Natalie drink lager?

Waiting for the kettle to boil, she sees the paramedic out front, on his phone. When he notices her watching, he turns away. Dee drops teabags into mugs and checks her phone again, even though she knows Frank hasn't called.

Time passes. The paramedics at last have Natalie ready to be carried up the perilous stairs.

Undrunk on the kitchen counter, the tea has all gone cold.

A police car has pulled up outside.

Dee's concerned about whether the ambulance crew might bump Natalie's head on their way up or even drop her, and thinks nothing of the police's arrival. Maybe it's standard procedure in emergency call-outs.

Two officers appear in the kitchen doorway. One of them is a big, bulked-up man who could be useful with the lifting. The other is a woman surely too petite for the job. She asks Dee if she's OK and what's been going on, but her colleague goes straight to the cellar door, peering down to announce himself to the paramedics, glancing round to make a professional assessment of the situation as a whole.

'Was it you who phoned it in?' he calls down to the paramedics, but their reply is muffled and Dee can't hear.

'Called what in?' she asks the female officer.

'Are you a relative?' asks the policewoman.

'I'm her mother.'

'How long's she been down there?'

'I don't know. She's fallen down the stairs in her ridiculous shoes. She'd probably had a glass of wine. That's Natalie all over.'

'Has she said anything to you?'

'No. When I found her, she was barely conscious. To be honest I thought she was dead. I'm so relieved she's—'

'Because the paramedics say she told them she was pushed.' Dee feels the room begin to spin. 'Pushed? Who by?'

'That's why we're here. Tell me exactly how you found her.'

'Isn't it a good thing I came?' says Dee. 'I keep thinking, what if I hadn't? And I nearly didn't come in, and I must have been in the house five or ten minutes before I even went down there. Well, I'd no idea she was there. Sometimes she drinks too much and I thought she might be hungover, so I went upstairs to look for her. She wasn't there, but I thought while I was here I'd put some laundry on. The washer's in the basement. When I opened the cellar door, there she was.'

'You opened the cellar door? You're sure about that?'

'Why wouldn't I be?'

'It's important that you're sure,' says the officer. 'Because if your daughter accidentally fell down the stairs, I don't think she'd have closed the door behind her.'

Fourth call, third message. 'For God's sake Frank, where are you? The police are here. Just pick up your damn phone.'

In a house miles away, a slender woman in jeans and fur-trimmed mules carries a cafetière of Costa Rican coffee into the lounge and places it on the glass table alongside the sofa.

'Hey, sleepyhead. Wake up.'

Frank's stretched full-length on the sofa. When the woman speaks, he opens his eyes. She lays his Nokia phone on the table beside the coffee.

He looks exhausted and burned out, rough and wrinkled. 'What time is it?'

'Just after eleven. I have to go soon. I've some errands to run before my shift.'

Frank pushes himself to a sitting position. 'I'm sorry. I'll get out of your hair.'

But the woman shakes her head. 'No rush. Stay as long as you like. Really.'

'I haven't been sleeping well. I've got things on my mind.' *Not least of all you.*

'Let me get you something to eat,' says the woman. 'You must be starving. An omelette or a sandwich?'

Frank gives her a grateful smile. 'Thanks. That would be great.'

'In the meantime, you'd better have a look at that.' She points to Frank's phone. 'Hope you don't mind me going in your pockets, but it's been ringing and ringing. Somebody's really keen to get in touch with you.'

SEVEN

'Where the bloody hell have you been?'

Dee looks like Frank's never seen her, grown years older in hours, face pale and swollen with crying, and an anger in her eyes he would never have thought she possessed. He's fast-walked and half run all the way here from where he left the car – without bothering to find a proper parking space or pay for a ticket, so that's no doubt going to cost him dear when it's time to leave – asking at the hospital reception where he should go, asking again and again because he seems to have lost the ability to retain information, to tell left from right, or remember whether they said second floor or third.

The way he was driving, it's a miracle he made it here at all: almost game over on two or three occasions, a near head-on with a BMW he's no idea how he missed, frighteningly close to taking out a motorcyclist who only just stayed upright. When you're in a desperate hurry, other drivers are maddeningly slow, taking their time and even blocking you out of spite, but he kept his foot to the floor and powered through regardless, taking risks which were borderline suicidal. And all the time he was ringing her, ringing her, trying to get an update, but she didn't pick up, whether because she had no signal or because he deserved a big fuck-off dose of her not picking up, except it wasn't the time, was it? This really wasn't the time.

Now here they are, face to face in this anonymous room with its white walls and institutional furniture, and she's going to give him the news, because he doesn't even know if there's still hope or if that ship sailed while he was on the road. They're in one of those defining moments in a life, in a marriage, when you really, really need to be able to depend on each other, and yet all there is between them is her anger, her rage at how badly he's let her down. And what the hell is he going to find to say to her anyway, in answer to the perfectly reasonable question she's just asked? All the way here he's been trying to invent a plausible story and all of it's just bollocks, just cock-and-bull bullshit, so he's even considering telling her the truth.

But the time for that isn't now.

Except that, right on the money, she says, 'Christ knows you've had long enough to come up with a story.'

Frank's desperate to skip all that, to bypass all the rancour and the squabbling because it isn't the time for that either, though for a split second he thinks, *If she's prepared to get into it with me, then maybe that's a good sign, a sign there's hope, because if she was gone, wouldn't she already have said so?*

In a moment of too-rare honesty, he says, 'You can break my balls later, Dee, for whatever it is you think I've done, but what about Nat?'

He's standing in front of her, and she looks up at him from the chair she's been sitting in for hours with her balled-up tissue and her desperate worry and aloneness, and says, 'They keep saying it's touch and go.' That sets her off crying again, not just crying but sobbing from the savage ache of her breaking heart, and he knows despite what's happening with Nat some of that crying is over him for being a bastard, and he's sorry for that, truly and deeply sorry.

So he dares sit down beside her and put his arm round her shaking shoulders. At first she tries to shrug him off, but without conviction, so he hugs her tight and she lets her head rest on his shoulder and does her crying into the jacket another woman fetched him to put on as he left her a couple of hours ago, and he's briefly anxious that she'll smell the other woman and then thinks, *What the hell, I'll deal with that shit later.*

He asks where Justin is, and she says he had to go and get Ruby – it's a decent drive from here and at this time there'll be traffic – but she's told him she'll ring the moment there's any change.

'Tell me what's happened,' he says, and she begins as she always does, going at it the long way round in ridiculous detail, why she did what she did and the exact time she did it, sometimes even what song was playing on the radio, when if it was him, he'd tell the whole tale in three sentences and we'd all be up to date. But he lets her do it her way because today he wants the details, he wants to know what time it was and how long the ambulance took to get there, and he wants to know (yet doesn't) how bad Nat's leg looked and the peculiar yellow of her skin, his baby's skin, how dry and sore her lips were and the scabbed blood on her head and how she'd pissed herself, poor baby, and that old bloke next door was watching from the garden and did Frank think he'd done it and Frank says, Hold on a minute, done what?

And Dee says, Pushed her down those stairs, and he says,

What makes you think anyone pushed her? Who the hell would do that? So Dee says, She said so to the ambulancemen. She said someone pushed her. I thought she'd turned her ankle in those daft shoes, I've told her before about them but she never listens does she, not Nat. And Frank asks, What are her injuries, what's the doctor said? And she says, I didn't understand all of it but a compound fracture of her left leg, which means internal bleeding and that's why she's in such a mess. They said about sepsis. And amputation. They might have to amputate her leg.

Frank feels suddenly sick, and finds himself about to say – absurdly – *Why didn't you ring me sooner?* but of course she did, she rang and rang and rang, and he slept through it.

The door opens. A man stands there in blue scrubs, and Frank's dismayed to see spots of blood on his trouser leg and wonders if it's his baby's blood, if it's Nat's, but of course that's not a question you can ask. The man's wearing a blue cap to cover his hair, frameless glasses dangling round his neck, and he has an intelligent face like you'd hope for in a doctor, but he isn't smiling as he gives his name and asks them to confirm who they are.

And Dee says, We're Natalie's mum and dad, and Frank wants to weep at the simplicity of that uber-important fact he so often loses touch with, that they're Natalie's mum and dad and Ruby's grandma and grandad, and after that, when you get down to it, not much else matters, and he wishes he could always keep those bare facts front and centre and give them the importance that they warrant.

The doctor closes the door carefully as if there's someone in the room with them he doesn't want to wake, and places a chair for himself in front of the low table where Dee's got her phone and the little handbag she calls her clutch and a whole farm of balled-up tissues all wet with tears for their daughter. And the doctor sits down with his knees spread, and leans forward with his elbows resting on his knees, and he clasps his hands together as if he's praying.

For whole seconds he doesn't speak.

And then he looks right at them, and says, 'I'm so very sorry. I'm afraid we lost her.'

EIGHT

At five years old, Ruby doesn't have a huge store of memories: nothing at all from the cotton-soft, milky time of babyhood; nothing bad but a bruisingly hard fall from a swing before the age of three.

In the next few minutes, that will change. One of her life's most consequential moments is looming close, and a disturbingly vivid and enduring memory is about to form. This coming hour will shape her future. When it's passed, nothing will ever be the same.

She's warm and comfortable lying on the sofa, but she's beginning to feel not quite forgotten but overlooked.

She hears Justin's phone ring shortly after 7.30 p.m. Ruby already knows she's on borrowed time, and that the unusual postponement of bedtime can't go on much longer. This whole evening's gone in interestingly unexpected ways: takeaway pizza – only normally allowed on Saturdays – for tea on a Monday, and afterwards her choice of sweets from the treat drawer; unlimited watching of CBeebies, unsupervised by Daddy while he does whatever he's doing in the kitchen; no bath in prospect, when normally at Daddy's it's an hour before bedtime, no ifs, buts or excuses. And why is she having another night away from Mummy's, when on school nights she always sleeps there, where school's only ten minutes away, not half an hour, like it is from here?

Probably that's Mummy ringing now, saying what time she'll pick her up.

Secretly, unexpectedly, Ruby's bored, and the evening without structure is becoming tedious. CBeebies finished at 7 p.m. and Ruby has no idea what to watch now. Flipping channels with the remote she's not often allowed to use, she finds only dull, adult stuff. She switches off the TV and wanders into the kitchen to find her father.

Justin's sitting at the kitchen table. They finished eating ages ago, but the empty pizza box is still there, along with their dirty plates, her empty juice glass, the unwanted crusts and dropped splurges of tomato sauce around her place.

He looks as if he might be sleeping, his head propped on his forearms, his phone on the table between his elbows. Whoever he was speaking to, he isn't speaking to them now.

Not realising she's there, he sniffs and wipes his nose on the sleeve of his hoody, in the way he's always told Ruby she mustn't do.

'Daddy. You need to get a tissue.'

He raises his head, and Ruby's disconcerted. She's never seen his face like this before, red-eyed and drawn with misery, as unhappy apparently as Ruby was when Daddy first left home.

Her daddy's always smiling, always making everything fun. This man is someone she doesn't recognise, a disturbing shapeshifter who resembles Daddy but can't possibly be him.

Can he?

Ruby's afraid. Standing close to him, she reaches out to touch his face but daren't make contact. Instead, she peers frowning round in front of him to get a confirmatory view.

'Daddy, are you crying?'

Justin knows this is his cue to pull himself together, put a smile on his face and reassure her. But he can't do it. Instead, his shoulders convulse in a sob and his head falls back into his hands, their heels rubbing at his eyes.

Ruby is dismayed but quickly decides she knows what will fix him. Remembering what he's always done for her, she crosses solemn-faced to the worktop. Standing on tiptoe to reach the tissue box decorated with jungle animals – the grinning orange tiger is Ruby's favourite – she pulls it towards her and places it on the table in front of her father.

'Daddy?'

Ruby pulls a blue tissue from the box and holds it out to him.

Raising his head from his hands, seeing what she's done, he takes the tissue and wipes his eyes. Ruby hands him a yellow one, and tells him to blow his nose.

'Why are you crying?' She has another idea to make him better, a thing that invariably works for her. 'Shall I get you some ice cream? We could share.'

He shakes his head, shoves his plate and the pizza box to the far side of the table, and turns in his chair to beckon her on to his lap.

'Come and sit with me, sweetheart.'

She hesitates. These days, he always says she's too big for this, and probably he's right. So this offer is disquieting, another off-moment in this perplexing evening.

But he picks her up and lifts her up on to his knee, so

she can smell his daddy-scent of aftershave and sawdust, and this evening something else she can't name, the faint animal odour of distress.

In a way he rarely does these days, he presses her head against his chest to breathe the treasured scent of his own child: shampoo and bubble gum and the last of the fresh air from her line-dried clothes, and melded with all that the indefinable smell which is uniquely Ruby.

Ruby's surprised by the neediness of his hug and uncomfortable with this disintegrating version of Daddy. She tries to pull away, but he won't let her go, and speaking directly into her ear, in a voice ragged with crying, he says, 'I have to tell you something.'

She knows then it will be bad; his broken voice and this soft lead-in give him away, because he always normally dives straight into what he has to say, and doesn't go round and round in flowery words before he gets to the point.

But now he is.

So she relaxes her head on to his chest as he seems to want her to do, feeling the warmth of him under her cheek and hearing the beating of his heart.

'It's something awful, Ruby. There's nothing I can do to dress it up or wrap it in ribbons, and I don't know how to tell you so I'm just going to come out and say it.'

She takes a breath and holds it, waiting to hear what this bad thing is, but he's lost momentum, or lost his nerve.

So she waits until he's ready to go on, not recognising, of course, the approach of a moment that will turn her whole life inside out or that she'll remember his coming words forever, believing in her naivety that the worst a bad thing could be is never, ever being allowed to have a kitten, or that he's lost all his money and they'll have to go and live on the streets like the dirty, crazy people she's seen begging near the station, or that he's ill in some way and needs an operation, and if it were this last, she wouldn't mind, because she could get a nurse's outfit and take care of him.

But none of these things are what's wrong.

'Ruby, you won't be seeing Mummy any more.'

This, quite simply, she doesn't understand. Pushing away the hand that's stroking her hair, she tries to look up into his face, but all she can see is the dark-stubbled underside of his jaw and the tears running down it.

'What do you mean?' She remembers Sasha Coombes's mother, who left Sasha and her dad and baby brother to go and live in Scotland with a man who was a footballer, as if him being a footballer was a reasonable excuse. In a small voice, she asks, 'Do you mean she's left us?'

'Not on purpose,' says Justin. 'She didn't want to go. She had an accident, fell down some steps. The ambulance took her to hospital and the doctors and nurses did their best, but they couldn't save her.'

His short account of these momentous events is bewildering. 'Save her from what?'

She feels his chest rise and fall as he sighs, deciding to try another way. 'You remember what happened to Mrs Dixon's cat when it got hit by that car?'

'Jasper.'

'Yes, Jasper. He was OK for a while and Mrs Dixon took him to the vet, but the vet said he was too badly injured to come home.'

Ruby does remember that, the awfulness of it, the squeal of tyres and the thump as Jasper hit the bumper. Surely that can't have happened to Mummy?

She feels her lower lip begin to quiver.

'Jasper died.'

'Yes.'

She feels a growing sense that something overwhelming is happening here, too horrific to be possible. She wants to ask for clarity, but if she's right in what she's thinking, then clarity will mean the end of her world.

'Ruby, do you understand what I'm saying to you?'

Ruby listens to her father's heart, how it goes on steadily and reliably, and decides to lean on that, rest in its rhythm a while.

'Ruby? I'm so sorry, sweetheart. I'm so, so sorry.'

She's afraid to get it wrong, but she must be wrong, and needs to check.

'You don't mean Mummy has died, do you?'

He nods his head, and his grip around her grows tighter.

And Ruby wants never again to leave his arms.

PART 2

Watching the Detectives

NINE

From the spare-room window of Nine Brethren House, Wilf is watching what's happening next door, and on his mind is a song they used to play on the radio decades ago, Elvis Costello's 'Watching the Detectives'.

Because that's what he's doing.

They come and go in their white suits, carrying their cases with contents unknown, probing and processing what was Ruby's home.

What they're looking for, God alone knows.

Chilly, but at least not freezing; cold, but not in that pinch-your-toes, hands-in-pockets way. A watery sun the colour of a cut lemon is dissolving the Gothic mist that hangs low over the water, and the emerging sky is clear and wide, reflected silver in the rippled mere. Dew lies heavy, glossing the muddy grass, and a light, shiversome breeze bends the bleached, downy heads of last year's reeds.

Along the bank where the moorhens are busy, Owen Laflin makes his cast. The rig drops into the water a little closer than where he wanted it, though not far enough to make him reel in the line and cast again. If he's going to be lucky, he'll be lucky. A metre or two to left or right won't change the outcome.

Besides, catch or don't catch isn't the point. The intention is to be immersed in the near silence and the invigorating air, to be vigilant for the otter he might glimpse if he's still enough, the water rat or coot, the overflying heron or crying geese. The point is the lesson of patience, to enliven and clarify the mind.

As she approaches, Gabby can see how engrossed he is in the watching and waiting. Even when she's close behind him, he doesn't know she's there, and she lets a minute pass before she disturbs him, entranced herself by the calm, quiet peace.

In the end, she interrupts him by breaking a twiggy stem of teazle.

He turns his head and smiles at her. 'Hello, beautiful. Aren't you a sight for sore eyes?'

His daughter's looking exceptionally well, he thinks, sophisticated in her London clothes: a cobalt-blue coat over black leggings and a black polo neck; those expensive Irish equestrian boots townies wear when they come down to Norfolk, which actually do a good job of keeping out mud and water. Her skin's as white as always, despite her recent skiing holiday, so she's at least taken his advice on the use of sunscreen at altitude on fair skin. And her hair blazes its constant red, wild and untameable as he hopes she'll always be, the alter ego to his own conventional self, who never found a way to escape his conformist nature.

Gabby returns his smile, always a daddy's girl, always pleased to see him. Almost always, anyway.

'It's a fabulous morning for a ride out. Mum said I'd find you here.' She holds up a paper bag. 'I brought lunch, brunch, whatever it is. Bacon sandwiches, red sauce and brown. Payment for disturbing you. What are you after?'

Owen begins to wind in the line. 'Carp. They say there's some decent-sized specimens in here, but time will tell. Here, come and sit down.' He moves to offer her a seat on the wheeled box under whose lid he keeps all his paraphernalia.

'Stay where you are, I'll stand. I've done enough sitting down for one day. I had a horrible drive, roadworks, accidents, you name it.'

'So how was the holiday?'

'Good. Relaxing, but way too much to eat and drink.' She puts her hand in the paper bag and offers him a foil-wrapped sandwich, screwing up the bag as she removes a second for herself. 'I'm eating super-healthily just as soon as I've finished this.'

'You're an angel,' her father says, taking the sandwich. 'Double sauce, eh? Don't tell your mother.'

'I won't.' Gabby brushes her hair back over the shoulders of her coat, and takes a bite of her sandwich. Winter or summer, rain or shine, her hair always works its way back to the cursed frizz, regardless of what straighteners and oils she uses. These days, she's learned to live with it, after seeing John Everett Millais's depiction of Ophelia at the Tate Britain and realising there can be beauty in red frizz, even if not everyone appreciates it. Her father's one of those who does, sharing the curse himself, though under his hat his own is reduced now to sandy grey. A league of firebrands, he used to call them, though he was never a firebrand that she can recall.

'So,' he says, feigning uninterest, scanning the water for bubbles and ripples as he takes a second bite. 'To what do we owe the pleasure?'

'You're such a cynic, Dad. Does there have to be a reason for me to be here?' She waves an arm over the view. 'Isn't this enough to call a body home?'

'Not you, and not after a week away from the office on snowy Alpine peaks.'

She laughs. 'OK, you're right. It's the Natalie Cutter case. They sent me because they reckon I've got local knowledge. Except I've never been to Wickney in my life.'

'Not many people have. It's way in the back of beyond. Perfect place for a fenland murder.'

'The senior staff think the story's a crowd-pleaser because she was a very good-looking girl. But I've seen the post-mortem report and actually it's grim and very ugly.'

Her father frowns. 'I won't ask how you got access to that, but I can't deny I'm interested in what they found.'

'On the face of it, it's a no-fault domestic tragedy. Apparently the house had a cellar converted to a laundry room, and she fell down the stairs wearing absurdly high heels, which seems a bit odd, doesn't it? I mean, even the most dedicated fashionista swaps her heels for ostrich-feather slippers in the comfort of her own home, doesn't she? That's a detail I find interesting. Anyway, she fell and broke a leg in doing so – a very nasty compound fracture. And there she lay for almost four days, until her mother came and found her.'

'Poor woman. Imagine the suffering.'

'I'd prefer not to. By the time she was found, sepsis had set in – apparently this cellar was prone to ingress by rodents, and not kept scrupulously clean, either – and she'd have lost the leg anyway. But she was just too far gone – dehydrated, low blood pressure from internal bleeding from the fracture, and a nasty bump to the head which caused a bleed on the brain. But she did recover consciousness briefly, shortly after the ambulance crew arrived, and managed to say two words: *Pushed me.* A likely scenario confirmed by the pathologist, who found faint bruising on her chest which could collate with the partial imprint of a hand.'

Her father's eyebrows rise. 'And who did the pushing?'

'That's what got the police interested – that and the fact that the mother initially reported that when she arrived the cellar door was closed. Difficult to close the door behind you as you're falling backwards.'

'So here you are, dispatched to swap your journalist's hat for a sleuth's magnifying glass.'

'Don't take the piss, Dad. I'm here to do a job, get more and better information than any other media outlet. Which should be easy enough, since as far as I'm aware this has so far slipped under our rivals' radar. We think there's a big story here, and I'm going to find it. Apart from the push, it's astonishing the poor woman survived as long as she did, down there alone in the dark. Her will to survive was amazing. I'm going to suggest we call her a Miracle Mum.'

Owen tosses the last piece of his sandwich into the water.

'I hope you'll manage to do that without offending local sensibilities, Polly.'

Polly. A name from childhood, only ever used by him. What its origins were she can't remember.

'Meaning?'

'Your mother and I have to live here, remember. When you turn over rocks, you never know what you're going to find underneath. Tread carefully.'

'Don't worry, Dad. I'll be careful. Not my first rodeo, OK?'

'So where's your first stop?'

'Horse's mouth. I was hoping you'd help me with that. Where would I go to connect with the local constabulary, off duty and off guard? Where might the local CID do its drinking of an evening?'

He laughs. 'I'm sure I don't know. I'm hardly the man to ask about local watering holes. Last time I went in a pub, beer was 50p a pint.'

'But you might know a man who does know.'

'Who do you mean? You're not thinking of Kevin Saddler, surely? He retired from the force, must be five years ago now.'

'He'd still have a clue, though, wouldn't he? You could give him a call, ask how he's doing. Please. For me. Help me get my big scoop.'

He sighs. 'Go on, get out of here. You're frightening the fish.'

'I'll see you at home later on, then. But you will call Kevin Saddler for me, won't you?'

'I'll think about it. No promises.'

'Thanks, Dad. You're a star.'

TEN

Dee speaks across the silent table. Neither of them has eaten much. The food – a ready-meal lasagne – was barely edible in the first place, and certainly no temptation for failed appetites.

'I want to go to Norwich tomorrow. To do some shopping.'

Frank's expression is incredulous. He hasn't shaved since Natalie's death, and his growing beard of sorrow is emerging stone grey. 'Shopping? What on earth for?'

Dee was thinking she'd got it under control, but no. As soon as she thinks of her mission, the wretched tears begin to flow. 'You'll think I'm being ridiculous.'

'I won't think you're ridiculous. I just don't know why you need to go all the way to Norwich. C'mon, love. Look at the state you're in. You're not fit to go anywhere.'

'I want to get something for Natalie to wear.'

Now Frank looks confused. 'Wear where?'

Dee's embarrassed to explain; he'll think her plan fanciful and unnecessary. What does it matter, after all, when nobody will see? But Dee will know. For all time to come, she'll know.

'For the burial. The undertakers said we could choose anything we wanted, but all she's got in her wardrobe are those skimpy dresses and tight trousers. I want to get her something beautiful. I want her to look her best.'

'Surely you can find something? She's got acres of clothes.'

'No.'

Frank considers. 'All right, if you really want to go. I'll drive you.'

'You're not fit to drive. You haven't slept in days. I'll go on the train.'

He looks doubtful. 'Are you sure you'll be OK?'

'No.'

'Do you want me to go with you?'

Dee shakes her head. 'Not really. This is something I want to do for her by myself.'

On the train, Dee stares steadfastly out of the window she's sitting next to, praying there's no one on here that she knows. Conversation is almost certainly beyond her; she's suffering in a fog of otherworldliness, sluggish and fuzzy-headed in a time and space all her own.

The largest part of her died with Natalie. If it weren't for Ruby, she'd see no use in doing anything ever again.

Except this one task.

When the train arrives at the station, she waits for the carriage to empty before getting off herself. Beyond the barriers, some unconscious function guides her where she needs to go, making her pause at pedestrian crossings until it's safe to proceed, avoiding people on the narrow pavements. Life in the city, for everyone else, seems entirely normal, and the city itself brings memories to mind. Here's the baby shop where she and Nat bought Ruby's very first outfits, when the ultrasound confirmed she'd be a girl. Here's the branch of Costa she and Nat used to visit whenever they came shopping together, and Nat always had a caramel cappuccino. Here's the place on the pedestrian precinct where she and Nat once had a very public row about what shoes she could buy for a school dance. After that, Nat didn't speak to her for nearly a fortnight.

They weren't all happy days.

The shop she's looking for – Lulu's – is smaller and more intimate than she remembers, with nowhere to hide inside. She's been here once before, when she still believed the solution to Frank's cheating might lie with her being more outrageous in the bedroom and blew two weeks' wages on impractical but gorgeous French lingerie.

She's older now, and wiser. Judging from the window display, Lulu's doesn't have much for a woman her age anyway.

But she's not here for herself.

This is her one duty remaining. The last thing, the only thing she can do.

The doorbell pings cheerily as she goes through. Inside, it's pretty as fairyland, rosebud lights and vanilla carpet, the floral scent of perfume and chairs covered in gold brocade. Around the walls hang the prettiest items of underwear, silk and chiffon, saucy fripperies of lace.

Natalie would have loved this place.

The woman behind the counter is not much younger than Dee. She smiles and asks if she can help.

Dee starts to cry.

The woman's tag gives her name as Bella. She hurries to Dee's side and guides her to a chair.

Dee opens her handbag, apologising as she hunts for a tissue, but Bella isn't fazed.

'A good cry never hurts,' she says. 'Believe me, we see plenty of tears in here. Are you interested in our mastectomy lines?'

'Oh,' says Dee. 'No. Nothing like that.'

'Oh,' says Bella. 'I thought with your being so upset . . . Usually it's ladies who are trying to come to terms . . .'

'I'm looking for something for my daughter.'

'Well, that's nice.'

'She's died.'

Dee can see Bella wondering why she is there.

'I'm so sorry to hear that. How awful. What was her name?'

'Natalie.'

A flicker of eyelids is enough to tell Dee that Bella knows exactly who Natalie is.

'Oh.' A slight blush rises to her cheeks. 'You don't mean the woman over at Wickney, do you? I read . . .' She tails off, conscious of her insensitivity. 'I'm sorry. How awful. I've been following it on the news. Have the police any idea yet – I mean, do they know who . . . I'm sorry, you'll think me horribly nosey.'

But Bella is only awkwardly phrasing the questions which hang over Dee's every waking moment: the when and why of Natalie's death, and, above all, the identity of the scum who stole her life.

'It doesn't matter,' Dee says. 'But you will be discreet, won't you? I don't want everyone to know. This is a very personal thing.'

'We are mistresses of discretion here.' Dee can see Bella's become more animated now she knows she's dealing with an almost-celebrity, a murder victim's mother. 'What you must be going through . . . I just don't know how I'd cope. What can I show you? What do you have in mind?'

'I want to buy her a nightgown.'

For a few minutes Bella disappears, to return carrying over her arm long silky gowns on padded hangers. One by one, she holds them up for Dee to see and reject: apricot satin, white silk, black lace.

The last she holds up is a shimmering midnight blue, with slender straps and frastaglio embroidery around the neckline.

'This is gorgeous, isn't it?' asks Bella, stroking the sensual fabric. 'So classically elegant, it would flatter any woman.'

Dee brings a laughing Natalie to mind, and mentally dresses her in this exquisite garment, picturing the graceful lady she always knew Nat could be.

All the friction that came between them is no more. Love and loss are all that's left, and this will be love's final gift: a gown to sleep in as she turns to dust.

ELEVEN

The two CID officers – a brawny middle-aged man who looks like he'd be handy in a fight, and a plain, soft-spoken woman whose eyes say she's been here too many times before – have the same funereal dress code and careful manners as the undertakers who were here yesterday. They explain that Natalie's death is being treated as suspicious, but seem unwilling to be pushed on what that actually means. Resources are being allocated, they say, and they will be exploring every avenue. Frank and Dee will be kept up to date every step of the way. They ask a few questions as they finish their coffee, and take their leave with a quiet respectfulness which seems wholly genuine.

Dee closes the door behind them, the click of the latch signalling that she and Frank are shut in together alone. For a few moments, she stands in the hallway, unable to push away memories of when that click brought blessed relief: the times in Natalie's rebellious teenage years when she stayed out way too late, and how it didn't matter in those dark hours whether she was drunk or drugged or had shagged a dozen boys, she was here, back in the sanctuary of home where the world couldn't harm her, and whatever rows and arguments and tantrums daylight might bring, that was enough for now. That sound will never again announce Natalie walking in through that door, and Dee doesn't know how her absence can be borne.

Yet borne it must be.

Frank is gathering up the coffee cups to take them into the kitchen, and it's a sign of his emotional trauma that the last biscuits on the plate remain uneaten. Normally, he'd pop them in his mouth the moment the visitors were gone. Whenever he says he isn't hungry, Dee rarely believes him because Frank always has an appetite, though he sometimes denies it out of consideration for her when she doesn't want to cook.

You can't always rely on Frank's words alone to know he's sincere.

But knowing him as she does, this small thing has meaning. His failure to eat what's available is a window on his suffering.

She follows him into the kitchen, where he's loading the cups into the dishwasher. He slides the leftover biscuits into the bin.

'What did you make of that?' she asks.

He doesn't immediately respond, so she thinks he hasn't heard her over the clatter of the crockery, but as she starts to repeat herself, he interrupts.

'I heard you.' He straightens up and closes the dishwasher, then presses a fist into the small of his back where it sometimes gives him pain. 'I don't know what to think.'

'Was that true, what you told them, Frank?'

'Was what true?'

'About when you saw her last?'

'Why wouldn't it be true?'

Dee watches his face. 'Not everything you say is true, is it?'

He closes his eyes and shakes his head. 'For God's sake, Dee, leave it alone. Stop picking that scab, will you?'

'I noticed something when I went over there.'

'What did you notice?'

'In Ruby's bedroom. You didn't finish emulsioning the walls. You were that close . . .' She holds up her finger and thumb with barely a centimetre between them. 'Another ten or fifteen minutes and you'd have been done. So why didn't you finish?'

'You heard what I told them. She came home and wanted me gone. She was itching to do something online, some Zoom call. I don't know who she was wanting to talk to in such a hurry, or why I couldn't stay. Some boyfriend, most probably. You know Nat. I didn't like to ask. She'd have told me to keep my nose out.'

'You're sure it was that day that happened?'

'Yes, of course I'm sure. It was the Thursday. The Friday I was at work. What is this, are you angling for a job with those guys?'

'No.'

'Well, give it a rest, then. You're giving me a headache.'

The doorbell rings.

'I'll go,' says Dee. 'That'll be Justin bringing Ruby.'

Dee gives Ruby the kind of enthusiastic welcome she always has, kissing the top of her head, stroking her hair, admiring her pink unicorn backpack. Ruby, for her part, manages a smile, though the incessant chatter she always used to bring with her is gone. Overnight she's changed from gregarious to withdrawn. Outwardly, she seems much like any other girl her age. Only if you knew her before can you see how the light that used to shine from her has dimmed.

Ruby's always been keen on baking, but she turns down Dee's offer of making gingerbread men. Instead, she settles in the dining room with the colouring books and pens Dee keeps for her visits. Dee herself is grateful for the quiet, and sits down beside her, watching as the outlined picture – a mermaid in a sea improbably full of fish and dolphins – changes from monochrome to colour.

An hour goes by. Frank comes in and offers to make something to eat, giving Ruby her choice. She says she isn't hungry, but he says he'll make something anyway, and Justin goes to sit with him while he cooks. Dee finds the low murmur of their conversation comforting. Recently, she's not as good at being alone as she used to be.

When Frank calls them through, Ruby picks at her food moodily, leaving her sausages and beans and eating only a few of her chips. Her silence is contaminating, and long pauses in conversation hang heavy over them all. Dee asks Justin what's happening at work, and he says his mother, Freda, is keeping things ticking over, calling on sub-contractors to get the orders out on time.

'We're coping,' he says. 'At the moment, other things come first.'

As the table's being cleared, Justin looks at his watch and smiles across at Ruby. 'We should go soon, munchkin.'

A look of sadness crosses Ruby's face. When she asks, 'Can I stay at Grandma's tonight?' her voice is full of doubt, little more than a whisper.

Dee glances across at Justin to get his view, and when he shrugs *Why not?* she assures Ruby they'd love to have her.

'But I haven't got my pyjamas, Daddy,' Ruby says to Justin. 'I think I might have put some in the car, just in case.' Ruby's smile is wide and appreciative of his forethought. Just as if there were nothing wrong at all.

When Ruby's had her bath, she insists she wants to be read *The Gruffalo's Child*, a once-favourite story from her younger childhood.

Dee's happy to oblige; the child's welcome to whatever small comforts she can find. Settled under the duvet in the glow of the bedside lamp, Ruby seems soothed by the charming pictures and Dee's voice as she reads, and her breathing grows slow.

Not slow enough to sleep, though. When the story's finished, Ruby's still wide awake.

'Will I be living with you sometimes now, Grandma?' she asks.

In truth, Dee doesn't know, and says so. 'I expect you'll come and stay here sometimes, like you always have, but mostly I think you'll be living with Daddy and Grandma Freda.'

'Will Grandpa paint my bedroom at Daddy's house pink?'

Dee thinks of the bedroom at Turle's Cottage, with the painting almost but not quite finished. 'If you want your room pink, I'm sure you can have it pink. Daddy might do it for you, if he has time.'

'Grandma Freda says not. She says bright colours stop people from sleeping, but I don't think they do. Do you?'

'I shouldn't think so. Maybe Daddy could have a word. And I expect Grandpa would paint this room pink, so it could be like your bedroom at the cottage.'

A moment's pause. 'I didn't like that bedroom.'

Dee's surprised to hear this; the room seemed to her perfectly nice, filled to bursting with Ruby's cuddly toys and an abundance of other playthings, far too many for one child alone.

'Didn't you? Why not?'

'I didn't like that house.'

'Really? It was a nice house, in the country. You had that place to make your den, didn't you, under the stairs? I expect you were nice and cosy in there, weren't you?'

'It wasn't my den. And I was always by myself there. Wilf tried to be my friend but Mummy wouldn't let him.'

The house seems suddenly still, as if Ruby's mention of Natalie has conjured her ghost, provoking more of the grief neither of them wants to feel.

'Perhaps she thought he was a bit old to be your friend. Little girls like you want to be playing with boys and girls your own age, not old men like him.'

'But she wouldn't let me invite my friends to our house.'

Dee frowns. 'Why not?'

'Because of her work.'

Always Natalie's work. Dee wonders what to say about it, but Ruby cuts her off, asking, 'Why was everybody cross with Mummy, Grandma?'

'Nobody was cross with her, sweetheart. What do you mean?'

'You were cross with her sometimes. I heard you. And she was cross with everybody back. Except Eric. He smelled like toilet cleaner.'

'Did you meet Eric, then?'

'Only once. He gave me some chocolate eggs, even though it wasn't Easter. And Mummy made me go to bed before it was even dark. I didn't like Eric. Why did Grandpa fight with Mummy?'

Dee's taken aback. 'Did they fight? Maybe they had disagreements sometimes. People who love each other do argue, like when you and your friends have little spats in the playground, but they soon get forgotten, don't they?'

'But they were really shouting. I was scared, but when I went to see why, Mummy shouted at me.'

Dee's thinking on her feet, wondering how she can find out what's been going on without showing Ruby her concern. 'I think Mummy and Grandpa used to rub each other up the wrong way. Sometimes people do that when they're too much alike.'

'I don't think they were alike. Grandpa's always kind.'

The shocking inference can't be missed. Ruby thought her mother unkind. What has been going on?

For the time being, Dee decides to steer the conversation in a different direction.

'Well, then, maybe we should do something kind for Grandpa. How about getting up a few minutes early tomorrow and making him pancakes for breakfast?'

'Maybe,' says Ruby, but Dee can tell that's a subtext for no. Ruby's zest for life could be a long time coming back.

She's quiet then for a while, and Dee thinks she's falling asleep until Ruby says, 'I don't know what I'm going to wear for Mummy's funeral.'

Funeral: a word Ruby had no need to know until a few

days ago. After reading online guidance, Justin's talked to her about what will happen, how Mummy will be in a box called a coffin but won't feel pain or fear or need air to breathe. Ruby wants to be there, and Justin's told her she can wear anything she wants, as well as choosing something to put with Mummy in the casket. For her last gift to her mother, Ruby chose her much-loved Rumpletum bear, because he's always kept her company when she was afraid of the dark and she can't quite believe Mummy won't be a little bit frightened alone in the dark of a sealed wooden box.

'I wanted to wear my frilly dress Mummy liked me to wear, but Daddy and I can't find it.'

'Oh,' says Dee. 'That's odd. Where might it have gone?'

'We don't know. So now I'm not sure. Could I wear my blue party dress I wore for Sasha's birthday? I think it's really pretty, and I have blue shoes that match.'

'If that's what you'd like.'

Another silence, which Dee resists interrupting. Whichever roads Ruby's thoughts are following and however dark they may be, surely it's better to let her mind travel there, in the hope that she'll feel able to confide later what most troubles her.

Then, 'Will you hold my hand until I'm asleep?'

'Of course I will. Snuggle down.'

'Will you leave the landing light on?'

'Don't I always?'

'Sometimes Grandpa turns it off.'

'I'll give him strict instructions not to.'

But as her eyes close, a frown crosses Ruby's face. 'Grandma? You and Grandpa aren't going to die, are you?'

Dee squeezes Ruby's hand and raises it to her lips to kiss it. Questions about death have difficult answers. For now, she'll keep it simple and tell a lie.

'Of course we're not going to die. We're made of strong stuff, me and Grandpa.'

'Wasn't Mummy made of strong stuff?'

Dee hesitates, realising the lie was a mistake. 'Of course she was, but sometimes accidents happen. That's just the way life is.'

'So how do you know you won't die?'

'Because I promise you I won't.'

Immediately, Dee regrets making a commitment way beyond her powers to keep. But it seems enough to comfort Ruby, or at least to stop her asking questions, including the question which most troubles Dee herself: who killed Natalie? Who hated her enough to leave her dying alone in the dark?

For a while after Ruby's fallen into the steady rhythm of sleep, Dee keeps hold of her hand, praying her dreams will be sweet enough to bring some respite from the misery they must all face again tomorrow.

And going downstairs, she leaves the door open a crack, to shine a comforting sliver of light on the bedroom wall.

Dee finds Justin alone in the kitchen, staring at a mug of tea gone cold.

'You're still here.'

'I didn't want to rush off without saying goodnight.'

'Where's Frank?'

Justin points a thumb to the lounge, from where they can

hear a football commentary. 'He wanted to watch the match. I can't fake the interest at the moment.'

Dee sits down beside him. 'It's his form of escapism. His mind empties out while he's watching them play, even if they make a real mess of it. I only wish I could find something that would do the same for me, something that doesn't come out of a bottle. You want a drink?'

Justin shakes his head. 'Not for me, not when I'm driving. You have one, though.'

'No, not tonight. I want a clear head in case Ruby needs me. How are the nightmares?'

'She's still having them. Maybe she always will.'

'Maybe so. And you, Justin. How are you doing?'

He puts his head back, and she sees tears in his eyes. 'Look at me. Isn't it time for me to man up? She wasn't even really my wife any more.'

Dee reaches across and covers his hand with her own. 'You loved her, same as we did.'

'I'd been hoping she and I might get back together again. Now I'll never know, will I?'

'She'd have seen the light, in the end. She had some wild oats to sow, that was all.'

Justin looks at her intently, hoping to find truth in the platitude, but Dee avoids his scrutiny by standing up.

'I'll make you a fresh cuppa.' She takes the kettle and holds it under the tap, and with her back to him says, 'The police were here today.'

'Oh yeah? They came to talk to me yesterday. They have to ask us questions, I suppose.'

'Just filling in the details, they said.' She switches on the

83

kettle, picks up Justin's mug from the table and tips the cold contents down the sink. 'There were things I wanted to ask, but I didn't quite dare. Do you feel that too? Things that weigh on my mind about how she – went – but which might weigh heavier if I know. They said if there was anything we wanted to know about the post-mortem, they'd tell us, but I could tell by their body language they really didn't want to discuss it.' She hesitates. 'They didn't quite say it, but they think it was murder, don't they?'

'Yes,' he says. 'I think they do.'

'I can't believe that. They only think it because of what the ambulancemen thought she said, that someone pushed her. But she wasn't in her right mind, was she? She was barely conscious, never mind in a state to make accusations. And who on earth would do that to my beautiful Natalie?'

As soon as the words are out, she realises she shouldn't have asked the question of Justin, when the answer probably lies among the men Natalie bedded after she decided he wasn't enough for her.

Unsurprisingly, he offers no opinion on who might be a suspect, answering instead with a deflection. 'What does Frank think?'

'He doesn't say much,' admits Dee. 'While the police were here, I don't think he said ten words. I think he's still in shock. But it must be always on his mind, of course it is, and I know if it does come out that someone hurt her, he's going to be mad enough to kill. Which I understand. Sometimes I feel I'd put a knife in his hand, until I think of the blame I carry myself. I lie awake at night and I can't get away from the fact that she was there all alone, and I was here in my nice warm bed, all tucked up and annoyed at her because she hadn't called.'

'If it's any consolation, I feel the same way.'

'Misery loves company.'

Justin nods his sad agreement. 'Can I tell you what I feel worst about?' he says. 'So bad I can hardly stand it? I tried to ring her to agree a time to take Ruby over there, but Nat didn't answer and I thought . . . I just thought she must have been on some bender or off with one of her new men.' Dee hears a catch in his voice: hurt, or jealousy, or anger? Possibly all three, which would be justifiable. 'I tried a couple of times and then – I'm so sorry – I just thought, what the hell, and I told Ruby she'd be staying an extra night with me and I made a fun thing of it. I dropped her off at school the next morning and I was going to ring Nat later on, and if I'm honest, I was going to give her hell. And then you rang me.'

He stares at the tabletop while she makes tea, listening to the spoon rattle in the cups, the opening and closing of the fridge.

Dee puts a mug in front of him and sits down. In the lounge, the crowd roars as United score.

'You don't only lose the person, though, do you?' she says, almost to herself. 'You lose all your hopes for them, your ideas of how it's all going to be. I suppose it's the same for everyone. We have plans for our kids, who they'll be, what they'll do. I always wanted Natalie to be something in the medical profession, a doctor or a nurse. You think you can plan it and control it, but you can't. Your kids are people with their own ideas, their own plans, and there's nothing you can do to make them be airline pilots or teachers any more than you can make them be nice to other people or honest or share your taste in curtains. You can't even make them like the same food you do, or remember your birthday. They're nothing like you, and they may not even love you or want to spend time with you, so I'm grateful that we did at least have that. Because you give them all those years you brought them up, but they don't owe you anything, not in their eyes.' She sips her tea. 'I read a story in the paper once about a woman who'd lost her teenage son. He'd walked out the door and never come back, fifty years before. And all that time, most of her life, she'd been beside herself with grief and worry about her boy, scared to death every time there was a knock at the door in case it was the police come to tell her they'd found his body. And you know what? On her seventieth birthday, she got a phone call, but it wasn't the police, it was him, her son. Just like that, out of the blue. And you know what he said? That he was ringing to wish her happy birthday. He'd been living not a hundred miles away all that time, never been in touch, never even let her know he wasn't dead. And you'd assume, wouldn't you, he was only getting in touch because she'd be dead any minute and he wanted a mention in the will. What a bastard! All those years, he never gave a damn about how she'd worried. Ruined her life and never gave it a thought.

'So you can't make them be doctors or nurses and you can't make them be nice either. Jack the Ripper had a mother, didn't he? Fred West, all the rapists and crooks and the kids who beat up old ladies, all the paedophiles and people traffickers you read about, they've all got mums and dads and not all those parents can have been bad people. Maybe some were, but not all. And we did our best with Natalie but we couldn't make her nice, Justin. Sometimes she seemed nice, but now I wonder if that was her acting. She was a good little actress, was Natalie, very clever at making you believe her untruths. Even so. She didn't deserve to be there alone all that time, lying at the bottom of those stairs, hoping somebody would come.'

She begins to cry, tears running down her face, but it's become such a way of life in these past days she barely notices she's doing it until Justin stands up and pulls several tissues from a fresh box on the worktop, handing all but one to her, wiping his own eyes with the last.

'You were brave to take her on. I've always said that.'

He blows his nose. 'I never felt I had a choice. She knocked me for six from the moment I first saw her at school, and I thought I had to have her at any price. That was my mistake. I blame myself, because I wasn't honest with her. When we first got together, it was over at Holkham, at the Horse Guards.'

Dee dabs her tears and smiles. 'I remember. You went all that way on that moped that didn't do more than twenty miles an hour.'

He nods, remembering too. 'She knew I fancied her way before that, and I knew she'd be there, so I followed and made sure I bumped into her, and you. And I told her I was there because I wanted to join up, be one of those guys. That was pure bullshit, because I never even liked horses, but I was so nuts about her, I was prepared to give it a go, just to get her to look at me. When I applied, of course they saw right through me, that I didn't have the right stuff. I thought that wouldn't matter. We'd made a bond, she and I, and I thought it was strong enough, that she loved me the way I loved her, or if she didn't yet, that she'd learn to love me for who I am, rock-steady and reliable. Because I was happy, I thought she would be too. But she saw that Horse Guards thing as the first in a line of failures. She set the bar high for me, and I always failed to clear it. She said I didn't have ambition, but I did, I do. I want to be the best at what I do, a master craftsman. I want people to say, if you want the job doing properly, mate, you need to go see Justin. I had ambition to build a home with her and Ruby, a proper house we could be proud of. I thought us being a family was enough because it was all I'd dreamed of, but it wasn't enough for her. I don't know what would have made her happy, really, and you know what? I don't think she did either. As long as someone had something she didn't, as long as there was some place she wanted to go and hadn't been, she couldn't settle. Clothes, cars, holidays, she wanted the lot. I said to her, we've got each other, we've got Ruby, we eat well, we sleep well, we wake up to that view of a morning. But she wanted that view to be always changing, and that's not who I am.'

Dee pats his hand. 'Frank and I know you did your best. We always hoped she might have come around to realising what a gem she had in you. Given time.'

'We'll never know now, will we?'

Dee shakes her head. 'Not now, no. We'll never know.'

TWELVE

Dee has barely slept all night.

At 4.30 a.m., she gets up for the second time to make tea, drinking it alone in the almost-dark, waiting for the moment when the first birds sing and this awful day will properly begin.

When she takes Frank up a mug of coffee, she finds him wakeful as herself. As she sits down on the bed, he clasps her hand and asks, 'You OK?' and she nods to confirm she's holding it together, for the time being at least.

She takes a long, hot shower, painstakingly styles her hair, puts on her careful make-up and sprays on perfume, wanting to look her best, as if this is some New Year's Eve or birthday party.

But it's not that.

She dresses in her new clothes and shoes, and the expensive pair of ten-denier tights she prays that she won't ladder, and places the rented hat ready by the front door.

Frank's already in his suit, pulling down his shirt cuffs, fiddling with his tie, handsome and haggard. She notices he hasn't trimmed his mourning beard.

'You look lovely,' he says. 'I think she would approve.'

They both glance at the clock: two hours, at least, to wait.

'I could murder a drink,' says Dee, 'but at this time of the morning . . .'

'I'll have one as well,' says Frank. 'We'll have a brandy. Just a small one.'

Slowly, slowly, time passes.

Until the doorbell rings, and their daughter's funeral begins.

At the church, the crush of people is gratifying, yet overwhelming.

Dee sees it as a blur.

The long black cars, the sombre men in overcoats and hats.

The people gathered by the churchyard gate, the whirr of cameras, the woman she knows from TV with the BBC microphone.

The flowers and the sickly scent of lilies, the tolling bell, the organ wheezing dirges.

The dankness of old stone, the bitterness of candle smoke, the coldness of the place and the dead beneath the floor.

And worst, for pity's sake, her Natalie in that box.

What Dee aches for is to rewind time, to have a chance to make things as they were.

To have her daughter back.

That cannot be.

All right, then.

What Dee wants next most is for all this pomp and ceremony to go away, for all these people – who are these people? – to be gone, for there to be only her and Frank and Ruby and Justin, the people who truly loved Natalie. To be with them, in a hidden, summer place, with trees and soft, sweet grass and the babble of a stream: a place that looks like heaven, where her child can be at peace.

With all her heart, she wishes she had held out for that privacy, with all the time they need to say goodbyes.

People will want to pay their respects, the undertakers had said, gently. *There's significant public interest. We'll be by your side to guide you. We'll be with you every step of the way.*

Dee was eventually persuaded, but the steps are on a path she doesn't want to tread.

The last time she was in this church was for Natalie's wedding. So beautiful she was that day, all smiles on Frank's arm, glowing in sequins and white satin, diamante in her hair.

Today – though no one sees it – she's wearing midnight blue.

Aided by Frank and four strangers, the man she married is carrying her coffin. Justin looks sallow and ill, his black suit hanging off him and his eyes rimmed with red.

Dee walks behind the slow procession, holding tight to Ruby's white-gloved hand. In her party dress, Ruby's a blaze of light blue in an extravagance of black, clutching a single white rose.

Dee finds she doesn't care that all eyes are on her. She sees faces she recognises – her sister and brother-in-law, Frank's boss Jerry, her friends Tina and Julie, Natalie's friend Sarah. The female detective who's been to the house is standing at one side. Natalie's elderly neighbour is in a pew close by her.

All these others she doesn't know, are they friends of Natalie's?

Is one of these strangers her killer? Or worse, is it someone she knows?

She pushes that thought away, and ushers Ruby into a front-row seat.

Natalie's coffin is placed on trestles, and Frank and Justin join them.

The vicar welcomes the congregation and the service begins.

When Frank's turn to speak comes, he walks straight-backed to the lectern.

The church is silent.

Frank clears his throat. '"Warm Summer Sun", by Mark Twain. This is for my beautiful daughter, Natalie.'

His head drops, and he covers his mouth with a trembling hand. Ready to intercede, the vicar stands up from his chair, but Frank composes himself and begins to read.

> 'Warm summer sun,
>   Shine kindly here,
> Warm southern wind,
>   Blow softly here.
> Green sod above,
>   Lie light, lie light.
> Good night, dear heart,
>   Good night, good night.'

Through all the service, Ruby doesn't cry but sits solemnly between Dee and Justin, holding Justin's hand, blank-faced and pale.

Until the final hymn begins. As Justin and Frank move to join the other bearers to carry Natalie from the church, Ruby becomes agitated.

She pulls at Dee's sleeve and asks in a loud whisper, 'Where's Mummy going?'

Dee doesn't know what to say. The plan is Dee's sister will take care of Ruby while she and Frank and Justin attend the internment.

'They're taking her to a special place.'

'Can I go?'

'Not today, sweetie. You and Daddy can go another day.'

Ruby's eyes fill with tears. 'But I haven't given her my flower.'

Dee glances to the front of the church. The hymn is coming to its end and the bearers are all in place, waiting for the subtle order – at any moment – to lift the casket.

Dee helps Ruby into the aisle, and oblivious of protocol, she runs to her father. He bends down to her as she whispers in his ear.

Justin picks her up. Against the black of his suit, her party dress sparkles. Laying the white rose on the lid, she blows the casket a childish kiss.

The bearers hoist the casket to their shoulders, and Wiz Khalifa's 'See You Again' – the song Justin and Ruby chose for Natalie's exit – begins to play through the loudspeakers.

It's been a long day without you, my friend . . .

With his focus on the coffin, Justin doesn't have a spare hand to offer Ruby.

But, holding on to his suit jacket, she sticks by him anyway, taking care to match the bearers' pace with poignant gravity.

THIRTEEN

Sarah Osgood knows the route to school very well. For years as a child she walked it herself, and she does it again now for her son Riley's sake, because somehow, somewhere along the line apparently it became too dangerous for kids to walk to school alone, even in a place like Wickney, where strangers stand out like sore thumbs. Stranger danger is imprinted on them from the day they're born, yet even so they can't be trusted; children are naive, easily distracted and lured away. Sarah doesn't enjoy the walk, but she'd rather do it than be sitting at home watching the clock every afternoon from 3 p.m. You hear such stories these days, such terrible things. If anything happened to Riley, she doesn't know what she'd do.

So every weekday at this time – school holidays excepted, though they're never long enough – she puts on the capacious tartan coat Natalie used to call her dog blanket, fastens little Lizzie in the buggy and heads up the lane.

The school buildings sit between a flat, grassed field and a playground edged by high metal fences more suited to a prison than a place for children. At least Wickney has plenty of space for the kids to run around: a derivative benefit of cheap land prices and low population density. The playground is a blank tarmac canvas, with a few lacklustre clumps of daffodils poking through the grass around its perimeter and a pair of benches under a wooden shelter with its back to the prevailing wind. Fastened to the fence, a grinning cartoon child holds up a sign in coloured letters, wishing visitors *Welcome to Our School*.

Until recently, in spite of the walk, this used to be the best part of Sarah's day – a time for socialising, a bit of a chat, sometimes a good laugh.

Since Natalie's gone, that's gone too.

She misses Natalie. The good and the bad.

With all the weight she's put on – she crossed the line from overweight to obese some time ago, never losing the baby weight with Riley, never mind Lizzie – Sarah walks slowly, and gives herself plenty of time for the short journey. When she arrives just after three, the other school-gate mums are already gathering, standing behind their pushchairs like sentries behind a wall. Even though Easter will soon be here, an icy wind stings like November, and the women and their offspring too young to be at school are wrapped up in down jackets, with thick hats pulled down over their ears.

Sarah takes her place among her friends, gripping the handle of the well-used buggy, pushing it back and forth in a habitual motion, unnecessary since Lizzie's already asleep, snug under a Peppa Pig blanket, her head warm in a faux-fur bonnet.

'What's up?' she asks.

'How was the funeral?' The blunt question's put by a glowering, dumpy woman, whose hands are thrust deep in the pockets of a black coat.

The woman beside her nudges her. 'Subtle, April. It's polite to say hello first.'

'That's rich coming from you, Jess,' objects April. 'Weren't you just saying you were dying to hear how it was?'

'I don't mind,' says Sarah, going a little pink at being the centre of attention. 'It was OK, just really sad. Her dad did a reading and he could hardly get through it. He kept breaking down.' The memory of it provokes tears, and she wipes her eyes with the back of her hand. 'Look at me. I still can't believe she's actually gone.'

'She was a good friend to you,' says Jess, and April flashes her a look.

'Hi, all.' Hannah – prettiest among them, now Natalie's gone – joins the group. 'How was the funeral, Sarah?'

'She's just telling us,' says Jess. 'Were the press there?'

'I saw some TV cameras,' says Sarah. 'I don't think I was on, though.'

'You weren't,' says April. 'I saw the report on *Look East*. They showed the arrival of the coffin and Justin and Ruby with Nat's mum and dad. There were a lot of flowers. Her mum looked good, I thought.'

'She was wearing a lot of make-up,' says Sarah. 'Justin looked really handsome in his suit. And Ruby was a little angel in her frock, all solemn she was, poor kid.'

'They interviewed a policeman,' puts in Hannah. 'He didn't say much, just that they were continuing with their inquiries. Why do they always say that? It's completely meaningless.'

'Just means they're not getting anywhere,' says April. 'Cop-speak for *we haven't a clue*.'

'They came to talk to me, actually,' says Sarah, and she goes even pinker.

The women all stare at her. 'When?'

'Two days ago. A man and a woman. They just rolled up and knocked on the door.'

'What did you do?'

'I asked them in. Made them a cup of tea.'

'What did you tell them?'

Sarah shrugs. 'They asked me all about her love life, stuff like that. If she had money issues, seemed worried about anything at all.'

'What did you say?'

'I told them about her and Justin, how they split up.'

'She was thinking about getting back with him,' says Jess.

'No, she wasn't,' insists Sarah. 'She never said that to me. She really liked that new bloke she'd been seeing. Eric somebody. I don't know his last name.'

'Something Polish,' says Jess.

'Latvian,' says April. 'Same difference. Where'd she meet him, anyway?'

'Probably that club in Norwich,' says Hannah. 'Revolution, is it, Sarah?'

'She goes there sometimes, yes,' says Sarah. 'Went there. That's not where she met him, though.'

'What about the old man next door, did you mention him?' asks Jess.

'I did,' says Sarah, 'but they weren't interested in what I thought about him. They've already spoken to him.'

'There you go,' says April. 'I said it all along. Never any smoke without fire, is there?'

Sarah's gaze follows a very tall, very thin man walking towards the school. He's in a definite minority, one of only three men here, and he's keeping himself to himself, going to stand alone under the budding branches of a horse-chestnut tree.

'There's Justin,' says Sarah, as the pinkness in her cheeks deepens and spreads down her neck to her chest. 'I wonder if I should go and talk to him?'

A bell rings.

'Too late,' says April.

The school door bursts open, and children come pouring out, skipping, dawdling, running to the waiting parents. Sarah keeps an eye on Justin, who's soon joined by Ruby. She shows him a picture she's painted and they both smile. Coping, somehow.

A boisterous boy runs up to Sarah, knocking the buggy as he foists his schoolbag on to her.

'Careful,' she says, but without any serious reprimand, and she ruffles his hair. 'Had a good day?'

'Not bad. Can I get some sweets?'

'I suppose so,' says Sarah, thinking of treats for herself from the Spar's bakery shelves. 'We'll go the pretty way along the river, shall we?'

She pushes the buggy ahead of her, finding her way between parked and departing cars, ending up on the far pavement across from the school. Riley ambles a step behind. The footpath's narrow, following the line of the backs of a row of terraced houses, and Sarah's walking slowly, almost dawdling, but while Riley is wondering what he can do to hurry her along to the shops, Sarah halts and says, 'Hi, Justin.'

He's approaching a silver car, and that's where Sarah's stopped. Justin's straight blond hair flops in his eyes. He's too gaunt to be called physically attractive, gangling and skinny, wearing work-worn jeans and the rock-band hoody Natalie bought him for Christmas two years ago – close to the end for them – with the weird image of a tarot-card Death she said gave her the creeps. The hoody's just about wrecked now, fraying at the neck, the indelible stain of a drop of carelessly eaten curry on the chest, but still he keeps on wearing it, like a talisman, a statement of his tedious fidelity to a woman who threw him away.

With long, thin fingers – like a piano player's fingers, thinks Sarah – he beeps the key to unlock the car. His other hand holds tight to Ruby, and in her dark hair and striking brown eyes – nothing like Justin's blue ones – and her dimples when she smiles, Sarah sees Natalie and her heart turns over. Destined to be a heartbreaker, like her mother.

Justin's no heartbreaker, but he has a kindly face, and some women are smart enough to go for kindness over looks.

'Hi, Sarah,' he says, distractedly. 'Ruby, get in the car.'

She's got that blush again all over her face.

'How's things?' she asks him, and then does all the talking without waiting for any answer. 'Stupid question, sorry. I've been wanting to ask you if there's anything I can do, I mean like mind Ruby for you. She can sleep over if she wants, give you some time to . . . She likes coming to ours, don't you, Ruby? Or come for a meal, I don't mean anything special, you know, but if you're not wanting to cook I'm home all day, what else do I have to do, right? Or if you need to talk, I'm here, any time. I miss her too, it's like . . . You've got my number, haven't you?'

Justin's climbing into the driver's seat, and smiles wanly as he pats his pocket, indicating her number's in there.

'Any time, night or day,' says Sarah, and Justin slams the car door.

She watches him go. As he turns the corner, she lifts her hand in a wave he can't possibly see.

'Is Ruby coming to our house, Mum?' asks Riley, not really a fan of girls, or really caring one way or the other.

'Maybe one day,' says Sarah. 'But no, she's not coming today.'

FOURTEEN

Gabby finds Aldern's woodyard down a single-track road sign-posted Wickney Fen. The road's the same as too many others in the district, in poor repair, pitted by potholes that would break a car's suspension if hit at speed, especially a car like her low-slung Mazda. But she takes her time dodging the worst hazards, sometimes swerving so hard to left or right she ends up with two wheels hair-raisingly close to the steep banks of the dyke which gapes between the hardtop and the wide, flat fields of cabbages and winter wheat.

Ahead she sees a stand of the monstrous, pervasive evergreen trees used as windbreaks throughout the fens, and knowing it must mark her destination signals a right turn to no one at all. City habits die hard. Sure enough, she finds the triffid growth of the trees almost conceals a professionally printed sign, with an attractive logo of a log cabin among pine trees and the wording: *J. Aldern Timber Buildings*.

The dense perimeter of trees renders the yard gloomy even on this bright spring day. Gabby turns in through the gate and parks outside a log-cabin office, between a silver Seat and a company van painted an eye-catching orange, branded with the same logo as the sign and a photo of a very attractive summerhouse Gabby would covet for her own garden, if she had one. A 4x4 truck with its wheel arches dipped in what looks like farmyard slurry is parked alongside stacks of cut timber covered by weighted tarpaulins. At the end of the yard is a barn converted to a workshop, from where comes the whine of a power saw.

Climbing from the car, Gabby sniffs the antiseptic scent of sawdust and pine shavings. It's muddy underfoot, and she's pleased she's worn serviceable flat shoes rather than the kitten heels which are her daytime wear in London. Opening her shoulder bag, she checks she has her phone (used for work purposes as her camera and recording device) and her old-school reporter's notebook and pen, with which interviewees are generally more comfortable. Seeing her writing very little puts them at ease, makes them feel they're having a regular conversation. Especially if they don't know the recorder's running in her bag.

For a moment, the saw stops whining, and she hears instead the lumbering rumble of farm machinery running over the land at the back. A pigeon flies up from one of the trees, startling her. The flapping wings are a country sound she's all but forgotten.

Opening the office door, she walks into a fug of heat. A radio is playing, a talk station where a member of the public is giving a rambling opinion on North Sea oil production down a crackling phone line. The office is small, one wall taken up by samples of exterior paint finishes, another by wood samples, pale lime through dark walnut. The coffee machine in one corner gives her brief hope of refreshment, until she notices its unplugged power lead dangling.

Behind a desk fronted by two visitors' chairs is a woman in her late fifties, with short, practical grey hair, arms folded across her body over a beige Aran cardigan, as if she's trying to keep warm. Thin and sharp-featured, her thick-lensed glasses magnify her eyes like some kind of insect. No make-up, no welcome. As she reaches out to turn down the radio, Gabby gives her a smile.

She has her press pass ready in her hand.

'Gabby Laflin, *Daily Herald*. I have an appointment to speak with Justin.'

The woman doesn't introduce herself. 'He's in the workshop.'

'Thank you.' Gabby's turned to leave when the woman says, 'I'll walk down with you.'

'Really, I can find my own way.'

'I need to speak to Justin anyway.'

She stands up, and Gabby sees she's tall, wearing grey trousers that hang around her waist.

'Have you worked for Justin for long?'

She gives a sniff, as if Gabby's given offence. 'He doesn't pay me. I'm his mother, Freda.'

Now she's round the front of the desk, Gabby holds out her hand. 'I'm so sorry, Mrs Aldern. You should have said.'

Freda's handshake is cold and flaccid. 'You wrote that piece about my ex-daughter-in-law.' Not Natalie or Nat, Gabby notices. 'What did you call her? The "Tragic Miracle Mum"?'

That was Gabby's front-page piece, leading with the awfulness of Natalie's almost-four-day wait to be found, the superhuman resources she must have called on to survive. She herself had found the story harrowing and difficult to write, speculating on how Natalie must have felt drifting in and out of consciousness with no idea whether help would arrive in time. As it happened, alive though she was, it was already too late.

'Such an awful story,' she says. 'I'm sorry for your loss.'

'Not my loss,' says Freda, changing what Gabby now sees are house slippers for a pair of black Crocs. 'But Justin's taken it very hard, as of course has little Ruby. Such a tragedy for her. But she seems to be coping, bless her.'

'You say your ex-daughter-in-law,' says Gabby, as Freda opens the office door and leads the way back outside. The power saw is whining again. 'It's my understanding Justin and Natalie were not yet divorced. Technically she was still related to you, I suppose, and wasn't she legally Justin's next of kin?'

'She stopped being related to me the day she left my son, and very glad I was of it.' She closes the door behind them. 'No man could have done more for her than he did. And do you know what? She wasn't worth it. She was never worth it. Fur coat and no knickers, that was Natalie. Put that on your front page and print it.'

Walking a pace or two behind Freda across the yard, Gabby can hide her shock. In her experience, victims of tragic death are revered, dressed up in the ethereal colours of near-sainthood, any flaws in personality – even downright nasty traits and outright villainy – whitewashed for public consumption, with the deceased displayed as paragons of every possible virtue: best dad, most caring mum, hard-working, sober, generous, brave, you name it. Freda was Natalie's mother-in-law, and those relationships are often tricky, fair enough. But to make such a statement to a representative of a national newspaper is a clear invitation to dig deep. No tears for Natalie here, that's for sure.

By the time they're close to the workshop, the whine of the saw is painful in her ears. The workshop is lit by high-wattage fluorescent lights, no doubt to counteract the perpetual gloom cast by the looming trees. She can see only one man in the workshop, and concludes he must be Justin.

'Does he work alone?' she asks Freda.

'Mostly. He's got mates he can call on for bigger jobs, freelancers. He learned the golden rules of a successful business from his father. No credit and no staff.'

The sawing stops, and Freda takes advantage of the sudden silence to call out, 'Justin!' The man bending over the planks he's been sawing brushes off sawdust to check the finish, and removes his ear-defenders. 'You've got a visitor.'

Gabby steps forward and introduces herself. 'Thanks for seeing me. Please accept condolences from everyone at the *Herald*.'

Justin doesn't answer. He has a look about him that's lost, unanchored, adrift. And he's not what she expected for Natalie; he must be pushing thirty but is still rocking the overgrown teenager look in his work jeans and rock-band hoody, where Natalie was – as far as Gabby can judge – a dedicated clubber and quite a looker. Being unkind, she'd say he was punching above his weight.

But maybe – under normal circumstances where he hasn't suffered a devastating loss – he's every woman's dream man. Maybe he's attentive, considerate, faithful.

In Gabby's view, faithful would be a great start.

She's aware Freda's still standing behind her, plainly intending to be in on this conversation, wherever it leads. But Justin deflates that expectation by looking her squarely in the eye and saying, 'Do you think you could make us some tea, Mum?'

Freda doesn't quite harumph, but when she says, 'I'll see if I can find biscuits as well, shall I?' Gabby doesn't miss the bitter sarcasm.

As his mother walks, arms folded, back to the office, Justin says, 'There won't be any tea, I don't expect. She doesn't like to do what she calls menial jobs.'

'So who does make the tea around here?'

'Usually I do, or the lads if they're here.'

'And do you make your mother a cuppa?'

'She doesn't drink tea, except camomile or nettle.' He gives a wan smile. 'It's probably the nettles that keep her prickly. We can sit over here, by the bench.'

The workbench strikes Gabby as immaculately tidy. A vast array of tools – chisels, mallets, hand saws, files – are arranged by size in clamps on the wall, and along the back of the bench is an array of glues and varnishes, with many sizes of brushes clean and ready in pots. Three long-legged wooden stools stand in front of the bench, sturdy-looking but elegant with back supports.

He invites her to sit down. 'Comfortable?'

'Very.'

Pleased, he nods. 'All my own work.'

'Nice job.'

He hesitates. 'D'you want to see something else I made? Something I made for Nat?' His face softens with sadness, with his loss. 'I was making it for her birthday last year but I never gave it to her. She won't ever see it now.'

He disappears into a side-room, returning with an object the size of his hand wrapped in a piece of dark-blue velvet. Removing the cloth, he holds out a wooden heart, carved and polished, amazingly cut to hold a second heart suspended within.

'It's walnut,' he says, rubbing a thumb over the polished surface. 'See the grain here? I had a piece left over from a special job I was doing, and I thought it was perfect to make something for her. Two hearts beating as one, that was my idea, but turns out she was thinking different. I was still hoping that when she got over her fling, she and I might . . . you know. That she might see sense, and want to be a family again.'

'It's beautiful,' says Gabby. 'You've got real talent, Justin. Can I take a picture of it?'

'Yeah, course. Don't know about talent though, more like years of practice. Five years old I was when my dad gave me my first penknife and a stick to whittle. Best thing he ever did for me. I felt I could see something in that wood, see what it wanted to be. I've always felt that. Things don't always want to be the same, they want to change into something else. That's true of people too. Not much you can do about it.' He folds the velvet over the heart, as if he's exposed himself enough. 'Don't know what I'll do with it now. Maybe I'll give it to Ruby when she's old enough to look after it. Hours of work there are in that. Days, if you add it all up.'

Gabby can't help wondering where Natalie was, what she was doing while Justin was here, in the workshop, whittling his love token for the wife he'd already lost. Maybe he'd have been better buying her flowers like anyone else and spending more time at home, though as anyone knows, home isn't always a place you want to be, and that makes her think maybe Justin's wearing a pair of very thick-lensed rose-tinted glasses.

She gets her pen and notebook ready. 'Can I ask you a few questions? What we're aiming for is maximum exposure for the case, to encourage anyone who has any information to come forward and talk to the police. What we try and do is to get readers to engage, let them know what kind of person Natalie was, what you loved about her. For example, how did you two meet?'

Justin immediately looks tearful, but Gabby's used to that and switches off her natural response to want to make him feel better in favour of pushing him harder.

'We were high-school sweethearts. I was nuts about her, same as half the lads in our year. She was so beautiful, I thought she was out of my league, but we had so much in common. We used to laugh at the same stuff. She had a wicked sense of humour, could make a joke out of anything. Everyone knew her, round here. Everyone knew my Natalie.'

A wicked sense of humour, thinks Gabby, *is often kind-speak for a razor-sharp, waspish tongue. Did Natalie upset the wrong person?*

'When Ruby came along, I thought our lives were perfect. We were doing all right for money, the business was doing well. But she was ambitious, didn't just want to be a mum or work on some supermarket checkout.'

'When did you last see her yourself?'

He shakes his head, remembering. 'Not since the weekend before, when I dropped Ruby off. I had Ruby weekends, see, took her back to her mum's Sunday evenings, normally. That

Sunday evening when I thought Nat wasn't home, I took Ruby away and didn't even ring her, I was that mad at her for letting Ruby down. It wasn't the first time, by a long chalk. And now I know she was there, all by herself in that cellar. I'll never forgive myself. How could I? Biggest mistake of my life.'

Gabby thinks she's got her headline there. 'How have the police been?'

'Oh, absolutely brilliant, can't fault them. I know they're doing all they can, and they're keeping me in touch with the investigation, every step of the way.'

'And how's Ruby coping?'

'She misses her mum. We both miss her, every minute of every day.'

'Do you know who's on the police's list of suspects?'

A naughty question, this one, that she should be asking of the police themselves. But nothing ventured.

Justin himself seems to sense the impropriety of it. 'You want to talk to them about that.'

Gabby puts down her pen. 'Off the record, though, Justin, who do you think did it?'

He shakes his head. 'Not for me to say, is it? You don't print this, right? Off the record?'

'Off the record.'

'I got two theories. I know she'd got some bloke in tow, Lithuanian or Polish, I don't know which and it's all the same with them anyway. You've only got to read the newspapers round here to know they've got no respect for the law. Maybe she and him had too much to drink and things turned ugly.'

Gabby nods agreement. To her, it's the likeliest scenario. 'And your second idea?'

'Off the record? You swear?'

'I swear.'

'You don't write this down, right?'

'Right.'

'That old boy next door. Now, don't get me wrong, I've always found him alright, friendly, polite. But Nat, she wouldn't have anything to do with him. She didn't trust him, I know that for a fact. Ruby liked him though, and she kept asking me if we could go round and feed his ducks, play with the cat. Animal mad, Ruby is. But once when I went to pick Ruby up, Nat said she was going to have him checked out, see if he was on the paedo register or anything, and when I asked why – like I say, he always seemed harmless to me – she said he was always watching, trying to look in the house.'

Gabby frowns. 'At Natalie, or Ruby?'

'Hard to say. She didn't know, I don't think. I told the police though, because if she did try and find out about him, they'd have a record of it, wouldn't they? And that would put him at the top of their list.'

And if the neighbour found out she'd been asking questions, that might have made him angry, thinks Gabby. *Angry enough to become violent?*

'You won't print any of that, will you? The police said if I say anything to anyone it might prejudice the investigation.'

'Course not,' says Gabby. 'Can I get some pictures of you, Justin? Maybe over there, working with the saw?'

Freda appears in the doorway, holding a tray with three mugs and a plate of biscuits.

Mother tiger? wonders Gabby. *Or something else?*

'Tea's ready,' says Freda, putting the tray down on the

workbench. 'How you are getting on with your questions? Justin, it's nearly time to go and fetch Ruby from school.'

'I know, Mum,' says Justin.

'We're nearly all done,' says Gabby, relieved that it's true. 'Just a couple of photos and a cup of tea and I'll leave you in peace.'

FIFTEEN

Wilf is peeling onions for a beef casserole when he hears a vehicle pull up outside. A visitor at this time – not the postman, for sure – is a curiosity, and he rinses and dries his hands quickly before hurrying to the dining-room window to see who's here.

A car has parked on the grass verge, under the dangling pink blooms of the cherry trees overhanging the wall. A brisk breeze is pulling petals from the flowers and scattering them in the lane. Soon the blossom will be over for another year.

He doesn't recognise the car, nor does he know the two men getting out of it. As they walk up the gravel drive, he sees them give the house and garden a once-over, exchanging a *Nice if you can afford it* kind of a look. People don't appreciate the work that goes into it. They don't appreciate the responsibility and expense.

One of the men knocks rather too loudly at the kitchen door, and Wilf finds himself reluctant to answer. What if they're con men, and him here alone? He delays a minute or two, but they're patiently waiting, not speaking to each other, so in the breath-holding silence Wilf hears the trickle of water from the fountain in the duck pond.

When they knock again, he feels obliged to answer. Checking his tie is straight, he opens the door.

His first impression is of a comedy duo: one heftily built and balding, the other much shorter, bearded and with luxuriant, dark hair glossed with some kind of oil. Both are wearing the sort of chain-store suits Wilf's father would have frowned on. The balding one is smiling; the other's showing nothing on his face.

They both hold up leather wallets embossed with metal coats of arms, opening them to show laminated photos of themselves with *Norfolk Constabulary* printed overhead.

The bald one introduces himself as Dagless, his colleague as DC Bailey.

'We'd like a word, if you don't mind,' says Dagless. 'Just routine, nothing to worry about. Is now a good time?'

Wilf doesn't mind. A uniformed officer came to call on the first day the police were at Turle's Cottage, took his details and told him they'd appreciate him giving a statement. He's been expecting their visit ever since, and even bought shortbread biscuits in anticipation.

'Of course,' he says, and stands back from the door, holding it wide open. 'Please, do come in.'

The policemen are unapologetically looking around the kitchen, taking it in, while Wilf's wondering whether this is an occasion to bring out Grandmother's Royal Worcester cups and saucers, which so very rarely get an outing, or whether that's *de trop* under these sad circumstances and it might be better to stick to everyday mugs.

'Excuse the mess,' he says, even though there is none, only a chopping board and a few vegetables and a sharp-bladed knife. 'Shall I make tea? Or there's coffee, if you'd prefer. Only instant, I'm afraid. I'm not much of a coffee drinker myself.'

'Nothing for us, thanks,' says Bailey, and Wilf finds himself disappointed.

'Well, if you change your minds,' he says. 'Do go through. We can be comfortable in the lounge.'

The policemen take seats at opposite ends of the sofa, not relaxing back into it but leaning forward on their spread knees, as if preparing to reveal something of great importance. Mr Grimes is sleeping on the armchair. Wilf shoos him off to sit down himself, and Mr Grimes stalks from the room, offended.

Wilf has the same sense he had in the kitchen of their taking everything in, assessing, and he looks around with a feeling akin to anxiety, checking to be sure there's nothing – what could there be? – incriminating. But the rugs are vacuumed, the bureau's polished and the hearth swept; the marble bust inherited from Great-aunt Sophie of a very handsome Lord Nelson in full regalia looks pleasing in pride of place on the baby grand piano, alongside a vase of tulips cut yesterday.

'Are you sure you won't have refreshments?' he asks. 'It really is no trouble.'

'Thank you, no, Mr Hickling,' says Dagless. 'We've had our fill of coffee at the station.'

'It's an unusual name for a house, Nine Brethren,' says Bailey, showing an unexpected interest. 'What's the history behind that?'

'People often ask me, and it is intriguing,' answers Wilf.

'Before my family bought it, the house was a meeting place for Freemasons. Only a small lodge, reportedly inaugurated by the nine brothers in the name. I have a copy somewhere of a nineteenth-century history of Freemasonry in the county, and I'm proud to say Nine Brethren House has a mention in that from as far back as 1740.'

'Have you lived here long, then – Wilfred, isn't it?' asks Dagless.

'Wilfred, yes. Though I answer mostly to Wilf. And this house, I've been here all my life, quite literally since I was born here, in the bedroom over our heads. It was bought by my paternal great-grandparents, handed down to my own mother and father, and since their deaths, to me. Sadly, I'm the last of the line. There'll be no more Hicklings at Nine Brethren House after I'm gone.'

'Live by yourself, do you?' asks Bailey.

'Just me and Mr Grimes.' Bailey's eyebrows rise. 'My cat.'

Dagless clears his throat. 'Obviously we're here about the tragic death of your neighbour, Natalie Cutter.'

Wilf places his hand on his heart. 'That poor, poor woman! To think of her lying there all that time when I might have gone to help her. It's affected me quite badly, to be honest, badly enough to give me nightmares.'

'How long was she there, Wilf?' asks Bailey.

Wilf blinks. 'Exactly? I'm sure I don't know. The news reports suggest two or three days at least.'

'And in that time, you yourself never went to the cottage?'

'I'm sorry to say I didn't, no.'

'You weren't on friendly terms with Natalie, then?'

Wilf hesitates. 'What do you mean by friendly terms? We

115

weren't on unfriendly terms, if that's what you're asking. We weren't on any terms at all, really. She hadn't been living there very long, and we hadn't had chance . . . If I'm being honest, I found her a little stand-offish. I think she was being protective, but there really was no need.'

'Protective of what?' asks Dagless.

'Of her daughter, Ruby,' says Wilf. 'Ruby and I had spoken once or twice. She was keen to come and feed the ducks, which is understandable.'

'Where had you spoken to Ruby, Wilf?' asks Bailey.

'She came to talk to me once while I was feeding the swans by the bridge in Wickney village. Her mother wasn't happy about that, I realise, but what was I to do when the child approached me? We weren't strangers to each other, after all. She used to wave to me sometimes from her bedroom window, and we had spoken through the garden fence. She'd found a hole there we could chat through. She was going to ask her father if she could visit me. She thought he might be more amenable to the idea than her mother was.'

'So Natalie was unaware of this contact?' asks Dagless.

'I really couldn't say. Ruby is quite an eloquent child, so it's quite probable she would have mentioned our conversations in passing. I didn't – and don't – think it was anything to hide. We are both human beings, after all, and as far as I'm aware there is no law as yet preventing one human being communicating with another.'

'That depends on circumstances,' says Bailey. 'But you and she – you and Natalie, that is – you'd had no disagreement or arguments?'

'Absolutely not. She and I never spoke. Except for that one

time on the riverbank. You know, I am of course very happy to help with your inquiries, if that's what you call them, but I do think you're getting the wrong idea, asking me about my relationship with Natalie. I thought you'd be asking me about who I saw coming and going from the cottage.'

'Who did you see coming and going then, Wilf?' asks Dagless.

'Well, that's the thing, and I don't want you to think me unhelpful, but there are two gentlemen – no, three – who come to call next door, and I can't in all honesty say who was here when. There's the tall chap I assume is Ruby's father, since he usually has her with him, and a man who's been doing some decorating, who I've surmised is also a relative of some kind since he visits regularly too and at odd times, sometimes with an older woman I assume is Natalie's mother – the family resemblance is striking – and once or twice recently, a man I haven't seen before, a youngish man with a ponytail, maybe a friend or boyfriend. Those are of course aside from the postman and so on. I've been racking my brains since this – incident, you'd probably call it – occurred, and I'm afraid one day does rather run into another for me, retired as I am, and it's difficult to remember who was here on what particular day.'

'You seem to have been paying a lot of attention to the comings and goings next door, Wilf. Natalie was a very pretty woman, wasn't she?'

'Don't think me unkind, but she really wasn't to my taste. An old man like me, you know, your appetite wanes somewhat.'

'Do you have family, Wilf? Ever been married?'

'I never married, no. It's not for everyone, is it? My nearest relative is my sister, Margot. She has a place in Derbyshire, in the Peak District.'

'Nephews and nieces, then?'

'She never married either. It is a regret for both of us that neither of us had children. I love children. They're so full of life, aren't they? Inquisitive, curious, just a delight. Do you have children, Inspector?'

'Sergeant. Can you take us through your movements for the dates in question when Natalie received her injuries, specifically Friday and Saturday, the twenty-fourth and twenty-fifth of March?'

'Quite easily. I was at home. I'm rarely away from home these days, now I'm not working. Perhaps I might have done a little shopping, but apart from that I'm a homebody.'

'And who did you see call at the house on that day?'

'To be honest, I don't specifically recall any callers. There was what looked like a delivery van, a plain white van, one day, but I can't recall whether it was Friday or Saturday.'

'None of these three men you mentioned?'

'I don't believe so, no. But I'm not on sentry duty twenty-four hours a day. I do go out from time to time.'

'And did you go out on that Friday?'

'I don't think so, no.'

'Saturday?'

'I went to the library, if I recall correctly. That's easily checked, because I have the date stamps in the books I borrowed. Here.' He stands, and crosses to a small table where a book – a hardback edition of a John Boyne novel – is half read, with a page marked with a Norfolk Libraries bookmark.

Wilf opens the cover. 'Here we are. Stamped to be returned on the fifteenth. I think that was a Saturday, wasn't it?'

Bailey makes a note. 'And how long were you out?'

'A couple of hours, I suppose. I go to the central library in Norwich because they have a much better selection than our little backwater branches. And I like to take my time choosing, because it's a long way to take them back if I've chosen unwisely. So I was gone easily two hours, I'm sure.'

'On the Saturday.'

'I believe so, yes.'

Wilf can see them thinking it's a wide window.

'But on the Friday you were home and you saw no one visit the house?'

'Well, not no one. The postman came here, I think, but I don't know if he went next door. And the delivery van, but that might have been Saturday too, as I say. Oh. There was that woman.'

'What woman?' asks Bailey.

'A woman came on foot, with a young child in a pushchair. She told me she was one of Natalie's friends. I said Natalie was out, but I don't think she believed me. She said she was going to knock anyway, so I left her to it.'

'What did this woman look like?' asks Dagless.

Wilf hesitates. 'I don't mean to be unkind, but she was well-covered. Plump, you might say. She was wearing a tartan coat or cloak of some sort.'

'And this was on the Saturday?'

'That was the same day I went to the library, so almost certainly.'

'Why did you tell this woman Natalie wasn't at home?' asks Bailey.

'Because I thought she wasn't. The place was so quiet.'

'You didn't know it for a fact, then?'

'I suppose I assumed.'

Dagless sighs. 'What work did you do, Wilf?'

'I managed a hotel. Quite a nice one, Illingham Hall. It belonged – and still does, I assume – to the Goodrich family. They're related to royalty through Anne Boleyn, who had Norfolk connections as I'm sure you're aware. I was quite friendly with the family, though of course after I left that friendship fell away.'

'Why did you leave?' asks Bailey.

'I was lucky enough to come into some money, which enabled me to take an early retirement. If I'm careful, I'm in the happy position that I no longer need to work. My needs in life are modest, and I have no mortgage or rent to pay.'

'Are you an automated sort of a person, Wilf? Spend much time online?'

'Me? Good heavens, no, I'm a complete dinosaur. I used to have a laptop, but when it gave up the ghost I didn't replace it. It lives in that cupboard over there. I've never thrown it away because they have private details on them, don't they, and I'm afraid of it falling into the wrong hands.'

'Mind if I have a look?' Dagless is already rising from his chair.

'Not at all,' says Wilf, though his expression is of bemusement. 'I have a Kindle for reading – you'll see it on the armchair over there – though I do prefer a proper book. The Kindle has an internet connection for downloading, of course, but I rarely use it for anything else. I pay all my bills at the post office.'

Dagless opens the cupboard, peers in at the outdated laptop and shakes his head at Bailey. 'Do you have a mobile phone, Wilf?'

'Yes, but it's neither sophisticated nor reliable. I prefer the landline.'

Dagless returns to his seat. 'What about banking? Do you have an online account?'

'Not really my thing, as I say. I visit a branch if I need to. Though they make that hard these days, don't they? No one ever thinks of the technically challenged like me.'

'Indeed,' says Bailey. 'Is there anything else you'd like to tell us, anything else we should know?'

'I don't think so,' says Wilf. 'Do you have any idea yet who did it?'

'We're keeping an open mind,' says Dagless, giving Wilf a lupine smile. 'Very much an open mind.'

SIXTEEN

The hour after the kids are finally asleep is Sarah's sacred me-time, a small celebration of having got through another day.

Everything for her evening is in place. The wine, a bar of Galaxy and her phone are close to hand, and on the TV she's found an episode of *Say Yes to the Dress* she hasn't seen, presented by kind and inspiring Gok Wan. Sarah loves Gok. He's always so sensitive to how bigger women feel.

The wine was on special offer in the Spar shop, and it's not the best she's had, but one glass in she's feeling relaxed. Gok's giving advice to a bride-to-be who wants to wear pink, and has produced a fabulous dress of sparkle and marshmallow froth, though the bride is pulling faces, shaking her head. Sarah would say yes to it in a heartbeat.

As the programme goes to a commercial break, she mutes the volume to listen for the kids. Upstairs, all is quiet.

But there's a vehicle with its engine running outside.

That's unusual. This lane is a dead end, with only three cottages beyond hers. Maybe someone's taken a wrong turn, ventured down here by mistake and is struggling to turn round.

Curious, she leaves the sofa to pull back an edge of the curtain.

A white van is parked right outside her house, its headlamps throwing light to the lane's end, oily smoke from its exhaust creating a blue-tinted mist. As she watches, the passenger door opens and a man jumps out, slamming the door behind him. Sarah curses, thinking he'll wake the kids. The man walks up her path and knocks loudly on the door.

'For God's sake.' More annoyed at the prospect of wakeful children than interested in who her visitor might be, she opens the door. With the light behind him, he's a silhouette, average height, average build. She thinks she doesn't know him, but his heavy accent gives her a clue.

'Hello, Sarah,' he says. 'Do you remember me?'

She peers at him, trying to confirm her suspicion.

'No. Should I?'

'I am Natalie's friend. Surely you know me?'

'I'm guessing you're Eric.'

'I am. I am here to pay my respects to you, as Natalie's friend. You miss her, I know.'

Sarah feels a pang of grief. 'I do, yes.' She has half an ear on upstairs, listening for Lizzie's wailing, and decides to be blunt. 'What is it you want?'

He shakes his head. 'Nothing, I want nothing. Except for something you can maybe tell me. I have a watch, old and valuable. It was my grandfather's and my father's, and now it is with me. When it got broken, Natalie told me her father can fix it, if I give it to him, but I don't know where his company is. Natalie didn't yet tell me. Probably you know where I can find it?'

'I don't understand. What do you want to know?'

'The address. Of where her father works.'

Sarah shakes her head. 'Sorry, I don't know. Somewhere in Norwich, I suppose. If you want to know, why don't you get in touch with her father? I can give you his number if you want.'

'I don't think her father would want to speak to me.'

Peering through the glare, she does her best to get sight of Eric's face. 'No, probably he wouldn't. Not as things are.'

'Maybe you can find out for me?'

'You're not serious? I have to go.'

She's begun to close the door, but he puts out his hand to keep it open.

'Wait. Sarah. You know I was always good to Natalie. Between her and I, we were always friends, always laughing, having fun. She was always one for fun, wasn't she?'

'Yes, she was.'

'So I hope she never said anything bad about me. She and I were always happy together.'

'I don't know what you mean.'

'Then we understand each other. You and Natalie were close, the closest friends. So if anyone says to the police that I did something bad to her, I'll be thinking it was you who said it.'

'I've already spoken to the police.'

'They might speak to you again. And if they ask about me, I hope we can agree that you'll say nothing. Because I did nothing wrong.'

'Fine.'

'OK then. I wish you goodnight. I hope I don't come visiting again.'

Disquieted, Sarah stands in the doorway, watching him climb back into the van.

'Hey!' she calls after him. 'How did you find out where I live?'

But the van door slams shut.

SEVENTEEN

'We'll take good care of her, Mr Aldern.'

In her fluffy jumper and swirly skirt, the woman about to take Ruby away seems well-meaning and sympathetic, but she works for social services and is a designated appropriate adult, and so a substitute for Justin. He's already made clear his wish to stay with his daughter, but he's been politely rebuffed. Two female police officers specially trained to work with young children will be conducting the interview, in the unsettlingly named Vulnerable Suite.

'Shall we go, then, Ruby?' asks the woman, in a cheery voice which makes it sound like they're off to some party or jamboree.

But Ruby's smart and isn't fooled. Before she's gone even ten steps along the corridor, she turns back. Since Natalie died, all her facial expressions seem to be overlays on a backdrop of solemnity, and this one's no different: solemnity overlaid with anxiety, maybe even a touch of fear.

Justin aches to go to her, grab her hand and take her out of here, but this has to be done.

He gives her a wink. 'You'll be fine, munchkin. It's just a few questions, and we'll be gone.'

'Will you wait here for me, Daddy?' asks Ruby, and the uncertainty in her voice tugs at his heart.

'Of course I will.'

'Here *exactly*?'

He points to a couple of chairs outside a room labelled *Interview 3*.

'Just there. I'm going to sit there and not move until you come back.'

'Promise?'

'Promise.'

With his reassurances, she's willing to comply, and follows the appropriate adult to a bank of lifts at the corridor's end, making no reply to the woman's empty chatter.

The lift pings as it arrives and Ruby steps inside. As the doors slide closed, she gives him a brave little wave.

Justin takes a chair as he's promised, sitting with his head in his hands. Will she forgive him for letting them take her away when she plainly was afraid to go?

A police interview is too much stress for her when she's already overloaded with grief and loss, trying to assimilate – so young – the permanence of death. How can she not ask questions about why they're questioning her? After this, Ruby will surely realise there's something not right about Natalie's death.

And Justin's no idea what he'll say.

How do you talk to a five-year-old about the black business of murder?

Ruby's gone for well over an hour, during which time Justin – mindful of his promise – resists strong urges to fetch coffee and to go and find the gents.

Returned to him, she's silent and distracted, almost as if she's left part of herself wherever she's just been.

Walking through the car park, he takes her hand. In a nearby tree, he points out a squirrel springing from branch to branch, but though she glances up, she shows no interest.

In the car, she fastens her seat belt and sits quite still. Before Natalie was gone, sometimes he'd find Ruby's chatter annoying and crave the luxury of uninterrupted minutes of quiet. But this child is only a husk of Ruby before, and he'd give anything for the return of her prattle, her monologues on classroom happenings, her theory on why cows are black and white, discourses on why she should be allowed to watch more than one episode at a time of her favourite TV programmes. All that's been swept away, leaving Ruby lost and wounded in a world cruel enough to snatch away her mother without warning.

'Shall we get pizza?' he asks.

In the old days, she'd have beamed, and spent the next five minutes weighing up what toppings she should choose if she can only have three.

Now, she gives a nod and that's it.

Heading out of the car park, he tries again. 'So were those ladies nice?'

A shrug.

'I expect they asked you lots of questions, didn't they?'

'Not really. They gave me things to draw with but most of the pens were all dried up.'

'What did you draw?'

Another shrug.

'So was that all? That doesn't sound so bad.'

They drive for a few minutes in silence before she says, 'They asked me about Wilf.'

Justin frowns. 'What, Wilf next door? What about him?'

'If he ever came to our house. I said I wanted to go and feed his ducks, but Mummy wouldn't let me. And they asked about you.'

'What about me?'

'If you and Mummy ever had fights. I said since we moved house Mummy only had fights with Grandpa.'

Justin glances at her, but her face is hard to read.

'What did she and Grandpa fight about?'

'I don't know. Actually I don't think I want pizza today, Daddy. I don't really feel very hungry. Can we just go home?'

'Whatever you want, munchkin. If you change your mind, you let me know.'

Ruby doesn't reply. She's looking out of the window, staring at the view, but Justin has a suspicion that everything she's seeing is in her head.

EIGHTEEN

Wilmer and Braun boast a royal crest on their logo, earned after making repairs at Sandringham to a Cromwell-era clock.

But there's nothing quaint or historic about their workshops. Housed at the back of an industrial estate on the outskirts of the city, their unit's tucked away between a company manufacturing circuits for digital radios and a fledgling micro-brewery. The unit's signage is ultra-discreet, and the van they use for company business is anonymous white, with no signage at all, nothing to alert anyone to their line of work.

Which is the servicing and repair of high-end timepieces.

Patek Philippe, Rolex, Bulgari: if Wilmer and Braun's technicians are ever fazed by the value of the watches they work on, they're careful not to show it. Frank recalls once telling Dee – long ago, before they were married – that he was working on a Breguet worth almost two million, and straight away she said, *Steal it, sell it and let's run away to the south of France.* At the time he laughed, but sometimes these days he wonders how things would have turned out if they'd done exactly that, changed their names and left the country – except being on the run would never have been Frank's style.

Still, a watch is a very easy thing to slip in your pocket. Jerry Wilmer has to have total trust in the people he employs.

But Frank loves his work. The workshop's quiet and comfortable, the air-conditioning set cool in summer and warm in winter, since cold hands are inflexible and clumsy. Each technician has their own workstation, spending hours every day focused on the micro-engineering of the timepieces, cleaning, buffing, reassembling the intricate mechanisms, replacing the slivers of diamonds and rubies that fit inside.

Frank was introduced to the trade by his father, a hobbyist who tinkered in his shed on weekend afternoons, stripping down old clocks and watches he found in junk shops and at auctions, cleaning the cogs and springs in his special mix of Moebius oil, repainting the faces with Indian ink and lacquering the cases back to as-new gloss. Nothing gave him more pleasure than to hear one of his rescue projects begin to tick again or strike the hour. By the age of ten, Frank had caught the bug too, and could strip and reassemble pretty much any basic timepiece you could throw at him. Finding Wilmer and Braun on the doorstep was a happy accident, after his father got chatting to a mate of Jerry's in some pub.

'My son's got a watchmaker's hands,' he'd said. 'Steadiest hands I've ever seen.'

Jerry's mate told Frank's father the company was looking for an apprentice. Frank paid them a visit the next afternoon.

Thirty years later and he's Jerry's main man in an exclusive operation. Clients bring their timepieces in by appointment only, or occasionally Jerry or Frank pick up the bigger pieces in the anonymous van. Dee used to wonder where all the clients came from, who these people are who can afford five, six, seven figures for a watch. Frank's answer is straightforward. They come from everywhere and anywhere: London, Newmarket, Cambridge, the wealthy villages of Suffolk down into Essex. They're the gentlemen farmers of Norfolk and Lincolnshire's Wolds, and the gentrified landowners of the fertile fens. They come from anywhere there's money.

Today, Frank's working on a pre-war piece with the clean lines of 1930s art deco, a gold doctor's watch with a second dial for taking a patient's pulse. In cash terms, it's worth only two or three thousand, but it has sentimental value for the family who brought it in for servicing. Frank's reached the stage of reassembly and the moment when the watch will begin ticking again, ready for return to its owner.

The lights at his workstation are bright, so bright they render the space around him dark. He holds his miniature screwdriver, preparing to fit one of the tiny screws into the casing.

'Hey, Frank.'

Frank hasn't heard Jerry approach; at his station, he's in a world of his own. He starts, and drops the screw on to the leather pad on his bench.

Jerry helps himself to a stool, wheeling himself into the white glare of Frank's lights. His grey hair and beard give him a professorial look, an impression matched by the casual comfort of his clothes: corduroy trousers and one of his cherished collection of fading '70s prog-rock t-shirts. Today's band is King Crimson, paired with what is, for Jerry, a workaday watch: a vintage Omega Seamaster Chronograph, eighteen carat, with the original alligator strap.

Jerry folds his arms, leaning away from the workstation.

He knows better than to touch anything, or even breathe too close. 'How's it going?' Over the top of his glasses, he peers down at the doctor's watch, at the refreshed glow of the gold and the smoothed, scratch-free glass. 'Looks good. They'll be pleased. I've got something a bit different for you when you're done with that. Just come in via courier.'

'OK,' says Frank. 'Great.'

Jerry's expression becomes serious. 'Are you OK, Frank? Because you don't have to be here if you're not ready. If you need another week or two, another month even, take the time.'

Frank shakes his head. 'I'd rather be here. It gives me something to focus on.'

Jerry nods, as if he can really understand what it's like to lose your daughter, how life on the far side of such a catastrophe might possibly be.

'If you're sure. But any day you're not up to it, you don't come in, OK? The work's not going anywhere, and Robbie and I can pick up the slack. To an extent, anyway.' He puts his hands on his knees, preparing to rise, when he appears to recall something. 'One other thing. I had a call from the police yesterday, after you'd gone. Unbelievable, isn't it, that they're involved? Really not something you need to be dealing with. Anyway, I don't remember the woman's name, said she was CID, checking timelines in Natalie's case – they have to do these things, don't they? – and she wanted me to confirm what you said about being at work on Friday the twenty-fourth. Off the top of my head, I said if that's what you'd said, then I was sure you were here, but she asked me to check to be sure, and actually the twenty-fourth was the day I went to the Oxford sale, so I had to tell her I couldn't confirm or otherwise. I'm sorry, Frank. I don't want to make life difficult for you. I know it's only box-ticking, and it seems a bit mad to have to prove your whereabouts when your daughter's been . . . Well. I put her on to Robbie, or I said she might ask Marie. She'd have been here, wouldn't she, answering the phone?'

'No worries,' says Frank. 'They're just box-ticking, like you say. I'm sorry they've bothered you.'

'What are friends for?' asks Jerry, rising from the stool. 'Anything at all you need, Frank, you come straight to me.'

Traffic's heavy on the Northway as Frank heads home.

He's tired; he hasn't been sleeping. Things he can't talk about are weighing on his mind.

For ten minutes, he puts up with the stop-and-start, but the claustrophobia of being hemmed in on all sides is getting to him.

He's stuck behind a bus. On the back seat, a group of schoolkids are messing about, a silent movie of teenage banter and horseplay. The two girls are disturbingly like Natalie was at that age, rebellious and gobby and physically close to perfect.

But those two girls are heading home to the families that love them.

Enough of this. He needs a break.

As the traffic edges forward, he indicates a lane change and noses the car over to the left. About two hundred metres ahead is a Shell station.

He pulls in next to a pump and switches off the engine. The near silence offers comfort, a temporary haven of peace. He closes his eyes.

But not for long.

A Range Rover pulls up close behind him. Its driver's pushy, in a hurry. After waiting only a few moments, the driver beeps his horn.

And Frank loses it.

Flinging open the car door, he's supercharged with rage. Every last little thing in life is shit, and now here's this prick, pushing all his buttons, getting right up his nose.

Frank storms up to the Range Rover's driver's door, hammers on the window and starts yelling. 'What's your problem, mate? What is your fucking problem? Get off my fucking back, all right? Just wait your fucking turn, like a normal person, or I'll turn your face to pulp. You total fucking wanker.'

On the forecourt, other customers are anxiously watching. A woman is recording video on her phone.

Slamming his fist against the window one last time, Frank walks apparently calmly back to his car. He's energised, feels in control. Behind him, the Range Rover's tyres squeal as it reverses and zooms away.

Frank glares at the people watching. 'What are you looking at?' he demands, and gets back in his car.

Inside the kiosk, one of the cashiers is talking into a phone.

Probably she's calling the police, but Frank absolutely could not care less.

Sometimes you just have to let rip.

NINETEEN

They came before breakfast, while Wilf was drinking his first cup of Earl Grey, still in his John Lewis pyjamas and his burgundy faux-silk robe, before he'd even shaved or brushed his teeth.

They were not knocking but hammering at the door, and their presumptuous, heavy-booted arrival – were so many of them really necessary? – startled the ducks into a cacophony of alarm, upset the nesting blackbirds, who took flight, and caused Mr Grimes to shoot out through the cat flap, running between their black-trousered legs into the safety of the long grass behind the greenhouse.

Glancing out of the bedroom window before hurrying downstairs, Wilf was at first more annoyed at their inconsiderate parking than at their beaconing of their presence to all the world. Vehicles were parked on the rain-soaked verge, doubtless leaving deep tyre tracks and making the grass impossible to mow. Why couldn't people be more considerate?

But with his kitchen overrun by people in uniforms, the enormity of what was happening quickly became distressing.

'What do you want?' he asked a policeman who seemed

almost double his own size, though much of the man's bulk probably came from his body armour. 'What are you doing here?'

'We're executing this search warrant,' said the policeman, handing Wilf a piece of paper. 'That's a copy for you to keep. We'll be here most of the day, so I'll find someone who'll accompany you while you dress, and then you may leave.'

'Where should I go?' asked Wilf, bewildered, but the policeman wasn't listening.

Back upstairs in his bedroom, under the close observation of a young officer who refused to leave him by himself, Wilf found clean underwear and socks in the mahogany chest of drawers and took trousers and a shirt from their hangers. As he dressed, the young man wouldn't do him the courtesy of turning his back, so Wilf was forced to display his old man's inadequacies, his blue-white flesh and hollow chest, and caused the young man to smirk as he painstakingly tied his bow tie. Wilf was indignant. Was such an outrageous invasion of privacy truly necessary? Was this how the constabulary always behaved? With his jacket shrugged on and a brush run over his hair, he declared himself ready to be led downstairs, only to realise as he reached the bottom step that he had forgotten to brush his teeth.

Now, late in the evening, he is home, returned to a disgruntled, complaining Mr Grimes, whose breakfast was missed and whose dinner is late.

Wilf turns on the pantry light and stares as if entranced at the tins on the shelf, unable to bring focus to this smallest of tasks, failing to choose between tuna and chicken cat food, incapacitated by the traumatic memories of this extraordinary day.

Ultimately, he reaches out for tuna, and – forgetting to turn out the light – carries it on autopilot to the kitchen table, where he forks a plentiful helping into a dish, for once not chatting to Mr Grimes, who seems not to notice the omission.

Wilf sets the dish down in its usual place. Beginning to eat, the cat is at last silent. Wilf has time to look about himself and see what they have done.

The floor is marked with the muddy prints of unwiped boots, providing a snapshot of what they were thinking and where in the house they went. The prints cross the kitchen to go through to the lounge, but also lead to each of the cupboards, which when opened show a slight but unsettling rearrangement of their contents, as if mischievous sprites have played some malicious trick intended to confuse and disturb. Teacups which were on the left are now on the right; the plain flour is in front of the self-raising instead of behind. His favourite Royal Minton eggcup has migrated to the top shelf, illogically placed in amongst the sherry glasses.

Realising every single one of his belongings has been touched by strangers is deeply disturbing, and his distress is made worse by not knowing whether his most precious things were carefully handled, whether Granny Flora's teapot, for example – spirited from the shelf above the stove to the windowsill – was treated with the tender respect he always extends to it himself. He wonders what possible interest they could have in the teapot anyway, before the truth quickly dawns: they were searching for anything he might have hidden inside it. Realising what they probably had in mind, a momentary dizziness overcomes him. Most likely they were looking for anything taken from the crime scene, some ghoulish keepsake or souvenir.

Of course there was nothing to find, but their work has nonetheless been thorough. Every corner of the kitchen has been searched; everything has been pawed and defiled. What, then, have they done in the rest of the house?

In the lounge, his old laptop is gone and he wishes them joy of it. Apart from that, the room is as if recently tidied. The sofa cushions are plumped, the cocktail glasses in the cabinet are only slightly displaced. Similarly in the dining room, though the small changes there don't trouble him, nor what they may have snickered over in the bathroom.

But his bedroom is another matter. How far did they go in there?

Approaching the bedroom door, he feels violated, sick with anxiety. What have they done with his most treasured things, his cherished mementoes?

Of course they have been found. Opening that most secret drawer, he half expects to find it raided and his treasures gone. They're still there, but not the same; they're slightly rearranged, each carefully kept item defiled by interlopers who neither respect nor understand.

Have they been photographed? Probably. And his writings, have they been read? Almost certainly.

Is there any chance at all they'll be discreet?

TWENTY

Early evening, and the Flag and Whistle is busy. Gabby buys herself a sparkling water and finds space in a corner where she can appear to be waiting for someone, checking her phone from time to time for more convincing effect while she picks a likely target from the rest of the clientele.

They're not hard to spot. Even without her father's friend's tip-off to say they drink here, she's confident she'd pick them out of the crowd. This group – six of them, a seventh having just left – have an attitude she's come to recognise from close contact through her job: a little louder than everyone else, a little more self-assured, letting off a little more steam.

Guaranteed this is a contingent from the local constabulary.

And with them is a young man who just might be a gift. He's in on the conversation, but his eye's roving around the room, checking out who's arriving every time the street door opens, lingering on the backside of a girl making her way to the ladies, but turning away before she gets there. Obviously not his taste. Gabby can only hope she is.

Taking her glass with her, she follows the other girl's lead, making sure to sashay as she goes.

And by coincidence – or not – as she comes out of the ladies'
door a few minutes later, who should be walking towards her,
ostensibly heading for the gents?

She gives him a full-beam smile.

And he smiles right back.

He's attractive in a cocky, over-preened kind of way: hair
razored to nothing on the sides, an intricately clipped beard,
tight suit, sharp shoes. He's wearing no ring, but instinct tells
Gabby he could be married. He flirts, they chat, he tells her
his name is Glen, but when his mates call over to ask him if
he wants a drink, they call him Freddie. When she asks him
why that is, he laughs and says, 'Long story.'

He tells her more or less straight away he's in CID, but
doesn't ask what she does. She lets him know she's impressed,
but moves the conversation on – good places to go in the city
for someone like her who's spent a long time away, where he
went to school and uni, shared memories of the city when
they were kids.

She sticks to mineral water, he's on alcohol-free beer until
he comes back from the bar with shots of whisky. He doesn't
seem surprised when she declines, explaining it's a fair drive
to where she's staying, but tips hers into his glass.

'You not driving?' she asks, and he shakes his head. 'I've
got a friend who'll pick me up if I give him a ring.' *Him,*
wonders Gabby, *or her?*

They've done the small talk long enough when she says – as
if she's just thought of it – 'Hey, that woman murdered in
Wickney, you're not involved in that?'

He looks into his empty whisky glass as if wishing it were
full. 'Not directly, no.'

'Any progress?' she asks, and gambles. 'Don't tell me. The husband did it.'

The whisky seems to have done its job. He laughs and shakes his head. 'People always think that. Suspicious death, the husband did it, end of. It's a bit more complicated than that.'

'Who, then?'

She can see him think, *What does it matter?* before he says, 'They're saying the old boy next door probably had a real crush on either her or her daughter. Five years old.'

Gabby's eyes widen. 'A paedo?'

He nods his head. 'Could be. No one we know, though. Sometimes they operate a lifetime under the radar.'

'So has he been charged?' A question too far, which she dilutes with feigned ignorance. 'If that's what you'd call it.'

'Questioned under caution. Listen.' He leans forward across the table, changing the mood. 'I've got an early start in the morning, but maybe we could continue this another time?'

Gabby tilts her head and smiles, hoping her lipstick's still in place. 'I'm here for a few more days, so yes, that would be great.'

He takes out his phone. 'Let me get your number, then, and I'll give you a call.'

Gabby's editor won't run her story until it's been confirmed, though that's soon done with a call to the constabulary's press office.

But they're giving little away.

'A sixty-two-year-old male has been interviewed in relation to the case, but up to this point released without charge,' is all they'll say.

For Gabby and the *Herald*, that's good enough for now.

TWENTY-ONE

These days, Margot's appetite is small, and her supermarket shop rarely takes more than a few minutes. Today, her wire basket contains a stem of broccoli, a prepacked piece of eye-wateringly expensive cod, semi-skimmed milk and a packet of chocolate digestives. She's brought her own bag for the shopping, and chats to the woman on the checkout as she pays, remarking on the mildness of the weather and the ridiculous price of fish.

As she passes Customer Services, she sees there's no queue at the till and so decides to buy a lottery ticket, a small extravagance she occasionally indulges in because nothing ventured, nothing gained. But there, on the newspaper display, is something that stops her heart for a full second, before it restarts with an uncomfortable, irregularly fast beat. Her head feels light and she wants to sit down, but she sees there are no chairs. Instead, she reaches out to the newspaper stand, leaning on it for support.

'Are you all right, duckie?' The cashier – a young woman with her hair coloured silver, almost the same silver as Margot's own – has noticed her distress and is approaching.

Margot waves her away, giving her a weak smile.

'I'm all right, thank you,' she insists. 'The doctor's put me on new tablets and I don't think they agree with me.'

Gathering herself, persuading herself she's fine, she picks a copy of the *Herald* off the stack and hands it to the girl to scan. 'I'll just take this.'

She pays, and folds the paper before tucking it into her bag with the rest of her shopping, not wanting to broadcast its content.

Outside, shaken and upset, she can't remember where she parked the car, and to hide her confusion, she stands as though waiting for a taxi pickup. Then she remembers: the car's in her preferred spot, in the far corner by the trolley park.

The walk across the car park seems long. Safe at last in the driver's seat, Margot pulls the newspaper from her bag, and, resting it on the steering wheel, stares at the front page in horrified disbelief.

The headline's bold and black: *Is This Pretty Natalie's Killer?* And beneath it is a photograph of a well-dressed man on a riverbank, feeding swans. Thank God for small mercies, his back's to the camera, but his identity is, to her, perfectly plain.

She'd know him anywhere, and many others would too: it's her own dear brother, Wilf.

It's late afternoon before Wilf answers the phone, and his tone is unexpectedly gruff, so different from his usual polite self she isn't entirely sure it's him.

'Wilf? Is that you? It's me, Margot.'

There's a moment of silence and an exhalation of breath.

'It's you.' Another hesitation, and she senses him collecting himself. 'How lovely to hear from you. How are things?'

'Wilf, for heaven's sake, what's going on?'

A little stiffness comes into his voice. 'I'm sure I don't know, unless you tell me.'

'Stop that right now. Why haven't you been answering your phone? And I texted a dozen times and you haven't replied. I've been so worried.'

'I've been busy. I do have a life, you know.'

'For God's sake, Wilf. You're on the front page of the *Herald*.'

In the silence which follows, she hears him breathing, and pictures him where she knows he must be, standing by the sideboard where he keeps the phone. When he's talking on the phone, he always stands upright as a soldier, she assumes out of respect to the person he's talking to, or perhaps because of the importance to him of the few calls he receives. No doubt too there are flowers nearby, probably in that dreadful vase which was Mother's favourite, a hideous piece of Victorian majolica which Wilf says must be kept because the ugly has a place in the world as well as the beautiful.

Margot disagrees. Times many she's told him off for keeping the lounge as a family shrine, but Wilf insists the old furniture must stay. *Good quality lasts a lifetime,* he says. *Best quality will outlast me.*

She lets the silence down the line lengthen, not pushing him and not asking – at least not yet – the dozens of questions she has, but when it becomes really awkward, she says, 'I was worried about you when you didn't answer the phone.'

'I didn't know it was you,' he says, defensively. 'The damn

thing's been ringing off and on all day. I've even had people outside the house. I haven't dared go out, not even for a pint of milk. It's a good thing I've got UHT in the pantry.'

'You could have texted me back.'

He clears his throat. 'I don't have my mobile at the moment.'

'Oh dear. Have you lost it?'

'Not lost. Confiscated.'

'Confiscated? What on earth do you mean?'

'The police insisted on taking it for examination.'

'Good God, Wilf. This is serious, then? Do they really think you . . . Do they believe you were somehow involved in this woman's death?'

'Apparently so.'

'Surely they can't think that you . . . Have they been to talk to you, then?'

'They've been here, yes. And I've been interviewed – I believe the term they used was under caution.'

'But that's absurd! Can they do that?'

'I didn't mind talking to them. I only live a matter of metres from the poor woman, so I rather assumed they would want to speak to me at some point. If they're investigating thoroughly, of course they would speak to me.'

'I suppose so. But why did they take your phone? They're not likely to find much on there, are they? You barely use it.'

'I told them exactly that, but they seemed not to believe me.'

'Such an invasion of your privacy.'

She hears the unmistakeable sound of ice chinking in liquid, the rim of a glass touching his teeth, and she knows he's drinking. Which for Wilf, except for Christmas and birthdays, is a rarity.

He swallows and says, 'You have no idea.'

Margot's becoming alarmed. 'Tell me.'

'They searched the house. A battalion of people in uniforms and those strange white suits. I wasn't allowed to stay, so I just went and sat by the riverbank, and when I noticed people were staring at me I drove to the coast and sat in a car park there, staring at the sea.'

'Did they make a mess? If they did, you should sue them.'

'Not a mess, not really, no. They tried to put everything back, but it's all slightly out of place, so I know it's all been handled by strangers.' She hears a catch in his voice. 'Everything feels dirty. I know it's ridiculous, but the whole house feels tainted. And the worst thing is . . . They went through my things, my most precious, private things.'

Margot knows her brother's crying in that held-in, buttoned-down way he's had since he was a boy, no physical sign but tears running down his face, and probably now he's reaching for one of the ironed white cotton handkerchiefs he always has in his pocket, wiping away the tears, not wanting her to know of his dismay. She doesn't know what his most private possessions are, but she has her own, as everyone does, and understands completely the mortification she'd feel if anyone came across them, handled them, turned them over and raised an eyebrow, maybe even made a joke or laughed.

And she feels anger on his behalf.

'Why on earth didn't you ring me?'

She hears a sniff and knows she's right about the crying.

'What could I say, Margot, that wouldn't make you think

less of me? That the police have been round and I'm a suspect in the case? I thought they wanted my help. I even offered them tea. But now it turns out they think I killed her. For heaven's sake, I didn't even know the woman! What possible reason could I have had?'

A slight unease creeps over Margot, a slither, a barely audible rustle of doubt. He may not have known Natalie, but he was fond, perhaps over-fond, of her little girl, whose name Margot can't at this moment recall. He's spoken of her several times, and she'd put his interest in her down to his – call it by its name – loneliness, but what if there were more to it? What *is* in those most private possessions he's so upset about?

'Oh, my dear. How awful! But they're just being thorough, surely? They can't seriously think you had anything to do with it?'

'They're serious enough to have taken my phone. I can't help wondering what on earth Ma and Pa would think.'

'They'd think the same as me, that the police are only doing what's necessary to rule you out, and the sooner it's done, the better.'

'But what about the newspaper? Everyone will have seen it. What does it say?'

'You haven't read it, then?'

'I've been lying low all day.'

'Well, it's better you don't see it anyway. That paper's just a rag. No one takes it seriously.'

But Margot knows as she speaks that what she's saying is untrue. The *Herald* is well known both for its scoops and for shaping popular opinion, and, following its lead, there's a good chance other news outlets will pick up the story too.

'You don't know the people round here,' says Wilf. 'I know exactly what they'll say, that there's no smoke without fire. They already think I'm odd, an old man living by himself. What else could I be but some pervert?'

For a moment, Margot's uncharacteristically lost for words, because he's right. In a small place like Wickney, people will be all too ready to believe the *Herald*'s insinuation. She glances down at the newspaper headline and realises how clever they have been, or think they've been. *Is This Pretty Natalie's Killer?* Not exactly an accusation, but a question putting an idea into suggestible minds.

'Who's been outside the house?' she asks.

'I don't know who they were. Some of them had cameras, so I assume they were the press. One young woman was quite brazen. From upstairs I saw her go over to the cottage and peer in all the windows, as if she had a God-given right to trespass. I nearly called the police, but I didn't want them round here again. They're not to be trusted. There must be some kind of leak in their ranks, because who else would have given my name to the papers? Anyway, they gave up and left a little while ago. Over a dozen times they came and hammered on the door. Honestly, I'm at my wits' end with the worry of it. I know I shall never sleep tonight.'

'Why don't you come to me? Pack a bag and just come. The spare room's all ready.'

'That's very kind, but no. I'm guilty of nothing but living next door, and I won't be driven out of my own home. And I've Mr Grimes to think of. I can't just up and leave him here all by himself.'

Mr Grimes. Her brother's best friend in the world. Apart, that is, from herself. She hopes he knows that.

'Have another whisky, then, and watch something good on telly. But not the news.'

'It's not whisky, it's mother's ruin, and I shall have another. Will you ring me tomorrow?'

'Of course I will. We'll have a code, shall we, so you know it's me? Three rings and I'll hang up, and you ring me back.'

'All right. Thank you.'

'It's the least I can do.'

'I didn't do it, Margot. You know that, don't you?'

Their father always used to say, *Innocent until proven guilty*, an adage he didn't always observe in Wilf's case, when he'd fetch the strap a little too readily for the most minor of alleged infringements of the rules, and shut Margot and Mother out of the study where white-faced Wilf was granted scant time to plead his case.

Margot was certain on most of those occasions of Wilf's innocence, that his punishments were due to nothing more than Father's whisky-soured temper, and she's almost certain now that whatever's happened in the cottage next door is nothing to do with her brother.

Almost certain.

'Of course I do, silly,' she says, wishing that tiny, niggling doubt would go away.

TWENTY-TWO

Gabby knocks at the door of a Victorian cottage tucked down a lane only just wide enough for a vehicle to drive along. In the front yard, a child's tricycle lies on its side, wet from the rain and speckled with rust.

Her knock at the door brings a rapid answer: a young woman whose long hair needs a wash, wearing a baggy black tracksuit probably intended to conceal the almost inevitable weight gain of down-at-heel, struggling Britain. Slippers made to look like pink furry rabbits. Dull eyes and skin, no make-up. Behind her, music's playing, an upbeat track Gabby half recognises, and not what she'd expect from the woman facing her, who she'd have put money on being more into the post-grunge pissed-offness of Breaking Benjamin or the sullen, life-sucks Smiths vibe of Odd Morris.

Offering a glimpse of her press pass, Gabby gives a bright smile. 'Hi! Are you Sarah?'

Unsure whether she should identify herself, Sarah nods.

'Hi! It's so lovely to meet you. I'm Gabby Laflin, a journalist from the *Herald*. I've been told you were one of Natalie

Cutter's closest friends. I wonder if I could just grab a few minutes with you?'

'How did you get my name?'

'Old journalist's trick,' smiles Gabby. 'I asked in the hairdresser's.'

Sarah tuts. 'Lindsay Reeves. Biggest gossip in Wickney.'

'I hope you don't mind. I'm just trying to build a picture of Natalie, and the only way to do that is to talk to the people who knew her best. Lindsay told me that was you.'

'Me and Nat were pretty close, yeah. We met at school. Stayed friends ever after, really.'

Gabby can see the conflict in Sarah's face: the curiosity, the possibility of excitement in a tedious existence, the feeling of being special vying with the knowledge that, really, she shouldn't.

'We could make it off the record,' wheedles Gabby. 'You know, no names mentioned.'

So Sarah lets her in.

The house is like a hundred others Gabby's talked her way into: too cramped for its occupants, inconvenient in its layout, never properly warm whether winter or summer. The scent of clean laundry from children's clothes draped over a drying rack competes with the greasy fug of oven chips. Overhead, the steady and annoying ping of a computer game tells her there's a child somewhere upstairs.

Sarah rattles a poker in the lounge wood burner, and drops a couple of pine logs on to the red-hot ashes, blowing on them to raise a spark, puffing up a cloud of fine, grey ash, which makes Gabby cough.

'I'll make tea,' says Sarah.

'What's the music?' asks Gabby.

'Sorry, I'll turn it off. Beach Bunny, "Oxygen". That was Natalie's favourite track. She was always playing it. It reminds me of her, you know?'

With the music gone, a toddler asleep in a buggy smiles. Under the sounds of a kettle being filled and the chink of china, there's a stillness to the house which should be calming, but somehow makes Gabby feel she's intruding. This isn't a young woman's decor – green velveteen curtains at the windows, cross-stitch embroidery in frames on the walls – and she wonders if Sarah's borrowing it from a relative, if her tenure here is temporary.

Through the party wall, she hears a child running heavy-footed upstairs and a muffled woman's voice yelling, *Bethany, don't you dare! Come down here this minute!* The lack of privacy and peace is too familiar; Gabby's only recently managed to find a quiet place in London after years of living in houses sloppily converted into flats where the builders considered soundproofing an unnecessary luxury. No longer having to wear earplugs every night – and occasionally during the day, when she'd been working shifts – has been a gift she's given thanks for every day since.

When Sarah comes back in, she's carrying two mugs of tea. One's a Christmas mug, red and painted with Santa and reindeer. The other – which she hands to Gabby – depicts Marvel characters she doesn't know.

'I gave you Riley's mug, but he won't mind,' says Sarah. 'And I know it looks mad using a Christmas mug this time of year, but it was the last thing Natalie gave me, for Christmas just gone. It makes me think of her every time I have a drink.

Do you want sugar?' Gabby shakes her head. 'I have three in mine. Look at me. Shows, doesn't it? Natalie never had sugar in her tea. She loved her chocolate, though. Never had any trouble persuading her to eat a KitKat with her cuppa.'

As she takes the tea, Gabby gives in to her curiosity.

'Have you lived here long, Sarah?'

Sarah laughs. 'Only all my life, pretty much. It was my grandma and grandad's house. They brought me up when my mum couldn't cope. She had issues with addiction so I never saw much of her. Anyway, when Grandma died, she left the house to me. She wanted me to sell it, take myself and Riley someplace with a bit more life. But then I got caught with Lizzie, and it seemed easier to stay where I've got roots, where people know me, you know what I mean?'

Gabby does know; it's a familiar story, getting stuck. Time was she'd have thought Sarah wasn't giving herself a chance at life, sticking around in this backwater while a whole wide world of opportunities glittered and beckoned. But she's met so many rootless young people with nowhere to call home, drifting from place to place, Downham Market to Dubai and all points in between, and all of them with few exceptions seem to be lost, lonely and struggling with unhappiness. Maybe the price of having your lifetime of adventures is losing touch with who you are, who your tribe is, where you belong in this big, scary world. So if Sarah can find a level of security in the place she's lived all her life, let her get on with it.

She sips her tea: hot, strong, a perfect cold-afternoon brew. But the mug is interesting. Not at all a present which chimes with the view she's had of Natalie, who she'd expect to choose something contemporary, more sophisticated, if only to bolster her own view of herself. This choice of gift suggests one of two things: that Natalie had a soft, sentimental side and a nostalgic view of Christmas; or that she gave the gift little thought and grabbed the first thing that came to hand in some pound shop or supermarket for her supposed friend.

'You must miss Natalie,' she says, as Sarah sits down in an armchair whose chintzy upholstery is flattened and worn from years of wear. The cushions give off a sweet scent of old tobacco, and Gabby pictures an old man seated there year after year, puffing on a pipe as her own grandfather used to do. Ghosts cling to places sometimes, as tightly as those left behind.

'Would you like to see some pictures of her?' asks Sarah.

'I'd love to.'

Sarah picks up her phone and starts to scroll. 'Queen of the selfie, Natalie was. She was always sending me pics of herself. Have a look through those.'

Gabby flips through pictures of a good-looking woman who knows how to make the most of herself, posing and preening in what look like pubs and clubs, a couple with her dark-haired daughter, others with a pony-tailed man. 'Can I play this video?'

Sarah glances over. 'Help yourself.'

Gabby presses play, and the video lights up in a fairground scene, so vivid she can almost smell the hotdogs and candy-floss. On an old-fashioned roundabout, a pretty child smiles nervously on the back of a white-painted horse, holding tight to the barley-sugar-twist pole which raises it as the roundabout spins. The frame switches to Natalie on the horse beside her, laughing as her dark hair blows into tangles. In a tight t-shirt and jeans, she's beautiful, and Gabby can't help thinking it's no big surprise Justin couldn't hold on to her.

'She looks a very vibrant woman,' says Gabby. 'Like she lived life to the full.'

'It's hard to think she's not coming back,' says Sarah, wistfully. 'I really miss her. We went to that fair just before Christmas. If I'm honest, we hadn't seen each other that much since then. After she and Justin split up, she had other fish to fry.'

Such a quaintly old-fashioned expression. In Sarah's constricted life, the old folk still have influence. 'Was the split his choice, or hers?'

'Hers, one hundred per cent.' Sarah's face grows sad. 'He's still nuts about her, though I know he'd have got over it in time, given the right woman. He's what I'd call a solid bloke, you know? Steady, reliable. He's warm and kind, and great with kids. Some men love kids, don't they? He dotes on Ruby, absolutely adores her. Natalie was never that maternal, not really. When Ruby was a baby, it was always Justin that got up in the night, even though he had to go to work the next morning. Natalie was worried pregnancy was going to ruin her figure, especially her boobs. She was saving up for surgery, to firm them up again. And she had new ideas about what she wanted in a man. She got to be all about excitement, foreign travel, and that's not Justin. I told her she didn't know when she was well off, but she wouldn't listen to me. She was going through a phase where she picked up men from anywhere, spent a couple of weeks with them and moved on to the next one. Not a very safe way to behave, is it? Makes you think, especially after what's happened.'

Gabby points to one of the pictures on the phone. 'This guy she's with here, with the ponytail, was he one of those casual pickups?'

Sarah blinks. 'He was the last in the line. She said he was an agricultural contractor – a gangmaster to you or me.'

Gabby knows exactly what Sarah means. Early morning in any fenland town centre you see groups of landworkers, waiting for the vans that will take them to the fields for that day's labour, cutting pumpkins or daffodils, harvesting cauliflowers or sprouts. The gangmasters were rumoured to be hard men who took too big a cut of the labourers' wages for their services. Why was Natalie involved with a man like that?

'He always had plenty of money to spend on her,' continues Sarah, 'and of course she liked that. He was friendly for a while with a group of pickers who were staying on one of the farms, but I think they've moved on now. I hope he's gone with them. I didn't like him at all.'

'What about previous boyfriends? Do you know any names or where I might find them?'

Sarah shrugs. 'Not really. She changed them like she changed her knickers.'

Some disapproval there? wonders Gabby. *Or even a little jealousy?*

'What was Natalie doing for money since her separation?' she asks.

'She wasn't getting it from Justin, that I do know. He didn't want her to leave, so why should he pay for a second household, was what she told me he said, and by the way I think that's totally reasonable. He told her if she was leaving she could find herself a job and pay her own rent, and she did, an internet job. What they call drop shipping.'

Gabby understands the basic principle. Essentially, you set yourself up as a middleman, creating a website advertising clothes or saucepans or whatever you want to sell. You take an order and the customer's money, then order at a much-reduced price from China direct to the customer, who waits weeks for delivery of some cheap tat, but hey, what do you care? The profit's already in your bank and repeat custom's not part of the business model.

'Isn't that rather a crowded market? Was she making any money at it?'

'She was doing really well,' says Sarah. 'New clothes all the time recently, and a few trips to London. She was calling herself an entrepreneur. She was doing a bit on eBay as well, selling hair products. Low-cost things which add up when you sell a lot, pop them in a Jiffy bag and that's it. I was thinking I might have a go at it myself.'

'What did you think to her new place, the cottage? Seemed a bit remote to me.'

Sarah looks thoughtful. In the buggy, the toddler is stirring. 'I didn't go there very often. We had a bit of a housewarming with a bottle of wine when she first moved in, but it's not easy, is it, when you've got kids? Mostly she came here.'

'So how long is it since you were at Turle's Cottage?'

'Invited there, you mean? I can't remember, to be honest. She moved in there just before my birthday, so early October. I went a couple of times before Christmas, but not since then.'

'While you were there, did you see any signs of harassment by the neighbour, Mr Hickling?'

'Not really. He was in his garden once when I was over there. Natalie was watching him from the window, saying nasty things about him. He's got a duck pond with actual ducks on it and he was feeding them. I think he's alright.'

'You know him, then?'

'I only met him once. Like I say, he seemed OK.'

'Is he well liked locally?'

Sarah shrugs. 'I don't know much about him. Keeps himself to himself.'

'But Natalie didn't like him?'

Sarah gives a wry smile. 'She didn't like him because she thought he was a pervert, peeping and whatnot. But Natalie didn't like many people, to be honest.'

Which makes Gabby wonder how many people liked Natalie back. And what Sarah's said has triggered another thought. Gabby's been to Turle's Cottage, had a sneaky peek through the windows, and there was no sign anywhere of the paraphernalia necessary for internet selling, no Jiffy bags or boxes of stock. It would be interesting to ask at the post office how often she went in there. Because Natalie may have been making some kind of living online, but Gabby doubts it was by selling hair products on eBay.

TWENTY-THREE

After she leaves Sarah, Gabby's already writing the opening paragraphs of a story in her head. She thinks she's got a good angle, but she's going to need more than Sarah's given her. She needs to pick another brain.

She doesn't care if she comes across as pushy or over-keen. How she's perceived doesn't come into it. She has a job to do, and it's time critical.

So she gives Glen until 4 p.m. to call, even though she knows the timescale's not realistic, that no man would be so uncool as to call a woman casually met in a pub within twenty-four hours.

Regardless, at 4.05 p.m. she dials his number, literally crossing her fingers that he'll pick up, knowing there could be a hundred reasons – anything from being at home with his wife to being on some back-street stake-out – why he wouldn't answer.

But he does. 'Hello, beautiful.'

She can hear a touch of arrogance in his voice, his conceit that she's been bowled over by him, and she knows that when he hangs up he'll be crowing about his conquest to his mates.

Goes with the territory. Let him think what he likes.

'Is this a good time?' she asks.

'Depends what for.'

'I'm in the city this afternoon, and I was wondering if you might fancy grabbing a drink somewhere, if you're free. I know it's short notice.'

There's a silence, and she imagines him weighing it up, making calculations, wondering if he can make it work. 'Tomorrow would be better.'

'Mmm. Can't do tomorrow,' she lies. 'Maybe another time?'

She senses he doesn't want to let a juicy opportunity like her slip away.

'Hold on.'

He covers the speaker and she hears muffled voices in the background, another man, a deal being done.

He comes back on. 'Yeah, OK, sounds good. Can't do earlier than six, though.'

'Six is good. Same place?'

'No, not there.' So he doesn't want to be seen. 'Do you know Fisher's, on Lambert Place? They do nice tapas there, if that's your thing. Good for those of us who didn't get lunch. Wine list isn't bad either.'

'I'll find it,' says Gabby. 'See you in a while.'

Away from his mates, Gabby finds Glen more attractive, less laddish and more thoughtful, a good conversationalist with tastes in film and TV she shares.

The wine's pleasant, the tapas tasty.

When he asks what work she does, she tells him she's in publishing.

161

They chat a while, order food, finish a bottle of red. When their knees touch under the table, there's no sense of awkwardness.

As the plates are cleared and a second bottle is opened, she senses the time might be right to lead the conversation where she wants it to go.

'What's the news in the Natalie Cutter case? What happened with the old man next door?'

He seems to take her interest as quite natural. It's a major case, and it might even be unusual if she didn't ask.

'Guy's a total pervert is what I'm hearing. They searched the house and found a secret porn stash hidden away, really unusual stuff. And he's got this fixation, created like a shrine to . . .' As she's hoped, alcohol is clouding his judgement. 'You know what, I really shouldn't do this, but have a look at these.'

He opens the photo gallery on his mobile, scrolls through to find the pictures he's after and hands her the phone.

Gabby's seen official crime-scene photos many times, and that's not what these are. There are no markers or labels; these are not pictures to be submitted in evidence. These are just snaps, curiosities to show others, pictures of a suspect's private possessions, which no one should have.

Of course she shouldn't look, but who could resist?

She peers at the first photo. At first, it's not clear what she's looking at, so she expands it on screen.

'What is that?' she asks, and when Glen laughs, she sees it: two men in what you'd politely term a highly compromising position, the intimate details blurred in tones of brown and white. What's thrown her is that the men's underwear is archaic, like theatrical costume. From that, she assumes the photo must date to the beginning of the twentieth century.

She scrolls to the next picture: a different act, different men, but the same vintage style.

'Guy's got a huge collection of this stuff,' says Glen. 'Must have been collecting it for years. All old-fashioned like that, Victorian drawings, 1950s. The newest they found was from the '60s.'

Gabby keeps scrolling. 'It's almost innocent, isn't it?'

Glen grins. 'I wouldn't say that. But it's nothing like what you get now. Some of that would make your eyes water, believe me.'

'What's this? It looks like some kind of scrap book.'

'They found four volumes like that, all dedicated to the same bloke. He must have had one almighty crush. Starts with the beloved as a young man in his teens. The last ones are quite recent.'

'An old lover, maybe?'

'Maybe. Looks like he was worshipped from afar, since the old boy's not in any of them.'

As a youth, the collection's subject is heart-stoppingly hand-some, but time isn't kind. He grows fatter and balder until in the most recent image – a page from a brochure for the impressive-looking Illingham Hall Hotel – he's red-faced and unattractive, bursting out of his suit.

'No suggestion he's a paedophile, then?' asks Gabby. 'Not after the daughter?'

Glen shakes his head. 'Not looking likely.'

'And not after Natalie either, in all probability.'

'He looks like a man of peculiar tastes to me. I mean,

vintage gay porn, who gets off on that? But gay as you like doesn't rule out a dispute between neighbours, does it?'

'So he's still in the frame?'

'Hundred per cent he did it. Guy living by himself, barely speaks to anyone, red flags for an oddball to me.'

'Have you ruled out the husband, then?' asks Gabby.

'No one's ruled out until someone's banged up, are they? But sometimes they have guilty written all over them. You get a nose for these things, you know? Fancy sharing a dessert? Or how about an Irish coffee?'

One thing leads to another.

Gabby rings her mother to say she's staying with a friend, and she and Glen take a taxi to a flat in the suburbs. Taking off her coat, she asks for tea instead of wine.

Somehow, that tea never gets made.

In the early morning, she gathers up her clothes and uses the bathroom mirror to make emergency repairs to her sleep-deprived face. She barely registered it the night before, but in the cold light of day it's obvious a woman lives at least part-time in this flat: her hair and shower products make it undeniable. Gabby's inquisitive nature – isn't that the job she was hired to do, to dig where no one else goes? – tells her it's OK to open the cabinet on the bathroom wall, and in there are prescription meds in two names, a man's and a woman's.

But the man's name isn't Glen, it's Thomas Hines. Looks like Gabby's suspicions are correct. Probably Glen is married and has borrowed this place from a mate just to bed her.

She's a big girl. She can handle that.

When she comes out of the bathroom, he's in the kitchen making Nescafé. His phone rings, and he answers it straight away. After a few words, he says, 'Hold on,' then looks at her and says, 'Sorry, Gabby, I have to take this.'

'Oh.' She's being dismissed, and tries not to feel hurt. This was a one-night stand, no strings, and she has no right to expect anything more. 'No worries. Thanks for a good night. Maybe I'll see you around.'

'I've called you a taxi – he'll be outside in a minute. I'll be in touch, OK?'

Downstairs, outside the front of the block, it's spitting with rain and cold.

Waiting at the kerb, she shivers.

Business and pleasure are never a good mix.

TWENTY-FOUR

The side street where Gabby left her car last night has turned into a metred zone this morning, and she's already got a ticket taped to her windscreen, despite the early hour. Ripping it off, she shoves it in the glove box with several others. Better get them sorted when she gets back to London; the accounts department are sympathetic to the need occasionally to park first and worry about legalities later, but they take a dim view if fines have been neglected and begin to inflate.

Her brusque dismissal has made her ninety-nine per cent certain she'll get no further in her quest for info on Wilfred Hickling via Glen. She's not expecting him to call, and that's frustrating, given the tantalising glimpses she's had of Hickling's eccentric porn collection. What's her next move? This story could be a big break for her, but she needs something fast. If the police charge Hickling with Natalie's murder, every media outlet in the country will be all over it and her early advantage will be lost.

A glance at her watch tells her it's not too early to call Caro. Redemption Roasters will have sold her the day's first espresso macchiato, and she'll have boosted her sugar levels and dispelled any lingering morning-after hangover with an almond croissant. It's a good time to check in and find out what's going on at the office.

She dials Caro's number, pictures her hunting for her mobile in the depths of her capacious mauve Mulberry bag, swearing as she does so. The phone rings for a long time, and when Caro finally answers in that cut-glass, privileged accent, she seems distracted.

'Hi, sweetie.'

'Hi,' says Gabby. 'How's everything?' She hears rustling and crackling down the line and checks her screen, thinking she's been cut off. 'Caro?'

'I'm here, sweetie. Just finding a better spot where I can talk. Yeah, everything's good. Well, almost.'

Something's not right with Caro. Usually she'd rattle on non-stop and Gabby would struggle to get a word in. This terse, staccato version of her colleague is one she doesn't recognise.

'So what's not good? Come on, spill the beans.'

'Bean-spilling's not really my thing, though. Not really my place.'

'Caro, what the hell? What's going on?'

Caro sighs. 'I can't talk long, I'm on my way to an appointment.' At this hour, Gabby can guess where: the chic, invitation-only hairdresser who has sole responsibility for keeping Caro's hair its honey-blonde, shiny best. 'But maybe I should give you a heads-up. It's only fair you should have a chance to dodge the bullet.'

'What bullet? What are you talking about?'

'Look, it's not for me to say. And don't shoot the messenger.

I had drinks last night in the Fox and Grapes and I bumped into David at the bar.' David. Gabby's boss's boss. 'He'd been there a while, and he was well on the way to being drunk, but he asked if he could join us, so of course I said yes. How could I not? And I didn't want it to turn into a work meeting because that is sooooo boring when you're with people you don't work with, but then I thought, well, his tongue's pretty loose, let's just see whether he's got anything interesting to say. So I asked him who was in line for Mandy's job when she goes and I was expecting him to say you, but he said probably Callum. And I said I thought you were a shoe-in, and he said, *Au contraire*, those were his actual words, in the most non-French accent you've ever heard. *Au contraire, Michael's thinking it's time to let Gabby go.*'

Gabby feels a cold wave pass through her body.

'What? You're joking! Did he say why?'

'Well, of course I asked him, but he seemed to have a moment of lucidity and just said it was his round and off he went to the bar and never came back. Got talking to some of his disreputable mates, probably. You know what he's like. He knows everybody.'

Gabby does know what David's like, and he does know everybody. If she loses her job at the *Herald*, finding another when David thinks she's not good enough to be on his team would be impossible. Her future would lie with some online sweatshop pumping out click-bait, or a provincial paper somewhere out in the sticks.

Somewhere like this.

She isn't sure if she's more angry, or hurt, or embarrassed. Probably a good measure of all three.

'Anyway, sorry to be the bearer and all that,' says Caro. 'Gotta go for now. Drinks when you get back, yeah?'

'Course,' says Gabby, suspecting she won't be hearing from Caro much any more.

And yet, in truth, Gabby's seen it coming. Beaten to the scoop in the double Surrey murder last month. A dropped ball on the Ministry of Health scandal a couple of weeks before that. She hasn't been pulling her weight in the *Herald*'s terms for the last six months.

She really, desperately needs a big win, a front-page exclusive.

Either that or deal with the humiliation of being fired.

Better pray for a miracle.

Or create one.

Since she's already got the parking ticket, there's no hurry to move the car. Instead, she sets up a hotspot from her phone, grabs her laptop from the boot and pulls it from its case.

Maybe the best thing to do is to have a look at Hickling's background, see what she can find.

She opens a Google tab and types in his name, adds the word Norfolk as an afterthought and presses enter.

The name is unusual, and she gets a direct hit straight away. He shows up as general manager on a page of promotional photographs for – how interesting – the Illingham Hall Hotel. A few more search terms and clicks and she has him confirmed: younger, less grey, but definitely the same guy she photographed feeding swans by the river at Wickney. He's not listed as an employee now, and the most recent mention of him is seven years ago, so it seems likely he no longer works there.

But Google Maps tells her the hotel isn't too far away. If she sets off now, maybe she'll be there in time for breakfast.

She's putting her laptop back in its case when she's startled by someone rapping on the window. A young woman her own age is grinning at her through the glass, signalling her to open the window, and Gabby does.

'Gabby, is that you? Oh my God, how wonderful to see you!'

An awkward moment passes as Gabby tries to place the familiar face.

'Mona!' Gabby gets out of the car. 'I didn't recognise you. You look amazing!'

In truth, Mona is barely recognisable from the way she looked when they were at school. Back then, Mona rocked a unique and sassy '60s style, pulled together from jumble sales and the vintage clothes shops in the cobbled lanes around the market. She was a cool, audacious daredevil who knew where all the best parties were happening and had tickets in her cutesy clutch bag to every sold-out gig. So how did she become this plain, innocuous woman you wouldn't look twice at? What happened to the Bardot sunglasses, the pouting pink lips, the platinum hair?

But then, the morning after the night with Glen, Gabby wouldn't be surprised if Mona was thinking the same about her.

'What are you doing here?' asks Mona. 'I thought you were in London now.'

'I am, mostly. I'm just here for a couple of days, covering a story.'

'Ooh, exciting! Tell me more.'

'The Natalie Cutter murder.'

Mona is impressed. 'That's a big story. Well done you. I always knew you'd be a superstar.'

With the news she's had from Caro, Gabby's keen to divert the conversation away from her career. 'What about you? What are you doing these days?'

Gabby sees a trace of wistfulness in Mona's smile. 'Oh, nothing very exciting. I work part-time in that Italian café we used to go to for pizza sometimes, do you remember? Waiting tables mostly. Me and Rick got married, but you know that – you had the invite.'

'Yeah. Sorry I couldn't be there.'

Now Mona's eyes light up and her smile is bright. 'We have two beautiful kids. Teddy, he's three, and Lola, she's just turned one. You'll have to come and meet them. Rick would love to see you.'

'I'd love to see him too,' says Gabby, pulling a regretful face, 'but like I say, I'm only here a couple of days.'

'You staying at your mum's?'

'Of course. It's like being seventeen all over again.'

'Well, look, if you do get time, give me a call.' Mona finds her phone, Gabby recites her number and seconds later her mobile rings. 'So, we're connected again. It's so lovely to see you, Gabby. We all miss you. Promise you'll give me a ring if you have time.'

'I'll do my absolute best,' says Gabby, knowing she's not telling the truth.

TWENTY-FIVE

Like so much of England, Norfolk is at its idyllic best on a spring morning.

But Gabby's too preoccupied with her professional future to appreciate the scenery, driving past waterways and through market towns with barely a glance.

Illingham, she finds, is too small to properly be called a village but is at best a hamlet, a few cottages at a meeting of two lanes. Beyond them is the gated entrance to Illingham Hall, declared by a sign of welcome to be a four-star hotel.

Gabby follows a winding drive through parkland grazed by sheep until the hall – a rambling Elizabethan manor house faced with traditional Norfolk flints – comes into view.

The car park is off to one side, and the main entrance – a broad oak door overhung by a thatched porch – is reached by a pleasant walk through a rose garden.

In reception, Gabby gives her brightest smile as she approaches the young woman at the desk. 'Am I in time for breakfast?'

The young woman points to a low-ceilinged corridor to her left. 'In the buttery. I'll have someone come and take your order.'

Gabby helps herself to a hotel brochure before she follows the scent of coffee. The breakfast menu is extensive, and expensive. While she's waiting for her eggs Benedict, she sips orange juice that tastes as if it's been squeezed in Valencia that morning, and gives thanks she's on expenses.

Idly, she opens the brochure. Alongside the welcoming title on page one is a photo of a man she's seen before, though older and greyer, redder in the face and more portly.

This is the man Glen showed her on his phone: Natalie's neighbour's apparent crush, named here as Lord Illingham.

When Gabby's eaten, she visits the plush powder room to fix her lipstick. Paying her bill at the front desk, she's relieved – after what Caro said – to find her company credit card still works.

As she replaces the card in her wallet, she pulls out her press pass and smiles again at the receptionist. 'Gabby Laflin from the *Herald*. Would it be possible to have a few minutes of Lord Illingham's time?'

The receptionist regards her coolly. 'Let me check with his secretary. I don't know what his movements are this morning.'

She disappears through a doorway at the back, but quickly returns. 'Lord Illingham has a few minutes before he has to go out,' she says. 'His office is on the first floor.'

Climbing a creaking oak staircase, Gabby rehearses an opening line, praying that an idea of where she should direct the conversation beyond that will come to her. Winging it, her father would call it, but she needs to do better than that. Anyone holding a hereditary title will be more than well connected, and if it all goes wrong she'll be out of a job regardless of how strong her story is.

She knocks at a door marked *Private*, inhales and exhales, ready to go. She's in this job because she's good at it. If there's anything of interest here about Wilfred Hickling, she's the one to find it.

'Enter.'

Lord Illingham's office has the air of a gentleman's club: last night's cigars, this morning's muted aftershave and a trace of polished leather. A grey gun dog sleeps in front of a fire which has burned down almost to ash. In the latticed windows, discoloured diamonds of antique glass dim the sunlight shining on the rose garden below.

Lord Illingham sits in a wing-backed chair, wearing a blue suit with the wide pinstripe favoured by city traders, and hand-made leather shoes Gabby thinks are from Joseph Cheaney's. By his side, a small table is covered in papers weighted by an almost-empty cafetière and a bone-china cup and saucer. He doesn't stand or offer his hand, but points to a button-back sofa, half of which is covered by a dog blanket.

'I hear you're from the *Herald*,' he says, with candid disdain. 'To what do we owe the honour?'

She sits. 'Gabby Laflin. Thank you for seeing me.'

'I couldn't resist, but I'm afraid I have to leave soon for a meeting in London, so I only have a very few minutes. What can I do for you, Ms Laflin?'

'Do you mind if I record our conversation?'

'Not in the least, do as you wish, but you have my assurance I'm highly unlikely to have anything of interest to say to you.'

'I'm covering the murder of a young woman in Wickney, Natalie Cutter. You've probably seen something about it in the press. It's been big news, for Norfolk especially.'

'As a general rule, I restrict my news consumption to business and finance, since they tend to be areas where what's reported is broadly factual. So no, I'm not aware of any happenings in Wickney, nor am I quite sure exactly where that is.'

'It's about twenty miles away. And I'm here because Natalie's next-door neighbour has been questioned by police in connection with her death, and I think you may know him. His name's Wilfred Hickling.'

Lord Illingham's eyebrows rise. Beyond that, she can read nothing in his expression.

'Baiting me for headlines, Ms Laflin? I'm well acquainted with all the tricks you chaps use. Mr Hickling was an employee here for a number of years, if that's what you're getting at, but I don't see what you're going to make of it.'

'Were you aware of the nature of Mr Hickling's sexual tastes?'

Lord Illingham's eyebrows rise again, and he gives her a smile without humour.

'You people never fail to astonish. I wonder what you'd make of it, if someone came round asking your employer about your sexuality? I suspect it would make you rather uncomfortable and perhaps even somewhat angry. But there's nothing to hide, as far as I know. I think we all knew, or guessed, that Wilf had what my father would have called a depraved nature and unspeakable appetites. But we're rather more enlightened than that these days, aren't we? My father was the kind of man to string him up by his thumbs and cut off his scrotum, but Wilf was always very discreet, hardly the type to go pinching the waiters' bottoms, if that's what you're getting at.'

'The police have found some sensitive material at Mr Hickling's house,' says Gabby.

Lord Illingham frowns. 'Sensitive in what way?'

'Concerning you.'

'Me? Nothing compromising, I assume?'

'Not exactly. Mr Hickling appears to have had what you might call a crush on you. He has a collection of photographs of you, going back decades.'

At this revelation, Gabby is hoping for an emotional response, shock or distaste, amusement or egotism. Instead, Lord Illingham draws in a deep breath and slowly releases it, as if laying down a weight he's long carried.

'I feel quite touched. Poor old Wilf. Flattering, isn't it, in a way? I'm vain enough to think I was handsome in my day, but time is a cruel mistress. Maybe I should pay him a visit, show him what I've turned into. That would cool any remaining ardour, don't you think? Wilf always had such a charming manner and the guests all loved him. He started out in the restaurant but by the time he retired we'd promoted him to general manager, a post he held for almost twenty years. And we miss him still. Always a safe pair of hands, was Wilf. If anything wanted doing, from changing a lightbulb to organising a banquet, Wilf was our man. That was our mantra. Ask Mr Hickling.'

'So why did he leave?'

'Are you hoping that he left under a cloud, Ms Laflin? Well, he did not. He came into some money, decided he'd had a good run and that it was time for him to step aside and give a younger man a chance. If he'd wanted, we'd have kept him on to sixty-five, but he felt he didn't have his old energy and that it would be better for us if he went. Even so, he gave us thirty years of sterling service. Not many can say that, these days. I'm sorry if he's facing a bit of trouble. No doubt those idiots buzzing about with their blue lamps flashing have got it wrong as usual.'

'They say he was very friendly with Natalie's five-year-old daughter.'

'I wouldn't doubt it. He was very fond of children, and never missed an opportunity to spend time with mine. For many years he was our hotel Father Christmas. We used to sit him in front of the tree in the old library, and the children used to sit on his knee to have their pictures taken. What's that to do with anything? Are you asking if I believe he had paedophiliac tendencies? You people truly are beyond the pale.'

The door opens, and a middle-aged woman looks in.

'The car's waiting, my lord.'

'Thanks Siobhan, I'm just coming.' He looks at Gabby. 'I think this lady and I are just about done.'

Gabby rings her mother to tell her she'll be home before long, then finds a café with free Wi-Fi in the backstreets of Downham Market where there are no other customers at the tables upstairs.

She orders tea and what turns out to be a rather dry scone. Opening her laptop, she plugs her earbuds into her phone and locates the file of her conversation with Lord Illingham.

The piece doesn't need to be long, if the key elements are there. This is all about creating prurient interest, selling papers and winning eyeball minutes online.

The headline's not up to her, but she includes one anyway,

as a teaser to the editor: *Did Natalie's killer have paedophiliac tendencies?*

The rest is straightforward: bigging up Illingham's aristocratic credentials, Hickling's length of service, a description of the house and made-up descriptions of wealthy visitors. Then, a juicy thread is woven through, cherry-picked from Illingham's own words.

He was very fond of children, never missed an opportunity to spend time with my own. The children used to sit on his knee. My father would have strung him up by his thumbs.

When she's done, on one level she's pleased with her attention-grabbing story. Wilfred Hickling is of interest to the police and may indeed be a paedophile, in which case she'll be playing a valuable part in exposing his true nature.

But what she's written contains a percentage of out-of-context quotes and half-truths, and the impression it will give is unproven. She's putting meaning to Lord Illingham's words she knows he didn't intend.

Even so. She urgently needs a win.

Her fingers are crossed on two fronts: that Lord Illingham really doesn't ever read anything but the business and finance sections of any newspaper, and that Hickling is quickly charged with Natalie's killing.

The element of risk is significant. But if she doesn't file a decent story, her career's all but over anyway.

Attaching the file to an email containing a brief explanatory note, she hesitates.

Should she or shouldn't she?

She counts to ten, and presses send.

*　　*　　*

Forty-eight minutes later, as Gabby's driving back to her parents' house, her mobile rings. A name comes up on the car's display screen: her boss, Michael.

She presses a button to connect the call.

'Hi, Michael, how are you?'

'Gabby, hi. How's things down there in the country? Fresh air and pints of scrumpy? Sounds fabulous.'

Detecting a hint of post-lunch ebullience, she glances at the clock. Only 11.30. Rather early, even for him.

'Scrumpy's the West Country,' she says. 'But actually, it's all good. In fact, I think I'm done here. I'm going to head back to London later today.'

'OK, great. Listen, I've read your piece and I like it, I like it very much. The only thing I need to ask you is, how solid is your police source?'

That's a very fair question.

She sighs, knowing this could be the end of the road for her. 'Honestly? I think he's straight up, but there's been no official information. He's local CID, so I'm sure he knows what's going on.'

'On a scale of one to ten, how solid are we on this bloke as a suspect?'

Gabby hesitates, considering bulling it up, but what's the point? 'Five? Six? He lived next door to her.'

'Hmm.' She can hear the drum of his fingers, but the background noise is subdued, not the usual chatter and ringing phones of their busy office, and she wonders where he's calling from. 'Well, you know what, Gabby, sometimes in life you have to take a chance and say fuck it. It'll sell a few copies, no doubt about that. You've stuck with this story, and I like that tenacity, and if they make an arrest it'll be a real coup for us. So you know what? Let's run it. I'll tell them to put it on page one.'

Gabby knows she should feel ecstatic to have a front-page byline, but the feeling's not there. Instead, a pulse of emotion she can't quite name makes her heart sink.

'Michael, you know, thinking about it, to be honest I'm not sure it's right for page one. Maybe I should stay another day, dig a bit deeper and rewrite some of the more speculative parts . . .'

'No, no, you need to get back. Plenty of other stuff for you to get your teeth into.'

'But I'm just thinking that, on reflection, it might be better to hold off . . .'

'Gabby? Gabby, are you still there?' She hears him muttering as he examines the bars of signal on his phone. 'You're breaking up. Look, I have to run anyway. Let's talk when you get back in the office.'

And he's gone.

TWENTY-SIX

Tuesday morning, a day like any other.

The petrol station isn't busy. Margot's intending to put fifty pounds' worth of fuel in her little Toyota; for the bits of running about she does, it should last her the week. As she goes through the usual motions – unscrewing the cap, waiting for the kiosk attendant to reset the gauge – her mind's running through the inconsequential tasks she has written on her list: the return of an overdue book to the library; the posting of a birthday card to a friend living abroad; the buying of lettuce and tomatoes for a salad. But as the pump runs she glances over towards the newspaper stand fronting the kiosk, and a headline catches her eye: *Natalie's Neighbour's Unnatural Appetites.*

Seemingly of its own will, her hand releases the trigger and the pump clicks off. In a daze, she leaves the car with the pump nozzle still in the tank opening, and walking over to the newspaper stand, lifts the Perspex cover keeping off wind and water and picks up a copy.

The opening paragraph is printed in bold.

A former employer of Natalie Cutter's peeping neighbour has spoken of his 'unnatural appetites', pushing loner Wilfred Hickling to the top of the police's list of suspects in her murder at an isolated Norfolk cottage.

Margot stares at more words that she can't read for the trembling in her hands. Taking the paper with her, she returns to her car and presses the trigger to keep pumping. *Better fill it up,* she thinks. She might be driving further than she expected.

When she goes inside to pay, Margot unthinkingly hands the newspaper over for scanning with the headline on full view. The cashier's similar in age to Margot and probably assumes she's a kindred spirit.

'Looks like they've got him, then,' she says, nodding towards the paper as Margot holds her card against the contactless payment machine. 'Dirty old pervert.'

Tears prick Margot's eyes. 'Innocent until proven guilty,' she says, defensively, and the cashier gives her an odd look, as if doubting Margot's sanity.

Errands forgotten, she drives home.

Using the three-ring code they agreed, she tries to call Wilf, but he doesn't ring back. When she's waited ten minutes, she dials again, this time letting the phone ring and ring, picturing it there in its usual place, fracturing the dust-moted silence, wondering and then worrying where her brother could be.

Early in the evening, as dusk falls, the phone rings.

Relieved to see his number on the display, she mutes the TV.

'Wilf? Where on earth have you been? I've been calling all day.'

He sniffs, and she knows he's properly crying, which for him – a proud man, a man defined all his life by unfashionable standards of keeping emotions to yourself – is the epitome of weakness and disgrace.

'Wilf, whatever's the matter? What's happened?'

'They're outside.'

'Who's outside?'

'Listen.'

But she can hear only muffled noises – could that be music of some kind, and shouting? Then, a thud.

'What was that?'

'Eggs.' Wilf blows his nose. 'They're throwing eggs at the windows. I daren't put the lights on or they'll know I'm here.'

'You're in the dark?'

'Yes.'

Margot feels an amalgam of disquiet, anger and pity. 'But who's doing this? Who in God's name are they?'

'I don't know. Cars started going past the house this morning with their music really loud, the same cars over and over. Then they got bolder and parked outside, shouting and jeering, so I thought I'd better leave. They let me go by but they banged on the car as I passed. I couldn't ring you then because the police still have my mobile phone and I'm sorry, Margot, I couldn't quite remember your number. I've just been driving round all day. I went to a service station near Peterborough thinking I might get a sandwich and something to drink, and I saw the newspaper there. Who's said those things about me, Margot? Who would say that?'

'You didn't buy a copy?'

'I didn't dare go in. I ended up in a village tea shop instead. Less people, and I felt safer there, but I couldn't stay forever, could I?'

'You haven't read it, then?'

'No. Have you?'

'I'm afraid I have, yes.'

'So who was it? Such a malicious thing to say, I just can't think where they've got it from. It's been troubling me all day.'

'I'm afraid it was Lord Illingham.'

A short silence. 'I won't believe it. His lordship is too much of a gentleman. He would never speak of me that way. Would he?'

'It's just a rag, Wilf.'

'But people believe it, Margot. They're here, outside, wanting my blood. I really do think that's what they want. They're a mob, Margot, a proper mob.'

Margot's disquiet is growing. 'You've called the police, haven't you?'

'Of course. I rang 999 and said I was being threatened, and they said they'd send someone, but that was over an hour ago.'

'You must ring them again.'

'But I don't trust them. I've been thinking about it, and there must have been some kind of leak. Who else but the police could have identified me to the newspaper?'

The question is valid.

'How did you get past them to get home?'

Another thud.

'They'll break the windows if they keep on. I thought when it got to be about six o'clock they'd have got bored and left, but I could see from the end of the lane there were more of them. So I drove to Parker's Bridge and left the car there, walked home along the riverbank and sneaked through the back gate, but that was a mistake. I should have stayed away. I wouldn't have come back but I was worried about Mr Grimes. He needs to be fed, but he wouldn't eat his dinner. He's hiding upstairs under my bed, refusing to come out. They keep starting up with a terrible racket and he's terrified.'

From the recesses of memory, Margot recalls old stories of fenland vigilantes and the practice of 'rough music', hostile gatherings roused by disapproval of someone's conduct, where whole villages paraded to torment the offender with the banging of pots and pans. But surely that's an archaic custom, mediaeval? Can it be possible Wilf is being tin-panned?

If so, from what she remembers of her reading, Wilf could be in danger of physical violence. And only recently, Channel 4 screened a documentary about attacks on innocent men provoked by groups on social media. One poor chap mistakenly believed to be a paedophile was beaten almost to death outside a pub. Another falsely accused of rape was run over with a car. People across the country, frustrated by cuts in police numbers, form their own brigades to patrol the streets at night. Huge backlogs in the courts tempt victims' supporters to take the law into their own hands. Natalie, by all accounts, was very popular in Wickney. Wilf, it has to be said, probably is not. Now that newspaper has pointed the finger, it isn't fanciful to think the situation could easily go from bad to worse.

'I think I should come and get you,' she says. 'Will you be all right for a couple of hours?'

'But in the dark, Margot? You're no better at driving in the dark than I am, and it'll take you the best part of three hours.' He's right. As she's got older – or maybe as headlamps have got blindingly brighter – night-driving is a nightmare to

Margot, the oncoming lights a confusing dazzle that stops her seeing the road. 'I think I'd be best taking a torch and making my way back to the car, sleeping in it tonight.'

'You can't do that, Wilf. Why don't you find a hotel?'

'What if I'm recognised?'

What if he is? thinks Margot. *He might swap this mob for a worse one.*

'All right then, maybe the bridge is best. Pack a bag, put Mr Grimes in his carrier and make your way there. And take a blanket. It's bound to be cold. Be careful they don't see you, Wilf. I'll set off as soon as it's light, around five, so expect me about eight.'

'Thank you.'

'I'm going to call the police again for you. It's shocking they allow this to go on. And try not to get too upset. I'll be there as soon as I can.'

The drive to Margot's is long. At first, confined in his carrier, Mr Grimes's yowled complaints remove any possibility of talk, but by the time they reach the A1 he's given up and settled down, and what's left between Margot and Wilf are uneasy silences and stilted bursts of conversation amid the rumble of traffic.

They reach Margot's at lunchtime, though Wilf's so exhausted it feels like the middle of the night. Leaving Mr Grimes for the time being still complaining in the kitchen, Margot leads Wilf up the narrow staircase and shows him into a bedroom with a single bed and a chest of drawers.

'I'll go and put the kettle on,' she says as brightly as she can, 'leave you to settle in.'

He hears the stairs creak, the knocking of a pipe as she runs the tap. Sitting on the end of the bed, he looks out on a view very different to what he's used to, of stone walls running like scars across Peak District valleys and hills. This place has its beauty, but it isn't home.

How will they manage, he and she together?

Margot has picked a vase of flowers from the garden and put it on the chest of drawers, on a doily she no doubt embroidered herself.

Her kindness brings tears to his eyes.

In times of crisis, small things mean a lot.

TWENTY-SEVEN

Gabby arrives early at the office, grabbing herself a hot-desk and thinking she'll be glad to let someone else take over on the Natalie Cutter case, move on to something new.

She chats a few minutes to Jeannie, a fellow journo she worked with a few weeks back on a people-smuggling story. Jeannie's about to tell her the office gossip when Gabby's phone rings. She listens for a moment and says, 'Of course, straight away.'

She hangs up and raises her eyebrows at Jeannie. 'That was Trudi. Apparently I'm wanted upstairs.'

Gabby's only been in David McAllister's office once before, crowded in with a group of others to celebrate an award to a senior editor. David's reached the top of the tree after a long and largely distinguished career, punctuated by a couple of blips around the time of the Jimmy Savile scandal, and once when he served three weeks in an open prison for contempt of court after refusing to name a source in an exposé – an episode which only served to make him more of an industry legend.

Gabby isn't nervous about going to see him; he's personable with his staff, and approachable. His office is what you'd expect, a corner office on a high floor, Scandinavian blond furniture and a personal assistant who's both beautiful and a formidable gatekeeper. If Trudi says you can't see David, there's no seeing him.

This morning she's in one of her cooler moods, barely looking up from her keyboard as she tells Gabby she can go straight in.

David's behind his desk in his usual almost-casual style, though everyone knows if you checked the collar of his shirt you'd find a label from one of London's pricier tailors.

She gives him a smile and regrets it, because he doesn't smile back.

'Close the door, Gabby,' he says, and that's when she knows she's in trouble. 'Have a seat.'

He drops a copy of her headline edition on his desk, the words she wrote undeniable in black and white.

'Do you want to tell me about this?' asks David in a cold, quiet voice. 'Give me your version of events? Because I've had Lord Illingham's legal people on the phone this morning, demanding we print a retraction and a full apology. According to him, he was very clear indeed when he spoke to you that he always regarded Mr Hickling to be of exemplary – that is the word used – exemplary character, and he now has the difficult job of apologising to Mr Hickling for everything he never said. I haven't heard yet from Mr Hickling's lawyers, but I'm expecting the call any moment. This looks like libel of the worst kind, Gabby. It could cost this paper millions.'

'But I talked it over with Michael.' The moment the words are out, she bitterly regrets them: a cheap move to foist blame on to her boss. But where is Michael? Why isn't he here?

'Did you?' asks David. He pulls the paper towards him and reads out the date. 'Michael left the company the day before this went to print.'

He sees the shock in Gabby's face. 'You didn't know? He didn't tell you? Oh my God.' He laughs without mirth. 'I get it. A revenge piece. You've been set up, my dear. Bit of a bastard thing to do on his part, wouldn't you say? But no worse than what you've done, trashing Mr Hickling's reputation and dragging a peer of the realm into the mess for good measure. What the hell were you thinking? What in God's name were you thinking?'

'I had an off-the-record police source.' Gabby's face is burning redder than she can ever remember. 'Hickling is a suspect, and what Lord Illingham said seemed to confirm the way they're thinking.'

'In what way? Tell me, what exactly did Illingham say to confirm anything about Hickling?'

'He said Hickling was attracted to children.'

'Did he? Did he really?' demands David. 'And think very carefully before you answer, because our lawyers will most certainly be going over your records of what was and wasn't said in that conversation with the finest of fine-toothed combs.'

Gabby has nowhere to go. 'Not exactly that, no. But I was just trying to break new ground. If Hickling's arrested, everyone heard it here first. He could be a dangerous man, a predator. Isn't it our job to out him?'

David shakes his head in exasperation. 'You seem to have completely lost your way, Gabby. This piece is the kind of crap that wouldn't even stand up on Facebook.' He turns his back on her and crosses to the high window with its view of the

Thames. 'I'm sure I've no need to tell you you're finished at this paper. You can take leave of absence until your notice period is up, and don't you dare come asking me for a reference. Go on, get out of my sight.'

Somehow Gabby gets through her hugely embarrassing, trying-not-to-cry exit from the office, her notebooks and laptop stuffed into her bag and a terse *See ya* to a bemused and startled Jeannie. Caro, she notices, hasn't even looked up from her keyboard, and Gabby really hopes that wasn't a smile she spotted at the corners of Caro's lips, because if it was, she's going to have to kill her.

What else is Gabby to do but hit the nearest pub, earning her the dubious honour of being the day's first customer? Carrying her order from the bar, she retires to a gloomy corner to take stock with a large gin and tonic.

Halfway down the glass, the undeniable truth hits her: she's brought this on herself.

And that makes it so much worse.

When Jeannie comes in and sits down beside her, Gabby bursts into tears.

TWENTY-EIGHT

Two days later, Gabby packs a small suitcase and takes the tube to King's Cross station. Bad things always happen together; her Mazda's gone for expensive repair following the discovery of an oil leak.

While she's standing below the destination boards waiting for a platform announcement, her phone rings.

Glen.

Even though there's no reason – no work-based reason – to maintain the relationship, she can't deny she's pleased he's called.

'Gabby?'

'Hi.'

'How are you doing?'

She decides to lie. 'I'm great, thanks. How are you?'

A tannoy announcement overrides his reply.

'Are you busy?' he asks. 'I can call another time.'

'No, no worries. As a matter of fact, I'm just jumping on a train to King's Lynn.'

'Really? I thought you weren't coming back this way any-time soon? Can't stay away, eh?'

She manages a small smile. 'Don't flatter yourself. I've got some stuff I didn't get done, that's all.'

'Trading places, then. I was calling to say I'll be in London next week if you fancied a drink or something. Will you be back by then?'

'To be honest, I'm not sure. When are you down here?'

'Monday through Wednesday. A work thing, at Earl's Court. Is that anywhere near you?'

'Earl's Court? Latest developments in blue-light technology or something?'

'What? Oh. Right. Listen, sorry, I've got to go, call on the landline. I'll call you next week, then, see if you're free?'

'OK, great.'

'Bye for now.'

She stands for a moment, thinking. Thirty-five minutes before her train leaves. Time to find somewhere quiet and make a call.

'Norfolk Police.'

'Hello, I wonder if you can help me? I'm trying to get in touch with an officer from your CID team, Glen somebody. I'm sorry, I can't remember his last name.'

The operator falls silent. Gabby hears the clicking of the keyboard as she types.

'I'm sorry, we don't have a Glen in CID. Can anyone else help you?'

Gabby recalls the medication in the bathroom cabinet and takes a chance.

'Can I speak to Thomas Hines?'

'I'll put you through to his office.'

She's thinking this has gone far enough and is going to hang up when a voice says, 'DS Hines.'

Gabby hesitates.

'Hello?'

'Yes, hello. I'm sorry, you don't know me but I'm trying to get in touch with one of your detectives. His name is Glen.'

'Who is this?'

'Like I say, we haven't met.'

'There's no one called Glen working in CID.'

'Should I try another department, then?'

But DS Hines has hung up.

Gabby's father is where she knew she'd find him, at the wheel of his unfashionable Volvo, reversed into a too-small space at the far end of the station car park. Usually, he'd be listening to some obscure '80s or '90s CD, but today as she approaches she sees he's not tapping out a beat with his fingers but has his head back on the headrest, looking at nothing but the black-painted fence lining the railway track. The day's warm, his window's down and he hears her coming, dragging her suitcase behind her on its inadequate wheels like a penitent dragging the weight of her sins.

His smile lacks its usual warmth, and she realises he's trying not to show what of course he must be feeling, the weight of disappointment and – worse – the embarrassing taint of shame. Everyone locally will know, of course. Someone will have seen the retraction and the apology and connected it to her story. Probably he's been fielding prurient phone calls ever since.

Of course he still gets out of the car to put her case in the boot, because he's a gentleman; of course he still asks if she had a good journey, if she's hungry or thirsty and if she wants him to stop somewhere for refreshments on the way out of town.

But she shakes her head. She just wants to run away and hide.

Traffic's Easter-bank-holiday slow, clogged with cars and campervans heading for the coast. For a while, they hardly speak, not until they're well out into open country and across the Great Ouse, into the territory she'd call home. The empty land is soothing, moving through the seasons as it always does, immune to any small drama of those who pass through and undisturbed by anything she's done or ever might do.

And at that point she finds the courage to say, 'I'm so sorry, Dad.'

He glances away from the road to her profile. His hands on the wheel are beginning to show signs of age, the veins more prominent, the knuckles bonier through thinner skin. He won't always be here to help her pick up the pieces.

But today, thank God, he is.

'I'm not going to lie to you, Gabby,' he says. 'Your mum and I are disappointed at the way it's turned out. But most of all, I'm mad at you because you brought this on yourself. Didn't we always say to you, if you're going to do that job, do it for good, do it with honesty and integrity? You were going to be a warrior for social justice. I don't understand what you were thinking.'

Gabby's eyes fill with tears. 'I just got carried away. I heard a rumour they were going to fire me because I wasn't delivering. You've no idea what it was like, Dad. You're only ever as good as your last story, and I didn't dare go back there with nothing.

I thought I'd got an angle. I had a contact in Norwich, but I shouldn't have trusted him. I got it all so wrong, and I'm so sorry.'

'An apology is definitely required,' he says, 'but it isn't me you should offer it to.'

The following day, Gabby borrows her father's car and drives over to Wickney.

As she crosses the bridge, the swans are on the river, gliding in a line.

Nine Brethren House has an unexpected air of dereliction. The verge out front is a mess of beer cans and litter and the windows are filmed with broken eggs. Across the Georgian front door, someone has sprayed *PEDO BASTARD* in red paint.

She walks round the back and, damp-palmed with apprehension, knocks at the door.

Even though she can tell no one is there.

But, to be sure, she knocks again, and waits. Her speech is well-rehearsed, even though she's no right to expect him to listen, no right to expect anything except abuse and a solicitor's letter telling her she's being sued for damages.

She peers through the door's opaque glass and sees the distorted shapes of unopened mail on the floor.

The man she falsely accused is gone.

All she can do is try her very best to make amends.

Justin's mother Freda made him do it: leave Ruby in her care, have a shower and a shave, put on some respectable clothes and take himself out for a drink.

Justin's no stranger to the Admiral Nelson. He had his first pint here at sixteen, bought for him by an older lad he knew from school, who charged 50p commission to make the purchase. Justin and his mates sat round a table in the beer garden, pretending they preferred the bitter, hoppy Wherry ale to their usual lager shandies, smoking illicit cigarettes and watching girls on the sly. Even then, Justin only had eyes for Natalie.

When he opens the taproom door, everything seems the same: the portrait of Nelson hanging over the fireplace, the smell of chips frying in the kitchen, the same old boy playing the fruit machine, still thinking one day he'll win the unwinnable jackpot.

And Kevin, polishing glasses behind the bar. When he sees Justin, his smile is warm and broad. 'Well, look who's here! It's about time you showed your face, young man. How've you been keeping?' Without asking, he's filling a pint glass with the same Wherry ale Justin used to find difficult to stomach. As the beer foams, his face becomes serious. 'Listen, I'm sorry about what's happened, mate. It's hard on you and the little one, really hard. We came to the funeral, me and Julie, I don't know if you saw us? We wanted to pay our respects, of course we did, though we didn't make it to the wake because we had to open up this place. People are always asking after you. How're you doing, really?'

'I'm all right.' Justin takes a long drink from his pint. He's imagined how it will taste, but somehow it's disappointing. 'And Ruby, she's doing OK. As well as can be expected, anyway.'

'Well, it's the shock, isn't it?' says Kevin. 'It's not something you get over in a fortnight, is it? Listen, your mates'll be pleased to see you. They still come in on a Friday, regular as clockwork. You seen any of them recently, Joey maybe, or Sam?'

Right on cue, the door opens and here are Joey and Sam, delight at seeing Justin painted all over their faces. Joey puts an arm round Justin's shoulder and gives him a hug. Sam orders three pints and, when Justin thanks him, laughingly tells him he's paying.

'You're well behind on your rounds,' he says, 'but we'll soon get that put right.'

The evening rolls on. More of the local lads join their table, and Justin finds he's recovered his taste for the beer, since it seems to be effective in muting his heartbreak.

As Kevin calls last orders, Justin and Joey and Sam are left alone again, all with a fresh pint and a double shot of Macallan.

'I want you to know we've done our bit,' slurs Joey. 'Given him something to think about.'

Justin shakes his head. 'Who? What are you talking about?'

'That old bastard who did for Nat. We gave him a rough time of it, didn't we, Sam?'

'What old bastard?'

Sam's grinning. 'Him next door. He didn't much like it, did he? But we gave him a taste of what he can expect, once he's banged up.'

In Justin's eyes, the glasses on the table keep slipping into double focus. 'What d'you do that for?'

'He did it, didn't he?' asks Sam.

'I don't reckon so, no.' Though his reasoning's blurred,

Justin's thinking of Ruby, who's struggling to find reasons to trust anything in her upended world. She liked Wilf, saw a lot of good in him. If bad things happen to him, she'll be beyond persuading there's any order left. 'I reckon he's harmless enough. Just lonely, that's all.'

'Course he did it,' says Joey. 'They need to lock him up and throw away the key.'

''Bout time they nailed someone for it,' says Sam. 'Taking their time about it, ain't they?'

Behind the bar, Kevin is listening. 'Come on then, Justin,' he chimes in. 'Who do you think did it?'

Jason takes a long pull on his fresh pint, knowing it's unwise to drink more. 'I know fine well who did it. That scumbag Pole she was going with.' And there, he's said too much; the alcohol has wheedled out an admission that his wife slept with other men, a fact he'd never dream of acknowledging while sober. But his loosened tongue is out of control. 'He's the one we should be going after. If it weren't for Ruby, I'd track him down and kill him myself, string him up and cut off his balls.'

'Careful, mate,' says Kevin. 'Walls have ears, you know?'

'It was prob'ly Ruby that old perv was after,' says Joey, stupidly drunk. 'You ask me, Nat got in his way.'

'Could have been like that, I s'pose.' Justin picks up his whisky glass and raises it above his head. 'Here's to my mates. Here's to all of us. Whoever did it, I hope they rot in hell.'

TWENTY-NINE

The last remnants of a lost life are boxed and loaded in the van.

Dee would love a cup of tea but the kettle and cups are all gone, the kitchen worktops cleared and wiped down, the wall cupboards standing open to show there's nothing in there. Only two rooms remain to be cleared. One is what they keep calling the laundry room, actually the cellar where Natalie suffered and all but died.

Dee can't bring herself to go down there. Mad as she knows it sounds, she senses that something lingers, that echoes of her daughter's pain and distress are somehow imprinted within the walls. Whenever that door is opened, she breathes a miasma of despair which floods her heart and threatens a fresh tsunami of grief.

Frank tells her she's imagining things. Let him go down there, then, and do whatever needs to be done.

At this moment, Frank and Justin are struggling with the sofa, Natalie's grandiose teal velvet monster she got second-hand from some friend. It was always much too big for this cottage, but that was Natalie: if she wanted it, she had to have it, common sense and practicality be damned. As Frank's said several times, it came into the house so it's only logical they can get it out, but it's been stuck in the living-room doorway for over twenty minutes while they lift and manoeuvre and swear, hands getting trapped against the door frame and tempers growing hot.

Dee and Ruby are upstairs, leaning on the windowsill of what used to be Ruby's bedroom, looking down on the garden next door. Now the growing season's begun, the clean lines of the flowerbeds are disappearing and the lawns are shaggy and in need of a cut. The duck pond's becoming choked by reeds, the ducks themselves nowhere to be seen.

Ruby is much more withdrawn these days than she ever used to be, but coming back to Turle's Cottage has reduced her to near silence. When they first arrived, she climbed the stairs to her bedroom and sat down in a corner, watching without comment as Dee took down the pink curtains Ruby herself had picked out, making no comment as Dee dropped them into a bin bag.

The next hour was sad and slow, making judgements on everything Ruby owned – her toys, her books and clothes – granting some the reprieve of the 'keep' box, condemning others to what Dee said was the 'decide later' box, secretly destined for the tip.

With everything gone, Frank's unfinished painting stands out.

'Why didn't Grandpa paint that last tiny bit?' asks Ruby, as bemused as Dee herself.

'You'd have to ask him.'

'Can we go and say goodbye to Wilf?'

Dee finds the question odd. Even allowing for the over-hopeful optimism of a five-year-old, Ruby surely couldn't have missed the damage to the front of Wilf's house, the graffiti and dilapidation?

'I'm sure he's not living there any more, poppet. I don't think he'd have let the garden get like that if he was.'

'Oh.' She seems crestfallen. 'I thought because he was old, he might just have forgotten about the garden. Is Mr Grimes still there?'

'I expect Mr Grimes is where Wilf is.'

'Can we go and find him, then? Maybe he's got a new house near here.'

Dee seriously doubts that. If Wilf has any sense, he'll be as far away from here as possible. 'I don't know how we'd find out where.'

'I think we should put a letter through his door and give him our phone number. Then when he comes back he could ring us and we could ask him round to tea.'

'I'm not sure about that, pet.'

'Why not?'

'Things have been difficult for Wilf. Maybe he'd prefer to be left alone.'

'But I want to say sorry.'

Dee's surprised. 'For what?'

Ruby's suddenly tearful. 'I think when me and Mum came here, we spoiled his life.'

Dee feels a lump in her throat. Other lives have been spoiled besides Wilfred Hickling's. In Dee's eyes, he's most likely guilty of killing her daughter, but there's no reason to upset Ruby with that revelation until it's proven.

They'll cross that bridge when they come to it.

'You write your note, then,' she says, 'and I'll take it round when I'm done here.'

That way, Ruby will be let down gently.

But Dee has no intention of putting any note through a murder suspect's door.

Finally, the sofa's been loaded on the van. Natalie's bedroom alone remains intact, an anomaly now the rest of the house is echoingly empty.

Dee will go through Natalie's things by herself, perform this intimate last rite with time to reflect and privacy to cry. Frank and Justin have taken Ruby to a favourite place to eat, and she's left this house without the slightest hint of regret, jumping into the van next to her dad as if she couldn't wait to be gone.

Stephen Turle's portrait hangs again at the top of the stairs. Dee pauses to study it, seeing in his face a creature wounded by the solitariness of his occupation, by a life spent on the fenland waterways with no company but the wind and the birds.

The door to Ruby's room stands open. Her only legacies to the cottage are dents in the carpet where the feet of her bed used to be and the pink paint on the walls, but Dee can picture her leaning on the windowsill, hoping to see a cat she barely knows in next door's garden. A sharp splinter of realisation prods Dee's heart, that Ruby was lonely in this house, and Natalie's protestations that Ruby loved it were not true. This place, for some reason, suited Natalie. But it left Ruby isolated and unhappy. How had she been so blind as not to see that at the time?

On the threshold of Natalie's room, she hesitates.

She hasn't been in here since Natalie moved in. When she died, the house was subject to police searches and forensics. Since then, Dee hasn't had the fortitude to face it.

Until today.

Natalie was never big on housework, but this room is almost showhouse tidy, everything put away, the carpet vacuumed. This is essentially how she left it; after their search, the police have put everything back in its place, except for the bedding, which was taken for DNA testing. When the sheets come back, she'll never wash them again.

She opens the left side of the wardrobe and a whisper of Natalie's favourite scent drifts into the room, a complex, musky perfume Dee always bought her at Christmas, until Justin came on the scene and took over that duty. Oh, but it's so unmistakeably her, and Dee has to take a moment, sit down on the bed and rub away her tears until the wave of grief recedes.

Distressing though it is, she must get to work; the house must be cleared, the keys returned. For a while, she works with her mind closed to what she's doing, taking blouses and dresses from their hangers, folding them and placing them in a bin bag, trying not to recall when she's seen Nat wearing this jumper or that t-shirt, trying to believe these items have no meaning.

When that's done, she opens the other wardrobe door.

At first, she thinks she's looking at fancy dress, outlandish costumes bought for Halloween. But there's so much. Thigh-high red patent boots, sky-high heels in black and purple, peep-toe wedges in lurid pink. And some of these clothes, what was Nat thinking? The shortest shorts and mini-dresses, indecently see-through mesh tops, skimpy chiffon blouses that would show everything she's got.

A hot blush spreads over Dee's face as she realises what she's found: props for her daughter's sex games. She feels ashamed on Natalie's part, and boundless embarrassment for herself. This is another of death's awful gifts, the revelation of secrets best kept hidden. But now this dark Pandora's box is open, how can it ever be closed? How can she unsee what she's seen, unknow the kind of woman Natalie had become, a tease and a temptress dressing herself up like the most lurid of streetwalkers for the entertainment of . . . who?

She doesn't know. Plenty here, though, to make a peeper of the old man next door.

Unwillingly, she opens one of drawers in the bedside table, relieved to find perfectly normal underwear, the pastel Marks & Spencer's frills and thongs she expected of her daughter. In the drawer below, though, are more pornographic props – leather straps and lubricants, suspenders and stockings, an obscenely large sex toy Dee doesn't even want to touch.

Without warning, she's overcome again by crying, at first not knowing why. But as the tears pass, she understands her grief is for a new loss, for the daughter she thought Natalie still was.

This loss is hard to take. Dee herself has been naive – as many mothers are – holding her daughter in her heart as that biddable, long-ago girl who loved horses, and pizza, and *Friends*. That image – her heart's image – is now corrupted. No, not corrupted: corrected. The real-world Natalie was in many ways a stranger, a fully formed adult it turns out she barely knew.

Her embarrassment takes hold again when she realises the police search team must have seen all this, touched it, messed about with it, and laughed.

Oh, Natalie, Natalie, Natalie. What must they have thought?

There's nothing to be done but to get rid of it all. Opening a fresh bin bag, she begins to drop things in.

As the wardrobe empties, she finds a camera tripod, folded in the corner. No camera. If there was one, presumably the police have taken it. Dee shudders at the thought of what they might find on there.

Frank must never know.

She'll tie the bags up tight. He'll have no reason to look inside.

Because Frank would take it very badly indeed, if he knew everything she's just discovered about their little girl.

PART 3
The Long Road Back

THIRTY

Weeks have gone by since Natalie left them.

At breakfast, a local radio station is filling the void of silence between Dee and Frank. Dee's spoon clinks the base of her bowl as she listlessly finishes a small helping of muesli scattered with blueberries. Frank coughs and clears his throat after his first sip of coffee. In the utility room, the washer whirrs on its spin cycle.

The announcer is tediously upbeat. 'And finally, the weather. We're expecting a fine, bright day across most of our region, with just a chance of showers later on this afternoon, and highs of nineteen degrees. So get out there and enjoy some of that lovely sunshine . . .'

Dee stands up and turns off the radio, but instead of sitting back down she remains standing by the counter, staring at the wall in front of her as if suffering some loss of function.

Actually, she's focused on the calendar.

'This weekend,' she says, at last. She picks up her bowl, and carries it to the sink. Despite the small portion, she hasn't managed to eat it all. No wonder she's still losing weight. 'The last weekend in June, me and Nat always used to go to Holkham.'

Frank realises he's supposed to know what she's talking about, but he doesn't.

'What's at Holkham?'

'It's the weekend the Household Cavalry are there.' Her face has grown hard and sad since the funeral, but is softened to its old self by memories. Her mouth moves into an almost-smile. 'They come up from London for a holiday. She used to love going to see the horses gallop along the beach. They ride them into the sea. It's really amazing.'

'How come I never went?'

Dee shrugs. 'I don't know, why didn't you? Because you were never here. She and I went every year, from when she was eight until she was seventeen. Except the year we all went to Mallorca. We missed it then.'

'Well, it sounds worth a trip,' says Frank. 'If you'd like to go, then let's do it.'

She scrapes the remains of her breakfast into the bin. 'I doubt a bunch of lads on horses would float your boat.'

'Aren't there any girls? They have women everywhere in the army these days. Anyway, we could find a pub somewhere, have some lunch.'

She can read the subtext. They can't lighten the mood, because how can they ever do that? But the monotony can be broken. Nothing in the rules of grief says you can't do things to make the hours more bearable, bring a sliver of light into the dark.

'All right then, yes,' she says. 'I'll go and get changed, and let's go.'

*   *   *

Dee's been hoping against hope for the emptiness of sea and sky, but it's Norfolk in early summer and big crowds are already gathered.

As they search for a place to park, she can tell Frank's trying to contain his shortening temper, and she wonders what it is about men that makes them so quick to anger, how it always feels they're never more than a finger-snap away from full-on, punch-in-the-mouth rage, even over something as banal as parking the car. Why are they so hair-trigger? Though not all men are that way. Maybe she's thinking of the men she's known well: her father, her brother, sometimes Frank.

When he finally finds a space, he grumbles about the cost of a couple of hours' parking, and even though they pay what Frank complains is more than the rate in central London, the walk to the beach is long.

Rarely do they walk anywhere together. The breeze blowing in their faces carries the salty tang which since childhood has raised Dee's spirits in anticipation of the first sight of the sea. Frank takes a navy-blue beanie hat from the back pocket of his jeans and pulls it too far down on his head, covering his eyes so he looks ridiculous, making her smile.

Ahead of them, a trio of little girls chatter and skip along the path, just as Nat used to do. Dee remembers how she had a way when very young of walking backwards, talking with her hands as much as her voice, never looking where she was going, flushing red when she would sometimes bump into people and briefly walk more sedately at Dee's side, until the excitement of the horses and the sea grew too much, and she'd go running off ahead, calling back for Dee to follow her.

Years have passed since she and Nat last took this walk together. Much has changed during that time, but this place, this spectacle, no.

Breaking away from the crowd, Dee and Frank scramble up the dunes between the spiky stands of marram grass, thrown off balance by the cloying sand. Frank offers his hand to pull her up the last couple of metres, but she doesn't take it; then, when she sees his expression change from cheerful to stung, she wishes she had. The least they can do for each other is to be civil, be kind, be friends.

But the snub's forgotten when he sees the beach's expanse, honey-blond where the sand is dry, glassy at the shore where the waves run up and back. And, for once, the sea is almost the Mediterranean blue Dee always hopes for.

The crowd they were caught in amounts to no more than a scattering of people now it's spread across the vastness of the sands. Before long, the horses appear in loose double file, ridden by young men – and women – in maroon shirts and black jodhpurs.

A lump comes to Dee's throat, for the privilege of being here, for Natalie's absence, for times gone by and lost.

Without thinking, she links her arm through Frank's.

He pulls her closer.

The soldiers gallop away along the beach, throwing up spray as their formation breaks up and regroups.

'I can't believe they're so young,' says Frank. 'When you see pictures of them in those shiny helmets and boots, they look like fighting men, but most of them are teenagers. You couldn't send them into battle. Or maybe I'm getting old.'

'They do a bareback ride into the sea this afternoon,' says

Dee, watching the horses grow small in the distance. 'All in board shorts and trainers, and they look so fresh-faced.'

The horses turn, and Dee watches mesmerised as they gallop back along the beach.

'I think we should go now,' she says.

Frank nods and takes her arm again. She's happy to feel the warmth and strength of it and lets him set the pace as they walk away.

Frank doesn't take the obvious route home but drives the back roads to the Minstrels' Arms in a nearby village. The pub's a quaint and pretty place, faced in flints with red brick framing the windows.

Frank suggests they sit at one of the terrace tables with a view of the village green. 'You go and grab a seat, and I'll get us some menus.'

Going through the doorway, he almost collides with a waitress carrying out a tray of drinks. As he steps back, he says something that makes the waitress laugh, and Frank's still smiling as he goes inside.

Do they know each other? Has Frank been here before?

Dee pushes the thought away. It's not a day for picking fights.

He brings them both cider from the bar, and when the waitress comes to them, orders the fresh crab salad and a bowl of chips. Nothing wrong with Frank's appetite now; if anything, he's gaining weight, not hesitating to pick up a Mars Bar or spread extra mayonnaise on a sandwich. The worst life can throw at them has already happened. What's the point in worrying any more?

His chips smell good, sharp with vinegar, and Dee reaches across to take one. He offers her more, but one's enough, and she goes back to picking at her cauliflower risotto, which is underseasoned and bland. The cold cider, though, sparkles on the back of her throat, giving her a pleasant buzz which translates into a better mood, but also prompts a loosened tongue and reckless daring.

And so when the waitress smiles at Frank as she clears their plates and he can't resist – when can he? – making some little joke, the sting of her jealousy is a prod in the back, so the question comes out almost involuntarily, as if she might now be ready to insist on an answer.

'That night when Natalie was at the hospital, Frank. Where were you?'

The remnants of his smile disappear, and his brow lowers in a frown.

'Come on, Dee,' he says. 'Give it a rest. What are you asking me that for?'

'Because I want to know.'

'You know, I barely even remember. We'd had a fight, hadn't we? You were sick of the sight of me. I just went driving round. I didn't know where I was going. I left Jerry a voicemail to say I wasn't coming in and had breakfast at some McDonald's drive-through. Beyond that, I don't really know where I was. I parked up in some field to think things over and fell asleep. You know me, sleep on a clothesline, can't I? No crime involved.' She flinches. 'Sorry. You know what I mean. We were on the point of divorce, weren't we? Honestly? And I was pretty cut up about that, if you want to know.' Reaching across the table, he squeezes her hand.

'But we're doing better than that now, aren't we?' He nods, encouraging her agreement. 'Water under bridges and all that.' He looks up at the sky. 'Sun's still shining. Let's have another drink, shall we?'

He beckons the waitress back over and this time, as he gives their order, Dee notices he's careful not to smile.

On the way home, lulled by a double dose of alcohol, Dee sleeps. In their absence, the postman's called. Dee puts the kettle on while Frank sorts through the mail.

The tea's brewing when he joins her in the kitchen. He looks pale and unwell, and Dee wonders if he might be in discomfort, hopes there was nothing wrong with the lunchtime crab.

He offers her the letter in his hand.

At the top, she sees the embossed badge of Norfolk Police, and immediately assumes it's news about Natalie's case. Which, in a way, it is.

She hardly dares read it. If an arrest's been made, is this how you find out these days? Via a letter in the post?

She looks at him, appealing for a summary.

'They want to speak to me,' he says.

'To you? What do you mean? Do you mean us?'

He shakes his head. 'Only me.'

She scans the letter. A DC is the signatory, not someone she can remember having spoken to before. Frank's name and their address are top left, and the date, three days previously. And then a title – *Interview Under Caution* – and a polite request for Frank to get in touch to make an appointment to attend the police station.

He's entitled to take a solicitor to advise him.

'What does it mean, Frank?'

He shakes his head again. 'How should I know? You know what, I'm going to give Dougie Welch a ring, see if he can shed any light.'

'What would he know?' asks Dee. 'He's not the kind of lawyer you need. He's a conveyancer.'

'He could put me on to someone who can advise me. They must have people who deal with this sort of thing.'

Frank goes back into the hall. Dee sips her tea as she hears him ask a switchboard operator to put him through, then an exchange of bonhomie and pleasantries as the men are connected. After that, no more than a murmur as Frank goes into the lounge to continue the call.

Out of earshot.

Maybe he just wants to sit while he talks.

Or maybe he has something to hide.

Because an elephant seems to have blundered into their living room.

Dee doesn't know for certain, but doesn't an interview under caution mean the police suspect Frank's involvement in Natalie's death?

THIRTY-ONE

Eight days before Frank's formal police interview, he's five miles from home, sitting in his car on a riverbank.

This river's a lonely stretch of water, visited only by weekend fishermen and – judging by the rubbish lying about – youngsters with a taste for McDonald's. If Dee were here, she'd be picking up the burger boxes and empty soft-drink cups, piling them in the boot for disposal at home. Frank's not quite that public-spirited, thinking he pays his council tax for others to do that. Besides, how's he to explain where he's been to pick up other people's garbage? He's way off the route of his normal drive home.

The river flows sluggish and brown, the level raised by days of unseasonal rain, with high, dark clouds at the horizon threatening more downpours. Winding down both the driver's and passenger's windows, he lets the late-afternoon air blow through. A skylark is trilling over a field of ripening wheat, the song melancholy perfection, a token of what good remains in this ailing world.

He thinks of Ruby, of the spoiled legacy she's inheriting, and the thoughtlessly scattered rubbish suddenly offends him. On impulse, he gets out of the car, gathers up the cups and boxes and drops them in the boot. Exactly as Dee would have done.

Back in the car, he unlocks his phone. An array of apps populates the screen: WhatsApp, Messenger, Google, Gmail, Contacts, Phone, his banking apps. Those are the essentials, alongside the usual time-sucks like YouTube and a couple of games.

And Gallery: all his photos.

He hasn't thought about them.

He touches the Gallery icon, and tiny thumbnail images load. Some are work-related, before and after photos of time-pieces he's worked on, transformations of which he's proud. There are aide-memoirs he should have deleted months ago, shopping lists and photos of product specs and prices, still lying about in his phone files like the rubbish that accumulates at the backs of drawers. These he deletes.

Many of the photos feel irreplaceable, memories of precious moments he doesn't want to lose. Natalie laughing as she dabs fingerpaint on the end of Ruby's nose. Ruby holding the string of a Peppa Pig helium balloon, gazing up in wonder as it bobs above her head. Natalie and Dee raising a glass of Prosecco on New Year's Day last year.

Many of these Dee probably has copies of.

But there are others, the ones only he ever sees, the ones Dee would never find.

Opening Settings, he selects Show Hidden System Files.

And there they are. The ones he has of her in all her beauty, reminders of days before everything went to rat-shit.

He limits himself to twenty, then decides to make it thirty:

images he wants to keep for life, sent by the magical airwaves to the safety of his Google account.

What happens to them next, he's still to decide.

The dull stuff, though, he's decided to do old school, because a full back-up is bound to raise suspicions. Copying longhand from his contacts file into a notebook taken from work, he makes a note of everyone whose details he might need – mobile, landline, email address.

It takes him longer than he thinks, the best part of an hour.

When he's finished, he prises the back off the phone, and removes the battery.

Over the wheat field, the skylark still sings.

Standing on the riverbank, he flings the battery upstream, where it quickly sinks.

Without the battery, the phone itself is light. He tosses it downstream, and briefly he can see it below the water's murky surface, carrying away his secrets from the world.

He explains his late arrival home with a trip to Tesco, pulling the box from its bag and laying it on the table.

Dee turns from the pan she's stirring on the stove. 'You got a new phone. What's wrong with your old one?'

'Only went and lost it, didn't I?'

Dee's exasperated. 'Oh, Frank, you're always losing your phone. Why didn't you give it a day or two? It'll turn up. It always does.'

'Thought I was due a new one anyway. What's for dinner?'

'So much hassle,' says Dee. 'All your contacts. All the stuff you've got on there.'

'Pain in the backside, isn't it?' Frank switches on the kettle to make tea. 'It'll take me a while, but I'll get it sorted.'

'And if your old one turns up? You've spent that money for nothing.'

'Don't worry about it. I have a feeling it's gone for good this time. How was your day?'

Dee removes the saucepan from the hotplate and turns to face him. 'The police were here.'

'Again? Why? Aren't I going to see them in a few days?'

'They're only doing their job, Frank, as they should be. They came to give us some news, about Wilfred Hickling.'

'About time too. Are they charging him?'

Dee shakes her head. 'Exactly the opposite. They say he couldn't have done it. They've ruled him out.'

The kettle's boiled, but Frank ignores it. 'How can they be sure? I thought they were certain he was involved?'

'They got the forensics results from Nat's house, and there's none of his DNA anywhere. They say it's impossible he was ever in the cottage. Never set a foot across the threshold.'

'But that's ridiculous. He must have been in there. If it wasn't him, who was it?'

Dee returns the saucepan to the heat. 'That's the big question now, isn't it? I suppose they must have good reason to want to speak to you.'

THIRTY-TWO

Margot walks as quickly as she can up the hill from the house, passing under the overhanging branches of the wood that marks the village boundary into open country. At the roadside stile, she clambers over into a field where cows graze. The footpath is well-trodden, worn down by hikers' boots to a sandy base dotted with puddles formed from the rain of the wettest summer in twenty years. The sky is glowering with the threat of more downpours.

Margot's no runner, but she hurries across the field as best she can to the personnel gate at its far side. Once through, she's at the moorland fringes, on a plateau of almost level ground high above the river valley, whose steep rocky perimeter falls away in tumbles of boulders and bracken.

The path leads on through blooming purple heather, punctuated by copses of spindly silver birch and remnants of ancient woodland oak and beech. Up here, you understand why druids considered this place sacred. The dramatic view – across the English countryside and its grey stone settlements – stretches to similar high points miles away.

Out of breath, Margot looks around. In his red Craghoppers jacket, Wilf's easy to spot, a solitary figure at the heart of the stone circle, his back to her, his head bowed. Despite the season, the wind is brisk. Even in his jacket – which Margot bought him for his stay here, correctly insisting that he would need it in this unreliable northern climate – he must be cold.

As she walks towards him, his eyes remain on a horizon of gathering clouds, but she disturbs a jackdaw, which flies up from the branches of a birch tree. Wilf turns, and seeing his sister, summons a smile and wipes away tears.

'Hello, old girl. What brings you to this bleak place?'

'You do.' Margot breaks all convention between them and hugs him. He resists; through his coat, she feels his bony body stiffen with intense discomfort. Wilf has often said the only acceptable form of public human contact is a handshake, but she wants this to be the moment where his shell is broken, hugging him tighter until she feels some of the tension leave him, and for a precious moment he hugs her back.

She lets him go. He steps away, his guarded self still there, though perhaps not quite intact.

'How did you know I was here?'

'Laura Wright was up here walking the dog. She knocked on the door as she went by, wondering if you were all right.'

'Village life.'

'Human life.'

He turns back to the view.

'I'm all right. You know me, tough as old boots. Did you think I was going to throw myself off one of the edges?'

'Something like that.'

'Not quite my style, to be so dramatic. Anyway, I'm afraid of heights.'

'Shall we go home and have a cup of tea? How long have you been up here? You look frozen.' She takes a hat she knitted herself from her pocket and puts it on Wilf's head, pulling it down over his ears.

'I must look ridiculous.'

'You'll look ridiculous catching pneumonia at the height of supposed summer. So, tea?'

He hesitates, and nods. Hands in pockets, walking towards the approaching rain, they head back towards the village. She links her arm in his and he lets it stay there, and she lets him be silent, choose his moment, until eventually he says, 'I was thinking where I might hide, whether I should go abroad. How I'd do across the water. I don't like the heat, though. I was thinking Scandinavia.'

Margot's doubtful. 'They eat an awful lot of pickled fish in Scandinavia, soused herrings and rye bread. You hate pickled herrings, brother mine. And anyway, you don't speak Swedish, or Danish.'

'I could learn.'

As they reach the stile, she lets go of his arm and sighs. 'Wilf, don't you think you've hidden enough?' She senses his sideways look. 'Don't you think it's time to be you?'

'But I've always been me.'

'Have you?'

'And I'm notorious, sister dear. My life now will be running from one place to another. That's why I was thinking I should start a new life. Somewhere far away.'

'But I would miss you so much. Even when you're home in Norfolk and I'm here, I like knowing you're not too far away. Something will turn up, you know. Something always does. Remember what Father used to say? Everything flows and nothing abides.'

'Yes, but that's just a ridiculous platitude, isn't it?' says Wilf, angrily. 'Like patting someone on the arm at a funeral and telling them time heals all. Well, it might, but it's not weeks or months, is it? It's years and years.' He seems overcome, dabbing at his eyes with a handkerchief. 'I'm in a terrible mess, and I can't see any way out of it. And the worst part is, I committed no crime. I didn't do anything except live in the house next door, yet my life's in tatters, absolute shreds and tatters. Everyone in Britain knows my face and hates me, and everywhere I go I see people whispering and pointing at Wilfred Hickling the pervert. If you can think of a way I can disguise myself and start to lead a normal, anonymous life again, I'd be extremely glad to hear it, because short of facial surgery I have no idea what to do.'

'We'll find a way to fix things,' says Margot, following him over the stile. 'Isn't that what we've always done, stuck together? Let's do something to cheer you up. Shall we drive to Miller's and get a treat to have with tea? A Battenberg or a couple of scones?'

'You go if you like, but I don't want to,' says Wilf. 'People stare at me. Two days ago someone spat at me in the street. A woman, for heaven's sake, a middle-aged woman. What has my life become, Margot, that I am to be spat at?'

'If that happens again, we should go to the police.'

'And say what? That my life's in ruins?'

'We could ask them to make a public statement of your innocence.'

'They've already effectively done that, by saying I am no

longer a suspect and was released without charge. Nobody believes that means I'm innocent. They just think the police should dig deeper. No smoke without fire, is there? The never-married man next door. I'm bound to have done something wicked.'

At home, Margot puts the kettle on. 'You'll have a cup of tea at least, won't you? Go and sit in the lounge and I'll bring it to you. Shall I warm you some soup, or make you a sandwich?'

'Thank you, but to be honest I'm not very hungry.'

In the hall, Wilf takes off his jacket, but instead of hanging it on the coat stand, he carries it up to the room which has become his bedroom. A letter from the Norfolk Constabulary telling him he is no longer a person of interest in their inquiries lies on the chest of drawers. Before he hangs his jacket on the hook on the back of the door, he removes a bottle of pills and a pint of brandy from the pockets.

These, along with the letter, he hides among his underwear in the chest of drawers.

THIRTY-THREE

In the aftershock of Natalie's death, it seemed only natural that Dee and Frank should cleave together, reunited in the marital bed. There they could indulge their need to rerun their memories of Natalie, and, most importantly for Dee, confer over the question that burned bright and constant in her mind: who had killed their daughter? When would justice be done?

So, for a while, their tragedy reignited a spark of forgotten closeness. Mundane habits and routine shared over many years made a safe harbour when everything once taken for granted had imploded. Left with nothing but a blasted future, the paths which they had all but made up their minds should diverge seemed destined to continue to run together.

To Dee, that seems at first to be for the best. With everything changed, Frank appears changed too, no more absences and evasions, and her his chosen company. But gradually, perhaps inevitably, the distance is returning. First, a more cursory kiss goodnight, then more space between them on the mattress. Next, his bedtime less and less often coincides with hers, and so she leaves him downstairs to his own devices on his laptop, voyaging who dares ask where while she sleeps alone.

And now he's lost his phone. As people do.

But most people who do are pretty upset about it.

Frank, however, couldn't be more relaxed.

Something strikes her as she's heating up the frying pan, making bacon sandwiches, which are about the only thing she can persuade herself to eat.

Frank's heading out the kitchen door and she asks him where he's going.

'Out back,' he says, indicating with his thumb their small patch of lawn, which is for once bathed in sunlight and the warmth of a morning with the promise of a hot day to come. 'I'm just going to ring Neil. I owe him a call. We haven't spoken since Nat's . . .' He was, she knows, about to say *funeral*, but since that actual event the word is taboo between them, too emotive and too final.

Dee's genuinely curious. 'How have you got his number?'

And Frank hesitates before answering. Whatever he thinks, he's never been a good liar.

'It's one of those I remember.'

She slides the pan off the hotplate, ready to take him on.

'Go on, then. What is it?'

He recites a string of numbers beginning with zero seven, sort of rhythmic at the end, convincing enough.

But she knows him very well. 'Go on, then, smart-arse, ring it. Let's see who answers.'

'Don't be daft,' says Frank, as if she's absurd to doubt his usually poor memory. 'I shan't be long.'

'Ring him now,' says Dee, 'or I won't believe you.'

Smiling, he holds up his hands. 'OK, it's a fair cop.'

'So how do you have his number?'

'I wrote it down.' He half shows her a piece of paper in his pocket. Not one number, but dozens.

'You wrote down all your contacts.'

'Yes.'

'Why did you do that?'

He shrugs. 'Belt and braces. Common sense. In case I lost my phone. So I'm laughing now, aren't I?'

'When did you write them down?'

'Ages ago. Why? What's got into you?'

Being organised enough to write things down just isn't Frank, who has a thing about what he calls annoying scraps of paper. Frank's a phone addict, who keeps everything on there, every shopping list, every appointment, everyone's contact details.

'Did you know you were going to lose your phone, Frank?'

'What do you mean?'

'Did you lose it on purpose?'

'Why on earth would I do that? That's your old paranoia talking.'

I don't think so, thinks Dee, putting the bacon back on the hob.

But what reason could Frank have for deliberately losing his phone?

With a police interview looming, the answer, of course, is all too obvious: they believe Frank has something to tell them about Natalie's killer.

Not long afterwards, Justin calls. 'Hi, Dee. How's things?'

She can see Frank in the garden, still talking to whoever it is he's rung. 'I'm OK. How are you, how's my little princess?'

'She's all right. I had a meeting at the school yesterday. They wanted to talk to me about one or two behavioural issues. Nothing major, but they need to be addressed. I'll tell you all about it at the weekend, but actually I was wanting to speak to Frank. Is he OK? He's not answering his phone.'

Dee gives a derisive laugh. 'No surprise there. He's lost it.'

'You're joking. He must be frantic. I'd go totally mental if I lost mine. I run my life from this thing.'

'Actually, he doesn't seem too bothered. He's got a bright shiny new one, and a new number.'

'What? Why? He could transfer his old number. It's pretty easy these days.'

'That's what I said, but he's not interested. Shall I send you his new number? You can give him a call on that.'

'Yeah, please, that would be great. Are we still on for Sunday? Ruby's looking forward to seeing you.'

'We're looking forward to seeing her too, and you. Come early, and I'll make a proper lunch.'

'Sounds good to me,' says Justin. 'See you then.'

THIRTY-FOUR

Frank has a headache.

Partly, it's his own fault, since it began with a scramble to park the car in the town centre. Dee nagged him to be on his way ten minutes before he set off, but he decided to change his clothes from the *I'm relaxed about this* jeans and t-shirt he originally planned to something smarter, realising – again as Dee tartly suggested – as a father helping with inquiries into the killing of his daughter, he ought to make more effort.

But the change into a polo shirt and jacket took longer than it should have, and his arrival in town coincided with traffic queues and full car parks, making his arrival at the police station five minutes late.

It didn't matter. They kept him waiting another twenty-five minutes before questioning him for hours. Fluorescent lights, stress and bad coffee have all piled on the pain.

Now he's waiting with a somewhat better coffee in a Costa outlet near the police station while his lawyer ties up what he calls the loose ends, casually referred to as if Frank should know what that means, as if he's an habitual client of the UK legal system.

The lawyer arrives carrying two briefcases so overstuffed

with papers they won't fasten. The briefcases are embossed with his initials: *R. P.*, Robert Peasgood, an old-fashioned name that entirely suits this '70s throwback man in his black-rimmed Roy Orbison glasses and buff suede shoes. Frank remembers his father saying no gentleman wears suede shoes, but Peasgood has no pretentions towards being gentlemanly as far as Frank can tell. He looks like a man who drinks at lunchtime every lunchtime, dishevelled and untidy with his hair in need of a wash. But Dougie Welch says Peasgood's highly recommended, and under these circumstances what choice does Frank have but to accept Dougie's word?

As if Frank's not there, Peasgood drops his briefcases on an empty chair, then removes his jacket and hangs it on the chair back, so Frank knows this isn't going to be quick. He heads for the counter, where Frank hears him order a double espresso. When Peasgood returns to the table, he's also bought himself a sandwich.

There are damp patches on the underarms of Peasgood's grey shirt, and the muskiness of his sweat is escaping the sharp florals of a cheap aftershave. Frank recalls Ruby's claim that the last of Natalie's boyfriends – the one he's just tried to tell the police they should be looking at as prime suspect – smelled like toilet cleaner, and he understands now what she meant.

Peasgood sits and, workmanlike and serious, unbuttons and rolls up his shirt sleeves. Frank – now with no hope whatever of a short of debrief – starts to feel a niggle of unease.

'So,' he says, with more swagger than he actually feels, 'anything to report? All good? All cleared up?'

Peasgood regards him, and Frank notices the pale greyness of his eyes, the colour of soiled water in a fish tank.

'Not exactly cleared up I wouldn't say, no.' He takes a slurp of coffee and a bite of his sandwich and, as he's chewing, goes on. 'You're RUI, Released Under Investigation. Basically, they want more time to strengthen the case against you.'

Frank shakes his head. 'Wait a minute, what do you mean, strengthen in what way? What case against me?'

Still chewing, Peasgood opens the nearest briefcase and brings out a pad of lined paper, then reaches behind himself to draw a silver biro from his jacket pocket. He flips through a lot of used sheets on the pad until he comes to a sheet headed *Francis Trent Cutter – MURDER* double underlined. Beneath that title, he's made a lot of notes.

Peasgood swallows the bite of sandwich and washes it down with more coffee.

'There were one or two things where they really weren't too happy with your answers or, it might be better to say, your non-answers. What I have here are the notes I took during your interview, marked where I believe the investigating officers will have questions outstanding, bearing in mind that in some areas you will in no way have satisfied their natural curiosity. If we can just run through these now, we could go back to them voluntarily with more complete responses, tell them there are a few points you'd like to further clarify, and that way they might start to look elsewhere. They don't want it to be you, of course.'

'Don't want it to be me what?'

Before Peasgood answers, Frank has a sudden, chilling comprehension of what he's accused of.

'They can't think I killed her?'

The café is crowded with city-centre shoppers, but Frank's

outburst hits an unfortunate lull in both the tedious background music and the conversation of the other customers, so his words are unmissably loud. Almost everyone in the place – except for the baristas, who don't hear over the hiss of the coffee machine – glances towards their table, a bolt of excitement ricocheting between them as they realise they're in the presence of a man accused of murder. Thanks to the media coverage, several people recognise Frank, and a woman behind him leans across the table and whispers *Natalie Cutter* to her friend. The whisper travels, and people openly stare. Is this the man who killed her, her own father?

Blushing furiously, Frank drops his head. 'Of course I didn't do it,' he insists, more quietly. 'They must know that. You must know that.'

'They don't very often go on gut feeling,' says Peasgood dryly. 'Mostly they rely on hard evidence, though occasionally they go with circumstantial, if there's a lot of it. Which in your case, being blunt, there does seem to be.'

'What evidence?'

Peasgood consults his notes. 'I think the best thing for us to do is to run through it point by point, see how the land lies. So . . .' The notes are all numbered bullet points in a crabbed, cramped hand, the kind of handwriting Frank's seen in every accountant he's ever used. 'Number one, your failure to produce your phone.'

'I told them, I lost it.'

'I've dealt with a lot of people who claim to have lost their phones, Mr Cutter,' says Peasgood wearily. 'Of course, you may be the first of my clients with whom it's perfectly true, but even so. Now they have your old mobile number, I think it won't be too long before your phone is traced and probably recovered. Presumably you'd be delighted to have it returned.'

'If it's lost and the battery's dead, how can they find it?'

'You may not realise it, but we live in a surveillance state. You'd be amazed what they can do these days. Take my word for it that it's highly likely to be found, but let's put that aside for now and come to point two. You have no alibi for the date of your daughter's assault, and no one to vouch for you, or at least no one you're prepared to name.'

He looks at Frank, who shakes his head, signalling Peasgood should move on.

'Point three, the witness who saw a white van at Turle's Cottage on the day Natalie was assaulted. I think you have access to a white van, do you not, through your place of work?'

'I have access to the van, yes, but I didn't drive it that day. There's millions of white vans driving about.'

'That's one of those difficult things, though, isn't it, proving a negative? I refer you back to my previous point, your lack of alibi. If you could name someone who could confirm you were elsewhere?'

Frank shakes his head. 'What else?'

'At the hospital, the day your daughter was admitted, and of course sadly passed away. The police officer in attendance there reported that several hours passed before your wife was able to make contact with you, and even she had no idea where you were. It's not a crime to be away from the locality, of course, but you have, to date, offered no explanation for your prolonged absence. I've put a note here, see point two above.'

'Move on.'

'Your daughter's own words at the scene of the assault are

incriminating, by her saying someone pushed her. Unless someone as yet unnamed and unknown is guilty of the crime, you are the only person in Natalie's known circle without an alibi. See point two above.'

'It wasn't me.'

'As your legal advocate I have no reason to doubt you, Mr Cutter, but speaking bluntly, I'm afraid you failed to create a good impression on the officers today. There are a couple of other, minor points which they're bound to explore. Your granddaughter told the police you and your daughter were in the habit of arguing. Family life isn't a walk in the park, I think we can all agree. So they're bound to wonder why when asked about that you decided to go no comment.'

'I thought they might misconstrue it.'

'You're right, they might. Serious arguments before a suspicious death tend to make them seek out a connection. But you and I have a relationship of confidentiality, so you can tell me, I'll make a note of your side of the equation, and then we've got something I can go back to them with. So what did you and your daughter argue about?'

Peasgood folds his arms and waits.

Frank sighs. 'It was about her boyfriend, if boyfriend doesn't make him sound too legitimate. Since she left Justin – my son-in-law – she'd been what you might kindly call playing the field. This last one, Eric, he was the latest in a long line. The police have spoken to him about Natalie's death, but the liaison officer told us they've ruled him out. I don't think they should do that. I think he could be her killer.'

Peasgood takes another bite of his sandwich, and nods at Frank to encourage him to go on.

'The last time I saw her – which for your notes was not on the day she was assaulted – she said she had to tell me something. She's always known my work is not for public discussion. Our workshops handle some very expensive items – a single watch can be worth hundreds of thousands or even more, and we might have a dozen in the safe at any one time – and we keep the place totally anonymous, no signage, no advertising. If you need us you can find us via the internet, and anyone who comes to the site is vetted first. Anyway, she very shamefacedly decided to tell me that after a bottle or two of wine – maybe even three the way she was carrying on – she told this Eric about my job and about the workshop.'

Peasgood's eyebrows rise. 'And you were not best pleased.'

'I was livid. The company's whole reputation is built on trust, on security, on clients having faith that their property will be safe with us. It's not just the monetary value that's the issue. Some pieces we deal with have huge sentimental value or have been in families for centuries. And yet my daughter had let all the details slip to some itinerant East European she'd known for about a fortnight. She put me in a position where I would have to tell my boss – a man I regard as a friend – that a member of my family had put the security of his business at risk. And who knows who else this guy has told? Worst-case scenario, we'd have to move premises, and that would be a huge expense for which she was responsible. I had every right to be mad.'

'Not if your anger led to violence.'

'It didn't.'

'So you say. Unfortunately it becomes a matter of proving it, and that's where the difficulty lies.'

Peasgood is finishing his sandwich, watching Frank as he chews. The silence between them grows long, until Peasgood swallows and says, 'Of course there is also the matter of the messages between you and a witness on the day of the assault in which you stated you were in fact at Turle's Cottage.'

Frank looks at him sharply. 'What witness? What messages? They never said anything about that.'

'You may imagine that after twenty years in and out of that police station, I've made a few contacts, people I can ask questions of on the quiet. It wasn't brought up in the interview because without your phone it's not yet proven, but of course if those messages were sent and your phone proves your location when you sent them – treacherous things, mobile phones, people have no idea – then that would almost certainly move us from the circumstantial into the more solid realms of firm evidence. May I give you a piece of advice, Mr Cutter?'

'Of course. That's what you're here for.'

'Naturally, I don't disbelieve you when you tell me your phone is lost, but if there were any way for you to find it before the police do, I think that would go in your favour. If the police find it first and those messages place you at Turle's Cottage, I'm afraid the outlook for you may be challenging. Just one other thing, what did your boss – did you mention his name? I don't seem to have anything written down.'

'Wilmer, Jerry Wilmer. Jerry short for Jurgen.'

'And how did Mr Wilmer react when you told him what Natalie had done?'

Frank's expression is defensive. 'I haven't told him yet.'

'I see.'

'The time's never seemed right, not since Natalie . . . And the police said Eric wasn't in the area any more, that he was planning his return to Poland, Romania, wherever he came from.'

'You'll have to be hopeful, then, that he isn't planning to return there with his pockets stuffed with very expensive watches.'

'So far, so good.'

'On the contrary, I'm afraid,' says Peasgood. 'So far, in your case, I feel it's not too good at all. And one other thing I should mention: I believe the constabulary will be issuing a press release later on. They won't name names at this stage, but conclusions may be drawn. The press are notoriously good at guessing the identities of those referred to in the oblique phrasing the police tend to use. If, for example, they say they're speaking to a fifty-four-year-old male, it's not a big stretch to infer that might be you. And as you are the victim's father, that's going to be regarded as a big development.'

'But that's ridiculous,' objects Frank. 'As the victim's father, I should be protected. What about my rights to privacy?'

Peasgood is gathering up his belongings, slipping on his jacket. 'Under English law, rights to privacy without some kind of injunction are inadequate at best, I'm afraid, and I'm sorry to say your daughter's death has left you open to the public's most prurient interest. You may find yourself at the heart of a media frenzy over the next few days, so if that happens I suggest you keep a really low profile, curtains closed, don't answer the phone, the usual kind of thing.'

'Is that it?' asks Frank, incredulous. 'Just put up with it?'

'You might try crossing your fingers,' says Peasgood, 'and hoping the police are quick to find themselves a suspect more likely than you.'

THIRTY-FIVE

As she pushes open the door and readies a smile for the pretty receptionist, Dee's subconscious flashes her a message. The reason she can so clearly hear the uber-chilled Far Eastern jazz fusion music that usually plays unobtrusively in the background is because everyone in the salon – from the stylists and their clients to the junior sweeping the floor – has fallen silent.

At least they have the wit to paper over the awkwardness with rapidly switched-on smiles and a chorus of hellos, even though there can be no doubt that the subject of their abruptly halted chatter was her.

But Dee's used to that kind of reaction by now, to the pointing in the street, to the remarks not quite out of her hearing. On more than one occasion, she's seen women she thought were friends hiding in supermarket aisles to avoid her, browsing shelves of cereals or detergents or even toilet rolls they've no intention of buying until they think she's safely out of the way.

Before Frank's name was in the frame for Natalie's killing, they couldn't do enough for her. Now, they don't even want to pass the time of day.

Her hairdresser, Stefan, decides to brazen it out, leaving the woman whose hair he's blow-drying to come and greet her, air-kissing her on both cheeks so she can smell his limey cologne over the ammoniac smell of the bleach he's been mixing.

'Well, don't you look fabulous,' he says, gushing as he always does, ignoring the fact that she absolutely doesn't, that she looks washed-out and ten years older, that the lipstick she's wearing is completely the wrong shade for her now her skin's so drained and sallow. And as for her hair, under other circumstances he'd have pulled it through his fingers and told her she was a disgrace for leaving it so long between appointments, but instead he sits her in a chair facing herself in the mirror, gives the lightest tut at the length of her grey roots, and smiles at her through the glass as he asks, 'What are we doing today?'

'Well,' she says, dismayed at her brightly lit reflection, at being unforgivingly confronted by the way she's let herself go. If Natalie were here, she'd never have allowed it to get this far: the neglected nails and hair, the lazy, baggy clothes, the lack of proper make-up, which the lipstick only exaggerates. Realising she wants to cry, she fights to hold it together. 'You can see it wants some attention.'

'Shall we tackle those roots?' asks Stefan, and he's already reaching for a colour chart, flipping through the little tufts of blondes and brunettes and reds and even pinks and blues. 'And how about we try something a bit more muted, more caramel?'

She understands his meaning, that he's suggesting, kindly, that she can't take her usual strong colour any more, that she should switch to a shade that doesn't make her look half dead.

'Until you get your mojo back?' he adds. Their eyes meet

in the mirror, and Dee knows he understands her mojo is unlikely ever to return.

He touches her shoulder before returning to his blow-dry client with his usual energy, his outrageous flounce, calling to the receptionist, 'Lauren, I think Dee would like one of our fabulous cappuccinos, please, my love,' leaving Dee to flick the tattered pages of last month's *Hello!* magazine and pretend she's not making people feel awkward just by being there.

In the end, she does find the next two hours soothing. Dee sits quietly while Stefan combs and wraps and paints on colour, not indulging in his usual prattle about the clubs he's been to or how he's taken his mum shopping in Oxford Street but sensitive to her need to be silent as she listens to the wordless nothing-music. If she focuses on that, she's relieved to find her restless mind calms down.

When the colour's applied, Lauren brings more coffee and magazines. Dee flips through the pictures as if they were children's storybooks, sometimes thinking how Natalie would have loved some of the new products – a scented spray to gloss her hair, or a fleeting fashion for blue lipstick. If Dee's thoughts aren't exactly happy, they are at least neutral, until she recalls Natalie has no use for these things, that nothing can make her beautiful again, nothing can make her more than whatever she has become in her midnight-blue gown.

But she won't go down that road, not now.

When it's time to wash off the colour, she's surprised Stefan himself comes to do the job, instead of leaving it to one of the juniors.

Seated with her back to the basin, she feels warm water

run over her head, the stroke of Stefan's hand on her scalp. No one else is there.

'How are you really, my love?' he asks, reaching for shampoo, beginning to soap her hair. 'I just don't know how you're coping.'

'You learn to live with it,' says Dee, even though it isn't true, even though every day the pain she wakes to is the same. 'Somehow you just do.'

Then, feeling brave, not sure she wants to know, she asks, 'What are people saying about it all? I know there's talk by the way they look at me. Such a leper I've become.'

'No point in asking me,' he says glibly, massaging her scalp.

Her lips spread in a sour smile. 'Don't give me that, Stefan. This place is Rumour Central. Come on, spill the beans. I won't shoot the messenger. I just want to know.'

'I don't think you do.'

'Try me.'

He begins to rinse off the shampoo, and under the gentle splash of the water tells her people are saying it's Frank who's guilty, that he killed Natalie after they had a fight.

'I'm sure it's not true, though,' he finishes, slathering on conditioner which smells sharply of grapefruit. 'I don't think any man would do that, kill his own daughter. I'm not being insensitive, am I? Just speaking as I find. My money's on that old man next door. The newspapers had him down for it, didn't they? Except that I'd have put money on him being gay, actually. Takes one to know one, you know what I mean?'

Dee sits in near silence through the rest of the process, the cutting, the drying, the smoothing and perfuming. When Stefan's finished, as he holds up a hand-mirror to show her the back, she nods approval. That gutsy, ballsy Sharon Osbourne lookalike is gone.

Caramel was a good choice, a mid-brown camouflage, making her a nondescript nobody. No longer someone you'd easily identify as the wife of that most terrible of monsters, a man who would kill his own child.

THIRTY-SIX

Having no particular reason to get out of bed, Gabby's lying under the same flowered duvet she slept under as a teenager, staring up at the cracks in the ceiling she's stared at for countless hours already. Downstairs, she hears her father clearing his throat in that particular way he has as he moves between the kitchen and the dining room. Cutlery clatters on crockery as he gets his breakfast – a bowl of Kellogg's All-Bran, a sliced banana, semi-skimmed milk – and she knows her mother will be there too, sipping her decaf tea with a single slice of Benecol-buttered wholewheat toast.

Gabby's thinking she ought to get up and get on with whatever turns out to be the rest of her life when her phone rings. Caro. Gabby's not ready for her saccharine, poisonous conversation.

And yet, Caro might be calling with an opportunity.

Gabby sits up in bed and answers the call.

'Gabby, is that you? I thought you weren't going to pick up. What's happened to your "never let a phone ring more than twice" mantra? You're slipping in my absence.'

'Hi. How's things?'

'Oh, busy, busy, busy. David's put me on this latest MP

scandal. I can't say too much about it at the mo, but we've got a real scoop, right up your alley, sex, bribery and corruption at the highest levels. You'd love it.'

'Sounds like business as usual.'

'So what have you been up to? Have you found a new job yet? Because if not, I could put a word in for you, you know. Annabelle's always looking for good people over there. Do you want me to give her a call?'

'I'm working on a couple of things,' lies Gabby. 'Maybe, if they don't work out.'

'Your choice, of course. All you have to do is say the word. How's things down there in Norfolk? Bet you're having a whale of a time, aren't you, home-cooked meals and hanging out with all your old flames? Wish I could be there.'

'It's nice,' says Gabby, unconvincingly. 'I'm trying not to put on too much weight.'

'Very wise. Oh, listen, someone was trying to get in touch with you, some woman who wouldn't give a name. Said it was in connection with the Natalie Cutter case. Left a number and asked if I'd get you to call.'

'Me? Why me?'

'To be honest, I don't know. I said if she had information she was welcome to speak to me, but she seemed determined it should be you.'

Maybe someone I know, then, thinks Gabby.

'Can you text me the number?'

'Of course, I'll do it right now. Listen, if it's anything juicy you will let me know, won't you? If you can't use the info yourself, pass it to someone who can make something of it – that's what I always say.'

'Of course.'

'Brilliant. Sending it through now. Keep in touch, won't you? Let me know who the mystery caller is, I'm dying to know. Oh, train's coming, gotta go. Ciao for now, sweetie, ciao.'

THIRTY-SEVEN

Sarah has dressed baby Lizzie in a pink cotton dress and floppy hat and pushed her in the buggy the long way round, along the riverbank, to collect Riley from school.

The river level has dropped over the past few days, and in the heat the water is still as a pond. On the bank, the swans are resting in the shade of a willow tree, and Sarah wonders what happened to Wilfred Hickling who used to feed them, where he's gone. He seemed such a polite old gentleman – in some ways he reminded her of her grandad – but people in Wickney took against him. The way they treated him was harsh, but probably it was deserved. No smoke without fire, after all. If he was a danger to her kids, she's glad he's gone.

At the school gates, the mums are wearing strappy dresses and sandals, with the scalded red of sunburn on their shoulders and backs. The rare hot day has provoked a festive mood, and the chatter is of plans for barbeques and picnics, and trips to the pub for beer-garden drinks.

Everyone seems cheerful except Jess, who stands sullen and silent, nibbling at the bleeding skin around her bitten nails.

April turns to her. 'Do you want to come, Jess?'

From Jess's expression, it's clear the last few minutes of conversation have passed her by.

'We're going to meet up on the riverbank, give the kids their tea there,' April says. 'Just bring whatever you've got to eat. The kids will love it.'

'Maybe.'

'Ah, come on,' insists April. 'And don't you dare tell me Paddy won't let you.'

'Me and him aren't speaking,' Jess says sulkily.

'Oh, for God's sake.' Hannah rolls her eyes. 'What is it this time?'

'I caught him on this website. Turns out he's been on it for months, talking to this woman.'

'What website?' asks April.

'What woman?' demands Hannah.

'Some sleazy porn thing, Closefriends.com.'

'I don't think it's porn exactly,' puts in Sarah.

'How would you know?' asks Jess, bitterly. 'Since when are you an authority on internet porn?'

Stung, Sarah jumps to her own defence. 'Natalie told me. That's the one she was on.'

Comically, the tableau freezes as Jess, Hannah and April all stare at her.

'You what?'

'What do you mean?'

Sarah's sun-pink face turns violent red. 'Just something she said. That's all.'

'Oh my God,' says Hannah slowly. 'That was her internet business, wasn't it? She wasn't selling stuff on eBay at all. That's why she suddenly had so much money.'

'That's so disgusting,' says Jess, and her face is filled with revulsion. 'How could she do that, parading in front of those men with their tongues hanging out? How could she?'

'Oh my God,' says April. 'Do you think Paddy saw her on there? That would be messed up, if he'd actually seen Nat naked.'

'She didn't do naked,' protests Sarah. 'Only tasteful stuff.'

'There's nothing tasteful about what my Paddy was looking at,' says Jess. 'And nothing left to the imagination, believe me. Just some woman in fishnet with her legs spread. Nothing tasteful about that, is there?'

'Was she on the game, Sarah?' asks Hannah, wide-eyed. 'Because if she was, you should tell the police.'

Sarah's indignation on Natalie's behalf is making her angry. 'She wasn't on the game. It was just chatting to lonely old blokes, that's all.'

'You're so naive, Sarah,' says Hannah. 'You swallowed every word she said. You've no need to put her on such a pedestal. Not after the way she used to treat you.'

Sarah blinks. 'She and I were mates. Solid.'

'No, you weren't. Believe me, the things she said about you, you absolutely weren't.'

'Did Justin know about her selling herself?' interrupts April. 'He'd have been so mad if he knew. Maybe mad enough to . . .'

'Don't!' says Sarah. 'He didn't know. Nobody knew except me. I promised her I'd keep it secret.'

'The police will know by now anyway,' says Hannah. 'They'll have looked on her laptop, won't they? I'll bet it's all over there.'

'Poor Ruby,' says Jess spitefully. 'Having a whore for a mum.'

'She wasn't a whore,' objects Sarah. 'She was a woman cashing in on her assets, and why shouldn't she? And it was nothing to do with Justin.'

'No, I don't think it was,' agrees April. 'I forgot to say, the police are interviewing someone about Natalie's killing. I heard it on the news just before I came out.'

The other women all look at her.

'Who?' asks Sarah. 'Who are they interviewing?'

'They didn't give a name,' says April. 'A man aged fifty-four. That rules Justin right out, doesn't it?'

'What are you talking about?' Sarah scowls. 'Justin was never ruled in.'

'And the old man next door,' puts in Hannah. 'He's way older than that.'

'And Eric,' says Jess. 'So who's left?'

As they're considering this, the school bell rings.

'Here we go,' says Hannah. 'Here come our little darlings.'

'You don't think, do you,' suggests Sarah, hesitantly, 'you don't think it could have been her dad?'

THIRTY-EIGHT

The park where her contact's suggested they meet has plainly been chosen for its anonymity. Gabby barely knows this area of the city, an outer suburb you'd have no reason to go if you didn't live there. The car park has plenty of space, though there are people seated outside an attractive and busy café, and several teenage boys kicking a football on a pitch of sun-hardened grass.

Gabby parks under a tree, reversing into the space so she has a good view all around. She isn't nervous – meetings with strangers in new places have been commonplace to her – but she's curious to the point of impatience. And with the minutes ticking by – it's already eight minutes past the time that was agreed – she's wondering if she's been taken for a ride, or maybe scoped out and dismissed by the woman she's here to talk to, who could easily be hiding in plain sight among other people's comings and goings.

But then a small red Fiat pulls into a space close by her. The driver's in her late fifties, unremarkable and unmemorable in the unfortunate way of older women, and she seems to lack the confidence of someone who knows this place. Instead of gathering herself to visit the café or walk a dog, she's settling herself deep into her seat, wondering – Gabby can tell – whether it would be better for her to leave.

Gabby takes action to prevent that happening. Getting quickly out of her own car, she saunters as casually as she can towards the Fiat, fixes on a smile and taps on the driver's window.

The woman jumps, stares at her for a moment, and with obvious reluctance lowers the window.

'Sorry if I've got this wrong,' says Gabby, confident she's got it right. 'But I'm Gabby. Was it you that called me?'

The woman appears to be having serious second thoughts, and if she denies who she is, it will be no surprise. But then, sagging as she gives up the pretence, she gives a nod of confirmation.

'Thanks for coming,' says Gabby brightly. 'Shall we grab a tea or something and go and find a bench to sit on, somewhere we won't be disturbed? My treat.'

Gabby's gambling, praying she's not misjudging the situation. Tip-offs, whistle-blowers, whatever you like to call them, are the lifeblood of the journalism she's been part of. If there's a story to be had here – and her nose tells her there most definitely is – this woman is teetering between talking and doing a runner. If she drives away, Gabby will be gutted.

But the woman gets out of her car. As soon as she has a clear view of her, Gabby begins to suspect who she might be: the drawn face, the lightless eyes tell their own story. No point, though, in jumping to conclusions. She could be anyone, and her reason for being here could relate to completely new information on a whole new story.

'It's a lovely day.' As Gabby leads the way to the café, the woman still hasn't spoken. Inside, the tempting smells of brewing coffee and home baking remind Gabby she's hungry, and she asks for a piece of flapjack to go with her latte. The woman asks for tea. When Gabby offers something to eat, she shakes her head.

They carry their cups outside. On the far side of the football pitch are a pair of vacant benches, and Gabby suggests they head over there.

When they're seated, peeling the lid off her coffee Gabby says, 'So you know who I am. Can I ask your name?'

The woman answers, 'I'm Dee Cutter. You wrote about my daughter, Natalie. You called her a Miracle Mum.'

It's all Gabby can do to hide her elation at confirming who the woman sitting next to her is, but she keeps her face composed, her expression serious and concerned. This is a major scoop. If she were still working for the *Herald*, she'd probably get a front-page byline and celebratory drinks with her colleagues. But she's a freelancer now. This could be something she can make good money on, selling to the highest bidder.

Yet she feels the drag of a new restraint, an unfamiliar instinct to deal with this woman differently, to listen to her without writing copy in her head. The error she made with Wilfred Hickling – the damage she did – has made a deep impression, shed an unwelcome light on the effects of her actions on living, breathing, vulnerable people. Her view of right and wrong has shifted. Faced with the mother of a dead woman she's up to now regarded as no more than a subject for headlines, she can't help but recognise the familiar in Dee.

What if it were her own mother or father sitting here, grieving for her? Wouldn't she hope they'd be treated with compassion and respect?

'I'm so sorry for your loss, Mrs Cutter,' she says, and finds she actually means it.

'It's been hard.' Dee's words are unnecessary; the constant, crushing pain of bereavement shows in her eyes, in her habitual expression of perplexity, as though something incomprehensible has twisted her world into a pattern of misery and suffering she can make no sense of. And yet, as people mostly do, she carries on.

Briefly, Gabby wonders if Dee might be here to berate her, to demand a correction to something she wrote, or an apology. And yet she shows no anger. Instead, she seems subdued, reluctant to say what's on her mind.

'Is there something I can help you with?'

Dee's doubtful. 'I don't know. I don't think I should be talking to you, really.'

'Why do you think that?'

'How do I know I can trust you?'

Inwardly, Gabby acknowledges this as a fair question. Professionally, she's never been trustworthy, and her conscience never used to trouble her when she's reneged on promises of keeping confidences 'off the record' or 'between these four walls' if reneging made a better story. With Dee, though, she knows her word once given absolutely must be kept. Otherwise she has no hope of ever regaining her integrity, or her father's respect.

'You can trust me,' she says. 'And in the spirit of full disclosure, I have to tell you I no longer work for the *Herald*. If you're wanting to talk to one of their journalists, if you have something you want them to publish, I can introduce you to somebody, but I might not be the best person to help you with that.'

'It's not something I want to be in the papers. The opposite of that, actually.'

'OK.'

Dee takes a deep, decisive breath. 'It's about my husband, Frank.'

Gabby does a mental recap, recalls him from Natalie's funeral. An attractive man for his age, but on that occasion apparently broken by grief.

'What about Frank?'

Dee takes a drink of her almost-cold tea, still hesitant to continue.

'You give me your word this stays between us?'

'A hundred per cent.'

'I don't know who else to ask. At first when Natalie . . . when she was taken from us, I thought the same as you did, that it was the man next door. I saw that story you wrote about him, about him being a pervert.'

Except he wasn't. Gabby feels a flush of shame spread up her cheeks and lowers her head to hide it. All he was was a lonely gay man so inhibited he'd never found the courage to step out of the closet.

'I was certain it was him,' Dee goes on. 'I nearly went round to his house and put a knife through his heart. I'd even chosen which knife I would use. Then the police said it couldn't have been him, that they knew from DNA he wasn't ever in Natalie's house.'

'Do you know what line they're taking now?'

Dee looks Gabby straight in the eye. 'They think Frank did it. They think Frank killed our daughter.'

Gabby is taken aback. There's a word for such a crime she remembers from her journalistic training – paternal filicide. In baby- and childhood, sadly it's almost an everyday occurrence, but beyond childhood it's a very rare crime. Racking her brains, she comes up with only two cases she can think of, both involving stepfathers rather than biological fathers. But maybe Frank is a stepfather. The question is relevant.

'Is Frank Natalie's birth father?'

'What?' Dee looks confused. 'Oh, you mean rather than a stepdad? Yes, Frank's my first and only husband. There's only ever been him for me. If only I could say the same for him.'

Gabby senses a line of enquiry there that she'll park for later, if needed.

'Why do they think he was involved? There must be other suspects, surely?'

'Everyone but Frank has a solid alibi. They were looking at her new boyfriend at one point. He's got access to a white van, which they think was involved, but he was managing a team of pickers all day, with about thirty agricultural workers to confirm it. Justin, her husband, can account for his movements, and anyway he doesn't have the right kind of vehicle. That leaves Frank, and I can see why they're interested in him. Nothing he says about any of it makes sense. Adding it all up, it's hard not to think he knows more than he's letting on.'

'But why would he harm Natalie?'

'There's the mystery. He's been a dark horse recently, kept a lot to himself. Natalie was never the easiest of people to get on with, and she and he had some rows in the past. But I thought that's where all the bad stuff between them was, in the past. So as to why, I just don't know.'

'So where do I come in, Dee?'

'I don't want it to be him, for Ruby's sake. Ruby's my granddaughter, Natalie's only child. She's had a tough time with all this, as you can imagine, though Justin's a wonderful father and he's doing the best he can. I've asked Frank a million times where he was that day, and all he does is shrug and say he doesn't remember. Of course he remembers – it was one of the most memorable days of our lives. Him not remembering is nonsense, and the police are taking his poor memory as part of their proof he was at the cottage, and so am I. But I so don't want it to be true. The stigma of it, the scandal, will stick to Ruby for the rest of her life. I want him to be innocent for her sake.'

'But how can I help?'

'You're an investigative journalist, aren't you?'

'I was.'

'So you know how to get to people, how to get them to talk, how to get information, go through the back door.'

'I suppose. But the police have far more rights to do that than I do.'

'Yes, but they don't have time, and they don't have the motivation, do they? They want Frank to be guilty or they have to look elsewhere. They probably have enough to charge him already, but they're stretched so thin they take forever to get anywhere. We've had this hanging over us for months already. I need to know, one way or the other, if it could possibly have been someone else.'

'Like who?'

Dee looks away, and Gabby knows she's keeping something back.

'I'll just say there are other possibilities.'

'The boyfriend? Is that what you're thinking? But you said it couldn't have been him.'

'They ruled out Eric, yes.'

'So who else?'

'I'm not worried about who else. I just want you to find something which will get Frank off the hook. That's all.'

'That's a tall order, Dee. Why doesn't Frank get himself off the hook, if he has information that would do that?'

'I keep asking myself that exact same question. Why doesn't he just come clean? He's hiding something, and I want to know what it is.'

'So just to be clear, you don't want me to find out who killed Natalie. I'm pleased about that, because I'd have no idea where to begin.'

'I can give you a couple of pointers, but that's all. A white van was there the day Natalie was . . . assaulted. Frank has access to a white van through work, but thousands of other men do too.'

'You're certain it was a man?'

'Honestly, no. I'm not certain of anything.'

Gabby thinks of the conversation she had with Natalie's friend Sarah, and her obvious crush on Justin. A shove in the chest to push Natalie down the stairs – a woman could easily have done that. And a white van would be a brilliant disguise for a woman. No, it definitely didn't have to be a man.

'Have the police found anything on Natalie's phone or laptop?' asks Gabby.

'From what I know, there wasn't much of interest on her phone. It's amazing they got anything off it, it was so smashed up when she fell. But they haven't found her laptop.'

This is new news, and Gabby's eyebrows lift. 'They haven't found it? But she did use one?'

'Oh yes, she used one. But it wasn't in the cottage.'

'Maybe it was stolen. That could make the motive burglary and her killer a complete stranger, which opens up a whole new can of worms.'

'Except there's no DNA unaccounted for in the cottage, they say. That's how they knew it wasn't the old man next door. Apparently it's next to impossible to go in a house and leave no trace at all, so they knew he'd never been in there. Look, I just want to know where Frank was over that weekend. I think if you find that out, it would give him an alibi, no matter what it is, get the police off his back and on to the right one, if you get what I mean. I need to know what he's hiding.'

'What do you think it might be?'

Dee sighs. 'Frank has a serious problem with fidelity. He's cheated on me more than once. At first, I thought he was desperately trying to hide another affair, but now I'm not sure. Under these circumstances, I think he'd just come out and say. But if it's not that, what is it? Will you help me? I'm afraid I can't pay you very much.'

Gabby considers. Dee doesn't seem to be aware of the possibility she might turn up proof that her husband killed their daughter after all. Or maybe the need to know trumps everything else.

Then she thinks of Wilfred Hickling, of his home ruined

by graffiti and smashed eggs, and the part she played in that ugly drama.

'All right, I'll do it,' she says. 'And I don't want any money. If I help you, maybe it'll help repay a karmic debt.' She has a thought. 'It would help if you'd let me have a photo of Frank I can show around. And some personal data like a date of birth and previous addresses can help too. His full legal name, any social media accounts, what kind of car he drives and the registration.'

'Frank's full name is Francis Trent Cutter. He doesn't do social media, never has done.'

'Not even Facebook, Twitter, the obvious stuff?'

'Not as far as I'm aware. The rest of what you want I'll have to email to you, though God help me if he ever finds out. I've got a picture I can let you have now.'

Dee takes out her phone and scrolls through long reels of photos. Most of the recent ones are of Ruby; prior to that, of Ruby and Natalie. Eventually she finds one of Frank, holding up a pint of beer at some country pub.

Gabby's phone pings as she receives it. The photo confirms he's a good-looking guy, a few lines and a little grey hair making him interestingly rough around the edges.

Her phone pings again and a second photo arrives: Frank with his arm round a blonde woman. Both of them are smiling.

She looks at Dee. 'Is this Natalie?'

Dee shakes her head.

'So who is it?'

Dee shrugs. 'You tell me.'

'Where did you get this?'

'By unfair means. Frank's very careful with his phone – that's why it was unbelievable when he lost it.'

'He lost his phone? When?'

'Lost it or dumped it, a few weeks ago. I think that's why the police decided to really go for him, put him at the top of their list. I found that photo just before Natalie died. Someone knocked at the door, and Frank put his phone down on the kitchen counter without switching it off. When I heard he was talking to our chatty neighbour, I knew he'd be gone a good few minutes, so I grabbed his phone to go through it. Despise me if you like, but something was going on and I wanted to know what it was.'

'I don't despise you. I'd have wanted to know too.'

'Anyway, I found this in his hidden files. He probably thought it was safe there from me, but I raised a rebellious teenage daughter and I know a thing or two about how to find hidden things on phones. I hit the share button and sent it to myself. We had a row that evening which just about ended our marriage, though I never said I'd seen the photo. There was plenty for us to row about without bringing it up. I thought it was just another fancy woman. Now I'm not sure.'

'Forgive me for saying, but she looks a little young for him.'

'Punching above his weight, isn't he? She might be long gone by now, anyway. I certainly hope so. Probably it won't help you, but you might as well have it.'

'The more information I have, the better. You say you don't know this woman, but couldn't she be a work colleague of his, a casual acquaintance?'

'Not likely. Frank's a watch repairer, high-end stuff, so he works in a unit that's protected like Fort Knox. Only three others work there and I know them all. Marie's the only woman and she's been there years.'

Unless something's changed you don't know about, thinks Gabby.

'Anyway,' adds Dee, 'if she's nobody, what's she doing in his hidden files?'

'Fair point.'

'Where will you start?' asks Dee as they stand up to leave.

'It's difficult to say. I'll have a think, and let you know.'

Gabby tucks her phone in her bag, acknowledging to herself that her lack of honesty is a hard habit to break.

Because as they say goodbye in the car park, Gabby knows exactly what she needs to do.

THIRTY-NINE

Frank's latest meeting with Peasgood has overrun like all the others, not by minutes this time but by well over an hour.

When he finally arrives at work, Jerry's car is parked outside. That's unlucky (Jerry rarely shows up before 11 a.m.) and unfortunate, since Frank will now have to offer some plausible explanation for his late arrival. All the usual lame ducks – dentist, doctor, waiting in for a delivery – he's already overused.

He keys the PIN number into the keypad by the door and pushes it open. As always, it's impossible for those already inside not to be disturbed by the annoying beep the security system makes to alert them to someone's entry. Walking to his workstation at the back of the building, he sees Robbie at his table, a loupe in his eye as he bends over the workings of a Rolex. Robbie briefly looks up, giving Frank an apologetic shrug so he knows Robbie's attempt to cover for him has failed. Frank shakes his head to tell him not to worry.

Jerry's office door is closed, and for a moment Frank thinks he still might have got away with it. But as he's hanging up his jacket, he senses movement behind him, and when he turns round, there's Jerry.

'Morning, Frank.' Jerry's tone is casual, though he can't resist giving away his irritation by glancing at his watch – a very good-looking Chopard Alpine Eagle Frank hasn't seen before. He's wearing what he calls his 'at home' work clothes – camel chinos, Timberland deck shoes, a polo shirt and designer cardigan – so Frank knows there's no long lunch booked anywhere, and no clients to meet. If an atmosphere develops, they'll all be sitting in the fug of it all day.

'Morning,' says Frank. 'Sorry I'm late. I got held up.'

Jerry regards him over the top of his faux-wood-framed glasses. Frank really dislikes those glasses; they make Jerry look like he works for the BBC, especially when he pulls the face he's pulling now, as if someone's ordered the wrong wine to go with smoked fish or admitted they don't read the *Guardian*.

'The thing is, Frank . . . You know what, let's do this in my office.'

Jerry leads the way there, pausing to call out, 'Marie! Any chance of coffee?' in the direction of his PA. As Jerry and Frank go by, Robbie keeps his head tactfully low.

Behind his cherry-wood desk, Jerry leans back in his black-leather swivel chair, gesturing Frank to the sofa against the office's back wall. The sofa's low and soft, so there's no choice but to sink in and be swallowed by it, which puts all Jerry's visitors physically below his level, enabling him literally to talk down to them. When it's time to leave, he likes to offer a patriarchal hand to those struggling to extricate themselves from the sofa's grip.

Over time, Frank's developed his own tactics to deal with Jerry's power play. He perches on the sofa's front edge, leaning forward on to spread knees; experience has taught him this position will enable him to make a dignified exit when it's time to go and has the added advantage of making him look keen on hearing whatever it is Jerry's got to say.

For a few minutes, Jerry prattles on about nothing in particular: new work coming in, a sale he wants to go to in Stockholm. Marie brings in coffee – Jerry's favourite Brazilian that he picks up from H. R. Higgins, a place in Mayfair he pops into from time to time – and she gives Frank a commiserating smile as she sets a hand-crafted pottery mug on the low table in front of him.

At least the coffee will be good, thinks Frank, and he thanks her.

Marie closes the office door behind her as she leaves. Frank tastes his coffee, which is as expected excellent.

'So, to business,' says Jerry. 'There are a couple of things, one of them rather serious, I'm afraid. We had a bit of trouble in the night.'

'Trouble?'

'I had a call about three a.m. from the security team to say the alarm had gone off.' Frank's stomach sinks. He has a horrible suspicion he knows what's coming next. 'They followed the drill to the letter and the police were here in minutes, so by the time I arrived it was all over. Definitely an attempted break-in. They tried to get in from the loading bay, and we've sustained some damage. Looks like they drove a vehicle at the rear doors – the police think probably some kind of truck. Ram-raiding, don't they call it? Their vehicle will have sustained some damage for sure, but the safety doors held up, thank God. And our van's got a couple of dents, but they're saying that might be a good thing – not what I'd call it, depends on your point of view, I suppose – but they might be able to match paint chips if they find the vehicle the thieves were driving. All in all, most likely a professional job, and probably a dangerous bunch. No arrests so far, but there should be something on the CCTV. They smashed two of the cameras, but they didn't spot that one hidden in the tree. It doesn't give the best view, but it should show something.'

'That's very worrying,' says Frank. He's tried to arrange his face into an expression of grave concern, while inside he's dreading what Jerry's going to say next.

'It is extremely worrying,' Jerry agrees. 'And it presents us with a number of problems. Not least of all to find out where the leak is, where our integrity has been breached.' He raises both hands. 'And I'm not pointing any fingers, not yet anyway. It could have been any one of us, a careless word in the pub or to a family member. Of course I need you all to cast your minds back, think of anyone you might have spoken to and let something slip. And not necessarily recently. The police say with a set-up of this value, the raid could have been planned for months. So rack your brains, and please let me know of anything at all that comes to mind. If this gets out, it could kill the business, decimate it. I've said as much to the police, and they understand the need for discretion. Bottom line is we'll probably have to move premises, and that's going to be a very expensive business. The set-up here cost well into seven figures.'

Frank, of course, understands that this is his cue to come clean and tell Jerry about Natalie's drunken indiscretion. And the words are almost on his lips, but a whisper of self-interest persuades him to stay silent. Isn't he in enough trouble right now? Any hint of a connection to this attempted raid could bury him further. Better to keep his mouth shut, for the time being at least.

'Nothing comes to mind,' he lies. 'I'll let you know if I think of anything.'

'Troubling times,' says Jerry.

Frank drains his coffee. 'I'd better get to it. Plenty to do.'

'Before you go.' Putting his elbows on his desk, Jerry makes a temple with his fingers. 'You and I go back a long time, Frank. Above all else, we're friends. But when all's said and done, we need you to handle your workload. That's the nature of running a business. We can't afford to be missing delivery dates, falling behind. You know that.'

Not knowing whether he's supposed to respond, Frank simply nods.

'I've got to be honest, and say I'd hoped you'd come to me voluntarily, though I can see why you wouldn't. But I trust you to level with me. Of course I do. So cards on the table. Have you been charged by the police in relation to Natalie?'

Trying to discern what he's truly thinking, Frank studies Jerry's face, and sees beneath an overlay of sympathy and concern a spark of voyeuristic curiosity, a hand-rubbing delight at having a front-row seat for the show.

The coffee has left a bitter coating on Frank's tongue. 'Cards on the table?'

'I think we have to be honest with each other, don't we?'

'I'm released under investigation. They'll be making an announcement later today and my solicitor will be reading a statement. Dee's gone to stay with her sister for a few days.

I'm hoping to keep my head down here during the day, but on my lawyer's advice I'll be checking into a hotel in Wisbech.'

'Wisbech?'

'No one ever goes there, nothing ever happens. Best place in the UK to hide.'

'But what are you hiding from, Frank?'

'A media scrum. The outpouring of hate when people think I murdered my daughter.'

When Frank uses the M-word, Jerry flinches.

'I didn't do it.' Frank's suddenly weary. 'Just for the avoidance of doubt.'

Now he's heard the unadorned truth of Frank's position, Jerry appears shocked. 'But why on earth do they think you did? Do they have evidence?'

'Surely that's not something you'd expect me to share with you?'

Jerry shakes his head. 'Of course not, forgive me. And of course I know you didn't do it. That's terrible, Frank, really awful. Is there going to be a court case?'

'You mean a trial? If I'm officially charged, yes.'

'How far are they away from doing that?'

'I have no idea. The wheels turn very slowly these days, apparently. Staff shortages, pressure of work. They're under-funded, same as everyone else.'

'When are they making this announcement?'

'There's a press conference at four.'

Jerry looks thoughtful. 'I'm not sure this is the best place for you to be then, Frank. Wouldn't you be better off safely tucked away in Wisbech?'

'I don't think so. Work will take my mind off it.'

'But if they track you down? Security here is already compromised. I wonder if it might be best ... For your sake, while you process this, why don't you have a few days off?'

'I don't want a few days off. What about my workload? As you just said, we risk falling behind.'

Jerry takes a gulp of his coffee. 'I was just coming to that, actually. I've been thinking it's time we got someone else in, a youngster maybe, in on the ground floor. They could do some of the basics, the easy stuff while you're gone.'

'Where am I going, Jerry?'

Jerry pretends he hasn't heard. 'I've asked Marie to place an advert in the obvious places, so we'll see what kind of response we get, shall we? I think we'll both be more comfortable knowing we'll be covered if things ... If – well, you know.'

'If I get convicted.'

'It's not going to come to that, I know. Of course I do.'

'I wish I shared your confidence.' Frank stands, pleased he had the sense not to let himself get buried in the sofa. 'I'll get out of here, then, shall I? When do you want me to come in again? Sometime, never?'

'A few days, Frank, no more than that. Just to let things settle. Is Dee OK?'

'About how you'd expect.'

'I understand. You must tell her if she needs anything at all, she's only to ask. And you too, of course. We'll stay in touch.'

'Aye, let's do that,' says Frank, walking out the office door.

Frank spends his journey home thinking. Despite him telling Peasgood about the likelihood of Eric's involvement, plainly no arrests have so far been made. There has to be a way of prodding the police into action without giving away to Jerry Natalie's unforgiveable indiscretion.

For Frank, Eric's arrest would be personal damage limitation. If he and his mates have another crack at the workshop, they might do better this time, and Jerry will quite reasonably want to know why Frank didn't speak up. Frank suspects telling Jerry he didn't want to lose his job won't improve his long-term prospects.

In the end, he decides to write an anonymous letter. Realising he doesn't know Eric's surname, he describes him as being of East European origin, and a former boyfriend of Natalie Cutter.

He prints the letter, and seals it in an envelope he addresses generically to Norfolk Police at their headquarters. As he drops it in the postbox at the end of the road, he's praying he's given them enough to set them running back in Eric's direction.

FORTY

Gabby still loves the cactus-silk cushions she bought at Portobello market, and the Moroccan kilim which was a find at a car boot in Dalston. But some of the things she acquired while she was living in the flat she's leaving today – the Paula Rego prints she now finds angry and ugly, a vintage chair that looks good but which has never been comfortable to sit on – she sees no reason to carry into her new life, wherever and whatever that will be. As she pulls the door closed for the last time, the pictures and the chair are staying behind.

After she's handed back the keys, hungry and in no rush to begin her journey, she dials Caro's number.

Caro is gushing, as always. 'Hi, sweetie. Lunch? Great idea! I'm working from home, so just tell me where.'

Gabby suggests a pub in Stratford and Caro instantly becomes less keen, but then she recalls a deli in that area she's been meaning to visit and decides it's worth her while.

'Don't mind if I'm a teensy bit late, and grab us an outside table if you can. I'm so pale I look as if I've been locked up for months on a diet of gruel. I need to take advantage of this lovely sunshine, bump up my vitamin D before I develop rickets.'

Gabby takes that as concern the tan Caro worked so hard on during her trip to Ibiza only a couple of weeks ago is starting to fade, despite the self-tan top-ups. But the sunshine is warm and she's happy to sit outside. Fetching a tonic water and a couple of menus from the bar, she finds the only outdoor tables left are not park views but views of the car park. No matter. Sunshine is sunshine, whatever.

As expected, Caro is late, parking her sporty vintage Merc in a space almost too small for it, not caring that her door bumps the car next to her as she gets out. As she wanders over to Gabby, she raises her hand.

'Hi, sweetie, sorry to be late. Traffic was just awful, as you can imagine. Is that gin you're drinking? What a fabulous idea.' With her usual aplomb, she accosts a passing waiter with her huge smile, touching his arm as she asks for a Bombay and Fever Tree, lots of ice. 'Fancy another?'

Gabby's glass is empty. 'Straight tonic for me, please.'

'Are you ready to order?' Caro sits and delays the waiter. 'Because I know what I want. Just a green salad with feta, dressing on the side. Oh, and do you have any tapenade? A little dollop of that, and maybe a slice or two from a baguette, if it's very fresh.'

Typical of Caro to go off-piste, and typical of the waiter not to object. Gabby's eaten with Caro often enough not to be pressured by her abstemious choices and orders traditional sausages and mash with English mustard.

'I don't know how you can eat hot food on a day like this.' Caro pushes her sunglasses back on to her head.

'I'm hungry. And I've got a long drive back to Norfolk this afternoon.'

'You should take a taxi. Then we could spend all afternoon here relaxing.'

'Where would I find the money for that?' asks Gabby. 'I'm unemployed, remember? And I've just paid a hefty bill for repairs to the Mazda. It needs to earn its keep.'

'You're not unemployed, you're freelance. And God knows I've freelanced for enough of my chequered career. Just embrace it, darling. Ah, fabulous, drinks at last.'

The chat through lunch is mostly gossip: a scandalous office affair Gabby had suspected for months; the front runners for a senior editorial role and the lows to which some of the candidates were stooping to undermine the competition; rumours of a senior government minister's infidelity with a fellow minister's wife.

'Of course, we're not allowed to print that,' says Caro, reaching across with her fork to spear a piece of sausage from Gabby's plate. 'But everybody's talking about it, everybody knows. It can't be too long before it finds its way to Twitter and the general population.'

When the waiter comes to clear their plates, Caro orders coffee. Mindful of the long drive ahead and the inconvenience of service station facilities, Gabby declines.

'So come on,' says Caro, 'spill the beans. What have you been working on?'

The lie comes easily to Gabby. 'Nothing.'

Caro studies her intently. 'Really? How come I don't quite believe you? Have you got a story running out there in the back of beyond? Don't tell me – it's something to do with that murder, isn't it? What was her name, Natalie somebody? Haven't they arrested the father for that?'

'Nobody's been arrested.'

'Interviewed, then. You're playing semantics now.'

'He's a person of interest, yes.'

'Not like you to be so coy. Look, you and I are friends. If you're not going to make anything out of it, then you could give it to me. I could talk to David, we could get you a little sweetener, call it a tip fee. Do us both some good. We're none of us any more secure than you were, and I'm only as good as my last story. I've spent a load of time on the minister's wife scandal, but they won't let me write it. I'm really in desperate need of something that might have legs.'

'Write it anyway,' says Gabby. 'Someone would take it.'

Caro spoons demerara sugar into her black coffee and stirs it thoughtfully. 'You know what we miss about you in the office, sweetie? A bit of daring. I'm too set in my ways to take the kind of risks you used to. I like being able to make my mortgage payment each month. Really, couldn't we come to some arrangement? You feed what you've got to me, I'll get you an ex gratia payment when we get some kind of result. Save me traipsing all the way out there to the wetlands of Norfolk.'

'It's a beautiful place. You might like it.'

'I went there once. It rained, and we were stuck in some ghastly damp rented cottage all weekend playing Scrabble. No thank you. Look, if the father did do it, it'll be huge. Do you think he did?'

Gabby considers. 'Possibly, but it's a rare crime, a father killing his daughter. Stepdaughters, yes, but natural daughters . . .'

'She was his natural daughter, then?'

'As far as I know. But I doubt it's been DNA proven.'

'So many questions DNA tests open up.' Caro downs her coffee. 'Sorry, but I have to dash. It's been such fun. Have a think about whether you and I might work together, give me a ring.'

As Gabby watches her drive away, she smiles over Caro's brass neck. What is she saying except please do my job for me and I'll bung you a few quid? If there's a story to be found, Gabby prefers to be working for herself.

It's almost time to go, to leave behind the London life she thought was going to be her happy ever after.

Has she been happy here? Has it been all she expected, as exciting as she told those she left behind it would be?

It's had its moments. Time now to look forward.

Or back.

She recalls her recent meeting with Mona. Those friendships she made in school were rock-solid, shelter from the life-storms of broken hearts, parental rows and the uncertain, disquieting future. Unlike Caro, they were people she could rely on. Why has she made no effort to stay in contact over these past few years?

Mona and Rick's wedding: why didn't she go to that? Everyone would have been there. It would have been a blast.

Since she's heading home, a drink with the girls might be fun.

If they'll see her.

FORTY-ONE

Wilf has grown a beard.

The difference in his appearance is remarkable – which is, of course, the point.

'It makes you look distinguished,' says Margot. 'Like Prince Michael of Kent.'

To begin with, Wilf was reluctant even to consider the idea. Outdated conditioning throughout his life persuaded him facial hair is for con men and the lazy.

When he expresses this view, Margot laughs. 'In some ways you're such a dinosaur, Wilf. If it's good enough for royalty, surely it's good enough for you? Besides, it really suits you. I'd even say it makes you look hot.'

But to Wilf, an unwanted beard is another negative in his unwelcome new life. His morning shave was a daily ritual he enjoyed, using a razor and a badger-hair brush he saved up for as a teenager, and the same scented soap his mother used to buy for him. Shaving had the same sacred place in his mornings as the day's first cup of tea.

Margot had hopes this small step outside routine would make Wilf feel liberated, but the effect has been the reverse.

Routine is what he's clung to since he's retired. Cutting the rope to this particular anchor has left him testy and adrift, obsessing about all the sacrifices he's had to make since being acquitted, as he puts it, of the crime of living next door.

The unseasonal gloom of constantly overcast skies has depressed his spirits further. Certainly it's no incentive to venture outside. Margot persists, asking him to help her pick the few straggly runner beans dangling from the rain-blighted vine (*You do it, I don't know which ones are ready*) or deadhead the roses (*You're the dab hand with the pruning shears, old girl*). Instead, he sticks to his book of *Times* quick crosswords, each morning determined to beat his own record, and when he's bored with those he moves on to Margot's extensive collection of jigsaws, one bought every Christmas for more years than she cares to count.

Beyond that, he's on his Kindle tablet. If Margot asks, he tells her he's reading a book; in reality, he's trawling the internet for content about himself, perplexed and angry to find himself hated and despised when he's always been the gentlest of souls. Once thrown, mud sticks. When the hour rolls round for *Countdown* and a cup of tea, it's a blessed relief that Wilf takes it as the cut-off point for his self-torment.

Of course, Margot is worried. A prisoner of his anxiety, he barely leaves the house. Every suggestion she makes for any kind of outing – a visit to a nearby stately home, to the weekly market, even a much longer trip to the coast – he finds a reason to reject.

Out of other ideas, she brings him a selection of books on Peak District hikes from the library.

For several days, Wilf shows no interest.

Until towards the end of a dull afternoon, hopelessly bored by both crosswords and jigsaws, he picks up one of the walking books and begins to read.

That evening it's Wilf's turn to cook, and after they've eaten his meal of steamed salmon served with Chinese vegetables, he brings the book into the conservatory, where Margot is finding her needle and threads to start on the complex embroidery she likes to work on after dinner.

Moving a disgruntled Mr Grimes from a chair to make room for himself, Wilf sits down opposite Margot, his finger bookmarking a page.

He clears his throat, as if he has something of import to say.

'I was looking at the weather forecast for tomorrow and it looks as if it's going to be a nice day.'

'Well, that's good to hear.' Margot is trying to thread a needle with royal-blue silk. 'I definitely need new glasses. I spend more time threading this damn needle than I do sewing.'

'I thought I might go on an expedition. If I could borrow the car.'

Margot hides her surprise behind a frown of concentration, until she victoriously pulls the blue thread through the eye of the needle. 'Got it! I don't think that would be a problem. I have to go into town briefly, but I know Laura would give me a lift. Can I enquire where you're thinking of going?'

Wilf holds up the book, open at the pages of his finger-bookmark. 'I've been reading about this plane wreck from the last war, somewhere called Bleaklow. I thought I might try and find it. Do you know where it is?'

Margot pulls a face. 'That's way up there on the backbone

of England, over towards Glossop. Isn't it part of the Pennine Way? Are you sure you wouldn't rather go somewhere a little less . . . bleak?'

'I want to see if I can find the wreck. Something about it is calling my name.'

'Shall I come with you, then, keep you company?'

Wilf shakes his head. 'You don't have to worry about me. There's a map in this book, and I'll take a phone. If I get lost, you can be the search party bringing jam sandwiches and flasks of tea, maybe even a spot of brandy.'

Margot looks serious. 'But are you sure you should be going somewhere so remote by yourself, Wilf? There are so many other lovely places much closer to civilisation. Why choose somewhere so desolate? You're not thinking of doing anything stupid, are you? Because you know you'd break my heart if you didn't come home.'

Wilf sees the concern in his sister's face. 'Have no worries on that score. Really, I promise. I just have the feeling the time has come for me to give myself a kick up the backside, challenge myself a little.'

'Well, if that's the case, go with my blessing, but you'd better come back safe and sound.'

The morning, as promised, is clear and bright, at last a summer's day as it's meant to be.

Wilf drives through the lowland valleys towards the hills of Derbyshire's Dark Peak, feeling a bubbling exhilaration, a sense of freedom he hasn't felt in a long time. Out here, he's anonymous, a mere dot in the wild landscape. There's no one to point fingers. No need to be afraid.

Margot has warned him of the point in his journey where he'll leave the civilised world for the empty uplands.

'If you want refreshments, stop in Bamford,' she said. 'Beyond that, there's not much until you get to Lancashire.'

Emboldened by his feeling of freedom and having plenty of time, he makes a stop at a café. Walking in the door, his heart falters in a nervous palpitation, but the woman behind the counter calls a cheerful good morning as if he is a person of no special interest.

In preparation for his walk, he orders a second breakfast of tea and a bacon roll, and carries them out to a garden, where bees buzz among hollyhocks and crimson poppies. The sun is pleasant, and when he's finished eating he sits on for a while, rolling up his sleeves to warm his skin. At Nine Brethren House, at this season of the year his forearms would be tanned, his nails ragged and his hands rough from working in the garden. These unhealthily white hands aren't a gardener's; they're the hands of someone cooped up inside for far too long.

About some things, Margot has been right.

Driving on from the café, the road becomes the winding, rising Snake Pass. Before long, the dense, dark pinewoods of the lower reaches are behind him, and he's on the steep, bald moorland slopes, empty places a man could walk all day and never meet another soul.

Wilf winds down the window and lets in the fresh air.

Bleaklow, when he reaches it, is aptly named.

Beyond the point where he leaves the well-trodden path, he wades through knee-high heather and across steep gullies, wondering if he's on the right track. Maybe he should have brought a companion; up here, he's alone, and that aloneness makes him realise that, even though he wants to hide from the world, solitude and loneliness are two sides of the same coin.

All the way on this walk he's wondered whether he'll be able to find the crash site, but in the end he comes on it unexpectedly: the remains of an American B-29. He stops, and looks around the empty, lonely place where thirteen men died. Around him, the wind sighs. Overhead, a curlew cries.

For a while, he wanders among the wreckage. Parts of the plane remain complete, the steel buffed and shining as if the plane came down only yesterday. The landing gear, the engines, a gun turret: all are here as monuments to life's uncertainties, to how in a second things can go fatally wrong.

Wilf's mood as he walks away from Bleaklow is reflective. The site of such tragedy is sobering, makes a man think. Is it possible he's spent far too long in life acting a part he was never meant play?

So many things he's never dared. If he were to die today, what would his memorial say? *Here lies Wilfred Hickling, an overly cautious man.*

That's not the epitaph he wants.

And it isn't too late to change.

PART 4

Reading Between the Lies

FORTY-TWO

While Frank is away, Dee undertakes an errand on Ruby's behalf.

The drive across the fens to Wickney brings unwelcome déjà vu. She was hoping she was done with the place, with the reminders, but Ruby's so badly afflicted – despondency, melancholy, you might even call it full-blown depression – Dee wants to do something to bring some light into her life.

If Mr Hickling is at home, she isn't sure what she'll say. An apology for what he's suffered isn't appropriate; it wasn't her, after all, who roused the rabble, and who has suffered from Natalie's killing more than she has?

Yet he is owed something, some gesture from the family to acknowledge his innocence. What better gesture than Ruby's invitation to tea?

As she drives by, she's unsurprised to sees Turle's Cottage is still abandoned. A sign offering the property for rent is hammered in among some nettle-infested roses, but the landlord is surely dreaming. No one who knows its history would live in that place now.

At Nine Brethren House too, the decline into dilapidation

has continued. The lawns she and Ruby saw in need of cutting when they were last here have grown up into hay meadows, swallowing the flowerbeds and the duck pond. A crop of fruit no one will pick weighs down the branches of the apple trees. No one has troubled to clean the red writing – *PEDO BASTARD* – from the elegant front door.

Dee can't help but feel a stab of remorse. She believed Mr Hickling guilty, once upon a time.

Pushing open the wooden gate, she walks across the gravel to the back door, finding it sealed with fine spiders' webs to its frame. No one has been here for many weeks.

Through the door glass, she sees a scattering of uncollected circulars and junk mail on the floor.

She pushes Ruby's painstakingly written invitation through the letterbox to join them, with no hope at all there'll ever be any reply.

Frank's budget accommodation stands beside a busy A-road, the major route for traffic heading for Norfolk's coastal resorts, and lorries carrying freight from East Anglia's farmland to the major urban centres of the Midlands and the north.

The misnamed Hotel Supreme is ideal as an anonymous hideaway, and lacking in almost every other way. The building's exterior – dreary even in bright sunshine – is perfectly matched to the corporate sterility of the lobby and the lacklustre bar beyond. The unending white-walled corridors are the kind you might get stuck in in a bad dream, and the flimsy plasterboard walls offer no discouragement to sound, so every voice going by, every wheeled suitcase or opening of the lift doors seems to be in his room with him, whatever the hour of the day or night. Even after paying the punitive daily charge, the internet's crawlingly inadequate, each page on his tablet loading in mind-numbingly slow motion down the screen.

At first, he thought the fake American diner across the car park would be a positive, but the novelty of eating hamburgers and chips and drinking Coke without Dee's *What about your cholesterol?* interference wore off with the heartburn that followed his first meal.

Just a couple more days, he keeps telling himself. *Stick it out just a couple more days.* But in such a place every hour feels interminable. Sometimes he's finding it hard not to cry.

Dee rings him twice a day, always angry that the police aren't doing more, aren't looking elsewhere for Natalie's assailant. Jerry has called him too, full of scoutmasterish bonhomie and encouragement.

'I saw the police statement on the news,' he said the last time he rang, and Frank knew he would have, knew he wouldn't have missed it for the world. Jerry was keen to reiterate his support, before telling him they'd be interviewing possible apprentice candidates the following week, and that he hoped Frank would be able to be part of the process.

Frank promised to do his best to still be at liberty, and with a hearty laugh Jerry rang off.

Today soon after Dee's first call, Frank's phone rings again. The caller shows up as Chris Marlowe, and he answers it very promptly.

'Hello?'

A woman's voice. 'Can you talk? Is it a good time?'

'Yes, of course I can. How lovely to hear you. How are you, my darling, are you well?'

He listens as she tells him little things, how her life is going, what she's been doing, until finally she draws breath and says, 'I'll shut up now. How are you?'

He draws in a deep, levelling breath, and lets it out.

'To be honest,' he begins, because the hours and days alone in this room have persuaded him the time for honesty is long, long overdue, 'I'm not that great. Promise me you won't be angry, but there's something I have to say.'

FORTY-THREE

Gabby's running to get out of the rain, which found her coatless and hatless on a city-centre pedestrian precinct, having believed the weather forecast which told her it was going to be fine right through the day.

For a few minutes, she shelters inside Superdrug, happy to test the make-up and browse the home hair colours, wondering if she'll ever dare go full-on fuchsia or steel grey. But when there's no sign of the rain passing, the matter of car parking becomes pressing. The car park on Spendlas Street doesn't usually attract much attention from traffic wardens – especially not in the rain – but even so, better safe than sorry.

She heads in that direction at a quick walk and takes less than four minutes, just in time for the rain to stop. At the entrance barriers, she finds her keys in her handbag, then looks round for her car, not quite remembering where she parked.

Away in a far corner is a vehicle she recognises: an orange van with a photo of a summerhouse on the side.

Justin. She hasn't seen or spoken to him since she visited him at his workshop. And there he is, helping a little girl down from the driver's side.

No sign of any parking wardens. She's got a couple of moments to say hello.

'Justin?'

As he looks at her, she can see him trying to place her but failing to come up with a name.

'Gabby Laflin. I interviewed you after Natalie passed away. I used to work for the *Herald*.'

Recollection brightens his face somewhat, though he's changed since she last saw him, the anguish of the bereaved written in new lines around his eyes. Ruby stands slightly behind him, holding on to his jacket for security. She's a very pretty child, but so solemn, her father's unhappiness mirrored in her face.

'This is Ruby,' says Justin. 'Ruby, say hello.'

Ruby hides her face.

'It really doesn't matter,' says Gabby. 'I'm parked over there and I recognised the van. I just thought I'd say hi.'

'I thought you were from London,' says Justin, with what Gabby realises is justified suspicion. 'What brings you back this way? Because if you're still on Natalie's story, I don't have anything else to say. It's up to the police now. You should speak to them.'

Gabby blushes, embarrassed at having been taken as a professional stalker. And yet, she can't blame him for thinking that way. For several years, that actually was her job.

'Oh, please, don't worry. I don't work as a journalist any more. Well, not at the moment. I got fired, actually, so I've crawled home to stay with my mum and dad while I find some gainful employment.' She holds up her shopping bags. 'Retail therapy.'

Justin appears to relax. 'Sorry. I didn't mean to be rude.

But I have people coming at me from all sides, all wanting exclusives. We get sick of it. We just want to be left alone. Don't we, Rubes?'

Ruby nods. The way she's looking at Gabby is positively hostile.

'I totally understand,' says Gabby. 'And as someone who might have been doorstepping you in the past, please accept my apologies. I'm a reformed character, or trying to be.'

'I'm pleased to hear it.'

'Anyway, I'll let you get on. I just wanted to ask how you're doing.'

'We're getting through it, one day at a time. Right now we're off to find a chocolate milkshake.' He looks down at Ruby. 'They were always Mummy's favourites, weren't they?'

'Your mum had great taste, Ruby,' says Gabby.

'See you around, maybe,' says Justin, and Gabby watches his stick-thin form lead his sad, shy daughter away.

After dinner, Gabby tells her mother and father she has work to do and makes her way upstairs to her old room. Beyond the window, dusk is falling on the familiar view, and she turns on the bedside lamp, making herself as comfortable as she can on the lumpy mattress before opening up her laptop and her phone.

The task Dee wants her to take on is daunting: basically, to establish plausibly that, with Frank, the police have got the wrong man.

Or the wrong woman. Gabby thinks of Sarah, who's well below everyone's radar, as far as she knows.

And there's someone else on the periphery, with – so far – no established connection to the investigation: the young woman in the photo Dee found on Frank's phone. Maybe she's no one of interest but Gabby's time among the *Herald*'s dirt-diggers and chancers have taught her one thing at least: those in the shadows, hidden in the background, can sometimes be mined for rich pickings, and turn out to have very interesting stories indeed.

She opens an app on her phone and starts to make a list of points of interest.

Number one, track down this woman, find out if she has anything to contribute.

Number two, the missing laptop. A simple theft to make a few quid selling it in some local pub is ruled out, because there was no unaccounted-for stranger's DNA in the house. So the removal of Natalie's laptop from the scene screams that it represents a significant risk to someone, who's either hidden it or got rid of it. Who might that be?

Number three, Frank's lost phone. Nothing says *Guilty* louder than a suspect whose phone is conveniently lost. Though she didn't say so to Dee, Gabby believes this alone could be enough for the police to press on with trying to nail Frank, and maybe rightly so.

So, where to begin?

With the obvious.

From her phone, Gabby sends the photo of Frank with the mystery woman to her laptop and uploads it to Google Images. It's not the best facial recognition software, but there's an outside chance she might get lucky.

She doesn't.

Next stop social media. She puts several versions of Frank's name into LinkedIn, hoping for an account, but draws a blank. Perhaps that's not surprising, since Frank's held the same specialised job for many years and has no obvious need for business networking. Dee's told her he's not on Facebook, but that doesn't stop Gabby checking. So many people have accounts the people closest to them know nothing about and have never bothered to search for. Chances are high that the police have already trawled this pond, but they're not in possession of this photo.

A search by name for Frank Cutter brings up dozens of accounts, many of them rarely used, some never even activated, no photos or posts. If one of these is Frank's, how would she know?

She considers. If she were Frank and trying to keep something under the radar, would she use that everyday name? Probably not. How about Francis Cutter? Not much comes up for that search: a few accounts, some of them again little used. Frank could be behind any of them, or none.

The task seems hopeless. If he's on here at all, if it's to communicate with someone he shouldn't be talking to, he still needs to be identifiable. And doesn't Facebook these days demand some kind of ID?

One more try. She keys *Trent Cutter* into the search bar, and hits the *Photos* button. An array of photographs populates the screen and she begins to scroll through them.

The name's uncommon, and she doesn't have to go far. There's Frank, tagged as Trent Cutter, and the blonde he's got his arm round is the same woman as in Dee's stolen photo. And they're standing in front of a café whose name and landline phone number she can clearly read from their sign: *Vanilla Velvet*.

A very good place to start.

FORTY-FOUR

The riverbed search is a significant operation, two divers and a support unit, all the usual crowd. Conditions are optimal: the calm, sunny weather is providing the best possible visibility, though in muddy water like this nothing's ever clear. But they've been here four hours, and so far they've found nothing.

On a break, Big Mike's warming his hands on a mug of tea, mask pushed back on his head, stinking of the river water dripping off his wetsuit.

'We'll do one more pass,' he's saying to the young DC who's nominally in charge. 'But there's a load of silt on the bottom and it could have got buried in that. Plus the river here is at the tail end of being tidal, so when it's been running high there's a decent current down there, easily enough to carry something as small as a phone downstream. Could be miles out to sea by now. At the same time, it might have got lodged in some weeds or something and still be where it went in. If it went in. There's thousands of acres of fields around here. How do you know he didn't just bury it?'

'We don't, for sure,' says the DC. 'Suspect says he threw it in the river, so that's where we thought we'd start. Whether he's telling the truth or not, only time will tell. All we know is, it was switched off somewhere in this area, and number-one choice of phone off-loaders, as we know, is chuck it in a river.'

'Even so,' says Big Mike. 'Needle in the proverbial haystack this one is, mate. If you want me to narrow it down, I'd say if it went in this river it's somewhere between here and the coast of Denmark, unless it's missed Denmark and got carried all the way to Norway.' He takes a drink. 'They've not been very generous with the sugar in this tea.'

'We might get lucky,' says the DC. 'Sometimes we do.'

Big Mike finishes his drink, and as his colleague is helped out on to the muddy bank, slides into the murky water for his last dive of the day, along the thirty metres marked out for him on the far side of the bridge.

The visibility is abysmal, but the riverbed near the bridge is rich pickings, cluttered with the detritus of fly-tippers too lazy or criminal to visit the local tip not five miles away. From the surface, you'd never know this stuff was here, but down below it's a regular junkyard: an old toilet, a couple of tyres and a car battery, a child's ride-on tractor missing two wheels, a couple of hanging baskets now growing waterweeds instead of flowers. Someone's thrown in an armchair, which being heavy enough to resist the undertow has settled midstream.

Purely for his own amusement, Mike sits on it.

Something hard presses against his backside. He reaches round to see what it is.

Even in the underwater gloom, it's unmistakeable.

Big Mike's just found a mobile phone.

FORTY-FIVE

'Sorry I'm late.'

Frank's been in the Costa Coffee by himself for almost an hour, nursing the dregs of a flat white. He's not surprised Peasgood is late – every meeting they've had, he's kept Frank waiting – but today he's pushed it to the limit as far as Frank's concerned.

'You might have let me know,' he says. 'I only paid for an hour's parking. It's just about time for me to leave.'

Peasgood drops his tattered briefcases on a chair, and sits down opposite Frank. The man looks tired, run into the ground, and his shirt might easily have been slept in. Not for the first time, the thought crosses Frank's mind that someone this unkempt might not be the best person to represent him.

'I got stuck at court,' says Peasgood, glancing over at the queue for service and then at his watch, 'and then because I was late on your behalf at the police station they kept me waiting as punishment. Anyway, here I am. I'm going to grab a coffee. You want anything?'

Frank declines. Peasgood gets up and joins the queue, while Frank silently nurses his worries of a £50 parking ticket.

Peasgood comes back with a whipped-cream-topped coffee and a toasted panini. The panini smells good, and Frank regrets not asking for one.

As always, Peasgood takes a bite before speaking, as if he thinks better while chewing.

'So, the first thing to say is that the police appreciated our telling them where they might find your phone. Inevitably, there were remarks about it not being a good idea to get rid of it in the first place, but we are where we are.'

'It's not illegal to dump a phone.'

'That depends on whether the phone contains evidence of a crime.'

'So did they find it?'

Peasgood takes another bite of his panini. 'As a matter of fact, they did, though they were keen to point out that it took them all day, resulting in a considerable drain on their limited budget.'

'I hope they think it was worth it. There's hardly going to be anything recoverable on there after it's been in the water. Is there?'

'You'd be surprised.' Peasgood takes a drink of his coffee, leaving a smear of foamy cream on his unruly moustache. 'It's amazing what they can do these days. Makes me wonder why anybody bothers trying to get away with any crime. You're probably not aware they have a specialist team to retrieve data from waterlogged phones. No doubt yours has gone straight to them.'

Frank manages to appear unconcerned. 'So what happens now?'

'We wait for them to see what they can find. Obviously, in

the case of a damaged phone, it's going to take longer than a straightforward job. Stands to reason.'

'How long?'

Peasgood shrugs. 'Hard to say. There's public interest in your case, of course, so that might bump it up the list. You can't blame them for the delay. It wasn't them who threw the phone in the river, after all.'

'And in the meantime?'

'Your status remains the same. You're still RUI.'

'For God's sake,' says Frank. 'Aren't I under enough stress without this hanging over me? What solid evidence is there against me? Can't you force their hands?'

'In my long experience, they're not people who like having their hands forced. Better just to bide your time and wait it out.'

'Wait what out? Them deciding if they're going to send me to trial or not? I can't sleep, I can't eat, my wife's barely speaking to me. How long is this going to go on?'

Peasgood takes the question seriously. 'Longest I've known them drag it out is just over two years. But like I say, I think we can hope for better than that, with the interest in the case.'

'And in the meantime, what are they doing about looking for other suspects? You seem to forget, my daughter's been murdered. They need to be looking for whoever killed Nat, not messing about trying to pin it on me.'

'Now that I can't comment on with any certainty.' Peasgood's almost finished his panini. A spill of breadcrumbs tumbles down his tie. 'Except, to be brutally honest, I don't think they're pursuing any other lines of inquiry at this exact moment.'

'Why not?' asks Frank, exasperated. 'What are they messing about at?'

The look Peasgood gives Frank is pitying. 'I wouldn't say they're messing about at all, honestly. They're just pursuing with all available resources their most promising line of inquiry. What you have to understand is – and I know you won't like this – they still seem very confident the man they're looking for is you.'

FORTY-SIX

Gabby doesn't know the countryside she's driving through, and the places whose names she's seeing on the road signs are intriguingly unfamiliar. Her sense of adventure is heightened; she's glad to be on a trail which might lead somewhere or shed at least a glimmer of light on what Frank's hiding from his wife and possibly from the detectives investigating his daughter's murder.

The satnav prods her into a turn off the A-road she's been following, and three kilometres further on to turn again, eventually guiding her to the heart of a large village. The high street looks prosperous, a thriving community whose rural origin has effectively morphed into a suburb of the nearest town, where commuters who spend their working weeks in air-conditioned offices can make-believe a country life at weekends.

Vanilla Velvet isn't hard to find; it has a prominent place between a pub and a gift shop and appears welcoming and popular. Gabby parks in a free space down a side street and walks back to the café, taking her place in the short queue inside. The place smells delectable, of good coffee and a mix of the warm brownies resting on the counter and bacon grilling in the back.

In her mind, there was an outside chance she'd spot the woman she's come to find behind the counter, making her job almost too easy. But it isn't to be. The pleasant-faced girl making coffees and cutting quiche and cake is a long-haired brunette, nothing like the woman she's looking for.

It's been a long drive. Gabby's hungry and thirsty, and so she scans the chalkboard menus, settling without too much difficulty on the café's lush-looking signature vanilla velvet cake.

When her turn comes, the girl's smile is genuinely warm and she moves immediately to start making Gabby's caramel latte, giving off all kinds of signs she's someone who enjoys her job. When the noise of frothing milk stops, Gabby decides it's the right time to start her enquiries.

'This is a lovely place,' she says. 'I haven't been in before.'

'It's my aunt's,' says the girl, pouring syrup. 'She makes all the cakes. Are you not local, then?'

'Me? No.' Gabby's digging in her pocket for her phone. 'But actually I'm looking for someone who might be. Maybe you can help me.'

The girl sprinkles cinnamon on the latte and turns back to Gabby. 'If I can. You wanted vanilla velvet, right?'

'Yes, please. Do you know this woman?'

Reaching for a knife, the girl glances at the phone's screen. 'Oh, yeah. That's Bethan.' She cuts into the cake. 'My sister was in her year at school.'

'Does she live locally?'

The girl's sliding a large slice of cake on to a plate. 'Yes, here in the village.' Suddenly she seems uncertain. 'I don't know if I should tell you exactly where.'

Gabby smiles. 'Course not. I might be a mad axe murderer or anything. Listen, can I give you my number and maybe you could ask her to call me? Do you have her number?'

'My sister will.'

Not wanting to hand over a business card giving away her credentials, Gabby grabs a napkin, asks for a pen and scribbles down her mobile, writing only her Christian name.

She pays with a card, but the transaction is slow. As they're waiting for the payment to go through, the girl studies Gabby's number and asks, 'Shall I tell her what it's about?'

'I'm a friend of a friend,' says Gabby. 'I was told she might be able to help me with a little mystery.'

Bait the hook. Curiosity is the fastest way to get people to connect.

'OK,' says the girl. 'I'll ring my sister when I get a minute.'

Gabby has no idea if that means in half an hour or the middle of next week. Taking her cake and her coffee, she finds a secluded table and takes her time with her less than healthy lunch. The cake's as divine as it looks, and the coffee's good too, persuading her to have a second before she leaves. What she'll do now, she doesn't know. This village isn't the kind of place she can hang around inconspicuously, but there's no point in driving straight back home. If Bethan lives here, she can surely be found, whether or not she takes the bait.

But she doesn't have long to wait. Just as she's about to stand and approach the counter for a refill, her phone pings with a message.

Unknown number. *Hi, who is this please?*

Gabby has her story ready. *Hi, is this Bethan? Sorry to get in touch out of the blue. I believe we have a mutual friend and I'd really appreciate a few minutes of your time. Chat on the phone or meet in a safe space, you decide. Don't mean to be pushy but I'm only in the area today. Thanks so much, Gabby.*

She reads it through and presses send.

By the time she's fetched a fresh coffee – thanking the girl behind the counter for helping her out and leaving a generous tip – her phone's pinged again.

Prince's Park, 4 p.m., says the message. *I'm wearing a red blouse.*

See you then, replies Gabby.

FORTY-SEVEN

Prince's Park turns out to be an area of flat land with a pair of goalposts set out for football, a kids' playground with climbing frames and a slide, and a community wildlife garden overgrown with summer weeds.

Bethan would be easy to spot even if she weren't wearing the red blouse. Too early for schoolchildren, there's no one else there. Gabby puts on her brightest smile and approaches with the show of confidence she's learned makes people more accepting of what you're asking them to say or do. Old habits die hard.

'Hi Bethan, thanks so much for coming to meet me.'

Close up, Bethan's a strikingly attractive woman: late twenties, beautifully cared for blonde hair, a great figure in designer jeans and the red blouse which is perfect for her colouring.

But she's not smiling back. 'You're lucky I'm free. I'm not usually off on Tuesdays.'

'That is lucky, then. What is it you do?'

Bethan looks at Gabby coldly. 'Can I just ask why you wanted to see me?'

Suspecting she'll get no further if she doesn't, Gabby decides she might as well come clean.

Taking out her phone, she holds up the picture Dee sent her of Bethan and Frank. 'It's about this.'

Bethan nods. 'I had a feeling it might be. Are you some relation?'

'Of Frank's? No. I'm a friend of his wife's.'

Bethan's eyebrows rise. 'Really? Because I can't help wondering if you might be from the press.'

Here's the moment where the old Gabby would have extended the lie, spinning the tale she thought would gain her maximum information. But there's something about Bethan that's vulnerable, hurting, and she finds that's not where she wants to go.

'I can assure you I'm not here to get a story I can sell. But I'm in the difficult position of not knowing how much you know.'

'As of yesterday, probably everything,' says Bethan. 'Look, it's crazy us standing here like a couple of Cold War spies. Why don't you come to mine, and we can talk there?'

Bethan's driving a red Mini whose colour matches her blouse, zipping too fast through the village so Gabby struggles to keep up. She pulls up outside a newly built mid-terrace townhouse, prettified by a mauve clematis growing over the porch. Bethan parks on the drive. Not wanting to presume, Gabby pulls in at the kerbside.

Inside, the house is pleasantly furnished but seems to lack the personal touches of a place that's a proper home. On the lounge wall, though, is a large colour portrait photo of Bethan with a handsome young man, her leaning on his shoulder under the coppery shade of an autumnal tree, both of them in green wellies and Barbour wax jackets. Is this her brother, or a significant other? Gabby's more intrigued than ever on where Frank fits in.

Two coffees is definitely her daily limit, so Gabby asks for tea. Bethan brings in their drinks, sits down on the sofa and says, 'I'm going to be blunt about this. Who are you, really?'

Gabby sighs. 'Like I said, this is awkward. I don't want to give away anything you're not already aware of.'

'About my father?'

The revelation is totally unexpected, which makes Gabby feel a fool. Why did a parent–child link never occur to her? She looks sideways at Bethan, points at her phone and says, 'Frank is your father?'

Bethan laughs. 'Now I've given too much away. You didn't know that? Yes, he's my father. Don't tell me. His wife – my stepmother, as I suppose I must get used to calling her – sent you because she thought Dad and I were having an affair.'

'Maybe. Kind of, but not exactly.'

'Full disclosure, remember. Why?'

'Your father's got himself in a bit of bother. Dee – your stepmother – thought I might be able to help get him out, given my background in . . . let's call it digging out the truth.'

'Are you the police?'

'No.'

'Ex-police?'

Gabby shakes her head. 'Not likely. Far worse. I was an investigative journalist, until I got fired. I suppose these days I'd have to call myself freelance, but you have my word everything we talk about here will not be used for any story. Cross my heart and hope to die. I don't know how else to make you believe me. I'm here doing Dee a favour. I owed someone a debt, and helping Dee out is my way of trying to repay it in some small way, karmically at least.'

'Who did you work for?'

'The *Herald*.' Bethan's face shows her distaste. 'Not good, I know. I promise I've seen the error of my ways. And by the way, I notice you haven't asked what kind of bother Frank's in, so can I assume you already know?'

Now Bethan sighs. 'I spoke to him yesterday. He and I haven't been in contact for long, a year or so, that's all. I was brought up by my mum. Before she died last year, she wanted me to know who my dad was. I knew his name from my birth certificate, but that was all I had. She'd never told me much about him, got a bit tight-lipped if I ever mentioned him, but when she knew she didn't have long, she had a change of heart and decided she wanted me to find him so I wasn't alone in the world. As far as I know, they hadn't seen each other since before I was born. Blood's thicker than water, though – isn't that what they say?'

'How did you track him down?'

'She had a phone number. It didn't go straight to him, but to one of his mates she was still in contact with. He was happy enough to give me Dad's number, once he'd got over the shock of hearing who I was. It took me ages to pluck up the courage to ring Dad. I thought he wouldn't want to know me, but I had an incentive to get in touch. I'm getting married in a few months and I wanted to ask him if he'd give me away.'

'Wow. Well, I mean congratulations. How did he react to that?'

'This is the hard part, though I didn't know it at the time.

We met up and he told me he was delighted I'd got in touch with him, that he'd be delighted to give me away. He told me I was the daughter he never had.'

'But . . .'

'Yeah, but. Until yesterday I thought he was unmarried – divorced, he said – and I was his only child.'

Gabby frowns. 'He lied? But those are not small lies. Why on earth did he do that?'

'I can only tell you what he said to me yesterday, in between the over-and-over apologies. Apparently he thought he could handle two separate lives, thought it would be easier not to rock the boat with his wife and daughter. Problem is, you see, I'm younger than Natalie was.'

'Ah.'

'At the very least, I'm evidence of an extra-marital affair, and, at worst, of a lie that lasted all of Natalie's life. When he told me yesterday what had happened and the trouble he's in . . .' Bethan's words trail off. 'I'm sorry. I'm still processing everything. I thought finding my birth father was a cause for celebration, and now I feel I'm sinking into a great pit of deception. I'm sure Mum didn't mean things to turn out like this, but if she'd never told me about Dad, I'd have got on with my life none the wiser.'

Gabby nods. 'I see that.'

'So what will you tell Dee?'

'I don't know yet. Did Frank talk about telling the police about you?'

'Why? Am I relevant? I really don't want to get dragged into a murder case. I've got my professional reputation to consider.'

'What is your profession, if you don't mind me asking?'

'I'm a junior doctor. You know, one of those poor sods you see on the news from time to time, complaining about long hours and lack of pay. That's me.'

'Congratulations again. That's impressive.' Gabby means it. If she'd taken a different path, maybe she could have done something to help people instead of wrecking their lives with half-truths and lies. 'Can I ask you something? Has your dad ever been here to stay, you know, overnight or longer?'

'Once or twice, yes. He came to meet Mark, my fiancé. He stayed in the spare room. Once he rang in the middle of the night on his way home from somewhere and came and fell asleep on the couch.'

Gabby's bullshit radar kicks in. 'He rang just passing in the middle of the night? Didn't that strike you as odd?'

'Yes, very. But when he got here, he looked so exhausted I didn't have the heart to grill him. And we didn't really speak before he left. Someone was trying to get hold of him urgently, so he said a hasty goodbye and left.'

Gabby frowns. 'When was this, approximately?'

'I don't know. A few months ago.'

'Do you think you could check your calendar, narrow it down?'

'Maybe. It was around the time . . .' Bethan's hands go to her face. 'Oh my God. You're not thinking . . .?'

'I am thinking,' says Gabby, slowly. 'And what I'm thinking is it's very possible you might be the alibi Frank's been hiding.'

FORTY-EIGHT

Dee's morning has been a clone of her old normality, a couple of hours shopping in the way she used to enjoy. She's thinking of it as a necessary step in moving forward. She can't stay locked in grief forever.

But driving home with her expensive skin products and her new top and a few treats for dinner from Marks & Spencer's, she can't fight the awareness that whatever she tries her old normality is never coming back. That good feeling, the buzz she used to get from her retail therapy hasn't kicked in, and the perpetual ache left by Natalie's loss is still there. Surrounded by all those people on the high street, she felt self-conscious and conspicuous, troubled by the feeling everyone was looking at her, recognising the wife of a notorious man who – in their eyes – killed his own daughter. Now she thinks the trip was completely pointless and is annoyed at herself for blowing all that cash.

As she turns the corner into their road, she's surprised to see Frank's car is in the driveway. Her first thought is anxious, and she wonders if he might be ill; with all the stress he's been under, it's a miracle he's gone this far without some kind of physical collapse. Her second thought is that he shouldn't be here; they agreed he would stay away from possible press harassment for four days at least, and this is only day three. Her third thought is that he might make things very awkward. Gabby's supposed to be arriving any time to report on what she's discovered. How she'll explain Gabby to Frank if their paths cross, Dee has no idea.

But she's reluctant to cancel Gabby's visit. Gabby's texts say she has news which needs to be explained in person. Fingers crossed Frank won't be staying home for long.

Though he must have heard her car pull up in the drive, he doesn't come to open the door. Annoyed, she dumps her shopping on the porch while she fumbles for her key.

Stepping into the hallway, she calls out. 'Frank? Are you there?'

'In here.'

She leaves the shopping and follows the sound of his voice into the lounge.

'Frank?'

He's sitting on the sofa, not relaxing but on the edge of it, elbows on his knees, his chin resting on his steepled hands, one of his feet tapping the carpet. He looks utterly, irrecoverably exhausted, and she wonders how long it is since he slept. The way he is – agitated, apprehensive – tells her there's something weighty on his mind, and her heart sinks as she can't help thinking, *He did it.*

'What's going on? What are you doing here? Didn't we say four days? They could easily still come back, Frank. You know what those newspaper people are like.'

He gives her what's supposed to be a smile, though there's nothing behind it but desolation. 'We have to talk.'

Her heart sinks further. Somewhere inside, she knows he's going to confess.

'There's something I have to tell you. Come and sit down.'

Seeing how serious he is, she gives him no argument but sits down in an armchair opposite him, mirroring his pose. And it occurs to her that maybe this isn't about guilt, or confessions, but that the thought she had when she saw his car might have been the correct one, that he might be ill, and afraid of breaking the news.

'What is it, Frank? For God's sake, tell me. You're scaring me.'

He lets his head drop, as if the effort of holding up whatever burden he's carrying is all too much. 'I haven't been truthful with you, not for a while.'

Dee gives a bitter laugh. 'Well, that's not news. I know you well enough by now to know when you've got something to hide. What is it, another of your women?'

'Dee, please. I know I've not treated you the way I should have, and I'm sorry for that, more sorry than you know. But this is bigger than that, and I should have told you before. I've got a daughter, another daughter.'

He looks directly at her, like a soldier who's pulled the pin on a grenade and dropped it at his own feet, waiting to see whether the damage will be survivable.

In Dee's face he sees the hurt he's seen there too many times before. But there's something else too, something formidable. Her jaw's clamped to contain her rising, furious rage.

When she speaks, her voice is icy. 'You what?'

He hesitates before he dares repeat himself. 'I've got a daughter, Bethan. I should have told you before, but I just didn't know how.'

312

'So when you were comforting me, telling me we were going to get through the loss of our only child together, that was all bullshit?'

'It wasn't bullshit, of course it wasn't. I meant every word. I still do.'

'Except Natalie wasn't your only child, was she? Of the two of us, it's only me that's childless now, isn't it? You had a spare waiting in the wings. How old is she?'

'Twenty-six.'

'So she's younger than Natalie. Which means you had a child with another woman after our daughter was born. You've had twenty-six years to tell me, and you decided not to bother? Is that what you're saying?'

Hopelessly, Frank shakes his head. 'It wasn't like that, I promise. I didn't know about her, not until recently.'

'But I assume you knew you'd shagged her whore of a mother? You're not going to try and tell me that just slipped your mind?' She stands up. 'You really are a piece of shit, Frank, a lousy, rotten, stinking piece of shit. And you know what? You can get out of this house right now, and go back to your stinking hotel, and you can stay there for the rest of your life, as far as I'm concerned. I hate you, Frank. I absolutely, totally loathe you with all my being.'

As she heads for the door, there are tears – of rage and hurt – in her eyes. He reaches out and grabs her wrist.

'You have to listen to me.'

'Let go of me. I don't have to listen to any more of your bullshit lies ever again. You're nothing but—'

The doorbell rings. He loosens his grip on her, and she shakes her arm free.

'Who the hell's that?' he asks.

She doesn't answer but goes into the hall and opens the door to Gabby, who takes one look at her and asks, 'Are you OK?'

'Not really,' says Dee. 'Sorry, I should have let you know. Can we do this another time?'

'Who's this?'

Frank appears behind Dee in the hallway. Gabby sees a man who looks exhausted beyond measure, beaten down and grey.

She raises a hand. 'Hi, I'm Gabby. Look, I don't want to intrude. Dee, give me a ring when you're free.'

She's turning away when Dee stops her. 'You know what? Why don't we do this now? No time like the present. Come on in, Gabby, come and join the party, grab yourself a seat through there. But you'd better be prepared for a stormy ride.'

Apprehensively, Gabby follows Frank into the lounge, sitting down in the armchair where Dee was seated. Frank sits again on the sofa. Dee prefers to stand.

Frank looks at Dee for some explanation of Gabby's presence.

'I asked Gabby to do a little job for me,' says Dee, bitterly. 'I thought it would be in our family's interests – in Ruby's interests, specifically – if someone could help give you an alibi. Because I'm still hoping, Frank Cutter, that despite what the police think, you might be innocent of our daughter's murder. Are you?'

Wearily, Frank nods. 'I didn't kill her, I swear it.'

'Well, we both know that you swearing anything is meaningless, so I was rather hoping Gabby might come up with something more solid. Have you, Gabby?'

Gabby's doubtful, afraid to proceed. 'Look, maybe it really

would be better if I came back another time. You two obviously have things to talk about.'

'No, no,' insists Dee. 'If you found something, let's all hear it.'

Gabby looks at Frank with appeal in her eyes to get her off the hook. But Frank is staring at his feet, not seeming to care.

'I'm sorry,' she says to Frank, and then to Dee, 'He has a daughter, your stepdaughter.'

Instead of the shock Gabby's expecting, a manic grin spreads over Dee's face. 'The same bombshell, twice in five minutes. Actually, Frank has just seen fit to tell me himself, and as you probably gathered, Gabby, I am not too pleased. In fact, I have just invited my husband to pack his bags and fuck off, never to return.'

'I will,' says Frank resignedly. 'I'll do whatever you ask. But first I want to tell you the whole story.'

'Really,' says Gabby, moving to stand, 'I should go.'

'Stay,' insists Frank. 'Because if you're here to help me prove my innocence, this is part of it.'

'She's mixed up in this, isn't she?' asks Gabby.

Frank nods. 'I wanted to keep her out of it for so many reasons, but most of all so I didn't hurt you.' He looks at Dee. 'She came out of nowhere, I swear. I didn't know anything about her until a year ago.'

'What about the conceiving of her?' asks Dee snidely.

'That's water under the bridge, surely?' asks Frank. 'I know I haven't been a saint, and I'm sorry for it. But I stuck with you, Dee, didn't I?'

'Just tell the story.'

'Bethan got in touch with me after her mother died. She

315

left Bethan a note to try and put her in touch with me, to let Bethan feel she wasn't alone in the world. And I was pleased to hear from her – delighted, actually. I'm not going to lie about that. You know I didn't always see eye to eye with Natalie, and it felt like another chance to have a relationship with a child – not a child, a daughter – who I didn't already have a lot of history with, a lot of pain and complications. So I met her . . .'

'All the while keeping it secret from me.'

Frank nods. 'I admit that.'

'Why?'

'Because of this. I knew you'd be livid. I thought I could handle it, compartmentalise it.'

'Does she know about me and Natalie?'

Frank's silence answers Dee's question, and Dee shakes her head. 'You really are a piece of work. What did you tell her?'

'It doesn't matter what I told her.'

'I know what you told her,' chimes in Gabby, indignant herself on Dee's behalf at Frank's dishonesty and deception. 'You told her you were divorced with no kids.'

Finally, the expected tears roll down Dee's cheeks. 'You absolute bastard. You disowned me and Nat, your own wife and child.'

Gabby hands Dee a box of tissues. 'Why did you do that?' she asks Frank. 'Honestly, I'm intrigued.'

'No other reason than self-protection. If she knew she had a half-sister, she'd have wanted to meet her. And that would have caused problems with Dee, and with Nat.'

'I don't see why Nat would have been a problem,' sniffs Dee. 'She always wanted a sister. She'd have loved to have known.'

'Take off your rose-tinted glasses,' says Frank. 'Nat never wanted to be anything but the only centre of attention.'

'Frank! Don't talk about her like that.'

'Why not? It's true. And I'll tell you how I know – because she did find out about Bethan. She and I had a massive row about her just before she died. You asked why I didn't finish that last bit of painting in the bedroom? Well, she came home absolutely spitting feathers, wanting to know who this second daughter was. She was so angry. I mean, she had a temper on her, but this was worse than any tantrum I've ever seen.'

'When was this?' asks Gabby.

'On that Thursday.'

'So you and she argued.'

'Yes. But I never touched her. I just left her to it,' says Frank. 'Years and years of that I had from Natalie, her berating me for something or other I'd done. It was water off a duck's back to me, in the end. Anyway, I got a couple of messages from her to prove I left her very lively after I left. She couldn't have sent those if her phone had been smashed.'

'Neither could anyone else,' says Gabby thoughtfully.

'Except you don't have your phone,' says Dee. 'What exactly did happen to your phone, Frank? Full disclosure.'

'I threw it in a river.'

'For God's sake! Why did you do that? What was the point? They already had Nat's phone, so they had records of all your messages. Didn't they ask you about what had been going on?'

'Of course they did. I told them we rowed about her telling that dead-beat boyfriend about the workshop. Which was true, only that was a week or so before. And for the record, there's been an attempted robbery, so Jerry has her to thank for that. I haven't dared tell him, not yet anyway. My job's hanging by a thread as it is.'

'If you've already told them about that, won't the police put two and two together?' asks Dee.

'Not so far.'

'It's not really any of my business, I suppose,' says Gabby, 'but I don't understand why you didn't just come clean?'

Frank's face softens into an expression of hopeless dejection. He looks up at Dee.

'I wanted to protect you. I knew how hurt you'd be about what I'd kept from you, and I felt so guilty. I couldn't come to terms with how unfair it felt, that I still had a daughter and you didn't. Not of your own blood, at least. I thought it was best if I tried to keep her hidden, but it was getting more and more complicated, and now it's come to the point where if I don't tell the truth, I'll probably go to jail.'

'So you'll go so far to protect my tender feelings, but not so far as going to jail?' demands Dee. 'Is that it? I have to handle it now so you can save your skin?'

Frank shakes his head. 'You make it sound like I'm a terrible person, and maybe I am. But you have to believe me when I say I was thinking of you and I didn't want to hurt you. I've been so conflicted. Bethan, she's . . . well, she's a lovely girl, beautiful and clever. I was thinking there might be some way we could all be a family, one day.'

'No,' says Dee.

'All I'm asking is that you keep an open mind.'

'If you're thinking she might replace Nat, you can think again. I have one daughter, and nothing will change that.'

'Please, Dee, just—'

'No. Never. She was your dirty little secret before; she can stay that way now.'

'I have a question,' says Gabby. 'How did Natalie find out about Bethan?'

Frank glances at the door as if he's considering walking out.

Noticing his body language, Dee says, 'Oh, here we go. Come on, spit it out.'

'She had a mate – I don't know which one, she didn't say – who works at the registry office. And this woman took it into her head it would be a good thing to tip Natalie off that my name was on the birth certificate of a woman who'd been in to do the paperwork for her wedding.'

'Wedding?' asks Dee, incredulous. 'What wedding?'

Frank's head sinks lower, as if preparing for a blow. 'Bethan's getting married.'

'She's what?' There's a quiet rage in Dee's voice Frank's never heard before. 'My daughter's dead and your secret child is planning a wedding? You disgust me, Frank. Just get out of this house, and never come back.'

Tears come to Frank's eyes. 'For God's sake, Dee, I've said I'm sorry. And I've done my best, my very best to shield you. I would have told you, of course I would, if Natalie was still here. I just wanted to do it in my own way, in my own time. Since Nat died, there's never been a good time. You can see that, can't you? I love you, Dee. You're my life.'

Dee glares at him, shaking her head in disbelief.

Gabby intervenes. 'So what will you do now, Frank? The cat's out of the bag and the big secret's out in the open. Presumably you'll go to the police and tell them all this?'

'Are you sure that's a good idea?' asks Dee. 'What about

the witness they've got who spoke to you while you were at the cottage on that Friday? What if that call makes a total mess of your story?'

'That's not possible because I wasn't there on the Friday. I've already told them that. I know you don't believe me. You think I killed her, don't you?'

'In the absence of another candidate, I think there's a reasonable chance,' says Dee. 'I hired Gabby hoping she'd find something to prove you didn't do it. But, by your own admission, you and Nat had one bad fight after another, and she brought you another damn good reason to be mad at her. As far as I can see, all Gabby's brought us makes the case against you stronger.'

'Don't give up on me, Dee,' pleads Frank. 'I didn't kill her, I swear.'

'So where were you on the Friday?' demands Dee. 'I've asked you a thousand times and you've never answered. Answer now. It's your absolute last chance.'

Frank looks down at his feet. 'I was doing what I told you I was doing on the Monday, when Nat was in the hospital. On the Monday I was at Bethan's. I drove to hers after we had that massive row, asked if I could sleep a few hours on her couch. Obviously I couldn't tell you that, though, could I? The Friday was the day I was driving round. I had a lot on my mind, you and me, Nat and Bethan. I took the day off work to go and see a solicitor, but in the end I didn't turn up for the appointment. I was just driving. Thinking, driving, trying to get things straight in my head. Nothing that gives me an alibi.'

'Why did you want to see a solicitor?'

Frank shakes his head. 'Don't make me say it. It doesn't matter now.'

'Just lay it all out there, the truth in its proper sequence,' says Dee wearily. 'It's over between us anyway.'

'I just wanted to ask some questions, in case we decided to separate. And I told you, I didn't go. I wish to God I had. At least I'd have had some kind of alibi.'

'You were wanting a divorce.'

'Be honest: we weren't happy.'

'You think we're happy now? You're out of your mind.'

'I haven't even thought about divorce, though, not since Nat . . . You have to believe that.'

'I don't have to believe a single word you say, ever again.'

'You're right about having no alibi,' puts in Gabby. 'But I still have a couple of ideas I want to pursue. Innocent until proven guilty, remember?'

'He's guilty of so much already,' says Dee angrily.

'Of many things, but not murder,' says Frank. He looks at Gabby. 'You go and do whatever you can for me, because I swear on my own life and Nat's memory, I did not kill my daughter.'

FORTY-NINE

On the outside, only one thing has changed at the house down the back lane in Wickney. Last time Gabby was here, a little girl's tricycle was lying on its side in the front yard. Now there's a boy's bike in its place, one of its tyres flat. Everything else – from the dirty windows to the hopeless air of a life steeped in monotony – remains the same.

When she answers the door, Sarah Osgood looks the same too – the same dull-eyed, pasty face, the same scraped-back, greasy hair, though the oversized t-shirt she's wearing looks new. Gabby reads the sequinned slogan running across Sarah's plump breasts: *Don't Waste My Time*. Gabby has the feeling Sarah's taking care of that all by herself.

'Hi, Sarah.' Gabby can see in Sarah's eyes that she doesn't remember her. 'Gabby Laflin. We spoke a while back, when I was working for the *Herald*.'

Now the lights come on. 'Oh, yeah. Hi.'

Gabby sees the slightest change in Sarah's stance, a subtle shifting of her weight to make herself more effective at blocking the doorway.

'Is now a good time?'

Sarah looks blank. 'For what?'

'I was in the neighbourhood and I just wondered if you might have time for a quick chat about Natalie. You know, from a personal point of view. I don't work for the paper any more.'

'What about her?'

'Cards on the table, right? Dee asked me to help the family out. They've got some trouble and, very between us, the police are fixated on the idea that Natalie's dad was the one who assaulted her. I promised I'd do what I could, so I was thinking you and I could go over old ground, see if anything new came to mind.'

'After all this time? I doubt it.'

'Her mum and dad are desperate, Sarah. Dee's lost her daughter, and the thought of losing her husband as well, of him being put in jail for something she's convinced he didn't do – you can imagine how she's feeling. Five minutes, tops. For Natalie's sake.'

Sarah is wavering and Gabby pushes home her advantage. 'No one need know I spoke to you if you don't want them to.'

'Five minutes, then,' says Sarah. 'I've got to pick the kids up in a bit.'

She leads the way into the same old-fashioned room Gabby remembers from before. A fresh load of children's clothes are drying on a rack, and the scent of fabric softener is bonding with smells of baked beans and sausages from the lunch leftovers on the table.

This time, there's no offer of tea or coffee.

'Excuse the mess,' says Sarah, picking up a half-dressed doll from an armchair so Gabby can sit. She herself slumps down at the end of the sofa where the cushions are most worn and a mobile phone and TV remote lie on the armrest. 'So what's going on with Frank?'

Gabby's not surprised that the bait has been so readily taken. In places where very little happens, fresh, reasonably reliable information is solid-gold currency. With a tempting insight into the Cutter household, Sarah's social standing will soar for at least a couple of days, especially if she's mysterious about where her information has come from.

'He's got himself in a bit of bother,' says Gabby, 'trying to keep the lid on at home. Turns out there were a couple of things going on in his life he'd have done better to mention early on.'

Sarah nods, so uninterestedly Gabby realises she already knows – or believes she knows – what's going on. She looks at Sarah closely. 'This isn't news to you, is it?'

'Depends what you're talking about.'

'About Frank's other daughter. How did you know?'

Sarah shrugs. 'Nat told me. She was pretty pissed off about it, actually, and I can't say I blame her. I mean, if I'd got a sister, I'd want to know about it. Most people would. She found out from a mate who works in council registrations. She'd done an interview with this couple for a marriage licence – what do you call it, a certificate of non-impediment – and she saw Frank's name on the woman's birth certificate. Well, there aren't that many Francis Trent Cutters about, are there? So she rang Natalie and asked if it was her dad. Like I say, Nat was really angry about it, being kept in the dark.'

'And did she tackle him about it?'

'I don't know. I think she'd have told me if she had, texted me or something. She always used to have a rant in my direction if something was bothering her, but I never heard anything about that.'

Which might not be good for Frank, thinks Gabby. *If Natalie never contacted Sarah after her row with him, maybe she was already injured and unconscious.*

'Have you mentioned this to anyone else? The police, maybe?' she asks.

'No. Why should I?'

'You didn't think it might be relevant?'

'No. If there was anything to say about it, I assumed Frank would tell them. Nobody ever asked me.'

A thought comes to Gabby. 'Maybe there was something about it on Natalie's missing laptop. Did anyone ask you about that?'

There it is: a flush of pink rising across Sarah's face. She ducks her head to hide it, pretending to urgently review messages on her phone.

'Sarah? Do you know anything about the laptop?'

'Course I don't. Why would I?'

Gabby can sense she's touched a nerve. Without even thinking about it, she switches to a method she hoped she'd left behind her: the blatant untruth. 'That's good. Because Dee told me the police are really concerned about where it's got to, and they're going to be doing full searches of several properties to rule them out. All Natalie's close contacts are on the list, and you were her best friend so I suppose that includes you.'

'What? When? They can't do that.'

'Well, of course they can. That's how they work when they

get stuck, they cast their net wide and see what turns up. But you've got nothing to worry about, have you?'

'No. Why should I have?'

'I've been wondering myself why someone should have taken it from Natalie's house,' muses Gabby. 'Haven't you wondered the same? There must be something incriminating on there someone doesn't want the police to find.'

'Maybe she got rid of it herself.'

'Why would she do that?'

'Same reason you just said. If she had something on there she didn't want anybody to see.'

'That doesn't make sense, though, does it? It presupposes she knew someone was going to push her down the stairs. Hey, speaking of not wanting people to see things, you'd better have a good tidy up before the police get here. They go through everything, your knicker drawer, your phone, all your private stuff. Your bank accounts. Hope you haven't got any income the DWP don't know about. They'll be passing on your details if you have.'

'That's not legal. Is it?'

'It's their duty. They're the police. By the way, what exactly was Natalie selling on the internet? She was making good money, Dee tells me, but there was nothing she could have been selling in the house.'

Silence.

'I thought you would know, since you and she were close. Speaking of which, how's Justin doing?'

Again, a blush spreads over her cheeks. 'He's alright.'

'You see much of him?'

'No. Why should I?'

Gabby shrugs. 'I just had the impression you and he were, you know . . .' She holds up two fingers intertwined.

'He's busy, most of the time. He's got his work, hasn't he? Ruby's been here for tea a couple of times. He knows he can rely on me if he needs anything.'

'Good for you. People need all the friends they can get, these days.'

Sarah gives her attention back to her scrolling, clearly disinclined to talk further, so Gabby rises from her chair. 'Well, I've taken up enough of your time. I suppose you need to go and get the kids.'

Sarah's phone pings with an incoming message. 'What? Yes, right.'

'Thanks for talking to me, then. I'll see myself out.'

Gabby decides to play a hunch. Climbing into her car, she drives it out of the lane, reparking out of sight of Sarah's windows but with a view of both ends of the lane.

She doesn't have long to wait before Sarah come out of her house.

Gabby's not sure what she's expecting, but isn't surprised that Sarah, in her idleness and lacking imagination, does the totally obvious.

If she'd been lucky, it would have been enough.

But Gabby's here to make sure Sarah isn't lucky.

Sarah's in her slippers, carrying a bag of household rubbish in one hand. In the other, she's holding a Tesco carrier bag containing a single object with a distinctive shape.

A laptop.

A council wheelie bin stands by the gate, already almost

full. Collection day must be close. Sarah drops in the wrapped laptop, dumping the bag of rubbish on top, then forces the lid shut as far as it will go, and wanders back inside.

Gabby continues to wait, not wanting to approach the house while Sarah might spot her. Thirty slow minutes go by before Sarah appears again, dressed in leggings and outdoor shoes, pushing Lizzie's buggy in front of her as she disappears down the lane.

The moment she's out of sight, Gabby hops out of the car.

Wrinkling her nose at the stink, she grabs the Tesco bag and hauls it out from under the mess of household waste.

FIFTY

Six weeks after his trip to Bleaklow, Wilf's taking his walking seriously. In new boots and waterproofs, he's developed a routine where Margot drops him off at the start of the route he wants to walk and – God bless her – picks him up when he rings her from the endpoint.

Walking, he finds, clears his head, helps him keep what's important in life to the front of his mind, lets him push his anxieties to the back. The places he chooses are out of the way, and he rarely meets more than one or two people in a morning, though as time's gone by he's become comfortable passing the time of day.

His fear of being recognised and abused is abating, and not only that: another change is underway. Slowly, his homesickness – his longing for the straight rivers and flatlands that are in his blood – is being displaced by his attachment to these rugged northern landscapes. And, with it, that change has brought an insight: the realisation that even at this late stage in his life there exists in him the ability to adapt, to evolve, to grow.

By planning his walks with care, he can usually end up at

a village with a place to buy refreshments to enjoy while he waits for Margot to arrive.

One Wednesday afternoon, following a hike through one of the lesser-known dales, he's pleased to reach the Black Bull public house.

He puts in his lunch order at the bar and carries his pint of lager to an outside table. The sun's coming out to brighten what's so far been an overcast day, and the warmth is pleasant on his face. A group of hikers is arriving – a chatty, cheerful bunch in muddied boots and gaiters, who drop their packs outside the pub door. In an organised fashion, two of the men write down a drinks order, while the rest of the group settles down in available seats.

Time to call Margot. Wilf bends down to find his phone in a pocket of his rucksack. When he raises his head, someone is standing next to him.

'Mind if I join you?' The man is a little younger than Wilf, lean and tanned from being outdoors, in the way Wilf used to be and is again becoming.

The man smiles, and there's something in his eyes Wilf has rarely seen: the light of interest.

Wilf smiles back. 'Please, do.'

The man sits and offers his hand across the table. Wilf takes it, finding the handshake firm and warm.

'I'm Laurence.'

'Wilf.'

'Delighted to meet you, Wilf. Pardon my barging in on you like this, but there's a lot of us today. Are you by yourself?'

'Yes. I generally walk alone.'

'I see the attraction,' says Laurence as a burst of laughter erupts from his companions at the next table. 'Sometimes I crave the peace and quiet of solitude. You local?'

'Not far away, for the time being. I'm staying with my sister. The arrangement's become rather more permanent than either of us intended. You?'

'About thirty miles, as the crow flies. You walk a lot?'

'Once or twice a week, if the weather's kind.'

Someone hands Laurence a bottle of dark ale, which he pours carefully into a glass.

He holds up his glass to Wilf. 'Cheers. Here's to fellow travellers.'

For a while they chat about favourite routes they've walked, places they've ambitions to go.

Before long, Laurence's group is ready to move on and they call him to join them.

'I'll catch you up,' he calls after them.

When he sees Margot arrive a few minutes later, Wilf finds himself sorry to be leaving.

As he picks up his backpack, Laurence says, 'Listen, maybe we could walk together sometime, get a bite of lunch after. If you'd like.'

'I would.'

'Is there somewhere I can ring you?' Laurence grabs a beermat and searches his pockets for a pen, writing down Margot's number as Wilf recites it.

'Maybe we could think about Monday?' suggests Laurence. 'Weather permitting.'

'I don't mind a bit of rain,' smiles Wilf. 'I've weathered more than my share of stormy weather recently.'

As he climbs into the car, Margot's eyes are wide with curiosity. 'Who was that? He was very handsome.'

'That was Laurence,' says Wilf. 'And, you know, I thought he was rather handsome too.'

FIFTY-ONE

Gabby's knock is tentative.

'Hey, Dad.'

Her father is in what's grandly known as his study – a cramped bedroom that years ago would have been referred to as a boxroom and nowadays estate agents would call a single bedroom, even though the smallest child's bed would leave no space for any other furniture at all.

But her father's made the most of it by fitting it out almost floor to ceiling with shelves, filled with reference books and his collection of vintage die-cast toy cars. As long as Gabby can remember, this collection has been Owen Laflin's passion, especially its highlights from the 1930s and '40s, including several originally owned by his own father as a boy. All have been painstakingly restored – wheels straightened, paint glossed – so every one of them looks fresh out of the box.

Under the narrow window is the workbench where he keeps his modelling tools, and propped up on the windowsill where he is the only person who regularly sees them are what he refers to as his past-life memorials, framed degrees and diplomas certifying his qualifications as an engineer.

He turns round from his bench, and smiles. Gabby can't help noticing how every time she sees him there are more lines in his face.

'Come in, come in. Pull up a chair.'

She does so, and as she sits he continues with what he's doing, frowning in concentration.

'What are you working on?' asks Gabby.

'I'm trying to get this old hairdryer of your mother's going again, though I'm afraid it's on its last legs. It's not the first time I've repaired it. Obviously I didn't do a very good job last time.'

'It's just a hairdryer, Dad. Bin it, tell her to get a new one.'

He regards her over the top of his glasses. 'Well, I could just send it to landfill, but I can think of a dozen reasons why I shouldn't. Anyway, I like a challenge, even if this one has probably got me beaten. If it needs new parts, that's when it makes no sense either economically or in the hours it would cost me hunting down what I need. But don't you think we throw too much away, that we're addicted to new stuff? Do you know, there are young people in Japan who own nothing that won't fit in a single suitcase? Imagine that.'

Gabby laughs. 'Says the man sitting in a roomful of battered old toy cars. I'd love to be like that, owning nothing.'

'Except for your twenty pairs of shoes.'

'Shoes don't count. They're a necessity, not a luxury.'

'If you say so. What can I do for you?'

Gabby reaches out for one of the little cars and turns it in her hands, admiring the detail and care in the paintwork, the intricacy of the tiny seats and steering wheel inside. 'I've got myself in a difficult place.'

Her father's eyebrows rise. 'Again? Seems to be becoming a habit.'

'This time it's different.'

Owen puts down the hairdryer and gives her his full attention. 'Tell me.'

'People do bad things to each other sometimes, don't they?'

Her father sits back in his chair. 'That's a very jaded view. I can honestly say I've never deliberately done anything bad to anyone, and I don't believe your mother has, either. Of course there are plenty of bad people in the world, but there are plenty too who do bad things because they're backed into difficult corners. Who are we talking about here?'

'Frank and Dee Cutter. The parents of that girl who was killed.'

'Natalie.'

'Yes. Turns out her father had a second daughter he never told Natalie or her mother about. Which might be understandable, I suppose, though a bit unfair on the second daughter as well, because he told her he was divorced and had no other children. Why would you do that?'

'Simple answer? For a quiet life. Men will move heaven and earth for that, you know, to avoid confrontation with the woman they live with.'

'Are we such dragons, then?'

He considers. 'I think women take their responsibilities more seriously. A lot of men live for playtime, whether that's on the football pitch or the golf course or shut away like me in the spare room playing with toy cars. Life would be much easier if we could all be a bit more like each other, if men could be more focused on the work which needs doing, and women could learn to relax a bit more, go with the flow.'

'Smell the roses.'

'Exactly.'

'He told his wife that he'd put everything on the table, but he didn't tell her he's going to his daughter's wedding. He's giving her away.'

'That's quite an omission.'

'Someone's going to get hurt, aren't they?'

'Almost certainly. His daughter if he doesn't turn up and his wife if he does. Tricky.'

'I thought I should tell Dee, but I couldn't quite persuade myself to light that particular blue touch paper.'

'It wasn't your place. You're learning the art of diplomacy, and not a moment too soon, if I may say so.'

'What do you think his wife will say when she finds out?'

'Is she invited to the wedding?'

'I don't know.'

'Regardless, the man sounds like a serial liar.'

'That's what I thought. And, that being the case, if he'll tell lies like that to his family, what're the chances he's telling the truth about whether he killed Natalie or not?'

'I'd say it's odds on he isn't. But if he did kill her, that would be terrible and unnatural. What father would do such a thing?'

'That's what I was thinking.' Gabby sighs. 'After that business with Wilfred Hickling, I decided I'm only going to do good works. I know it sounds twee, but I thought I could make reparations to him somehow – only karmically, I realise – by helping others. That's why I decided I'd help Dee keep Frank out of jail, for her sake and for their granddaughter's.'

'Ruby.'

'Ruby, yes.'

'It's the kids who suffer so badly in these kinds of affairs. The adults have every right to ruin their own lives, but when it impinges on the children, that's different. I hate to say it, Gabby, but the children of the most notorious killers can be pursued for decades by your colleagues looking for a story.'

'I know. And I'm trying not to be that person any more. Hear me out, though. I don't think Frank did it. I think I've inadvertently cracked the case, and I don't think it's him after all.'

'You've cracked the case? Really? I'm all ears.'

'A while back, when I was over-focused on Hickling, I went to interview one of Natalie's friends, Sarah Osgood. Natalie was a very good-looking woman, and I think her friendship with Sarah was one of those weird ones, where a beauty pairs with a beast to make themselves shine even brighter, because Sarah and Natalie were chalk and cheese. Sarah's overweight and unattractive, couple of kids and no future outside Wickney Fen. It was plain to see at the time – though I didn't really register the fact or give it much weight – that Sarah had a massive crush on Natalie's husband, Justin. I wasn't looking for that because I was – rightly or wrongly – after dirt on Hickling. Now I'm certain Sarah wants Justin for herself. So what was to stop her being the one who pushed Natalie down those stairs, in a fight over him, a catfight? The police talked to her at the time, looking for background on Natalie, looking for a guilty man. But why couldn't it have been Sarah? She's the kind of woman you'd never notice, unattractive and uninteresting. The police were focused on the untraced white van, but what if the van's got nothing to do with it? Sarah could have put the baby in the buggy and walked round there. Hardly anybody goes down Stickpike Lane, and she might have been totally unobserved. And if anyone did see her, she'd just be a young mum out for a walk round to her mate's, totally under the radar.'

Owen frowns. 'It's a plausible theory, but where's your evidence?'

Gabby hesitates for a second, knowing this is a moment of commitment. 'I think it's on the back seat of my car.'

Her father looks shocked. 'What are you talking about? Gabby, what have you done?'

Gabby raises her hands in her defence. 'Hear me out. I did a good thing, not a bad thing. I went to talk to her again, going over old ground really, just to see if there was anything else which might help Frank's case because, to be honest, I was getting desperate. We were talking and I mentioned Natalie's missing laptop, and I saw something in her – call it experience in talking to serial liars – which made it clear she wasn't telling the truth. So I wound her up a bit, turned the screws. Don't judge me, Dad. I told her she was on a list for a full police house search, that they might be round at any minute. It was a long shot, but it shook her up. Five minutes later, when she thought I was well on my way, she dumped a laptop in the bin outside her house.'

'You're not serious.'

'Deadly serious.'

'What did you do?'

'I did what any citizen would do. I ran over and grabbed it.'

'So you're holding potential evidence in a murder case?'

'The thing is, though, I've come full circle, haven't I? There may be incriminating stuff on the laptop, or the laptop itself may be evidence that Sarah killed Natalie. But Sarah's a mum with two young kids. I set out to help Dee and especially Ruby, but what I've found might ruin the lives of two children rather than one. What if Ruby's grandpa's innocent but Sarah becomes a notorious killer and her kids end up in care? I wanted to make things better, but whatever happens now, looks like I'll mess up somebody's life. Have you ever wished you could turn back time and never get involved?'

'Rarely,' says Owen. 'But I'm not bull-headed old you, Polly.' From downstairs, the old dining-room clock striking the half hour reminds Gabby of easier, simpler times, when she was too young to be worried by life's complexities. 'It's not easy I know, but try not to think too much about what happens next. All you can do is take the laptop to the police and explain how you came by it. That's it. And remember, nothing you've done makes any difference to who's guilty or innocent, only to how quickly the case is proven.'

'Those poor children.' Gabby looks stricken. 'They're too young to understand.'

'Life is full of tragedies,' says Owen, 'and undeniably that's hard. The gods roll the dice, honey, not us. You'll have to think of it like you said, as karma.'

Gabby nods.

'When you go to the police station, I can drive you over there, if it will help.'

'Thanks, Dad. I'd appreciate that.'

'And don't be too hard on yourself.'

'It's hard not to be,' says Gabby. 'I thought I wanted to get to the truth, but now I feel really bad about what I've found. I should just have said no to Dee in the first place.'

'But that's never been your way, has it, daughter of mine?'

Gabby manages a weak smile. 'No, Dad. That's never been my way.'

FIFTY-TWO

At the moment, work is the only thing keeping Frank sane.

And that's despite Jerry's out-of-character geniality, expressed in a manly slap on the shoulder every time he wanders by, and upbeat chats about football, even though Jerry's a rugby man at heart. Frank's becoming suspicious of the constant cheerfulness, suspecting it's masking secrecy and dishonesty. If Jerry's hiding a P45 in his pocket or putting together a package for Frank's very early retirement, Frank won't be surprised.

Despite Jerry's behaviour, Frank's workstation is a place of calm, where he can focus his overtired brain on the mechanisms laid out before him. Timepieces are predictable, logical, usually repairable. If only the same could be said of his relationship with Dee, and now Bethan too.

Today he's working on a Tissot lady's watch: an 18-carat yellow-gold casing, a diamond surround on the face, date of first purchase 1959. In monetary terms, the value isn't high, but a family is paying for its repair following the death of its owner, and Frank thinks – as he always does in these instances – how much better it would have been to have had it repaired while its owner was still here to wear and enjoy it. Kept in the dark, watches – like people – lose their lustre.

The silence and concentration are healing. Placing a loupe in his eye, he bends into the brilliance of his spotlight, removes one of the minute cogs and puts it to one side.

His phone's on silent to prevent interruptions, but it's vibrating with an incoming call.

Removing the loupe, he picks it up.

Peasgood.

'Hello?'

'Robert Peasgood here, about your case.' Like Frank doesn't know why he'd be calling.

'Yes?'

'Just to let you know.' Peasgood sounds as if he's at a railway station: Frank can hear a tannoy announcement in the background. 'As you're aware, the police have had forensics look at your phone. Your lost phone, that is. I'm surprised they've got round to it so quickly, but it's no bad thing, considering what they've found may somewhat weaken their case against you.'

Frank's waiting, breath bated, for him to go on, but Peasgood falls silent, and Frank wonders if the connection's been broken.

'Hello?'

'Yes, I'm still here,' says Peasgood. 'Just finding a spot where I won't be overheard. So, they've managed to recover data from the phone – amazing what they can do these days, absolutely mind-boggling – and what they haven't been able to do is confirm the messages their witness claims were exchanged with you at Turle's Cottage on the Friday.'

'The messages I said I didn't send.'

'Indeed.'

'So their witness was lying, not me.'

'As things stand, that's the conclusion we have to draw.'

Frank feels a lightness in his head, and weakness in his legs which make him glad he's sitting down.

'I told them that. I told them, and they didn't believe me.'

'They had superficial evidence, I believe, from the witness's phone.'

Frank shakes his head. 'How can they have evidence if the messages weren't sent? And what do you mean, superficial?'

'Anything can be faked these days, Mr Cutter. The things I've seen, you'd be surprised. There are apps which will prove to the casual observer that you made contact even when you didn't, most often used I believe to soothe the wrath of neglected wives and girlfriends. But open to misuse, of course. Maybe that's what's happened here. You can fake messages on one phone, but of course there'll be no reciprocal record on the other.'

'So what will they do?'

'No doubt they'll go back to their witness and have a closer look at their data.'

Frank is suddenly angry. 'Who is this witness putting me through this? Who is it?'

'I don't have that information, I'm afraid.'

'Well, as my lawyer, I want you to get that information, and I'll be paying them a personal visit.'

'I strongly advise you against that, Mr Cutter. Interfering with witnesses is a criminal offence. Anyway, I thought I should let you know. Perhaps we should meet next week, see how things are progressing. I have to go now – my train is arriving.'

Frank hangs up and slams his fist on the desk.

In his usual silent manner, Jerry has appeared behind him.

'Everything all right, Frank?' he asks.

'A bit of good news, that's all.'

'Anything you'd like to share?'

'Not really.'

'Well.' Jerry takes off his glasses, peers at the lenses, rubs one of them on his shirt and puts the glasses back on. 'It's a day for good news all round, then. I've had a call from the police and they think they've got the gang behind our break-in. Arrests were made this morning, so I think we'll all sleep sounder in our beds.'

'Did they say who they were?' asks Frank.

'Not so far. I expect I'll have to go to court, give evidence. One more thing to worry about, but I'm thinking perhaps we won't have to move premises after all. That, of course, is a huge plus. How are you getting on with the Tissot?'

'Almost done,' says Frank. 'Should be ready by the end of the day.'

'Excellent. Well, I thought you'd be pleased to know that our unwelcome visitors are in the right hands.'

You have no idea, thinks Frank, as Jerry walks away.

FIFTY-THREE

Gabby can remember, when she was still at primary school, how proud her father was of his old Volvo when it was brand new. These days, the car's looking its age, the bumpers scraped in places, the hubcaps rusted, and the burgundy paint has long ago lost its gloss.

But inside, it still smells of the once-luxurious leather seats, now sagging and scuffed and in need of replacement. Owen turns the key in the ignition but the engine's reluctant to fire. When eventually it starts, it's with shuddering hesitation, like an old beast reluctantly prodded awake.

'Don't you think it's time for a new car, Dad?' asks Gabby.

Revving the engine to keep it running, her father smiles.

'Not at all. Plenty of miles left in the old girl yet. You can't just be getting rid of stuff because it's got the patina of age. Look at me, I'm fraying at the edges. You wouldn't throw me out just for that, would you?'

Gabby doesn't need to look at him to know what he means about fraying. Every day she notices the changes in him: how his hair has changed from distinguished grey at the temples to almost white; the droop of his eyelids and the heavy lines around his mouth; the stoop in the once-strong shoulders he carried her on when she was small.

Everything, everyone changes.

In contrast to her usual brash confidence, on the way to the police station she's feeling the flutter of nerves. She's grateful he's driving. While he's thinking about what route to take into the city and where best to park, she's free to gaze out of the window and think about not much at all.

Her father, bless him, is full of chat she's too keyed up to want to hear, but she responds out of politeness. Just before midday, the city's arterial roads are busy, and crawling through the inner suburbs, she has plenty of time to look around. Everything's changing around here too, and not all those changes are for the better. The gutters and pavements are scattered with litter no one's bothered to pick up, and many of the houses have paved over gardens for the parking of multiple cars. A pub she has great memories of – where she and Mona and the rest of the gang used to drink sickly alcopops – has been turned into a supermarket.

She'd like to see Mona again, and Isla and Becky. Time she gave Mona a call.

A place that used to sell discount tyres has become a sig-nage business, advertising vinyl wrapping for cars. On the forecourt, an old-model Renault has had the treatment and looks amazing in bright yellow with the company's logo down both sides.

'You know what, Dad,' Gabby says absently, 'that's what you need for the Volvo. Get it pimped like that. I'd get mine done, if I had the cash.'

Her father laughs. 'It'd do wonders for the paintwork, but

it wouldn't go far to fixing the carburettor and the oil pump. Anyway, that sounds like a secondhand car salesman's dream to me, covering the flaws and doubling the price.'

'I think it's cool,' says Gabby. They stop at lights, and a driving-school car pulls up alongside them, wrapped in red and splashed with cartoon road signs. 'There you go, like that. You could make your boring old car look really funky.'

'Looks great, I have to concede,' says her father as the lights change. 'I'll park in the multistorey, but I can drop you before I go in there, give you a shorter walk. I've a couple of errands to run while you're occupied, sorting something out for your mother's and my anniversary. Thirty years, we'll have been married. Our pearl anniversary, so I thought a necklace might be nice, if I can find something affordable. Here OK?'

He's offering to pull over right outside the police station, and she wants to decline, to get out instead at the far end of the block and walk back, give herself time to plan what to say.

But he's already stopped.

'I feel so bad about this, Dad.' She faces him, appealing. 'I feel such a heel giving them her name, wrecking those kids' lives. Wouldn't it be better to leave it anonymously, let them figure it out for themselves?'

Owen raises his eyebrows in stern disapproval.

'OK,' she says, 'I'm going.'

'Do the right thing, Gabby,' he says, handing her the carrier-bag-wrapped laptop. 'Be a good citizen and tell them everything you know.'

Gabby can remember a time – not so long ago – when police stations were open to the public 24/7, but she knows from her time with the *Herald* that those days are gone. The central police station's inquiry office keeps the same office hours as an accountant or bank, nine to five Monday through Friday, half day on Saturday, closed on Sunday. If you're running from a rapist or being robbed at knifepoint outside those hours, there's no point in coming here.

The building's locked up like a fortress, the old front door sealed permanently shut against the citizens, the street on the building's west side closed to all but police vehicles. Are they really so in fear of drive-bys? Do the men and women wearing that uniform really feel themselves so at risk? In all her time as a journalist, she can't recall a single incident of an attack on a police station, and yet a solid steel fence encloses the car park (there's no public parking available, she notices). Such levels of defensive precaution might reflect irrational levels of paranoia, but when you deal night and day with the worst of humanity, maybe it's excusable that your world view's slightly skewed.

She finds a public entrance and is buzzed in. The desk sergeant – safe behind Plexiglas – is offhand. She asks for Detective Thomas Hines.

The sergeant knows the name. 'What's this regarding?'

Gabby finds herself blushing, as if she's being melodramatic. 'I have some evidence in the Natalie Cutter murder.'

The sergeant nods, and moving with a languor suggesting he's heard it all before – probably several times already today – he picks up a phone, dials and speaks into it with his back to Gabby.

The call is short. He hangs up and says, 'Have a seat.'

Twenty minutes go by before one of the men she saw in

the pub the night she met Glen appears. Plainly he has no memory of her, and she decides it would be better not to mention the fact they've spoken before.

He gives a tight, professional smile. 'Can I help you?'

She stands, and holds up the carrier bag. 'I thought you might be interested in this. I think it's Natalie Cutter's laptop.'

Naively, Gabby had expected Hines to take the laptop, thank her profusely and walk away.

But he makes no move to take the package from her.

'Can I ask your name?' he asks.

'Gabby Laflin. I used to work for the *Herald*.'

'Where did you find this laptop, Gabby?'

His use of her first name feels patronising, and without her permission, inappropriate. She feels she's already been judged and found guilty of wasting his time.

'Long story. Shall I just leave it with you?'

He considers. 'Why don't you and I go and have a chat?'

An hour and a half later, she meets her father at the Sanctuary café in St Alban's Church. She's always liked this place. Isn't using the church as a gathering place better than keeping it locked and silent six days a week?

Even though it's warm outside, the church is cool. Her father's already here, sitting at a table covered in a gingham cloth, drinking tea from a mismatched cup and saucer and finishing what had been a large piece of date-and-walnut cake.

She leaves her handbag with him and goes to the counter to order, feeling the need to up her blood sugar, choosing black coffee and chocolate-fudge cake.

As she sits, her father asks, 'How did it go?'

Gabby rubs her temples, hoping to fend off a developing headache. 'Honestly? I felt a bit of an idiot. They took down some details, but the CID bloke was at pains to say that well-meaning members of the public frequently bring them items they believe are evidence when they're not. I don't think for one minute he believed it was Natalie's laptop, but he's going to have someone look into it. So there you go, that's me – officially well-meaning.'

'Ah.' Her father lowers his head. 'Well, you can always blame me. I pushed you into it.'

'No, you didn't, Dad. I explained to him why I thought Sarah was a candidate for the assault on Natalie, but he said they'd already spoken to her and ruled her out of their inquiries. I told him I thought her feelings for Justin might give her a motive for wanting Natalie off the scene, but he didn't make much of that. I think they're too used to people beating each other up for a shot of heroin to have much experience of crimes of passion. I should have suggested he might read more French novels.'

'Maybe they're just too plodding to think in those terms.'

'Maybe. Anyway, I've done my bit. He said they'd be in touch, but I won't hold my breath. How did you get on?'

Her father reaches into his jacket pocket. 'I got this, which I hope she'll like.' He opens a jeweller's box, where a string of glowing pearls lies on deep-blue velvet. 'It's antique, from the 1930s. Do you think she'll like it?'

Gabby reaches across the table and squeezes her father's hand. 'More men should be like you, Dad. It's really beautiful. I'm sure she'll love it.'

FIFTY-FOUR

Wilf is standing in front of the full-length mirror in Margot's bedroom, surprised to see that the man he's become – so different inside to the man he used to be – on the outside isn't changed at all.

'Do I look all right?' he asks.

Wilf's voice has an edge of nervousness and self-doubt, and Margot can see why. His choices from his ultra-conservative wardrobe – the moss-green sweater, the beige trousers, the sober tie and the well-polished, traditional brown shoes – suit a man who doesn't want to be seen, a man in hiding.

Wilf has had two outings with Laurence, long hikes through the Dales, a sandwich and a pint at the end.

Today is different. Today could be the move from walking companions to something more.

Margot stands behind his shoulder. 'You look lovely, dear. Very handsome.'

'But I don't look very appealing, do I? I'm afraid I look rather dull.'

'That's just first-date nerves. If he's anything about him, he'll see past the exterior and fall madly in love with the man inside.'

'I am nervous,' admits Wilf. 'My tummy's all aflutter with butterflies. Isn't that ridiculous, at my age? But I feel as if this isn't just a first date with Laurence, it's my first date as me, as I really am. I don't want to go full-on Michael Portillo, but I don't want to put him off by arriving dressed like a retired accountant.'

'You could do with a bit more colour,' admits Margot.

'What time is it?'

'Stop asking me the time. You've plenty of time. You don't need to leave for another forty minutes.' Margot considers, smiles. 'I have an idea. You wait here.'

While she's gone, Wilf crosses to the window and looks out on the view he's become accustomed to. These hills are easier to love than the cultivated, featureless fens, and he's been content to stay here. But the weeks have turned into months, and, though she denies it, Margot must be ready to have him gone. He really should be thinking about going home.

If home it still is.

From downstairs, Margot calls to him. In the living room, she's thrown a pile of clothes on the sofa.

'I got these from Evelyn two doors down. Her Tom's a snappy dresser, but he's put on a load of weight since he retired and he's got a wardrobe full of clothes he's barely worn. Have a look, see if there's anything you like. What about this?'

She holds up a tan jacket with a cobalt-blue lining, and he touches the sleeve. The cloth is soft, feels expensive, but the style is too flashy, in Wilf's view, for a man of his age.

'I don't think it's really me.'

'It may not be the old you,' says Margot, 'but it can't hurt, can it, to try it on? And there's this.' She shows him a casual needlecord shirt with silvered buttons. 'You could wear this, and not need a tie.'

'I always wear a tie.'

'You always used to wear a tie. But Laurence has no expectations of you, Wilf. He doesn't know what you've always done in the past. Be bold, and let him think you're a man who only wears a tie on formal occasions. You're going out to lunch, not to a funeral.'

Upstairs, in front of the mirror, Wilf sees a man in well-cut jacket and shirt who looks as if he's going out to enjoy himself.

'You look so dashing,' smiles Margot. 'Unrecognisable.'

'That's good to know.' Wilf feels the pricking of tears. 'You've been so kind to me. I couldn't have asked for a better sister. But I've been thinking, I really should go home. I've trespassed on your good nature quite long enough.'

'You're always welcome here, you know that. And let's not talk about that now. Now is the time for you to get out there and knock him dead.'

'I think I'm a little past that.'

'Nonsense. A wink and a smile, and he'll fall at your feet. Let me give you a kiss for luck, and you go and have a fabulous time.'

According to Laurence, Bradley's is the best restaurant in the county.

Approaching the reception desk, Wilf can't help wishing he'd worn a suit. Without a tie, he feels underdressed.

But as the waiter shows him to their table, he starts to relax. Laurence is already there, drumming his fingers on the table, as if he might be nervous too. When he sees Wilf, his smile is like sunshine breaking through clouds. He gets to his feet. He isn't wearing a suit, or a tie. He's wearing a jacket and open-necked shirt, just like Wilf.

Margot truly is a marvel.

The waiter turns back to the kitchen, and Wilf and Laurence embrace.

'I'm so glad to see you,' says Laurence.

They sit, a white cloth laid with silver and crystal between them.

'It's a lovely place,' says Wilf, looking out on a garden of white roses.

'It's romantic,' says Laurence. 'Perfect for this special occasion.'

Reaching out, he squeezes Wilf's hand.

FIFTY-FIVE

The knock at Sarah's door annoys her. Lizzie's got a cold and the morning's been filled with tears and clinginess not resolved even by an extra dose of Calpol. Finally, though, she's fallen into an uneasy sleep, covered by a blanket next to Sarah on the sofa.

Sarah's engrossed in her phone, and her first thought is to ignore the knock and hope whoever it is just goes away, but it comes again, more insistently, more confident than anyone selling something. She wonders if it could be someone from the council come to do something about the rats, which seem to be everywhere since they started operating the grain-dryer at the farm two fields away.

Anyway, the knocking's disturbing Lizzie, who's moving in her sleep as if she might be about to wake. Sarah puts down her phone, hauls herself off the couch and heads down the hall to open the door.

There are two women outside. One of them is familiar, though difficult to place. She's smiling and holding up an ID card.

'Hi, Sarah,' she says, with what Sarah regards as unwarranted familiarity. 'Janet Desmond, Norfolk CID. We spoke just after Natalie died.'

Did they? Sarah isn't sure. Those early days after Natalie's death are a blur.

As Desmond goes on, Sarah's heart sinks.

'Can we come in for a moment?' asks the detective. 'Some new information has come to light in Natalie's case, and we have a few more questions we'd like to ask.'

'It's not a good time,' says Sarah. 'My little girl isn't very well.'

Desmond's smile this time is different, more practised, less honest.

'Maybe you can get someone to come and sit with her, then. If it's not convenient here, we're quite happy to talk to you at the station.'

Sarah blinks.

'Whichever you'd prefer,' says Desmond, not quite kindly.

'You'd better come in, then,' says Sarah.

It's been a while since Justin's seen Sarah, but the seasons don't change her; she lumbers from month to month in the same lumpen way, never changing her hair or even, really, her clothes. She is, he thinks, one of life's punchbags, always indignant at her perceived problems but too stupid – or lazy – to step out of range of the fist coming her way.

She's standing in the workshop doorway, pasty and lank-haired, hands in the pocket of the tartan coat Natalie always used to call her dog blanket. For years, for Natalie's sake, Justin tried to like Sarah, but something about her makes it hard.

Will and Marcus are at the back of the workshop, putting together the frames for a summerhouse's windows. They turn and nod at Sarah, then go straight back to their work, not even interested enough in her to make a joke between themselves.

Justin switches off the sander he's been using and produces a smile. 'All right?'

She glances at the two men behind him. 'Can I talk to you a minute? In private?'

He hesitates, weighing up the inconvenience of breaking off what he's doing now against the possibly bigger inconvenience of a meeting with her later, which might involve a trip to her house, or even a drink somewhere.

He lays down the sander and leads her outside, and as she follows him, she's already talking. 'I can't stay long. My neighbour's looking after Lizzie, and I have to pick Riley up in an hour. Well, you know that, you have to get Ruby too. Your mum said you were in the workshop. It's lucky I caught you.'

He leads her round the far side of the van where his mother won't be able to see them, even if she peers through the tiny kitchen window at the back of the office. Unless she's bought herself a periscope, which he frankly wouldn't put past her.

'What's up?' he asks. 'I've got to get on.' For the first time, he notices she's close to tears. 'Sarah? What's the matter?'

He hates to see a woman cry. Instinct tells him to put an arm round her, make her feel better, but he holds back, afraid of being misconstrued, of her making it something it's definitely not.

But suddenly there are floods of tears, and she's standing there weeping with her face in her hands as if the dam of all the sadness she's always carried is finally breached, shattering her heart into too many pieces ever to be whole again. What else can he do? He steps forward and draws her to his chest; he does it as he would for an upset child, or for his mother, if she were ever so weak as to cry, but as he feared she takes it as so much more, and throws her plump arms around him.

She's talking into his hoody so he can't hear her clearly, but the gist is plain, even though she's started in the middle.

'When she said that the police were coming, I didn't know what to do. I didn't want to ring you or message you because they trace everything, don't they, and you told me it wasn't safe to get in touch. I had to think quickly. I didn't know when they'd be here. And I know you wanted me to take care of it, but how would I have explained it if they'd found it in the house? I thought I was doing the right thing, and it seemed like a God-sent opportunity because it was Wednesday afternoon, and that's when the binmen come. I thought it was better if neither of us had it, then there was nothing to be found. So I put it in the rubbish, and they came and emptied it and I thought that would be that, but I didn't dare ring you to tell you because you told me not to.'

Her grip on him is tight, but he pulls her arms from his sides and holds her at length.

'Stop crying, Sarah, and tell me what you mean. What did you put in the rubbish?'

'The laptop. I put Natalie's laptop in the rubbish.'

He lets her go and rubs his face.

'When? When did you do this?'

'Last week. They empty the bins on Wednesdays.'

'So it's gone?'

'Yes.'

'OK. Well. Maybe it's for the best.'

'But that's just it.' Sarah wipes a mess of snot and tears on her sleeve. 'They've got it. I don't know how they got it. I saw the lorry come and empty the bin, I watched them do it from the kitchen. I didn't give it to them, Justin, I swear. I wanted to help you. You know I wouldn't do that.'

Justin's face darkens. 'Who's got it?'

'The police. They came to the house today. I had to let them in, and anyway I didn't see the harm. I didn't know what they wanted – how could I? I thought they'd send a search team, not just two women, so I let them in. And they didn't need to do a search because they already knew it'd been at my house. They said there were fingerprints and DNA, which would match mine, and I knew they were right. They said I might be arrested and I was scared, and it just slipped out.'

'What slipped out?'

'I said you asked me to look after it.'

'Fuck!' Justin slams the van's side. 'Fuck, Sarah! What were you thinking?'

'I didn't know what else to do. I'm sorry, Justin, I didn't mean to let you down. Anyway, after they left I came here straight away. I wanted you to know that they were coming.'

'When?'

'I don't know. I didn't ask. They probably won't take long. But it'll be all right, won't it? You just have to tell them the truth, about hiding those pictures. You did it for the best, and they'll understand, I know they will. You're not mad at me, are you? I couldn't bear it if you were.'

Justin looks at her. He shakes his head. 'I'm not angry with you, Sarah, I'm angry with myself. I shouldn't have asked you to do that, and I'm sorry. But you have to go now.'

'What are you going to do?'

'Nothing. Wait for them to turn up. Like you say, I had my own good reasons.'

FIFTY-SIX

Gabby's driving towards Wickney Fen when her phone rings.

Dee.

Gabby considers letting it ring. She hasn't spoken to Dee in a couple of weeks, and she hasn't told her about the laptop because she's still not sure she hasn't made a total fool of herself. She's had no contact from Norfolk Police to update her on whether it's evidence of value. She's tried ringing Hines to ask what's going on, but all she gets is his uninterested colleagues telling her he's out of the office. In other words, that it's in their hands now and nothing to do with her.

But Dee doesn't deserve the same kind of treatment.

Gabby presses the dashboard answer button. 'Hey, how's things?'

'Not bad, actually.' In fact, Dee does sound quite bright; there's an optimism in her voice Gabby can't recall hearing before. 'Do you have a couple of minutes?'

'Of course,' says Gabby. 'I'm driving, so all the time in the world.'

'We've had some news. Frank had a call from his lawyer. He says the police witness who claimed to have messaged Frank while he was at the cottage that Friday – they've found out that's not true. There weren't any messages.'

'Oh my God.' Gabby takes a moment to process the information, realising that she's surprised, and that until this moment she really believed Frank was guilty. 'That's – well, it's brilliant for Frank, but how?'

'They've been having a very close look at his phone, now they've dragged it out the river. And I don't quite understand how this is possible, but Frank's phone apparently doesn't show any messages to match the ones on the witness's phone. They were faked.'

'Faked? How? Why?'

'His lawyer's guessing to incriminate Frank.'

'Oh my God. But who's the witness? Who would do that?'

'We still don't know. The lawyer's asked for full disclosure, but he says it could turn this so-called witness into a suspect.'

'Who do you and Frank think it is?'

'We just don't know. We've racked our brains and can't come up with anyone.'

Gabby's thinking of Sarah sitting there on her phone, and of the laptop.

She takes a deep breath. 'I can.'

'Who?'

Gabby's approaching the turn to Wickney Fen. 'I think it might be Sarah.'

'Sarah? Why on earth would she do something like that?'

'Question is, is it possible it could be her? Could she have had Frank's mobile number?'

Gabby can almost hear Dee thinking. 'I doubt it. Why should she? No, hold on, wait a minute. Of course she does.

Frank's picked Ruby up from Sarah's a few times, when Sarah was minding her for Natalie. She must have had his number, mustn't she? But why would she want to incriminate Frank? What possible reason ... You're surely not thinking ... Natalie?'

'I don't know what I'm thinking, Dee. Let's wait and see what the lawyer comes back with. But it's got to have been someone who knew Frank well enough to have his personal mobile. Look, I'm sorry to do this to you, but I'm arriving at where I need to be. Can I ring you later on?'

'Don't forget,' says Dee, and hangs up.

The tall trees outside Aldern's yard stand like sentries. Gabby drives into the yard and parks in front of the office, but the office itself is empty, with no sign of Freda.

Round the back, the workshop is silent, the wide sliding doors across its front closed with a chain and padlock. Probably the men are out on a job – but the three vehicles she saw before are all lined up in a row: the big 4x4 truck, the silver Seat and the company van in its vinyl-wrap livery.

A van which might once have been white.

She can hear voices: a man, a woman and a little girl.

Justin is closing the boot of the Seat. Freda is crouched down beside Ruby, who's wearing jeans and a hoody and clutching a polar bear toy. Her thumb's in her mouth in a way far too childish for her age, and she looks as if she might have been crying.

Justin looks at Gabby warily, seemingly not remembering – again – who she is, though Freda looks like she remembers all too well and doesn't relish a repeat encounter.

Nobody is smiling.

'Sorry,' says Gabby. 'Is this a bad time? Justin, I came to ask you a personal favour. I can come back another time, if you like.'

Justin walks towards her as Freda opens the car door for Ruby to get in.

'How can I help?' asks Justin.

'I wanted to talk to you about a personal commission. When I was here, you showed me the heart within a heart you made for Natalie, and I thought it was so beautiful. My mum and dad have a special anniversary coming up, and I wondered if you'd make one for me to give them as a gift? I don't thank them enough for all they do – you know how it is – and I wanted to give them something personal they could cherish.'

'That's a nice idea, but I can't help at the moment. Really, I've just got too much on.'

Gabby nods her understanding. 'Well, it was worth an ask.'

Her reporter's instinct is kicking in. She sidesteps Justin and takes a few paces closer to Ruby and Freda.

'Hi, Ruby. Do you remember me? We met in the car park in town. Aren't you a lucky girl, having a day off school?'

'She's got a tummy ache, haven't you, sweetie?' Freda answers on Ruby's behalf. 'Daddy's taking you on a little trip to cheer you up, isn't he?'

'Daddy's having a day off too?' asks Gabby. 'Lucky Daddy.'

Justin's standing behind her, arms folded, obviously willing her to leave. 'Sorry you've had a wasted journey.'

'No need to worry about that,' says Gabby. 'A drive across the fens is always grounding, helps me think straight. Oh, and can I just ask you, the artwork on your van, I think it's brilliant. It's vinyl, right? Thing is, I've been thinking about getting my car done and I've been trying to find somewhere reasonably local – can I ask you who you used?'

Justin frowns. 'Actually, I don't know. Mum arranged all that, didn't you, Mum? She even drove it there and back. My mother will drive anything. She used to drive double-deckers, back in the day. The van disappeared one day and came back looking like that the next. Looks good, doesn't it? Where did you take it, Mum?'

He turns to look at Freda, but Freda is busying herself with Ruby in the back of the car and doesn't seem to be listening.

'Mum?'

Freda's head appears. 'What?'

'The van. Where did you get it done?'

Freda pulls a *How should I remember that?* face. 'Somewhere in town, I don't recall exactly.'

'In town?' asks Justin. 'Didn't you say it was out at Parson's Drove?'

Freda appears not to have heard and bends back down to mess with Ruby's seat belt.

'Well, we're not much help, are we?' says Justin. 'There's plenty of places around. I think they're all pretty much of a muchness.'

Gabby nods. 'OK. Well, I won't keep you. Enjoy your day off.'

'See you around, maybe,' says Justin, and he turns away.

FIFTY-SEVEN

'Can we stop here for a moment?' asks Wilf.

Margot pulls over at the side of the road, opposite the Spar. When she turns off the engine, the quiet of the place offers a sense of Wickney's past: the river's endless run, the ripple of a breeze through the trailing branches of the riverbank willows, the listlessness of a backwater community. But the place can't help but lift Wilf's heart: man and boy, it was his home.

His hand goes to the lever to open the door.

'Are you getting out?' asks Margot, alarmed. 'Do you think it's safe?'

'Only one way to find out.'

She watches him disappear inside the shop. He's changed a great deal, looks younger and – at last – happier, and she hopes he won't be recognised, that the inbred animosity that drove him from his home has lost momentum. She shares none of his nostalgia for Wickney; to her, it's always been a dreary, backward place, poisoned by tongues that would rather find fault in their neighbours than friendship. How Wilf stuck it out so long she'll never know.

He comes out of the shop and, holding up a bag of sliced

white bread, points down the bank-side. Sure of his footing in his new shoes, he makes his way down to the water's edge, where a small flock of swans are dabbling among the reeds on the far bank.

She hears him call to them.

The largest bird – a male, she assumes – raises its head, and makes a cry which rouses the others.

Raising itself up, the male spreads its huge wings and scutters across the water towards Wilf as if to attack him, the others close behind.

But Wilf is perfectly calm, unfastening the top of the bag, breaking slices of bread into small pieces and dropping them at his feet.

The birds scrabble from the water and waddle honking towards him, gobbling down the bread as if half starved. Wilf is surrounded by the creatures, who seem to be chattering as they eat, and a grinning Wilf talks back to them, chastising those which are too greedy, making sure the more hesitant get their share.

If such a thing is possible, the birds are welcoming him back. And Wilf's delighted to see them too.

As he should be.

For a long time, he has confessed to Margot, he felt they were his only friends in the world.

Stickpike Lane is changed only by the season, summer's brazen colours fading into a palette of ochre and rust.

As they approach Turle's Cottage, Wilf says, 'There's the scene of the awful drama.'

Unashamed of her curiosity, Margot slows the car as they

pass the frontage. The uncurtained windows look darkly inwards. The driveway is empty, and dandelions and couch grass have broken through the gravel.

'Looks empty to me,' she says. 'Which is hardly surprising. Who'd want to live there after what happened?'

'They'll find someone in the end,' says Wilf. 'But it looks so awfully run down. It makes me even more nervous about what we're going to find.'

The gate at Nine Brethren House is closed. Margot waits with the engine running while Wilf opens it, taking in his first view of the damage and neglect: the graffiti settled into the walls as if tattooed there; the garden overgrown and ruined, his once meticulously cut lawn a weed-infested tangle of knee-high grass. Choked by reeds, the pond is all but dry. The ducks, it seems, are gone.

Returning to the car, he speaks to Margot through the window. 'I can't go in there. It'll break my heart.'

'You have to do this, Wilf. If not now, when?'

She drives through the gate and parks the car. Wilf finds his keys, familiar yet strange, like objects remembered from a dream.

Margot touches his shoulder. 'Ready?'

'Thank you for coming with me.'

He turns the key in the door.

Inside, there's a fungal smell of damp, of dust and cobwebs, of rooms too long closed. The pile of post on the mat is mostly circulars, a couple of bills delivered before the mail redirection kicked in.

Wilf picks them up and sifts through them, finding nothing of interest but a folded sheet of paper.

The note is short, in a child's hand, expressing a hope that he and Mr Grimes are well, and an invitation to tea: if he'd care to come, please ring the number below. Signed *Ruby*, with a recognisable drawing of a cat.

He finds himself uncommonly moved.

'She must have thought me terribly rude not to have replied to her invitation,' he says to Margot.

'You can still respond. I'm sure she'll understand, when you explain you've been away.'

Wilf agrees, and puts the note in his pocket. 'Shall we proceed?'

He leads the way down the hall, into the lounge. On the walnut sideboard under the window, a half-brick lies with shards of glass from a shattered pane. Rain has come in; the sideboard has suffered water damage and may be beyond rescue.

Margot picks up a library book left open on the seat of an armchair when Wilf left and checks the date stamp. 'I think you're in trouble,' she says. 'It's so overdue you probably owe them thousands.'

Wilf sits down on the couch he remembers from when he was a boy. Now he's been away, he's come to understand that others don't live this way. Over the years, his shrine to those he loved became his own mausoleum.

'Why did I hold on to everything for so long?' he asks Margot. 'I thought all these things were precious. I see them now and I'm not so sure.'

Margot sits down beside him, and picking up a silver-framed photograph from a table at the end of the sofa, holds it up for Wilf to see: herself and Wilf and their father, waving from a boat on the Broads, their father shirtless and relaxed with his hand on the tiller.

'Happy days,' she says. 'Do you remember that holiday?'

Wilf smiles. 'Almost every moment of it. I think that was the only day it wasn't raining. My wellies were leaking, and I spent the whole time with feet so damp I kept telling Pa I was in danger of contracting trench foot.'

Margot places her hand across her heart. 'You see? You carry all the important stuff round with you, in here. All these things, they're just inanimate objects that can be ruined by rain or stolen or burned. If everything in this room disappeared tomorrow, you and I could still laugh over that holiday in Walsham.'

Wilf sighs. 'You're right, of course. Can I tell you something? I really don't want to come back here. I'd far rather be nearer to you, and to Laurence.'

'So sell it.'

'I feel I'd be letting them all down. They passed the legacy to me. There have been Hicklings at Nine Brethren House for two centuries.'

'Is it a legacy you want, though?'

'I was proud of it before. Now . . .' He looks around at the antique vases and solid furniture, at the worn Turkish carpet in front of the fireplace and the fading velvet curtains at the windows. 'Now I'm not sure it fits the new me.'

'Time to move on, then,' says Margot. 'Besides, I'm sure you don't want to spend the rest of your life with a view of Turle's Cottage.'

'No. That terrible thing, that poor woman. I still can't forgive myself for not going to help her, but how could I have known she was there? And yet, awful as that whole time was, miserable and hounded and humiliated as I felt, it gave me a shove, didn't it? I hate to think it, but I might have died stuck in this rut if that hadn't happened.'

'We'll find an estate agent then, get it listed.'

'I'll have to stay here a while, I suppose. There's so much to do, with the mess that's been left. The garden alone will take weeks.'

'We'll hire a couple of beefy blokes to do it, and sip tea while we watch them get hot and sweaty. And I'll help you, of course. Maybe Laurence would too. And I think the house would be grateful. It should be a family home again, full of noise and children and dogs.'

'Not just a stuffy old bachelor like me.'

'You're anything but stuffy, dear brother.'

'But what about all these things? What will I do with them?'

'You can choose what to do with them, one by one. Some things you'll take with you, and some you'll leave behind.'

'Out with the old and in with the new.'

'It's long overdue,' says Margot.

FIFTY-EIGHT

The thing about a wild-goose chase is, when you're on one, you never know it.

After her conversation with Justin, Gabby was convinced she was on to something with the Aldern's van being transformed from day-to-day white. If she can find out when that was done – if it was done after Natalie's death – could it rule Justin back in as a suspect?

Could it rule in Freda?

Justin has a solid alibi – Dee told her that. And beyond the natural antipathy which seems so often to exist in these relationships, what possible motive could Freda have for killing her daughter-in-law?

Shouldn't she just take the view now that it's none of her business, that she's done as much as can be expected to help Dee, and go on with her life, whatever it turns out to be?

When she leaves the Aldern's yard, she drives slowly back to Wickney, crossing the bridge over the river. On the far bank, she pulls over and parks, gets out of the car and wanders over the grass down to the water.

Watching the swans, she recalls taking a picture of Wilfred

Hickling as he was feeding them, stealthily and without asking his permission, as part of a plan to present him to the British public as a killer, whether he was guilty or not.

What had she been thinking?

Her debt isn't yet repaid.

In the Spar shop along the road, she buys a Mars Bar and a can of full-fat Coke – cheap, fast energy she might need. Back in her car, she googles car body shops in Parson's Drove. Unsurprisingly for such a back-of-beyond place, there's only one.

She sets up Google Maps for directions and follows the female robot voice down dead-straight roads, across flatlands she's never travelled but which look identical to those she knows well.

Parson's Drove is in many ways similar to Wickney, except smaller and noticeably more down-at-heel. The roof of the Wesleyan chapel at the village's perimeter has long ago collapsed and a twisted hawthorn has grown up where congregations used to gather. A weathered estate agent's board is nailed to what's left of the chapel door. A row of terraced cottages runs along the roadside, and at their end a scruffy pub advertises a meat raffle every Friday.

She finds the body shop on the far side of the village, inside a barn on the yard of a derelict farm. Parking her car beside a rusting tractor, she doesn't bother to lock it.

Inside the barn, it's as she expects: Radio 1 on full volume, the heavy smell of oil and the sharpness of fibreglass, three lads in dark overalls in a corner drinking tea, scrolling through phones. A red Nissan Micra is up on a ramp; off to the right, the front wing of a vintage Jaguar is masked up ready for spraying. But this is a traditional, low-tech operation. No sign of the kind of equipment she's looking for.

One of the youths spots her and nudges another, who reluctantly puts down his phone and saunters over.

'Help you?'

She gives him her brightest smile, thinking feminine wiles are probably the way to go.

She has a story ready. Fingers crossed it's plausible.

'I hope so. I'm Jenny Barker, I'm a freelance accountant working for Aldern's woodyard over in Wickney.'

A look crosses the youth's face, so she knows something she's said has resonated.

'Oh yeah?'

'I'm sorry to bother you, but I'm chasing up paperwork prior to filing a tax return, and I'm missing an invoice for some work done on a van.'

He's shaking his head.

'You do know Aldern's, I assume?'

He pulls a face. 'I know Justin; I was at school with him. But we've never done any work on his van. What sort of work?'

'A paint job. Signwriting, that sort of thing.'

He shakes his head more emphatically. 'Think you've got your wires crossed somewhere. We just do bodywork repairs. You know, filling and spraying, a bit of polishing out. Not really equipped for signwriting, as you can see.'

'I'm sorry,' says Gabby. 'Crossed wires for sure. Anywhere else round here I might try?'

Now his eyes narrow with suspicion. 'Seems to me you'd be best off asking Justin, if you're working for him.'

She flashes the bright smile again. 'Of course I will. Sorry to have bothered you.'

'No worries.'

Gabby walks away, hoping he's already forgetting her, but even without turning round she can feel his eyes still on her, watching her mistrustfully until she drives away.

The takeaway from Parson's Drove is that if she hasn't quite been lied to, she's been given a steer intended to put her off a scent. Justin's a local man and he must know that a farmyard body shop isn't capable of the kind of service she asked him about.

Which only makes her more determined to dig out what he doesn't want her to find.

That means a potentially long and time-consuming slog.

Happily, she's nothing else pressing.

Investigative journalism 101: make your list of targets and go through them, one by one. If your first list doesn't contain your target, widen your net and start again.

She's glad she's got the Mars Bar and the Coke.

Google lists five places in and around the city where the artwork on Justin's van could have been done.

By the time she's visited the first three, she's about ready to decide this is a waste of time and not her job. It would be far easier to tip off DS Hines, get a knock-back for her unwanted interference and walk away.

But her dogged nature won't let her do that.

Number four on the list is at the back end of one of the city's more notorious housing estates, an area that features more often than statistically it should in the local press.

This workshop doesn't appear prosperous but it is busy, with a collection of discontinued model BMWs on the forecourt, some with the kind of heavily tinted windows that scream drug dealer to most law-abiding citizens. Several teenage boys in baseball caps and Reebok trainers are sitting on the low wall surrounding the forecourt, drinking Red Bull out of coloured cans. As Gabby climbs from the car, they watch her silently and closely in a crude attempt at intimidation.

Gabby isn't fazed. As she walks by, she looks them in the eye one by one, calling out a friendly *Good afternoon.* Her politeness doesn't thaw their attitude, but at least she doesn't hear laughter after she's gone by.

Inside, the workshop is split off from the reception area by a long counter, and behind that a wall-to-wall glass screen. The seating in the customers' waiting area is empty. Loud music is bleeding through from the workshop, but not so loud that Gabby has to raise her voice to speak to the young man behind the counter.

'Help you?'

'I hope so.' Gabby tells her fake story for the fifth time, claiming to be Justin's accountant; by now she almost believes it herself. The young man listens attentively, and not questioning her credentials – why would he, after all? – moves across to a monitor and keyboard and asks for the date when the work was done.

Gabby's flying a kite here. She gives the date of Natalie's assault.

'Name?'

'Aldern Limited, in Wickney.'

He scrolls, pauses, scrolls again, shakes his head. 'Nothing in that name.' He scrolls again, frowns. 'Maybe this is it.'

Gabby's heart misses a beat.

He's pointing to the screen. 'It's not that exact date, though. It's three days later.'

Makes sense, thinks Gabby. *That would be the Monday after the assault, and probably the absolute earliest the job could be booked in.*

'Full-colour vinyl wrap and signage on a white Ford Transit long wheelbase van, reg number beginning DRT? But it's not in the company name. This invoice is in a personal name, F. Aldern.'

Freda.

'That's it,' says Gabby calmly. 'Thanks so much.'

'No problem,' says the young man cheerfully. 'Give me a minute and I'll run you off a copy of the invoice.'

In her car, Gabby stares a long time at the innocuous piece of paper in her hand, realising it could be the last piece in a hugely complex jigsaw and the final payment in her karmic account.

The problem's not hers to solve, but she has in mind her father's mantra: *Always do the right thing.*

Taking out her phone, she finds the number for DS Hines and dials.

FIFTY-NINE

Frank has been granted a deferment.

Supposedly, there's only one reason Dee's allowed him to remain in the house: Ruby. Dee concedes the child should not suffer more disruption in the form of Grandpa's disappearance from the haven Ruby loves; she and Frank are a crucial constant, a touchstone of dependability and routine. Whatever the cost to Dee, that must remain unchanged.

But the gulf reopened between them is no match in width or depth for what was there before Natalie's death, when they were within touching distance of divorce. Dee's long silences feel contrived, lacking the underpinning of real anger. Sometimes there are still small acts of kindness: Frank's favourite dish for dinner, an ironed shirt ready for work.

Frank's wondering if, like him, she fears a lonely future.

He's hoping that, in time, he might win her round.

In the meantime, Ruby's visits are a welcome distraction for them both.

'Can I have a drink?'

Frank's thinking Justin doesn't look at all well. Though it

hardly seems possible, he's lost weight; where he used to look gaunt, now he's skeletal.

'Course you can,' says Frank. 'I'll put the kettle on.'

'I mean a proper drink. Can you spare a drop of your single malt?'

Justin's request piques Frank's curiosity. Ruby's always Justin's top priority, and he insists it's his parental duty to be sober at all times when he has care of her. His own father was a drinker, so Frank's heard. Presumably Justin's learned hard lessons from his own upbringing.

Frank wanders into the kitchen and decides he'll have a drink too. He places a pair of tumblers on the counter. In the garden, Ruby's helping Dee refill the bird feeders, loading them up with peanuts and the niger seed which draws the chattering goldfinches Natalie used to love when she was small. A perfect bird for Natalie, he thinks now: colourful, flighty, gregarious. Ruby's become far more thoughtful than her mother ever was; her soulmate in the bird world would be some solitary creature, a kingfisher or an owl. Twilight is approaching, and in the fading light the physical likeness between Ruby and Natalie at that age is striking, and Frank feels the familiar tug of grief reminding him of what's been lost. He pushes the darkness away and pours the whisky.

In the lounge, he hands Justin a glass and sits back down in his armchair.

'Cheers.'

Justin's sitting forward on the sofa, his bony elbows resting on his thighs, his right foot – the perpetual teenager, always in trainers – tapping on the carpet.

Straight away, he downs half his drink.

'So what's up?' asks Frank. 'You don't look yourself. Is everything OK?'

Justin drops his head. 'I don't know how to say this. I've been wanting to talk to you for a long time, but I don't know where to start.'

Justin's nervousness is disquieting. Frank thinks of illness, of something wrong with Ruby. 'Try the beginning and take it from there.'

Justin fixes him with his eyes, and Frank sees his normal placidity has been displaced by the kind of volatility you might see in a drunk ready to smash up a room.

Something is very wrong.

'I need to ask you the biggest favour ever,' he says. 'I mean, like, so huge you could hardly even imagine I'd have the balls to think it, let alone actually ask you. But it's not for me, it's for Ruby, because she's the one that counts; she's the reason this whole thing happened. And I'm not saying I did right because I didn't, but I swear it was never my intention, I never meant for it to end up like it did. I needed her to listen, to see the wrong in what she was doing, but it all got out of hand. She never liked to be told what to do. But thousands of men have done worse than me and got away with it. I was just the unluckiest man alive, and that's the truth of it.'

Frank is bemused. 'Slow down, mate. What are you talking about?'

Justin holds up his glass for another drink. Normally Frank would talk him out of it, but he isn't sure what Justin will do if he refuses.

'If you have another, you sleep here on the sofa or you get a taxi, OK?' he says.

'Deal.'

With his refilled glass half emptied, Justin seems calmer, more together, or maybe the Dutch courage has kicked in.

'So come on,' says Frank, 'spill the beans. What's eating you?'

Justin takes a huge breath, exhales and says, 'I knew something wasn't right because of Ruby. When she came to me from that place, she wasn't the same. She was too quiet and clingy, following me round like a little ghost. She didn't want to sleep in her own bed. She had to have a light on. I got it out of her in the end, though, and I was mad as hell. Turned out Nat was having her boyfriends over from time to time, and when they were there Ruby had to go and play in the cupboard.'

Frank thinks he's misheard. 'Cupboard? What cupboard?'

'The cupboard under the stairs. Natalie tried to con her that it was some Harry Potter game she'd come up with, told her it was a den with chocolate and all the videos she wanted to watch. Truth is, I reckon, she put her in there so she wouldn't hear the noise she and the boyfriends were making. But Ruby was scared to death in there, all by herself in that dusty old hole. I can't believe anybody would do that to a child, any child, let alone their own kid.'

Frank can't believe it either. 'Are you sure about this, mate? It doesn't sound like something Nat would do. Not to Ruby.'

Justin looks despairing. 'Of course you wouldn't think so – she was your daughter, I get that. But I need you to believe me. You don't know the half of it, Frank. Not even the half of it.'

If there's more and it's worse, Frank doesn't want to hear it. Natalie was no angel, and he doesn't need any more dirt shovelled on her memory. He's the one who'll have to live with the knowledge, after all. And what's the point in that? Ignorance, in Frank's book, is bliss.

'Look, mate,' he says, 'why don't we just leave it? Don't speak ill of her now she's gone, eh?'

But Justin shakes his head. 'I don't want to tell you, but how else can I explain everything? If you don't know the worst of her, the rest of it makes no sense.'

The worst of her. His poor, maligned daughter, never what everyone thought she should be. A challenge to love, even for him.

But he did love her, to the depths of his soul.

And Justin is going on, regardless.

'What you have to ask yourself is, what was she doing living in that cottage? It just wasn't Nat, was it, cut off down some country lane away from all her mates? I thought when she said she was moving there she had something to hide. Then Ruby started acting all weird, not wanting to go home, asking if she could stay longer with me, but of course Nat was never one to make that easy. Even though she didn't want to make time for Ruby, she didn't want to do anything to make me happy either.' His whisky-red eyes fill with tears. 'You know what, though? Hand on heart, all I ever wanted was to put a smile on her face. She was the light in my world, and I had this mad idea that if I kept on trying, she'd come back to me, we'd all be a family again. Shows how wrong you can be, doesn't it? The more I tried to do nice things for her, the more she wanted to stick it to me. So I kept taking Ruby back there even when she didn't want to go, even though Nat didn't really want her, just to keep the peace. That's something I'll never forgive myself for. I should have stuck to my guns and kept her with me.'

'Where are you going with this, Justin?'

Like a pistol, Justin points a finger at Frank. 'To the Sunday the week before she died. I was behind on an order and I needed to spend a couple of hours in the workshop. Mum wasn't around, so I had no choice but to take Ruby back to the cottage a bit early. I tried ringing Nat to tell her I was coming, but she didn't pick up. I took Ruby anyway. Nat knew we were coming at some point, so I figured the latest boyfriend would already be on his way. And he was. When we got there, her car was in the drive, lights on in the house, all good, except she didn't answer the door. So we went in. I didn't want to be prying, but how could I have left Ruby without checking Nat wasn't in some alcoholic coma? Man, the place was a total tip, pizza boxes and empty bottles everywhere, like she'd had some party over the weekend and not got round to clearing up. Seemed like she missed my talent for keeping the place in order, if nothing else. I was worried then about what might be going on, whether she'd lost track of time completely and was still in bed with some bloke, so I told Ruby to go and wait in the car and I went upstairs by myself. And there she was.' Justin drops his head again. 'I didn't want to see that. I really didn't.'

Clearly, he doesn't want to go on. Dreading what's coming, Frank waits.

'She was all dressed up, like a hooker. Thigh boots, a corset. You don't need to know. And there was a camera, she was playing to a camera. My wife, putting on a show for some dirty old men.'

One hundred per cent, Frank doesn't want to hear this, wants to put his fingers in his ears the same way Justin must have wanted to cover his eyes. Yet it's his duty as a father to defend his daughter, stop Justin smearing her memory with sleaze. 'I know that must have been hard, but she was a free woman at that time, you know?'

Justin brushes away tears. 'Please, just wait a minute. Long story short, right? We had a massive fight. I told her she was an unfit mother, which I believe she was. Anyway, one mystery was solved. No, not one, two. First, the reason she'd buried herself out there in the backwoods was so she'd got a quiet place to make her videos and entertain her clients.'

'Clients?'

'Yeah, clients. She was on that website, Closefriends. com. Blokes pay what they call sponsorship money to watch women – well, you name it, there's somebody on there doing it, whatever gets you off. And that's where she'd been getting all her money, because she was pretty flush those last days, wasn't she? New clothes and handbags, that car. She was coining it, all those blokes with their tongues hanging out watching her writhe around the bedroom. I was beyond angry, man. I just couldn't understand it, why she'd leave me with a good living and a respectable job to be a hooker, because what else was she if she wasn't that? That's who my wife was. That's what your daughter became.'

'Stop.' Dee's standing in the doorway, rigid with anger, jabbing a finger at Justin as she speaks. 'Don't say those things about her. Whatever she was, we loved her.'

Justin pulls his eyes into focus to look at her. 'I'm sorry, Dee. I'm really sorry. Where's Ruby, is she OK?'

'She's fine. She's upstairs, playing on my tablet. What the hell's going on here? Frank, what's he been saying?'

'Come and sit down,' says Frank. 'We have to listen to what he has to say, even if we don't like it.'

Justin covers his face with his hands and begins to sob. 'Please don't hate me, I couldn't bear that too. I loved her with all my heart. I loved her as much as you did.'

His distress resonates with Dee; on this hateful journey, Justin's been a trusted companion into the black wastelands of grief. Sitting down beside him, she puts an arm around his shoulder. 'Don't. Don't get so upset. Ruby needs you to be strong.'

'I can't be strong any more,' Justin sobs. 'I just can't do it.'

'He was telling me about Nat,' says Frank, quietly. 'He says she was making money doing online videos.'

'What kind of videos?'

'Sounds like porn to me. Kind of an online peepshow.' At this revelation, Dee appears not shocked but resigned. 'Dee? Did you know about this?'

'I had an inkling. I found some stuff when I was clearing the house, kinky clothes, that kind of thing. I thought they were personal things, you know? There was a camera tripod, but I couldn't find a camera.'

'I took it,' blurts Justin. 'I got rid of it. I thought it was best.'

Dee and Frank look at him.

'When was this?' asks Dee.

'The Sunday before she died. I found Nat doing her online thing, so I took Ruby away with me again. Nat was in a stinking mood from our row, and I knew she'd only take it out on Ruby.' He wipes his nose on his hand. 'The next couple of days it was all I could think about. You'll tell me I was jealous and I was, I was mad with it, but mostly my heart was all broken. My beautiful girl, my Nat, selling herself cheap that way, because however much those bastard punters were paying to get an eyeful, it wasn't enough. It could never have been enough. I couldn't eat, I couldn't sleep. I had to know what she was showing them, so I did a crazy thing. I signed up to the website, and I had a look.

'This is the worst part.' He holds up his glass. 'A drop more, Frank, do you mind?'

'I'll get it.' Dee takes his glass and heads to the kitchen. The garden is in darkness now, and before she turns on the light, she looks up at the sky where a million stars twinkle. To this family, this drama is life-changing, monstrous; by the scale of the cosmos, it is nothing, less than nothing, less than dust. The pain of this fresh knowledge is oddly cathartic. Natalie made her own decisions. Dee was not to blame.

'Silly girl,' she whispers to the stars. 'You silly, foolish girl.'

When she takes the refilled glass back into the lounge, Frank is silent. Justin is still crying. She hands him the whisky and he takes a sip, then wraps his hands round the glass, a priest with his poisoned chalice of knowledge she and Frank don't want.

'It was worse than I could have thought.'

Frank feels his shoulders tighten, ready for the blow.

'It wasn't just her. In some of the videos, she was using Ruby.'

A ringing starts in Dee's ears. She wants to scream at Justin, tell him he's lying, but he's only the messenger. If Natalie's committed vile acts, that isn't Justin's fault.

Franks feels sick. He should ask exactly what Justin means, but he doesn't want to know.

Justin's going on anyway. 'You might say it wasn't too bad. Nat was there with her. She'd got Ruby dressed up in a party frock, and she was making her do weird things, parading her and making her twirl and pose with her finger to her lips, and I thought of all those perverts watching, all those paedos she was being sold to. I just cried. I cried for hours. I told myself nobody saw it, but this voice in my head kept telling me maybe hundreds did, maybe thousands. How do you know? And how could she have done that? I couldn't bear anyone else to see them. I thought about you, I thought it couldn't be long before someone in Wickney got hold of it, and then what if social services came? What if they took Ruby away because of what Natalie was doing? That was too much of a risk, so I took them both, the camera and her laptop.'

'Wait a minute,' says Frank, confused. 'When did you take them?'

'I went to see her. I wanted to tell her I was going to make a formal application to stop her having care of Ruby, to have full custody.'

Frank is seeing the light. 'You were there on the Friday.'

'I wanted to be reasonable, offer her a freer life, but when I got there she was still blazing from what you'd said the day before and spoiling for a fight. She told me you had another daughter and she was jealous. That temper of hers, sometimes she was frightening, but I was ready for a fight too. I told her what I knew, and she went mental. She flew at me, went right for my eyes with her nails. I pushed her off. I wasn't going to stand there and take it. I was tired of being her punchbag.

She wouldn't see that what she was doing with Ruby was wrong. She said Ruby should earn her keep, and that made me so angry. In my whole life, I've never been that mad. I had to stop her doing it, I had to get that laptop, but she was screaming at me, fighting me, telling me I had no right to take her stuff. It didn't seem that big a deal. I pushed her in the chest, and she staggered backwards in those daft shoes she always had to wear. Always the glitz for Nat, wasn't it, in case the postman came or some guy to read the meter. She fell through the cellar door and that was that. You'd say it was a tiff, a domestic, and I thought she'd be fine. It's not like she was dead or anything, not the way she was yelling and screaming. I thought she was being a drama queen, because she was always good at that, making a drama out of nothing. So I went upstairs to find the camera, and her laptop was up there too, on the bed. I took them and I left. And I'm so sorry.'

Franks voice is hoarse. 'What did you do with the stuff?'

'I ditched the camera in a bin at McDonald's. The laptop I didn't dare. All day long I expected her to come after me, to get it back, and I knew she'd kill me if I didn't have it. But she never came. I picked Ruby up from school, everything was normal.' He looks at Dee. 'It was only when you rang me on Monday to say you couldn't get in touch with her I began to think something might be really wrong.

'I took Ruby over there on Sunday night like I always did. I didn't want to. I nearly didn't go, but I thought it would be OK for her to be there, because I'd taken all Nat's kit. I thought if I didn't she'd be straight to her lawyers Monday morning, hauling me back into court over breach of our agreement. But she didn't answer the door, and that just made me mad all over again. I thought she was at some boyfriend's, late coming back. It wouldn't have been the first time. So I took Ruby home.'

'And all that time, she was down the cellar.' Frank closes his eyes. 'Jesus Christ.'

Justin begins to cry again. 'I'm so sorry, so very, very sorry. I didn't mean to, truly I didn't. I loved her. She was the love of my life.'

'Why didn't you say something, though?' asks Dee. 'When I rang you, you said you'd no idea where she might be. That was a lie.'

'It wasn't a lie. I never thought for one moment she might still be down there. I thought the moment I left she'd be back up those stairs, ringing her mates and telling them what a prick I am. I didn't know, Dee, really I didn't know. But when you rang again and said what a state she was in, I was worried then. I talked to Mum about it. I told her what had happened, about Ruby. She said to keep quiet, see how things panned out. If Nat had . . .'

'If she had what?' demands Dee.

'If she'd been OK, anyway she'd have told the police it was me, and I'd have fessed up. I'd have had no choice. But Mum said, if it's bad they'll be looking for the van, a white van. There'll be CCTV or something. I wasn't worried. There's no CCTV on Stickpike Lane. Why would there be? But she said, everywhere you go someone's watching, and they'll definitely be looking for the van. She said she had a way to fix that problem, and even if it wasn't a problem it was still a good thing to do. It was an idea we'd talked about for the business and we'd just bring it forward.'

'Bring what forward?'

'She called in a favour at a place in town. When they were opening up, their contractor let them down. I stepped in and got them up and running, put in counters and a load of shelving so they could open on schedule. So she came up with some artwork, asked if they could fit us in ASAP, and they said bring it in. Like a vanishing trick, it was. The van turned orange, and the white van was no more.'

'Jesus Christ, Justin.' Frank's shaking his head. 'You let me go through months of suspicion, all that stress and worry, and you never said a single damned thing to help.'

'I couldn't, Frank. I can't leave Ruby. That's why I'm here, that's what we have to talk about.'

'But how could you have been there?' asks Dee. 'You had an alibi. That's why they thought it was Frank.'

Justin nods. 'I know. But Will and Marcus, they're loyal lads and focused on the job, so they were easily persuaded what happened on Thursday happened on Friday and don't even know they're wrong. And my mum's stood by me; she's said I was at the workshop till three, and Sarah knows I was at the school gates at ten past. Sarah's got a bit of a thing for me, so it was easy for her to forget I was a few minutes late. I owe Sarah a lot, or I did. When things took a turn for the worse, I dropped Nat's laptop off with her for safekeeping. I didn't want to get rid of it, because it had the evidence on of what Nat was doing with Ruby. Because you know what worried me most of all? That those videos would get leaked. You can't trust the police these days, can you? Everything gets leaked, turns up on YouTube, so I needed to keep it somewhere safe, and that was at Sarah's place. Until she panicked. She dumped

389

it in a bin, but someone fished it out, so the police have got it anyway.'

'They've got the laptop?' Dee looks at Frank. 'Why didn't Peasgood tell you?'

'How should I know? This whole thing is a mess.'

'They've got your phone now, haven't they?' asks Justin. 'That's the thing that's changed everything.'

'Why?' asks Frank. 'What's changed?'

'Shot myself right in the foot, didn't I? I had this plan, and it was never going to work, I see that now. But Mum persuaded me it might keep me out of prison, that we could keep them off my track even if you had to take the heat for a while. It's them that's screwed this whole thing up, them being useless. I thought they'd take one quick look at you and write you off, move on to thinking it was some boyfriend of hers, or some stranger. I only wanted to point them in your direction for a while, keep the heat off me. You dumping your phone made it easy, honestly, especially when I knew you'd had a row with Nat.'

'What did you do?'

'I downloaded one of those apps which lets you put fake messages in your phone history,' says Justin. 'I got the idea from a story on the news. This schoolboy who wanted to get a teacher into trouble, put a load of fake messages from her on his WhatsApp, made it look like she was sexting him. So I did the same thing, put messages from you in my phone history, told them I'd spoken to you on that Friday and that you were at the cottage mid-afternoon. With your phone being lost, how would they ever find out? I've got the messages on my phone proving I was telling the truth. Except when they found your phone, that all fell apart, pointed the finger right back at me.'

'You're kidding me, right?' Frank's red with rage. 'You're not saying you let me go through all that, the worry and the strain, after what we'd been through with Nat's death? What were you thinking? I thought we were a family, in this together.'

'We are a family. I love you guys, and I love Ruby. But I can't leave her, I just can't. I tried to do a runner, take her away. I drove her to the airport, thought we'd get a flight to Spain, make a new life. But she didn't want to go, and I couldn't bring myself to make her. She would have missed you guys so much. I would have missed you. So now we don't have any other option, far as I can see, but to build a workable story, say you did it. Because we have to take care of Ruby, all of us, look after her best interests, and the way to do that is to keep her with me. If she loses me too, she'll never get over it. Say it was you who pushed her. Go for manslaughter without intent and you'll only get two to four. Please, Frank, for Ruby's sake. Because you have to look at it this way. We both had rows with Nat, didn't we? We both know how easy it was to lose your rag with her. It was an accident, pure and simple, but it could just as easily have been you that did it as me, and then you'd be in the same boat. It's true, Frank, and you know it. It was an accident, and it could have been either one of us.'

'He can't do that,' says Dee quietly. 'It wouldn't be right.'

'It isn't right for me to lose Ruby for trying to save her from what was wrong,' insists Justin. 'There's no justice in that. And my mum, they might charge her too, and she was only trying to help me and Ruby. What mother wouldn't do that? What am I going to do? It was a roll of the dice. It could have been either one of us.'

Frank is overwhelmed. In the last half hour this bad situation has got exponentially worse, and all their futures – his and Dee's, and especially Justin's and Ruby's – appear desperate beyond anything they can bear.

And looking at Justin – his daughter's killer and Ruby's saviour – he feels both pity and rage.

PART 5

Lean on Me

SIXTY

Three a.m., and Dee is wide awake.

This is the recent pattern of her nights: a couple of hours deep sleep when she first goes to bed, then a wide-eyed waking in the smallest hours, her brain an endless treadmill, slogging again and again through every possible worry.

But long hours of undistracted thinking have slowly changed her mind. Maybe Frank was telling the truth when he said he didn't want her to be hurt over his daughter. The sin of that woman's conception is way back in the past. She's just another ingredient in this overwhelming turmoil.

Tonight, though, is true déjà vu, a flashback to that long-ago night before everything fell apart, before Frank drove away to take refuge with Bethan, when there was still time – if only Dee had known, if only – to save Natalie's life.

Except tonight, it's not the sliding of the patio door that's woken her. She's been awake for hours, ranging in her mind over what Justin did, devastated by what Natalie was doing to herself and – worse – to Ruby. Part of her wants to kill Justin for not checking Nat was OK before he left that day. Part of her knows that Justin was right, Frank might have easily been the one to get physical with Natalie. Under those circumstances, rage about Ruby might have goaded her into it too.

But one small detail doesn't fit with Justin's story.

Justin left a little while ago; even though he was trying to be quiet as he closed the front door, Dee heard the click of the latch, and moments later his car as he drove away.

Shortly after, Frank left the bed.

The deep-blue hours after midnight stretch interminably, rendering it impossible to measure their true length. Dee's heart aches to imagine how much longer those hours must have felt to Nat, in pain, alone in that cold, dark cellar.

She wonders where Justin's gone. Home, probably, to wait for what happens next, for the drama and the fear. Thank God Ruby is safely shielded from all that, sound asleep in the room next door.

Unless . . .

Climbing from the bed, she hurries to the spare room where Ruby sleeps, relieved to find her still there. Her mother's lost; how will she face the loss of her father too? So much heartbreak for such a young child. Can she and Frank even begin to fill either of those voids?

Back in her bedroom, Dee puts on a robe and crosses to the window. Frank's down there, as he was that other night, wrapped in his old dressing-gown, a mug of tea in his hand, staring into the darkness. She taps on the glass, and when he looks up, beckons him upstairs.

He brings her tea, and in the light of the bedside lamp, for the first time in a while she cuddles up close to him.

'You should try and sleep a little,' says Dee. 'Or make up your mind to give work a miss.'

Frank shakes his head. 'I daren't do that. Jerry's ready enough to push the "fire Frank" button as it is.' He's silent for a moment before he says, 'You know what I can't shake, what troubles me the most? I can't help asking myself who was the real criminal.'

Dee tenses. 'What do you mean?'

'Look, forget I said anything. I don't want to upset you any more than you already are.'

'Just tell me, Frank. Things could not possibly be worse than they already are.'

'Maybe they could, though. Justin told me something, before you came in. About Ruby.'

Dee feels a shiver of dread and closes her eyes, but Frank hurries to take her worst fears away.

'Not that,' he says. 'Not that anyone touched her. Something else Nat did. She shut Ruby away, under the stairs.'

In a flash of memory, Dee recalls a morning at Turle's Cottage, the duvet left under the stairs, Ruby's resistance to the place, and she knows there's no point in trying to push away the truth of what Frank's said.

If she dares to be totally honest, that behaviour goes beyond unkindness, crossing into the dangerous borderlands of cruelty and abuse.

And that's bewildering.

'But why? Why would she do that to her own child? To our beautiful Ruby?'

Frank shrugs. 'I suppose to get her out of the way while she was entertaining upstairs.'

They're silent together, failing to find acceptable answers.

'Justin was right, you know,' says Frank, eventually. 'If I'd found out what Nat was doing, I don't know what I'd have done. Everyone has their limits. When Nat was Ruby's age, if I thought someone was doing her harm, I reckon I'd have been angry enough to get physical. I might very easily have done what he did, and when he said it could have been me as easily as him, he was right. And I played my part, indirectly. She was mad at me before he even arrived on the scene, and I left without calming her down. I'm sure she was all fired up for a fight before he even arrived. He was just petrol on her bonfire.'

'Do you think that will help him? When it comes to court, I mean?'

'I don't know. He's going to need a good lawyer.'

'I veer from wanting to kill him with my bare hands to wanting to give him a big hug and thank him for saving Ruby from worse harm,' says Dee. 'My head's all over the place. But you know what troubles me more than anything? What kind of person was Natalie, deep inside? Was she a bad person? Everything we tried to teach her about values and how to live a decent life, none of that seems to have stuck. Was it something we did? How could she have been so wicked?'

Frank sighs. 'I've asked myself that question a million times, and in all honesty, I don't know. The only thing I can think to say is the world is full of bad people, and every one of them has a mum and dad.' He glances at the bedroom clock. 'I'm going to be wrecked today, aren't I?'

'I mean it, Frank. Don't go in to work.'

'If I'm honest, I want to. Work clears my head. All those cogs and wheels, they make sense. Put them in the right places and the watch will run like clockwork, like it's supposed to. Unlike real life.'

Dee reaches across and turns out the lamp. The darkness where they lie shows the first grey of dawn.

Frank takes Dee's hand. 'Are you still awake?'

Dee squeezes his fingers. 'Yes.'

'Are we going to be all right, after all this? You and me, I mean.'

'We weren't so good before it.'

'What doesn't kill you makes you stronger. We should give it a go, though, shouldn't we? For Ruby's sake.'

'For Ruby's sake, we have to.' Dee is silent for a moment. 'There's one other thing I thought of, about Justin. About whether his story is true.'

'Don't you believe him, then?'

'I do believe him, yes. But there's something that doesn't fit. That cellar door. It's months ago now, but I think I remember it was closed when I first got there. Doesn't that say there was malice behind his anger, that he'd close the door on her down there?'

'Maybe he just slammed it in a rage,' says Frank. 'That's what I would have done.'

'Maybe,' says Dee. 'I don't suppose we'll ever know.'

SIXTY-ONE

In the hours before they come for him, Justin has time to think.

The dread of imprisonment casts shadows on every last moment of his liberty. The life that he insanely took for granted and thought mundane, he sees now was bright with pleasures and freedoms he's going to be devastated to lose. He can't yet bring himself to contemplate long-term separation from Ruby.

Every small thing he did for her yesterday – finding her school uniform, pouring her breakfast cereal, slipping a chocolate treat into her lunchbox – was the last time, for who knows how long. Driving his car, making a call on his mobile, settling down to work – all soon to be gone. He tells his mother he's fine, even though he's vacillating minute to minute between hope and despondency, acceptance and mad plans of escape, optimism and depths of despair he's never known before.

Freda knows him better than he thinks. She sees his pain.

What disturbs Justin most, though, is the fear of being imprisoned among men who've done unspeakable things, who'd rob him, pummel him, shank him if he gives any offence, who'll torment and brutalise him and change him, forever, for the worse.

He doesn't want to become a hard man. He doesn't want to come away with scars.

And what about his mother? What has he dragged her into? She took radical action to protect her only child, as he did. Now she faces the catastrophe of incarceration herself. *It won't be so bad,* she says. *I can take care of myself.* But he's caught her with a look on her face he's never seen before. She is afraid.

Before he left Frank and Dee's, he sat down on Ruby's bed as she lay sleeping, trying to commit to memory every detail of her face and hands, the rise and fall of her chest, terrified of how quickly she'll change in his absence.

At that other house, Dee will be waking his daughter for school.

In the kitchen – his kitchen – he takes time to make himself tea just the way he likes it, and sits down at his own table to drink it.

Through the window he can see across the unending spaces of the fens, where a man could walk all day and never meet another soul, flatlands running towards those vast, empty skies, always changing and, though he never realised it, consoling.

Sunlight is spreading across the land.

A police car is pulling up outside.

SIXTY-TWO

Ruby's on the floor of her bedroom at Grandma Dee's house, trying to complete her fairies jigsaw puzzle but finding it difficult by herself. Really, she needs help, but Grandma's downstairs cooking tea and it's too early for Grandpa to be home from work. If Daddy were here, he'd be glad to help.

She misses Daddy so much.

The fairy faces on some of the jigsaw pieces are laughing and smiling. Ruby tries to put one in place, but it doesn't fit.

Downstairs, Grandma Dee's phone rings. Ruby hears her answer with a cautious hello, and an exclamation of surprise. Then she's coming up the stairs, saying how pleased Ruby will be.

In the bedroom doorway, she holds out the phone. 'It's for you.'

Ruby jumps up. 'Is it Daddy?'

'Not Daddy, no, my sweet.' Ruby's face falls. 'But it's someone I think you'll be pleased to hear from. Shall we put you on video?'

She hands Ruby the phone. On the screen is an old man in an armchair. A sliver of light falls on the grey cat sitting on his knee.

'Hello, Ruby,' says Wilf. 'I hope you remember me?'

'Wilf! And Mr Grimes!'

'He's only sitting nicely on my knee because he knows I'm talking to you,' says Wilf. Ruby thinks he looks different, a little plumper, wearing nicer clothes. 'I'm ringing to say hello, but also because I need to apologise.'

'What for?'

'Because, very rudely, I didn't reply to your invitation to tea. I'm so sorry, but I didn't find your note until a few days ago. I've been staying with my sister the past few months, and I'm back at her house now, so I wouldn't be able to come for a little while. But if I'm still invited, I'd love to come. Do you think there would be cake?' Ruby looks at Dee, who smilingly nods yes. 'Because I'm definitely coming if there's cake.'

'Will Mr Grimes come too?'

'Now he's an animal who actually doesn't enjoy afternoon tea,' says Wilf. 'That's because he's so grumpy. Anything that anyone else would think a treat, he doesn't like.'

'Does he still bite?'

'Given half a chance, I'm afraid he does. It's all part of his grumpiness.'

'Grandma says she might let me have a cat, maybe even a kitten.'

'Well, that would be lovely. Don't get one that bites. You want one who'll settle on your knee and be good company.'

'I want a ginger one, or ginger and white.'

'I think they're the friendliest kind.'

'When might you come for tea?'

'I don't know for sure, I'm afraid. But I hope it won't be too long. Shall I give you a ring when I know when it might be?'

'Yes, please.'

'In the meantime, will you send me a photo if you get a kitten?'

'Yes, I will. If it's a girl, I'm going to call it Mrs Grimes.'

'I think Mr Grimes would be deeply honoured to know that, Ruby. I'll wish you goodbye for now, and we'll speak again soon.'

'Goodbye for now,' says Ruby politely, and as she's passing the phone back to Dee, her face shows the beginnings of a smile.

SIXTY-THREE

The Crown Court is an unimposing redbrick building, a piece of unimaginative architecture you'd drive by without a second glance.

Yet decisions made here in these coming few days will impact everyone Dee cares about, forever.

For some – the lawyers with their legal bundles, the clerks in wigs and gowns, the belligerent, foul-mouthed families come to give moral support at sentencing hearings – nothing happening here is out of the ordinary. Under normal circumstances, Dee would find it fascinating. But these circumstances are light years away from normal.

As a witness, she's barred from watching Justin's trial until she's given her evidence. *We'll let you know when you'll be needed*, the well-meaning family liaison officer told her.

But Dee has been in the building since the beginning, waiting, talking in her mind to Natalie.

Because somewhere, somehow, Natalie must understand that Dee has to act in Ruby's interests. Even if that means not doing right by Natalie.

* * *

On the morning of the trial's third day, Dee sits alone on a bench outside Court 6, hands shaking, sick with nerves. Frank gave evidence yesterday and has been escorted today to a seat in the public gallery reserved for the victim's family. She misses having him here beside her. She wishes he were here to hold her hand.

With a swish that has become too familiar, the courtroom's soundproofed door opens. A black-robed usher looks around at the waiting public, spots Dee and smiles.

'Mrs Cutter?'

Dee feels suddenly lightheaded, and prays that she won't faint. 'Yes.'

'They're ready for you now, if you'd like to come with me.'

Familiar faces in unfamiliar surroundings. Among the crowd of people — she didn't realise there'd be so many — she sees Frank watching her anxiously from the gallery and, sitting in a glass-screened box, Justin.

He looks so pale, so scared.

The usher is giving her instructions, telling her she must read the oath. Everyone else in the courtroom is silent. In Dee's hand the laminated card is trembling, but the time-honoured words stay clear. She understands their implications. To lie under oath could mean jail time for her.

But she reads them out anyway. 'I swear by Almighty God that the evidence I shall give shall be the truth, the whole truth and nothing but the truth.'

The usher takes away the Bible and the oath. Around the court, Dee hears the shuffling of papers, light coughs behind hands, the mumble of an exchange between two clerks. She glances across at the jury and sees they're as mixed as you'd hope for in Justin's position, youthful and elderly, prosperous and down-at-heel. Twelve strangers who hold her family's fate in their hands.

At the far side of the room, underneath an imposing coat-of-arms, the judge is a severe-looking man in red robes and an antiquated wig. The smile he gives Dee is not warm. He offers his condolences for Natalie's death and tells her she may have a chair if she needs one. Dee declines and says she prefers to stand. That much at least she can do for Natalie. She glances up at Frank, who gives her a surreptitious thumbs-up.

When he first rises to his feet, Dee doesn't recognise the barrister, but he is known to her. In his black robe and wig, he looks older and more distinguished than he did in a pinstripe suit, and she and Frank have spoken to him about Justin's prosecution, discussing the line he should take. He's confident of a conviction and a lengthy sentence, promising the full weight of justice for Natalie's murder.

And yet.

Dee answers his questions on her identity and her relationship to Natalie, about Natalie's relationship to Justin and their divorce.

Then the barrister moves on.

'I don't mean to distress you, Mrs Cutter, but I want to ask you about the day you found Natalie injured, on the twenty-seventh of March last year. Can you tell us exactly what happened?'

Dee's been through this with the police many times and was given her statement to reread before she came in here.

Following the prompting of his questions, she recounts her version of events.

When she begins to talk about first entering the kitchen, the barrister interrupts again. This is, she knows, the key point in her evidence, where he's planning on detonating the bombshell that will put Justin away for life.

The barrister glances across at the jury, making sure he has their attention.

'When you entered the house, Mrs Cutter,' he says, 'can you tell the court how you found the door to the cellar?'

Dee is ready with her answer, knowing any hesitation will fatally signal the lie.

Confidently, she says, 'It was open. I closed it without thinking . . . without even thinking she could be down there.'

A shadow crosses the barrister's face. From the corner of her eye, she senses Justin watching her from the dock.

The barrister picks up a stapled document from the desk in front of him. 'I wonder if you might want to reconsider your answer, Mrs Cutter? Because I'm looking at the statement you made to Norfolk Police on . . .' He fakes a need to check the date, flipping through the stapled sheets, buying himself time to think. 'Here we are. You made a statement on the twenty-eighth of March, and here you say – for the benefit of the jury, I am reading verbatim from Mrs Cutter's own words – *When I went in the house, the cellar door was closed. I opened it to take down some laundry I found in my granddaughter's bedroom.* Isn't that what you said at the time?'

'Yes, I did say that at the time. But I've been over and over it in my head and I'm certain I misremembered it. It was definitely open when I arrived. I closed it so I could move about the kitchen more easily.'

'And yet you told the first police officer in attendance – PC Alison Williams – that you had found the door closed.'

He's interrupted by the judge. 'Is PC Williams on the list to give evidence?'

'I don't believe so,' says the barrister. 'I believe she's left the service and has moved away from this area. Of course she could be called . . .'

'Let's move on,' says the judge.

The barrister, scowling, turns back to Dee. 'How then do you explain the error in your statement?'

'My daughter was seriously injured. Actually she was dying, I knew she was dying and I was in shock, not thinking straight. I've had time to relive that day many times over, and I'm sorry for my mistake, but I can't lie. My statement was wrong. The door was open when I arrived at the cottage. It was me that closed it, not knowing she was down there, and for that I shall never forgive myself.'

SIXTY-FOUR

For Jess, Hannah and April, the hole Natalie left at the school gate has recently been filled by petite and funny Ella. Ella's recently moved here from Birmingham, following her husband's transfer to a managerial position at a trailer manufacturer. Ella's husband drives a BMW, and she wears clothes bought in city boutiques. When she expresses an opinion, the other women listen.

The school term is ending, though the weather's not playing fair. This afternoon a storm's brewing. Some have brought umbrellas, though the rain is holding off so far, contained in banks of purple clouds massing across the fields.

As so often these days, Sarah is last to join the group. Lizzie, now aged three, prefers to ride her tricycle than go in the buggy, and that slows Sarah down. The close, humid air is making her sweat, and she's removed her baggy cardigan and tied it round her waist. As she approaches her friends, she sees Ella is wearing a crop top with her skinny white jeans, showing off her fake-tanned stomach and the diamante piercing in her navel.

'Hi,' says Sarah, in her downbeat, tired-of-life way, as Jess and April make room for her in the circle. 'God, it's so hot today I can barely breathe. Lizzie, get over here.'

'Oh, it can never be hot enough for me,' counters Ella. 'Hot as an oven, that's how me and Ben like it.'

Sarah ignores her. 'I was just listening to the news before I came out,' she says, directing herself towards April, Jess and Hannah. 'They've reached a verdict in Natalie's case.'

Jess's hands go to her face. 'Oh my God. What did they say?'

Ella frowns. 'What's this?'

'Natalie,' says Jess. 'They've reached a verdict.'

'Oh,' says Ella. 'That woman who died, right?'

'She was our friend,' says Sarah. 'And they've decided it was manslaughter.'

'Oh my God,' says April. 'Not murder? Oh my God.'

The school bell rings for the end of the day.

'That's so lucky for Justin,' says Hannah. 'Why did they decide that?'

'Pretty much because he didn't intend to kill her. I always knew he didn't. Justin isn't like that.'

'He murdered his wife and he's got away with it,' says Ella. 'Wow. I'll say he was lucky. Wife-beaters like him should be strung up.'

'He didn't beat her,' said Sarah. 'There was stuff involved you don't know about.'

Ella studies Sarah's face. 'Fancy him yourself, do you?' she asks. She's voicing a thought none of the others have ever dared put into words. 'From what I've heard, you're not his type.'

Hannah notices the hurt on Sarah's face and tells Ella not to be such a bitch.

'What will he get?' asks April. 'Will he still go to jail?'

'Definitely,' says Sarah. 'I don't know how long for. I googled it and it says with everything taken into account, probably three to six years.'

The women fall briefly silent. Six birthdays, six Christmases. Six years of Ruby's life missed.

The school door opens and the first of the children emerge. 'That's still a long time,' says Jess thoughtfully.

'What about Ruby?' asks Hannah.

As if conjured by their thoughts, Ruby steps on to the schoolyard, moving slowly and oblivious to the knocks and bumps of other kids pushing past her, her eyes looking nowhere but the middle-distance.

'She's coming home with me,' says Sarah. 'Dee and Frank and Freda are all at court.'

'She'll be fine,' says Ella glibly. 'Kids are tougher than you think. I grew up without a dad and it didn't bother me.'

'What have you heard about Freda?' asks April. 'When does her case come up?'

'Sometime next month, according to Dee,' says Sarah. 'They reckon she could get a custodial sentence too.'

The group's broken up by the arrival of the children. Sarah gathers up Riley and Ruby and Lizzie and guides them as best she can on the slow walk home.

She thinks of Justin, and wonders how he'll cope inside.

She thinks of Ella, and decides she's a spiteful little cow.

In many ways, if the truth be told, Ella's a lot like Natalie,

So how come Ella's someone she'd never have as a friend?

SIXTY-FIVE

Every day, Gabby still checks the *Herald* website. Like picking at a scab, she can't leave it alone.

She isn't looking for anything in particular, but she reads Caro's florid pieces with amusement and – in fairness – admiration. Caro keeps her job for a reason. She conjures a gripping story out of nothing much at all.

But it's not Caro who's penned the headline which catches Gabby's eye this morning. Justin's conviction for Natalie's murder is yesterday's news. This short item Gabby's found by scrolling well down the page is the *Herald*'s final chapter in her story.

She studies the words for a few moments, taking on board the implications for the family, especially for Ruby.

Tragic Natalie's husband handed five years.

Gabby doesn't click on the article; that headline tells her all she needs to know. Closing her laptop, she picks up an envelope from the bed and heads downstairs.

Her mother and father are in the kitchen eating breakfast. Her mother's in her bathrobe and pyjamas, with the string of pearls her father bought round her neck. Gabby goes to each of them in turn, kisses them on the cheek and wishes them happy anniversary.

She hands her mother the card. 'I just want to say I think you guys are amazing, sticking with each other so long.'

'You mean putting up with each other,' laughs her father.

'I wanted to get you something really special,' Gabby goes on. 'To say thank you for all you've done for me and still do for me. You're inspirations, both of you.'

'Really, Gabby, you shouldn't have.' Her mother tears open the envelope and takes out a card, on whose front two painted swans form a heart with their necks. A second envelope inside the first contains a voucher. 'Illingham Hall,' reads her mother. 'Gabby, what is this? This place looks very grand.'

'It's beautiful, and very special, and you deserve to spend some time there,' says Gabby. 'I took a chance on booking you in tonight. I know Dad hasn't got anything up his sleeve, have you, Dad?'

'I was planning a romantic takeaway,' says Owen. 'But your option sounds good too. Are you coming with us?'

'What, and gatecrash your dinner for two? I don't think so. Besides, I have plans for this evening. I'm going to a party at Mona's place.'

Her mother's eyebrows lift. 'Well, that sounds nice. Send our regards.'

'I will. I'm looking forward to seeing everybody. Mona says she might be able to get me a job at her place, until I find something permanent. Don't worry, I'll be moving out, but I think it would be nice to see more of you guys than I did when I was living in London.'

'Great idea,' says Owen. 'I could teach you to fish.'

'Don't push it, Dad,' smiles Gabby.

SIXTY-SIX

'Do you know, I've done the most damn fool thing,' says Wilf. 'I've left my reading glasses in the car. I'll have to go and get them.'

Laurence is already absorbed in his copy of the menu, running through the daily specials, vacillating between the mussels and the crab. As Wilf leaves the table, he tells him to hurry back.

This is to be a special lunch for a red-letter day. Earlier today, Wilf supervised the removal of his last belongings from Nine Brethren House and handed the keys in at the estate agents. Before he locked the door for the last time, he wandered alone through the empty rooms, saying his goodbyes to the place of his birth, the place where he lived from boyhood to retirement. Every room, it seemed to Wilf, had ghosts that clung, memories compelling him to stay. When the moment came, he really didn't want to leave.

But he has other paths to walk.

Lunch was Laurence's suggestion, but Wilf picked the venue: a little place famous for its seafood, beloved by tourists in the season but enjoyed by locals in the quieter months.

On the drive from Wickney to the coast, Wilf was quiet, watching the familiar flatlands as they drove by. Sometimes, he's been here in his dreams, so perhaps on some deep level it calls his name. But for the most part, he barely gives this part of the world a thought. Little by little, the cord has been severed.

Or so he believed.

The car is close by, in a public car park on the seafront. Wilf takes only a moment to unlock it, reach in and grab his glasses. As he's locking up again, someone calls his name.

He assumes it must be Laurence, having followed him for some reason from the restaurant. But when he turns round, he sees a familiar face.

Lord Illingham.

'Wilf!' Illingham holds out his hand and Wilf, blindsided and dazed, holds out his own and finds it tightly gripped and pumped in greeting. 'My God, I'm pleased to see you. I've been trying to get in touch with you for months, absolute months. Where on earth have you been hiding?'

'At my sister's.' Wilf is all but lost for words. Here is the man he loved in secret for so long, the same man whose betrayal wrecked his life, who cut him into small pieces and fed him to the gutter press. Should he maintain a casual coolness, pretend he wasn't broken? Or is this his moment to speak his truth?

But Illingham is going on. 'Listen, can we talk? Can I buy you a drink? Lunch? I owe you a massive apology, Wilf. You must think me an absolute louse. The blame is all on me. Of course I should never have let that bloody woman get a foot in the door. I thought I could handle her, but the moment that bloody rag came out I knew that I'd been had. I rang you straight away to apologise – I rang and rang every day for the best part of a fortnight. In the end I assumed you didn't want to speak to me, and who could blame you? I sued them, you know, and I hope you did too. Settled out of court, cost them a few quid at least.'

'I didn't sue, no,' says Wilf. 'I never thought of it.'

'Those people are absolute scum. Every quote they attributed to me was out of context. I praised you to the hills, Wilf, I promise I did. Told them I had the deepest respect for you, which I absolutely do. If you want to sue, it's not too late, you know. I can give you the name of the firm I use, they're absolutely top drawer. Come on, let me buy you a drink at least, for old times' sake. It's the least I can do.'

'I'm with someone,' says Wilf, though in truth his heart aches to go with this man, to bask for a while in his energy and confidence and humour. For more years than he can remember, he's dreamed of such a moment. But Laurence is waiting. 'We're having lunch.'

'Of course you are,' says Illingham, and he pats Wilf's shoulder. The gesture is meaningless camaraderie, though to Wilf it's so much more. But Laurence is waiting, and he should go. 'Well, in that case, another time. Come to the hotel, we'll have lunch there and a good old catch-up. When would suit you? Tuesday's good for me, or Thursday. Wednesday's no good, I'm off to see the cricket. Old habits, eh?'

Wilf risks looking into Illingham's face, long enough to see what remains of that once heart-stoppingly beautiful boy: the intelligent blue eyes, the noble nose, the cupid's bow of the top lip. Nothing else is left. Yet Wilf still feels the same.

Or perhaps not quite.

'I'm travelling back up north tomorrow,' he says. 'I'm buying a house with my new partner. Laurence. I'm afraid he's waiting for me now. I really should go.'

'Of course, of course. You mustn't keep him waiting. Send him my regards, won't you? Tell him I said he's lucky to have you. I can't tell you how glad I am to have bumped into you, Wilf. Sometimes I lie awake at night, thinking how badly you must think of me.'

'I'd never think badly of you, my lord,' says Wilf.

'No, I don't suppose you would. Don't put me on any kind of pedestal, you know. I really don't deserve it. Listen, we're going to have that lunch, I'm determined. You ring when you're next coming down and we'll get it fixed up. Give me your word.'

'Of course.'

'The children will be delighted that I've seen you.'

'Please send them my very best wishes, my lord. To everyone.'

'Don't be a stranger, Wilf. I mean it. I'm so pleased that I've seen you. You've made my day.'

'You've been gone a long time.' Laurence watches anxiously as Wilf retakes his seat. 'And you look very pale. Are you feeling all right?'

'I'll be fine,' says Wilf. 'I bumped into an old friend, that's all.'

Laurence studies him closely. 'An old friend, or an old flame?'

'Long story.'

'And you have all the time in the world to tell it to me,'

says Laurence. 'I think I'm going to have the crab, and then the plaice. I ordered a bottle of wine to get us started. This is a celebration, after all.'

'A kind of celebration, yes,' agrees Wilf, as Laurence fills his glass. 'And a day of reflection and goodbyes too, of course.'

'You seem a little sad.' Laurence reaches across the table and presses Wilf's hand. 'Please don't be. As one door closes, another opens. The best is yet to come.'

'I believe you're right.' Wilf picks up his glass, and holds it out across the table to chink against Laurence's. 'To those we leave behind, God bless them.' He takes a drink and offers his glass to toast again. 'To our old loves, and the new.'

SIXTY-SEVEN

On an unseasonably warm day, wishing Dee were with him, Frank takes a seat beside the other guests in a pew of an ancient church.

He won't be giving Bethan away. She has an uncle who's known her all her life, and Frank suggested the honour should be his.

However much Bethan might wish it so, these people are not Frank's family.

The organ strikes up; the congregation stands. Frank watches with a lump in his throat as Bethan, all in white, passes by. She's a beautiful woman, and he's proud to be her father, but she's someone he barely knows.

For him and Bethan, there'll always be best behaviour.

But Natalie – he knew her inside out, the laughter and the tears, the good, the bad and – as it turned out – the downright ugly.

He loved her with all his being, just the same.

Time moves on.

Dee and Ruby have headed to the coast to watch the

horses of the Household Cavalry gallop along the water-glossed sands.

As they follow the path to the beach, Dee pictures the ghost of Natalie ahead, walking backwards and bumping into people, chattering non-stop.

Ruby's not like that. She walks quietly and calmly, holding her grandma's hand, eager to see the spectacle, but undemanding.

As the horses go by, she's transfixed.

'They're wonderful, Grandma,' she whispers. 'Do you think I could do that?'

Dee strokes Ruby's dark head. 'If you wanted to, I'm sure you could, my love. You could do anything at all.'

Back at home, they make pastry for jam tarts for when Frank gets home, and Ruby makes a pastry man for Justin. He won't be able to eat it, but she can show it to him on their weekly video call.

Justin won't let Ruby visit him in prison, because he says it's not a place for kids. But every week, Ruby writes him a letter and sends it to him with a picture she's drawn, usually of her ginger kitten, Mrs Grimes.

When the baking's done, Ruby places the pastry man on a plate.

'This time next year, will Daddy be home?'

'Not next year, my love, no,' admits Dee.

'The year after?'

Dee remembers how slowly time goes by in childhood, how centuries elapse between one Christmas and the next. At Dee's age, the months fly by. Probably it's not that way for Justin.

'Maybe then, I don't know,' she says. 'Let's not wish the

time away, eh? Time's in short supply, and what you waste you don't get back.'

In the evening, Dee reads stories, and Ruby's content to listen. There aren't those exhausting scenes at bedtimes she used to have with Natalie. Perhaps, on reflection, the signs were always there.

Ruby's gentler than her mother. More considerate, more caring.

If she were growing up under Natalie's care, might she be a different person?

Maybe on some level, everything in life happens for the best.

That's something Dee would never presume to know.

ACKNOWLEDGEMENTS

My grateful thanks as always to the team at Headline, and in particular to my wonderfully wise and insightful editor, Toby Jones. A huge thank you too to everyone at Curtis Brown, and especially to my brilliant agent Cathryn Summerhayes – thanks for your acumen and guidance. My gratitude again to Ken Fishwick, whose time and care in tracing the complexities of timelines and plot logic are invaluable. And to ex-Detective Sergeant Terry Parry, thank you again for your patient guidance on police and court procedures.

Thank you all.

Discover more from Erin Kinsley . . .

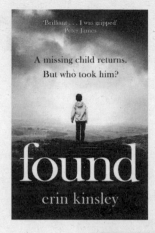

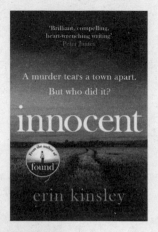

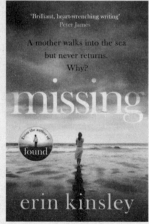

Available to order